DIVISIBLE MAN™
THREE NINES FINE

by

Howard Seaborne

Copyright © 2020 by Howard Seaborne

DIVISIBLE MAN is a registered trademark of Trans World Data LLC

This is a work of fiction. Names, characters, places, and incidents are the product of the author's imagination or are used fictitiously, and any resemblance to actual persons, living or dead, businesses, companies, events, or locales is entirely coincidental.

DIVISIBLE MAN - THREE NINES FINE contains adult language and is recommended for mature readers. A PG-13 version suitable for younger or more sensitive readers is available in the DIVISIBLE MAN - THREE NINES FINE - LARGE PRINT EDITION, available online.

ACKNOWLEDGMENTS

This is the Divisible Man's seventh mission. Lucky seven. Thank you, Stephen Parolini for editing that trims, tightens and teaches something new every time. Thank you, Rich Sorensen and Robin Schlei for being the beta readers who anxiously await each book, as much a treat for me as you say it is for you. Thank you, everyone at Trans World Data—David, Carol, Claire, April and Rebecca—who work to keep the the doors open so that I can keep doing this. Thank you, Kristie and Steve, for taking over so much of what kept me from doing this a long time ago. And thank you, Robin, for being willing to read each book so many times, nudging them closer and closer to perfection.

*For everyone who serves
with decency, respect and the
true bearings provided by
a moral compass.*

PREFACE

THE OTHER THING

It's like this: I wake up nearly every morning in the bed I share with my wife. After devoting a religious moment to appreciating the stunning, loving woman beside me, I ease off the mattress and pick my way across the minefield of creaks and groans in the old farmhouse's wooden floor. I slip into the hall and head for the guest bathroom two doors down—the one with the quietest toilet flush. I take care of essential business, then pull up to the mirror. The face offers no surprises. I give it a moment, then picture a set of levers in my head—part of the throttle-prop-mixture quadrant on a twin-engine Piper Navajo. The levers I imagine are to the right of the standard controls, a fourth set not found on any airplane, topped with classic round balls. I see them fully retracted, pulled toward me, the pilot. My eyes are open—it makes no difference—I can see the levers either way. I close my hand over them. I push. They move smoothly and swiftly to the forward stops. Balls to the wall.

For a split second I wonder, as I did the day before, and the day before that, if this trick will work again. Then—

Fwooomp!

—I hear it. A deep and breathy sound—like the air being sucked out of a room. I've learned that the sound is audible only in my head.

A cool sensation flashes over my skin. The first dip in a farm pond after a hot, dusty day. The shift of an evening breeze after sunset.

Preface

I vanish.

Bleary eyes and tossed hair wink out of the mirror and the shower curtain behind me—the one with the frogs on it— fills in where my head had been. The instant I see those frogs, my feet leave the cold tile floor. My body remains solid, but gravity and I are no longer on speaking terms. A stiff breeze will send me on my way if I don't hang on to something.

The routine never varies. I've tested it nearly every morning since I piloted an air charter flight down the RNAV 31 approach to Essex County Airport but never made the field. The airplane wound up in pieces and I wound up sitting on the pilot's seat in a marsh. I have no memory of the crash. The running theory is that I collided with something. If I did—whatever it was—it saved me and left me this way. I may never know how or why.

Since the night of the crash, whenever I picture those levers in my mind and I push them fully forward, I vanish. Pull them back, and I reappear. It applies to things I wear, things I hold, and even other people in my grasp.

There's one aspect of this *thing* that I may never understand. On a fogbound Christmas Eve I held a dying child in my arms and made us both vanish. I found out later that the child stopped dying. That when this *thing* envelops a child stricken by cancer sometimes—not always—it leaves the child whole and healthy.

Don't ask. I have no idea.

This *thing*—what I call *the other thing*—saved my life. It allows me to disappear. It defies gravity. It cures where there is no cure.

Those things don't scare me.

Far scarier things greet the dawn every day.

PART I

1

"What happened to you?"

Earl Jackson leaned back on his Army surplus office chair, challenging it to throw him over backward. He leveled his left leg on the only other chair in his tiny office. Ordinarily, I wouldn't have asked an intrusive personal question of the boss, but his open office door guaranteed a quick exit if any of the objects on his desk became projectiles.

"'S my goddamned arthritis. Woke up Sunday morning with that knee all swolled up. Hurts like a hot poker."

Rosemary II, the Essex County Air Service Office Manager and Goddess of The Schedule, leaned in the open doorway and gently nudged me aside. "He's not supposed to be here. And he's supposed to use this." She leaned a cane against the chair supporting his leg.

"Yeah, I'll use it alright," Earl muttered.

I grabbed the cane and handed it back to Rosemary II. "Best not to arm the man in this condition." She scoffed at me and returned it.

"I'm calling your doctor, Earl. I'll take you myself if I have to." She breezed out of sight, ignoring the withering glare that followed her.

"What's going on with the new bird?"

I shrugged. "They finished the pre-buy inspection on Friday. Dewey Larmond is wiring payment today. I planned on picking her up this week, but the pre-buy recommended a new set of tires and replacing one of the brake lines. Probably next week."

The search to replace the Piper Navajo belonging to the Christine and

Paulette Paulesky Education Foundation unfolded quickly after the FBI confirmed for the insurance company that the aircraft had been stolen and subsequently crashed in Lake Michigan. The Feds listed the cause of the crash as Dumbass Without Pilot License Loses Control in Non-Visual Flight Conditions Over Water at Night. My role in causing the crash that killed two mass murderers did not make it into the report. I mourned the loss of the airplane but had to admit to some excitement over her replacement, which had been found in San Diego.

"Compressions good?" Earl asked.

"Tip top."

"They check the lifters for pitting?"

"Yup."

Earl's blessing mattered. Earl Jackson has bought and sold more airplanes than I will ever fly. He can smell a good or bad deal across half a continent.

The new Navajo, a powerful cabin-class twin-engine airplane with seats for up to eight, would transport Sandy Stone and Arun Dewar on the Education Foundation's business, which typically meant day trips to small towns for on-site assessments—towns well beyond the sphere of commercial airline service. The aircraft would also fill in flying charters for Essex County Air Service, my previous employer, thanks to a lease/maintenance agreement. I planned to fly the Navajo for both the Foundation and Essex County Air, occasionally returning to my old job to take a charter when demand ran high or pilot staff fell short.

I figured being shorthanded prompted Earl to call me to his office this Tuesday morning, although it struck an off-key note that the call came from Earl, and not Rosemary II, who governed the air service booking schedule.

"So, what's up, Boss?"

"Close the door." I did as commanded. He made no move to shift his leg. I remained standing. "I need a favor. Off the books."

"Anything."

Earl glanced at the door as if he detected Rosemary II pressing an ear to the other side. He reached up and rubbed the sun-baked surface of his bald head with a gnarled, calloused hand. He lowered his voice.

"I need you to fly down to La Crosse and pick up a passenger. I was gonna do it, but…"

I pointed at his knee.

"That? Hell, I can fly one-legged. I flew for two months in South America with t'other leg in a cast."

Another Earl Jackson story noted for future inquiry.

"Then what do you need me for?"

Earl scratched his scalp. "They asked if you were available."

"Somebody I know?"

"Nope," he said sharply. "Prob'ly picked up your name from when you were famous. Can you take it?"

I didn't like being famous. I was less happy with the idea of someone thinking they were fixing the odds of a safe flight by choosing a pilot who fell out of the sky and lived. I imagined the passenger rubbing my head for luck—and me punching their face for fun.

"Sure. Out to LaCrosse and then what—back here?"

"Nope. Make the pickup and then she'll tell you where to go from there. Let her do her business. Then take her back."

"Back to La Crosse?"

"Yup."

Earl wears a perpetual scowl, but something in the granite angles and crevices of his face shifted. This request carried a personal priority.

"Wherever you take her, don't file. No flight plan. No record. Got it?"

"Okay. But I'm not doing this without asking questions."

"I wouldn't. Shoot."

"Her? Who is she?"

Earl checked the door again.

"Lonnie Penn."

I blinked. "*The* Lonnie Penn? The actress?"

"Actor. Don't call her an actress unless you want an earful."

Why on earth would an A-list Hollywood name call Essex County Air Service when she surely owned her own jet?

The answer jumped at me. "You know Lonnie Penn?"

"Knew her dad."

"Okay." I wondered if I would ever stop being amazed by the slowly revealed threads of Earl Jackson's life. "Equally impressive. You knew Dahl Penn? *The* Dahl Penn? Ran with John Wayne and John Ford? Said to have drunk Peter O'Toole under the table?"

"I knew some of 'em. I was a snot-nosed kid building time in the right seat with the old Honeymoon Express—Paul Mantz's air charter company." I added the famous Hollywood stunt pilot to the list of people I planned to ask Earl about. "Hauled Dahl Penn out of a Tijuana jail one night after we got the deputy hammered on tequila. We stayed in touch after that."

"Jesus Christ, Earl!"

"Get your head back in the cockpit, Will. This has to be done quietly."

I forced the bald wonder off my face. "Lonnie Penn called *you* for this?"

"Yup. Fly to La Crosse. Park at the FBO. Wait in the airplane for her and then fly her wherever she tells you. She takes care of business. You fly her back to La Crosse. Don't ask her any questions and don't pester her. Got it?"

"I guess."

"Take the Arrow. I had Pidge put it out on the line. Stay off the radio, except for La Crosse." He drilled me with a serious expression. "What? Spit it out. I gotta know if you're all in on this."

"I am. It's just…I have a thing on Thursday. With Andy."

"You meet Lonnie at ten in La Crosse. A couple hours out. Wait for her. A couple hours back. If it all goes right, you'll be home rubbing your wife's feet for beddy-bye."

If all goes right. In every hare-brained scheme I've ever joined, there's always a moment when a gremlin peeks through the fabric of the plan. I felt sure its arrival had just been announced.

Earl stared at me.

"Okay, Boss."

"Good. Get moving."

PIDGE SPOTTED me heading toward the flight line. She told the passengers boarding the Essex County Air Service Piper Mojave to go ahead and take their seats, then she ducked under the wing and trotted after me.

"Stewart!" She caught up as I dropped my flight bag on the wing root of the Piper Arrow, a four-passenger high-performance single-engine airplane. "What the fuck is this all about?"

No secret goes unnoticed at Essex County Air.

"You hauling drugs now? Smuggling guns?"

"Can't tell you. I'd have to kill you."

"Oh, c'mon!"

I shook my head. "Nope."

Pidge propped her fists on her hips. At twenty-three, she holds every rating on the books except seaplane and helicopter. She's the best pilot I've ever seen. Better than me, and I trained her. Her pixie size and appearance mask a stubborn streak that rivals that of my wife. She'll tear into you if you slide onto her bad side, but her loyalty is carbon steel. Pidge is one of a handful of people who knows I can disappear at will. Trust wasn't an issue. I simply didn't want to tell her about Lonnie Penn until I met the woman. The whole thing seemed odd.

"Honest truth? I don't know. I'll tell you when I get back."

"Fuck you," she replied, living up to the nickname she earned as a teenaged student pilot. Pidge is short for Pidgeon, so named because she talks dirty and flies. "Hey, are you still meeting up with the feds on Thursday?"

Pidge had been hammering me to do something meaningful with *the other thing* for months.

"If it doesn't get put off again."

"What?"

"It was supposed to be today, but the guy we saw in New York stalled it," I said. "Or his secretary did. Miss Carlisle-Plinkham, or some such. Sounds like a British nanny. Anyway, we got the call Sunday. She said her boss had meetings in Washington."

Pidge laughed. "Probably testifying before a Senate subcommittee on dumbshits who can disappear."

"Don't even."

She glanced back at the twin-engine Mojave crouched by the gas pumps, waiting for a pilot. "I gotta go. Call me tonight! I have GOT to hear about this!"

"You and me both," I said. She darted away.

I CONDUCTED a thorough preflight inspection of the Arrow. Fuel had been topped. I planned to refill the tanks in La Crosse. Without destination information, the best fuel status would be full tanks. I checked the weather again, using the iPad rather than calling Flight Service for an on-the-record briefing, adhering to Earl's mandate that the tail number of the Arrow only be used with LaCrosse tower.

The Foreflight app on my tablet told me a trough of low pressure extended from the Canadian province of Saskatchewan all the way to Tennessee, causing widespread areas of marginal VFR and in some places IFR conditions—low clouds and poor visibilities in drizzle and mist. This did not mesh with Earl's admonition not to file a flight plan. Getting to La Crosse from Essex didn't pose a challenge but depending on where my passenger wanted to go from there, I might run into lousy conditions for visual flight.

I tabled my concerns. Earl wouldn't have asked me to do this if he didn't think it could be done.

I loaded my flight bag and dropped into the pilot's seat of the Arrow. After plotting a course, I pulled the checklist and settled into pilot mode. Ten minutes later I lifted the landing gear and banked in a climbing turn toward La Crosse.

2

"Hey."

"Hey, you," Andy replied. Her warm voice came from somewhere in the center of my head, thanks to the Bluetooth connection between my headset and phone. I sat in the pilot's seat of the Arrow on the ramp adjacent to Colgan Air Services at La Crosse Municipal Airport. A light mist fogged the windscreen and glossed the wings. I landed under Visual Flight Rules, but the weather was marginal. The airport reported an overcast ceiling of 1700 feet and visibility of four miles. "What did Earl want?"

"Run an errand. I'm in La Crosse right now. How about you?"

"Office. Paperwork." The Clayton Johns prosecution was making the county DA as nervous as a bride's mother before the wedding. The former NFL star accused of rape mustered a high-powered defense team. At least one of the attorneys practically owned a box as a talking head on Fox News. The DA, in turn, applied constant pressure on Andy to ensure that nothing in the conduct of the investigation would blindside the prosecution. Andy described it as playing nursemaid to controlled hysteria. "Will you be home for dinner?"

"Better not plan on it. However, I hope to be there in time to rub your feet."

"What?"

"Something Earl said."

"That's gross...although..." I pictured dimples appearing at the corners of her lips.

"No. I'm not rubbing your smelly feet."

"What a thing to say to your wife."

I felt a strong urge to say more about my mission, but also knew that whatever story unfolded, it would be better whole. "Anything new about Thursday?"

"God, I hope not." Andy had been disappointed by the delay. We had discussed to death the decision to meet with the Deputy Director of the FBI. The call from his assistant lent it a feeling of low priority that made us both insecure. Andy more than me.

I tried to brush off her doubts. "Dee, what's the one thing we know about plans?"

"They change," we said in unison. I added, "I thought you might have heard from Donaldson."

"Not since this was set up. It's been radio silence."

"That's over two weeks. Makes me think he's got something up his sleeve."

"Will, you have to get over your distrust of the man," she said. Andy placed firm professional faith in FBI Special Agent Lee Donaldson, who had been the conduit to Deputy Director Mitchell Lindsay. She was wrong about me. My distrust of the man was long past its expiration date, chiefly because Donaldson had saved Andy's life, for which I owed him a deep debt. He also ranked among the handful of people aware of my ability to vanish.

"I think I've shown trust."

"Well, I expect he'll be there on Thursday as planned," Andy said. She paused for a moment, then asked, "Am I getting a hint that this errand you're running for Earl might disrupt our plans?"

"No," I said quickly, feeling a vague sense that I had just lied to my wife.

"Will! You can't. It's been postponed once. We can't just not show up."

"Dee, it's two days away. I told you. I plan to be home tonight."

"Rubbing my feet."

"It could happen."

I WATCHED the jet touch down. Symmetrical curls of spray spun into the air behind each wingtip. I had been watching the approach path to Runway 18. The landing light emerged from the low clouds about a mile out. That told me the ceiling was dropping. Not good.

Something else not good was my passenger's decision to arrive in a Gulfstream G650, the current pet jet and status symbol among Hollywood A listers. Not exactly discreet, although I was mildly amused by the idea of a pampered queen of the screen jumping out of her leather upholstered executive jet and into my single-engine Piper Arrow. I glanced at the seat beside me. No duct tape patching the upholstery, but the forty-plus-year-old airplane had seen better days. Champagne service on this flight consisted of two plastic water bottles lying on the back seat waiting to be served with a warning not to drink them early in the flight because there's no onboard toilet.

The G650 made a stately entrance to the general aviation ramp, enthusiastically waved to priority parking by a ramp rat wearing a reflective vest over a yellow rain slicker. The jet's nose bobbed to a halt and the ramp rat hustled to the unfolding airstair. He produced and opened an umbrella.

There was no mistaking Lonnie Penn. Blonde and trim, she wore a white leather jacket over black tights that advertised her figure. She followed a crewman down the steps and accepted his hand for the transition to the ramp, quickly ducking under the proffered umbrella and paying the ramp rat with a red-carpet smile. A cadre of young men and women hurried down the stairs after her. A woman wearing a ball cap and a long dark ponytail took the star by the arm to guide her forward. The entourage disappeared into the FBO.

If she wanted discretion, she had a funny way of showing it.

I waited in the cockpit of the Arrow. Earl's instructions had been clear. She'll find you. Sit tight.

I obeyed Earl for a fruitless fifteen minutes, maintaining watch over the jet and the FBO. I also had a partial view of the road fronting the FBO offices. When a pair of stretched black SUVs pulled away, I decided the whole plan had gone seriously wrong.

I let another ten minutes tick off the clock. Nothing moved on the ramp. No one emerged from the office. The jet crew eventually disembarked and made their way to the building. A fuel truck rolled up to fill the thirsty jet.

You learn patience as a charter pilot. Customers promise to be back at the airport for departure at a certain hour and then leave you twiddling thumbs for another two hours. It's tempting to call and ask what they're thinking, but I don't bother. Nothing I say or do alters their schedule, their momentum, or their perception of time. On several occasions I met the client at the door hours late and calmly explained to them that they could make hotel arrangements, since the weather window for departure had closed, precisely as I had explained to them upon arrival. Of course, such news is always my fault and the flight home the next day tends to be cold and quiet.

I waited, using the time to check the weather, which continued to deteriorate. Earl's restriction on filing an instrument flight plan weighed heavily on any outbound planning. If Her Hollywood Majesty needed a kale and cappuccino lunch before dashing off on her mystery mission, she was well on her way to screwing things up. I'll fly in marginal weather up to a point, but the derogatory term for it is "scud running" and the practice often generates an accident report.

I checked METAR reports for a two hundred-mile radius—since I had no idea in which direction my passenger would point. Head down in the cockpit, I nearly missed seeing the woman cross the ramp toward me. She wore a brown leather flight jacket over jeans. A ball cap and dark ponytail suggested Penn's assistant—no doubt headed my way to deliver bad news. The mist had turned to a drizzle, but she did not hurry or duck under an umbrella. Despite the low-hanging clouds, she wore aviator sunglasses.

"Come to tell me your boss is getting a pedicure?" I muttered to the empty cockpit as she rounded the wing. I leaned over and pulled the door latch. The door issued a shabby squeak as it swung open. I felt her mount the step behind the trailing edge of the flaps, then watched her jeans, artfully sliced and frayed at the knees, climb the low wing. A heavy leather attaché case dropped into the back seat. In one gymnastic move, she lowered herself into the seat beside me.

"Are you Will?" I instantly recognized the voice from a dozen movies. She put out her hand. "I'm Lonnie."

3

I'll admit to being starstruck. I've met a few celebrities in my life, and there is *something* about them. An alertness. A sense that they're operating with the On switch thrown at all times. An undefined possession of the moment that we mere mortals can't muster.

The woman sitting behind the copilot's yoke radiated that *something* in a measure off the charts. I didn't expect the effect it had on me and no doubt looked as befuddled as a thousand other idiots she has met in her life. Enroute to La Crosse, I imagined being cool when meeting her. I wasn't.

I stared until her expectant expression forced a few words free.

"I didn't expect a disguise," I said. She held up her hand until I belatedly produced mine. She shook it firmly.

"The price of fame," she said. She turned and pulled the door closed.

"I'm sorry." I collected myself and reached carefully across her chest. "There's a trick to it." I opened the latch and pushed the door out, then slammed it and locked the latch forward. I reached over her head and snapped the overhead latch. "If we need to leave in a hurry…to open this, flip the latch above you, then pull this one up and toward you."

"Is that the emergency briefing?"

"Part of it. The other part is that if we're in serious trouble the best idea will be to follow the back of my jeans because I'll be outta here *post haste*."

"Got it."

I heard an actor once say of making it in Hollywood that you have a better chance of becoming an astronaut. The alchemy of right place, right time, right face and voice may be even more secretive than producing gold from base metals.

Lonnie Penn held a patent on the magic formula. The face wasn't cookie cutter beautiful, yet she possessed a magnetism. She had morphed its smooth contours into dozens of vivid characters throughout her career—beautiful and sweet, vicious and cunning. Her body wasn't centerfold material, yet it stole men's breath when backlit in a love scene or wrapped in golden silk for one of her perfume ads. I'd seen most of her films and found it hard to reconcile the idealized star of the screen as a living, breathing woman in a worn seat beside me.

My wife's beauty and intensity can suck the air from a room.

Lonnie Penn would stroll in and steal the scene.

Focus, idiot, I told myself.

"Where are we going?"

"Wayne County, South Dakota."

"Roger that."

I concentrated on the aviating task at hand.

The flight planning picture looked grim. Heavy low clouds and poor visibilities draped our intended route. I couldn't climb up through the clouds to bright clear air above because the cloud tops were reported above fifteen thousand feet and we had no oxygen on board. Flying in the clouds meant talking to ATC, and that was a no-go.

The destination pushed the envelope, too. I had anticipated a short hop somewhere, possibly into a small municipal airport. One without runway length or services to accommodate her G650. Wayne County listed Prince Henry as its county seat. The Prince Henry Municipal Airport owned a single hard surface runway and offered self-service fuel. I touched off a flight plan on my iPad. It tallied up 255 nautical miles—just over two hours flying time.

I briefly wondered why she had flown to Wisconsin, only to backtrack to South Dakota. She could have landed at half a dozen closer airports.

I zoomed the iPad screen with my fingers and scanned the purple line describing the flight route. Along the way, I picked out obstacles. Towers. Where they touched the flight route, I planted a waypoint and created a deviation padding my path with a couple miles clearance. Then I looked for and noted safety valve airports along the way. The process took a few minutes.

I expected her to put pressure on me, but she remained silent.

At length, I said, "Well, you're going to get a low-level tour of Minnesota, but it'll go by fast and you won't see much."

She nodded.

4

I killed the engine and released the control yoke. My fingers had grown stiff with tension. I wanted to fill the sudden cockpit silence with something witty about disembarking, but the truth was, I was just glad to be on the ground. The last ten miles of the trip were flown below 500 feet, which is damned low. Worse yet, the visibility challenged the 1 mile minimum required for legal flight. I didn't see the airport until we were on top of it.

Before takeoff, she turned down my offer of a headset, which eliminated intercom conversation, for which I was grateful. The two-plus hour flight required all my attention and left me wrung out.

I worked to get feeling back in my fingers. She broke the silence. "Is this it?" She studied the airport.

What looked like a normal small town airport to me probably looked like a deserted movie set to Lonnie Penn. A self-serve gas pump sat at the edge of a small ramp containing half a dozen empty tiedowns, one of which we would soon occupy. A shack the size of a small RV bore a sign proclaiming the name of the airport and the field elevation of 1,235 feet. A row of simple T-hangars extended away from the edge of the ramp.

"I'm going to say yes," I answered tentatively. "Have you been here before?"

She shook her head.

"Is someone meeting you?"

"No. I need a cab. Or a rental car."

"Um…"

"There isn't one, is there."

"I wouldn't bet on it. But there might be a crew car." Her expression asked for explanation. "Somebody's spare wheels. They leave it at the airport for transient pilots to use."

"With the keys in it?"

"The keys are probably in that shack over there. Let's have a look."

They were. The shack door had a sophisticated magnetic lock with a numeric keypad. A small sign over the pad advised me to enter the VFR Squawk Code. Simple enough for any pilot. I tapped in the number and the latch snapped open.

The shack interior lay dark and still. I found a light switch, which flicked on a lamp with a brittle yellow shade. It cast a warm light over a small desk at the side of the room. A guest book on the desk invited pilots to sign in and take the vehicle. A set of GM keys beside the book confirmed that the single vehicle in the parking lot, a rusted Chevy Astro, awaited us.

"We're in luck."

"Do we have to sign it?"

"I have to write down an expected return time, which would be…?"

"I don't know."

My internal caution light flickered.

"Couple hours?"

"Less," she said. "I hope."

"Good. I'll put my name on this. Why don't you wait here while I gas up the airplane?"

"Well, no…that is…you can't come with me." She picked up the keys.

"Okay. Look, Earl made it clear that what you're doing here is none of my business and I'm okay with that. But something tells me that whatever you're doing may or may not go as planned." She didn't comment. "Which means I don't want to be sitting here in the dark wondering when you'll be back. I don't need to go with you for whatever business you plan to conduct, but at the very least, you can drop me at a local bar. I'll order Coke, I promise. You can take care of business and pick me up on the way out of town."

She hesitated.

"Fine," she said. "Let's go."

"Gas first. In case we need to leave in a hurry."

5

The aptly named Airport Road took us to a highway marked County H. A sign told us that Prince Henry lay four miles to the left. Lonnie let me drive the thirty-something-year-old Chevy van. The vehicle's worn interior smelled like pizza. She sat with her case on her lap, holding it just a little more possessively than seemed necessary.

On the way, her phone chirped. She lifted it and read the screen notification. I glanced over to try and interpret her expression, but she betrayed nothing. She worked the screen for a moment, then looked up.

"There's a place—it says it's on the west side of town on Highway H. White Bluff Motel. Take me there."

"Should be easy. We're on Highway H."

"It says there's a café. You can wait for me there."

Better yet. I was hungry. We ticked off a mile before I came up with a way to ask. "Miss Penn—"

"Lonnie."

"Lonnie…it's not my business, but it sounds like you're meeting someone. I'm no bodyguard. In fact, I'm a grade A coward when it comes to getting in a fight, but if you want some company."

She turned her head to watch the wet gray landscape flow past the van. Silence hung in the rattling van. Her pause struck me as overly dramatic. I wondered if she lived every moment as if a camera focused on her.

"No." Without turning her head back to me, she said, "I'm just here to get my Oscar."

6

We rounded a curve in the highway and I nearly missed the sign. Runnels of rust partially obscured the name. White Bluff Motel. Neither the word Vacancy nor the word No were lighted. In eight-foot letters mounted on a sign above it all, the word EAT. A diner occupied the bottom half of a two-story main building. Stretched in either direction, a one-story row of undersized motel rooms looked as if they were built into the hillside behind the establishment. The doors wore glossy blue paint with stupidly large red numerals near the kickplates.

"Park here." She pointed at the end space in front of the diner. No other vehicles graced the gravel lot.

I followed orders. She looked up and down the row of motel rooms, then checked her phone. She craned her neck to peer through the windshield at the second story above the diner. After a moment, she cracked the van door.

"My offer stands," I said. "If you need—"

"What?" she snapped at me. "Company? In a motel room? Just sit in the goddamned van or in the restaurant. I don't care. But if I catch you posting even a hint of this or my name on social media, you'll spend the rest of your life and every penny you ever saw in court. Got it?"

"Hey, all I—"

"I know what you were offering. Keep it in your goddamned pants." She slammed the door and stalked forward, past the grille of the van toward a metal staircase hung on the side of the building.

I watched her climb the stairs, pounding anger into each step. At the top she reversed and marched to the front of the building and counted off two of the doors. She stopped at the third. A glance over her shoulder satisfied her of something, then she turned the knob. To my surprise, the door opened. She slipped in.

"Well, okay then."

I decided not to take her outburst personally. My stomach reminded me that breakfast lay five hundred miles behind me. The scent of fried onions nudged aside the lingering smell of pizza in the crew van. I decided to implement a cardinal rule of charter flying. Never miss an opportunity to eat a good meal.

Roadside diners with no franchise affiliation rely on regulars. Regulars expect certain standards. My favorite breakfast stops usually have a dozen pickup trucks parked in front. Granted, the coffee can range from heavenly to something better used to grease an axle, but I will take the chance if the bacon is crisp and the eggs are not overcooked. When the refills are free, I feel rich.

I found a seat at the end of the counter. The lunch crowd had come and gone. The dinner rush, if they had one, had a few hours to wait. During the in-between part of the day you either got a chatty waitress who had no one else to talk to, or you couldn't find one.

My waitress was a wiry sixty-something man in a white apron and grease-stained t-shirt. He had thin, slicked-back hair and faded tattoos on skinny forearms. He smelled like cigarette smoke but had the courtesy not to dangle one from his lips when he approached to take my order. I took him for the head chef because he seemed none too happy to see me.

"Kinahgetcha?"

"A cheeseburger with bacon. Onion rings. And a coffee."

He didn't write any of it down. The coffee came swiftly from a pot sitting on a shelf under the Order Up window. He muttered something about the rest taking a few minutes.

"No hurry."

I'm just here for my Oscar.

My mind tapped out a B-movie screenplay centered on a famous actress who dallied with an opportunistic younger man, a leech whose affections only went as deep as her A-list connections. When she catches her lover straying with a scheming starlet, the Hollywood queen torches the affair along with the young man's hopes. Tossed off the gravy train, the rejected lothario grabs her Academy Award on his way out the door. She wants it back, but without fanfare. The kid bolts for East Nowhere, South Dakota with the gold statue wrapped in underwear and buried in a duffle bag. He demands a payoff. She shows up with a satchel full of cash.

I wondered if Lonnie Penn would give her former lover the same speech about posting on social media. I wondered why she didn't send hired muscle (one of today's body-builder actors got the part in my mind movie). Or a couple leg breakers scrounged up from a former romance with an underworld—

"Wancatchupwiddat?"

The cook shoved a plate across the counter in front of me. A burger hid under a mound of onion rings

"Um, yeah, thanks."

He grabbed a red squirt bottle and slid it toward me.

"Got mustard?"

He gave me a cold look suggesting that my request impugned the delicate flavor of his creation. Maybe yellow conflicted with his cuisine's presentation. He produced a plastic squeeze bottle from under the counter, then beat a sullen retreat to the kitchen.

While I painted red and yellow over the bacon hiding under the bun, the door to the diner opened and closed. I looked up to see a man studying me. Work boots. Cargo pants speckled with old paint. A camo t-shirt. Central casting sent a "rust belt construction worker" into my bad screenplay. He matched my height but carried at least fifty pounds more than me. Most of which hung over his belt. His face had paunch under buzz-cut black hair and eyes laden with baggage. I checked out his ride. The mud-spattered Dodge Ram pickup fit him like the pack of cigarettes accenting his t-shirt pocket.

Just about the time I wrote him off as a late-lunch customer, I caught movement past the window at the far end of the room. Someone large and dark climbed the stairs Lonnie had taken.

"Hi." The newcomer made no move to take a seat. "That your van out front?"

"Nope." I lie best when what I'm saying is true.

He took a long look at the van parked beside his truck.

"How'd you get here?"

The classic *Who wants to know?* danced on the tip of my tongue, but I decided to play a different role.

"Just waiting for my ride," I said. I used a hefty bite of the burger to prohibit elaboration. The cook had a point about the mustard. His burger was excellent.

The man at the door curled the corners of his lips downward and bobbed his head, letting me know my story was being considered, if not fully accepted. I feared he might pull up to the counter. Not beside me—men don't do that—but a stool away, now that we were such good buddies.

He put my fear to rest. He turned and strolled out. I watched the windows. He crossed in front of the van and turned to follow his companion on Lonnie's path up the stairs.

The gremlin peeking through the fabric of Earl's mission planning suddenly appeared, armed to the teeth. I put the burger down and considered my options.

The cook reappeared. He looked at the truck parked outside, then leaned on the counter toward me.

"That's eight-fifty. You want that to go?"

"Wouldja?" I caught myself adopting his one-word dialect. I pulled a ten from my wallet as I stood. "Keep it. You got a back door?"

He picked up the ten and pronounced my exit plan a good one by flicking his eyebrows toward the kitchen. "Follow me."

I paralleled him on my side of the counter until I came to a gap by the register. He turned and passed through an opening in the wall hiding the kitchen. I followed.

The kitchen showcased the cook's pride in spotless floors, shining stainless steel counters and orderly utensils. He dodged left behind a pair of steel prep tables, then right down a constricted hallway, past a small office and then past an open storage pantry. Light shined through a small mesh window topping a heavy steel door at the end of the hall. He pushed the door open and waved me out. The hillside I saw from the motel parking lot ascended abruptly from the other side of a narrow concrete walk.

"Can you put that burger on the front seat of the van out front?" I asked. "It's really good."

"Would'a been even better if you hadn't'a slathered it with mustard."

"Point taken." I touched the phone in my hip pocket. "What do you have for cops around here?"

This brought a clipped laugh. The door swung shut but not before he muttered, "You're funny."

The windowless back wall of the building and the close angle of a scrubby hillside gave the narrow sidewalk a claustrophobic feel. I moved to the side of the building where an alley between the diner and the wing of motel rooms offered access to the front lot. The diner's dumpster shared space with an ice machine; both nudged the side of the building beneath the stairs Lonnie and her visitors had climbed.

The diner parking lot contained just the two vehicles. Three other cars nosed up to the motel rooms. I wondered where the cook parked, but then considered that maybe he lived in one of the rooms above the diner. Maybe he owned the joint.

I moved to the wrought iron railing of the stairs and looked up.

No point in stumbling into someone.

Fwooomp! The cool sensation enveloped my body. I pushed with my toes and rose easily in defiance of gravity. The stairs climbed to my left while I ascended to the second floor. Fixing a grip on the rail, I performed a hand over hand move to the front of the building. I floated unseen over the van, then over the gray pickup.

The door Lonnie had opened and entered wore the numeral 9 above the kickplate. A single window to the right revealed nothing of the interior thanks to drawn curtains.

Just as I pulled myself over the railing and pushed across the narrow balcony, I heard Lonnie cry out.

"No! No, goddammit! *Get off me!*" Rising panic in her voice pushed the muffled words through the motel door. "*Just tell me and go! Get off me!*"

I grabbed the door and turned the knob to burst in. The knob resisted. Locked.

Lonnie's outcries became muffled. Something in the room thumped.

"Shuddup, bitch!" A man's voice, not the one from the diner, overrode the sound of stifled screams.

I began to push *the other thing* down my arm and into the doorknob. Sometimes if I push the cool sensation over metal and make it vanish, at the borderline the metal becomes frayed. Shredded. If I apply pressure, the metal breaks. It seemed the thing to do now.

And then what?

I stopped.

What if busting in on her was precisely what she didn't want? What if she wasn't looking for an idiot playing hero? What if she was engaged in a deliberate act that needed to be played out? The notion felt crazy, but it fit with the brief shot of venom she issued when she exited the van. What if she knew perfectly well what she had gotten herself into and me bursting in like The Lone Ranger ruined some carefully scripted theater?

"Ow! You miserable bitch!" the man cried out. I heard a sharp slap.

Nope.

I drew back *the other thing* before it spread to the doorknob. Instead, I fixed a grip on the knob and hammered my fist on the door.

"Wayne County Sheriff! Open up!"

I expected silence. I expected the warning to startle them into freezing, and maybe letting Lonnie go before getting caught doing something worse than they already had.

I did not expect the laugh that came from the other side of the door.

"Goddammit, Mallorin, I knew you'd want a piece," a voice—not the man from the diner—said from within. The knob turned. The door flew open.

He filled the frame, bigger than his rust belt companion. His dark brown skin competed with a black t-shirt to absorb what thin light seeped through the drizzly clouds. His face mounted a powerful jaw. Badly pocked skin marred cheeks with uneven beard stubble.

His grin jarred the moment. White teeth, just below eye level with me, looked more menacing than friendly. Yet for someone answering a door summons by law enforcement, he looked anything but worried.

The absence of a living soul outside the door stopped him in his tracks. He shot his head back and forth, checking the balcony in both directions.

"Not funny, Mallorin," he said loudly.

I could not see past him into the dark motel room, but I heard Lonnie issue a stifled closed-mouth scream. If she thought there were cops at the door, she seemed to want their attention.

The Black man leaned out, searching the balcony in both directions for someone named Mallorin.

I reached for and clamped a grip on his forearm. He jolted. He tried to jerk himself back, but before he could, I pushed the levers in my head hard against the stops.

FWOOOMP! The man in the doorway disappeared.

"*What the—?*"

I gave him no time to absorb what had happened. I planted my right hand on the motel wall and heaved him through the door with my left.

He may have weighed seventy or eighty pounds more than me when fully visible, but when I vanish, the influence of gravity and the rules of inertia vanish with me. He had no more resistance to me than a dandelion fluff has to the wind. The motel wall provided leverage. I yanked him across the balcony on an upward angle, lifting him over the railing. I felt him flail and jerk but without weight, leverage and inertia, his wild movements offered no resistance.

When I had stretched as far as I could, I let go.

Fwooomp!

He reappeared.

He screamed. He dropped.

Most of his body stretched over the balcony railing. His kicking legs slammed the handrail and flipped his body. I heard a metallic bang. A short scream ended when the hood of the pickup truck punched the air from his lungs.

I gripped the railing and looked down. He lay sliding slowly toward the truck grille with his legs splayed on the shattered spiderweb of windshield glass. His eyes were flat slits, pressed tightly shut against pain. I saw no blood. He clawed at the dented hood with his hands and gasped for new air.

I could not assess his damage, but his landing put a few hundred dollars-worth of body work in the truck's future.

A heavy crash inside the room jerked my attention away from the amateur skydiver. I heard Lonnie cry out, first in pain, then shouting, *"No! NO! NO!"*

Floating without weight or inertia means I have no force in a fight.

Sometimes a fight is just a fight.

Fwooomp! I retracted the levers in my head and reappeared. My feet dropped to the metal plates forming the balcony footing. I took a second to stabilize; a second I didn't have.

Rust Belt Man burst out the door and slammed into me. The collision caught me off balance. I ricocheted off his tucked shoulder into the balcony railing. For an instant, I pictured the old wrought iron giving way and sending me overboard to join the man below. The railing held and slammed me in the kidney. I folded sideways and went down. Stars danced across my vision. I felt the second man's pounding footsteps on the balcony as he sprinted away.

From darkness within the room, Lonnie Penn wailed like a wounded animal.

7

"Let me get some ice for that."

I knelt on the shabby carpet. The welt on the side of Lonnie's face didn't look bad. She'd been slapped. I made out lines from individual fingers. The red rims of her eyes made the injury look worse. That and the tracks of tears and wet snot running from her nose. She sniffled loudly and wiped both away with her forearm.

Her shirt was toast, ripped down the front to expose a black bra. Another series of welts tattooed the high side of her left breast. One of them had pawed her. Painfully.

She stared dully at the door, sniffling loudly.

I felt awkward and helpless.

"Wait here, okay? I'll be right back."

I stood and hurried out the door, down the stairs and into the diner, still empty. The pickup and its two occupants had departed quickly, spinning tires and kicking up parking lot gravel.

I ducked past the counter and into the kitchen where the cook unwrapped white butcher's paper containing meat.

"Got any ice?" I asked.

He lifted his eyes toward the ceiling, toward the room above the diner. I said nothing to answer the implied question. He finished unwrapping the package and extracted a slab of steak from the paper. Producing a knife, he sliced off a piece and handed it to me.

"This works better."

"Thanks."

I hurried back up to the room. Lonnie had lifted herself off the floor and found her jacket. She wore it zipped to her throat to hide the torn shirt. She sat on the bed. Her face flickered between dazed and angry. I added confusion to her expression by holding out a slab of steak.

"For your cheek. The swelling."

She flashed anger but took the slab and gingerly applied the red meat to her cheekbone. She closed her eyes.

"Are you going to ask?"

"Would you answer?"

She said nothing.

"Look," I said. "I understand how important it must be to you. It's the top award. But it's just a statue, right? Can't you get another? Isn't it insured?" I had no idea how those things work.

Her eyes remained closed, but her head moved minutely from side to side.

"Why don't you let me call the cops? Those guys can't be too far away." I reached for my phone.

"No."

She made no move to explain. She made no move at all. We sat in heavy silence.

Eventually I asked, "Are they the ones who stole it? Those guys?"

"No."

My wife taught me that when a woman has a problem, a man always wants to solve it, but a woman doesn't always want it solved. Sometimes she just wants to air out the problem.

Neither seemed to be the case with Lonnie Penn, so I pressed on.

"Does the Academy allow you to get a replacement? If it's stolen?"

"What?"

"Your Oscar."

She issued a two-note laugh and shook her head again.

"Oscar isn't a statue," she said softly. "Oscar is my grandson."

8

My cheeseburger sat in a bag on the table. The aroma ignited my appetite, but I left it untouched.

Lonnie had cleaned her face in the motel room's tiny bathroom. I expected her to argue in favor of chasing after the pickup truck. Instead, she followed me down to the diner. She closed her hand self-consciously around the steak and wore her hat and sunglasses when we entered, but the diner remained empty. I suggested a booth by the window. I wanted to keep an eye on the parking lot. A moment after we sat, the cook appeared with two glasses of ice water and my unfinished coffee. Lonnie sheepishly offered to return his cut of meat.

"You put that on your cheek, honey," he said. "I'll getcha cuppacoffee."

He sauntered off.

Lonnie drew a lungful of air, releasing it on a long slow breath.

"What was in the bag?" I asked. The man who ran a Packer Sweep on me outside the room had been clutching her attaché case to his chest.

Her sharp blue eyes lifted and narrowed, bearing down on me. "Hey, I don't know you. Okay? The poor damsel in distress tells all for the big strong man who will save her? That may be your fantasy, but it's not mine."

"Nope. You don't know me. You don't have to tell me anything. We can grab a cup of coffee here and beat feet for the airport and that's fine with me. Better, in fact, because as bad as that weather was coming in, you won't see me flying in it after dark. In fact, if you don't want to say another word, then all I want is to finish the cheeseburger in this bag and be on our way."

I gave back some of her icy stare.

She blinked.

The cook delivered a cup of hot coffee to her side of the table and poured a heat-up in mine.

"Kinahgecha?" he asked Lonnie.

She shook her head. "I'm fine. Coffee's fine. Thanks."

He left again. I wondered if he recognized the woman wearing dark glasses on such a gray and cloudy day.

"Half a million dollars," she said. I whistled softly. She pointed at the paper bag on the table. "That smells good. Go ahead. Really."

I pulled out the wrapped burger and onion rings. "Want some?"

"No. Well, maybe an onion ring."

I spread the meal on the table between us. I took a grateful bite of the burger while she picked up a small breaded circle of fried onion.

"That's a lot of money. Do you want to go after them?"

She shook her head. I tried again.

"I know people in the FBI. If those guys kidnapped your grandson…"

"No," she said quickly, then added, "he wasn't kidnapped."

I took another bite. She sat in silence.

"Okay, this is my last question. How the hell do you have a grandson? You can't be older than me. I'm only thirty-four, for chrissakes!" I made a gesture at her face, her body.

This brought a shallow smile. She lowered the meat slab to the paper on the table and pulled some napkins from the holder to wipe her cheek.

"I'm not. You're not supposed to ask my age, but when you were a senior in college, I would have been a sophomore."

"I didn't go to college so I can't do the math."

"Neither did I."

"A grandson? Really? How old is the kid?"

"Three."

I shook my head. "Impossible."

"That's my life, Will. The ten percent of the tabloid version that's true."

"Then let me help. I told you. I have connections with the FBI. Not just some acquaintance. Serious firepower. Plus, my wife is a kick-ass cop. A detective. Let us help you find him."

"I know where he is." She said it calmly, firmly. I wondered if this explained her lack of panic. I waited for her to explain. She didn't. Instead, she asked, "You're married?"

I lifted both hands to show the only two rings on my fingers. A wedding band on my left hand and an old Army Air Corps ring on my right. "Married to my wife. And to airplanes."

"Lucky for her. Lucky for me."

I wolfed another bite of the burger. "You really should try this. I don't know what that guy puts in it, but it's awesome."

She looked longingly at it. "Do you know how long it's been since I ate a cheeseburger?"

I held it out. She conjured a pained expression. I pushed it toward her. She stole a glance at the empty diner, then snatched it from my fingers and took a bite. She closed her eyes and savored it, humming erotically.

"Finish it. And now I know your second deepest secret. Why don't you tell me about your first?"

She thought it over while chewing. I leaned back and worked on the heap of onion rings.

"My grandson wasn't kidnapped. He's in custody. Here. In Wayne County at the Eastern State Detention Center." She spoke between bites. "He's an illegal. One of those murdering, raping immigrants you hear so much about. He's in detention pending deportation."

"To?"

"Mexico."

"We're a little far from the border here in South Dakota, aren't we? I thought those detention centers were in the border states."

"No. No, they're all over. ICE has facilities all over."

"And how did a three-year-old climb the mighty wall and get all the way to the Dakotas?"

"He was with my daughter." She finished the last bite of the burger.

"Was she keeping him from you?"

"She was." I watched her silver-blue eyes fill with water. "Until she died in ICE custody."

I froze, dangling an onion ring between us. After a moment, I mustered a soft, "I'm so sorry."

Lonnie took a drink of water, using the pause to compose herself. "She must have been sick. When they arrested her and the boy. I was told she was in a lot of pain. I don't have any details. I don't know if she got medical attention. I don't know what caused it. The officer I spoke to said she...uh, her remains...were cremated...and they will be returned with the boy to Mexico. Deported. They're deporting her remains along with her son."

"Can't you step in? Stop it? Do you have standing with the kid as a relative? Can't you send in an army of lawyers?"

"Doesn't work that way."

"How can it not work that way? You're her mother."

Lonnie trembled with a breathless laugh. "I never knew her."

"Then how...? What...?" I gave it a moment's thought. "You got a call. Somebody figured out who she was to you."

Lonnie nodded and her face darkened. I marveled at how quickly she moved from expression to expression.

"She knew who her mother was. She knew all her life but wanted nothing to do with me. I didn't even know she had a child. That I had a grandson. She probably would never have had anything to do with me. I...I...left her...when she was a baby. In Mexico. I left her with her father. She knew who I was...but I never...I never tried to reach out to her."

"How did she end up as an illegal alien?"

"I don't really know. Her father was on a long, slow path to failure, even back when I was infatuated with him. I heard he died a few years ago. I didn't know what had become of her until someone—I think it was one of those two men—called me. And that's not easy to do, you know. Big Hollywood star, you can't just pick up a phone and get past my agent, my publicist, my assistant, my lawyer, my whole goddamned—" She stopped and bit her lip. Her voice grew high and thin. "My daughter was dying and she couldn't get past my—"

I concentrated on the diminishing pile of onion rings.

"She must have been desperate—at the end. She must have told someone at the detention center who she was. *Who I was.* She told someone—I don't know who—he didn't identify himself. He finally got through. He texted me a picture."

She pulled her phone from the pocket of the leather jacket. After swiping the screen, she held it up for me to see.

The photo framed a dark-haired girl clutching a small boy. She looked afraid and in pain. Her hair was matted with sweat. Both faces in the photo shared Lonnie Penn's eyes.

"She named him Oscar. Probably to spite me. He was born the year I won—the second one." Lonnie gazed at the photo before putting the phone away. "I got a call from a man. He told me my daughter died in ICE custody and her child would be deported. He said if I brought half a million dollars here, to this place," she pointed at the ceiling, "he would get the boy out of detention and turn him over to me."

"Why not just go to Mexico and wait there for delivery? Then work out the connection with the authorities?"

"The caller said if I didn't show up with the money, they would have him sent back as an Unidentified Individual. He said that's what they do with kids who have no parents and no idea who they are. South of the border they get off-loaded into the Mexican orphanage system. He said if I didn't pay, he would see to it that I would never find him."

"He might have just been trying to scare you."

"And succeeding. I couldn't take the chance."

"This detention facility. You say it's an ICE facility?"

"It's a county jail. ICE uses it."

"Now it makes sense," I said.

"What?"

I lined up my thoughts before answering. She leaned forward. I saw the rapid transformation of her expression, from mournful to curious to demanding.

"What makes sense?"

"First, a question. What happened up there?"

The expression shifted to disgust.

"I was a fool. They told me to wait in that room. Alone. They showed up and I was supposed to give them the money. They were supposed to have the boy. I could tell right away they didn't have him. They took the money. They wanted more."

"Money?"

"No."

"Oh." I recalled the image of red skin on her breast. "They assaulted you."

"Not me. Some character on the screen that they probably masturbate to." She laughed sourly. "Do you know how often men grab me? They own Lonnie Penn on DVD. They think they own her body. That's what that was."

"I'm sorry," I said. "On behalf of the *not* slimy members of my species, I'm sorry."

She cracked a thin smile. It didn't last long. "What did you mean? You said it made sense. What made sense?"

"Did you hear what I said when I knocked on the door?"

"Not really."

"I told them I was the Wayne County Sheriff's Department. You sounded like you were being attacked so I thought cops at the door might scare whoever was in there into running away. But they didn't."

I watched realization dawn on her face.

"No, they didn't…"

"No. They thought it was someone named Mallorin. And I bet—"

"—that he's a deputy at the detention center!"

9

"You want to know *what?*" Andy asked.

"ICE. Immigration and Customs Enforcement. I want to know if you can find out if they have a child in custody at the Eastern State Detention Center in Prince Henry, South—"

"Will! Stop. What's this about?"

"Usual disclaimer?"

"Um...I'm not sure that applies. Is this the errand Earl sent you on?"

"Yeah."

Andy let dead air hang for a moment. Lonnie plucked an onion ring from the diminishing pile.

"Are you with someone right now?" Andy asked. I have no idea how she senses these things.

"I am."

"Can you talk in front of them?"

I knew what she was asking. "Not about everything."

"Can you tell me what's going on?"

"You know I will, but for now I need information and time may be short." I repeated my question. Andy thought it over for a moment.

"ICE uses regional detention centers. Usually through agreements with county agencies. One or two per state. The one you mentioned could be part of their program. We have one in Wisconsin, in Racine. I don't know much about it, though."

"Can you find out if they have a certain individual in custody?"

"I doubt it. Not quickly, at least. You said it's a child?"

"Uh-huh."

"Do we know the name of the child? Part of the problem right now is identifying tender-aged individuals. A lot of them arrive without ID. It got worse when they started separating adults and kids, especially when they got the bright idea to deport one or the other. In some cases, they lost track of who the kids are. It's a mess."

"That's not the deal here. They know who the kid is."

"Do you have a name?"

I held the phone aside.

"What's the boy's name?"

"Oscar Rilling."

"Oscar Rilling," I repeated for Andy.

"Middle name?"

I asked. Lonnie shrugged.

"Don't know," I relayed. "See what you can find out about the boy's mother, too. She died in custody."

"That's a big deal, Will. That's a huge deal. What was her name?"

I asked Lonnie. She replied.

"Gloria Rilling," I relayed.

Lonnie abruptly waved her hands, signaling me to pause.

"Hold on a sec," I said.

"When they called me, they told me my daughter was traveling under an alias. Um…Apalona…no! Apalacio! First name Maria—ach! No! Mira! Mira Apalacio!"

Andy heard the exchange. "Did the boy have an alias?"

I asked. Lonnie didn't know.

"Doubtful they recorded her alias if they knew her real name," Andy said. "I'll see what I can find out."

"Thanks. I gotta go. Love you!" I wanted to end the call before Andy asked me too many questions, like whether I still thought I'd be home before dark or not.

"LET'S GO," Lonnie slid sideways in the booth.

"Where?"

"Jail. We know where he is. Now we may know who set me up. I'll file charges. Bribery. Assault. Extortion. C'mon!"

She blew out the diner front door before I could slide out of the booth. I pulled another ten from my wallet to leave for the coffee and the steak.

"Hang on!" I called after her as she climbed into the van. I double-checked that the keys were still in my hip pocket. She slammed her door and waited for me.

I slipped behind the wheel. When I made no move to start the vehicle she spun her hand in a get-on-with-it gesture.

"Really?" I asked. "Where's the jail? And when we find it, where's the public entrance? What authority do we have? What are visiting protocols? Visiting hours? Are ICE detainees allowed visitors? Are they even acknowledged as detainees? Because from what I hear that branch of federal law enforcement is anything but transparent. Plus, we know someone on the inside just did something seriously illegal and ripped you off for half a million. How anxious do you think they will be to help you? Are you getting the picture here?"

"I can't just sit here. They're going to move him."

"And you know this how?"

"This!" She pointed at the room above the diner. "This meet! It had to be today. They made it clear that today was the only day they could get him out. They said he was being deported and today was the last day they would be able to get him to me. For all I know they're loading him up tomorrow morning."

I pulled out my phone.

"Who are you calling?"

"Not calling. Texting."

Find out what their protocols are for deporting. When? How? Transport?

I hit send, then pocketed the phone. I reached behind the seat for my flight bag and slid my iPad free.

"Now what?" she demanded.

"Unless you can give me directions, I need to know where the hell this county jail is located."

"Oh."

"And while we're driving there, you're going to tell me what you haven't told me yet."

10

Lonnie didn't tell her story. I interpreted her silence as obstinance.

We pulled out of the White Bluff Motel parking lot, turned east, rounded a curve that outlined the hill behind the motel and found the county seat of Prince Henry sprawled in front of us. The speed limit dropped. Gas stations and auto dealerships popped up alongside the highway. Stoplights hung on overhead wires.

Google directions led us onto a side street hosting the Eastern State Detention Center.

The jail looked like an elementary school. I expected to find a fence, but nothing more than a well-kept lawn separated the detention center from the street. A one-story façade spanned a parking lot. Behind that, the structure rose to a second story with walls containing narrow slit windows. The jail dormitory could have been mistaken for a school gymnasium.

One row of the parking lot was marked Reserved for county sheriff's cars. Beyond that and a simple sign at the street, a casual observer might see no reason to believe the structure housed prisoners.

"Are you turning in?"

"No." I rolled placidly past the sign and its driveway.

"Why not?"

"What were you thinking of doing? Rushing in and announcing who you are? Telling them you just paid an official half a million bucks to illegally spring a detainee and now you want your money back? Their counter-argument would be that you just admitted to a federal crime."

"So now this is my fault? I did what I was told to do!"

I looked for a place to turn around, then changed my mind. Not wishing to risk being seen driving past the building again, I took the next right and set out to drive a box pattern that would take us back through town.

"You were painted into a corner."

"Well, duh. They're moving the boy in the morning."

"Right. And if that's the case, I may have a way of doing something about it. But first, tell me what you're not telling me."

11

We parked the pizza-scented van in a Walmart lot.
I killed the engine and pocketed the keys but did not move.

"I was fifteen. Fifteen and pregnant. My dad, well you know who my dad was. The last of the Hollywood swashbucklers. You grow up in that world and learn an early lesson. What you see at home has nothing to do with the real world."

"Rough growing up?"

"Not at all. My dad was sixty-one when I was born. His first and only child. He gave me a fairy tale life. I had a loving father and mother, even if they hated each other and she didn't stay. I lived a lavish lifestyle. I wasn't spoiled and I wasn't left to run wild. But there were so many interesting people coming and going. Amazing people. Parties. Travel. It was a dream.

"I'm the one who broke it. I broke my dad's heart before he died. I thought I was so grown up, such a mature woman. I met Dominic Rilling, all dash and flamboyance. A Mexican television executive who swept a fifteen-year-old off her feet. I thought I was so far beyond my years. I thought it was love. The law said it was rape. The people around my father, who was beginning to decline at that point, said finding out would kill him. Rilling had more power and money than my father, and he had me utterly under his spell. My dad's people made a deal. I went to Mexico to have the baby in secrecy. Problem solved."

"Your father agreed to this?"

"My father...I told you. He was declining. Alzheimer's took him. I found out later that his managers knew for a long time and made deals to preserve what they thought they could get their hands on after he was gone. In the critical final act, the one thing they didn't want was a scandal involving the underaged daughter of the great Dahl Penn. Not until they had wrung every penny out of the estate. They shipped me off to Mexico to put a lid on the scandal and get me out of the path of the vultures circling the estate."

"Shipped you off?"

"Bad word choice. I was more than complicit. I went happily. I was a deluded princess swept away to a new castle. Rilling was all that, you know? Only, things weren't quite what they appeared to be. I won't play the sad violin. I deserved a lot of what I got."

"I doubt it."

"That's noble of you, but you weren't there. Having a baby wasn't what I thought it would be. The father wasn't a father. The castle wasn't paid for and the fortune wasn't real. I had my own issues and dealt with them ... poorly. I ran away from Rilling and my baby girl when I was just short of sixteen. Back to Hollywood. Just in time to find out my father's life and fortune were both drained. Tough break, kid, they said. Things got…let's just say *dark* for a while. Then I started catching eyes, getting noticed. I shamelessly used what was left of Dad's connections and landed a few good parts. The first Oscar nomination came when I was nineteen—and that's when the real ride began. I got the statue when I was twenty-three. I showed them all. And I convinced myself that I had done it on my own, which, of course, is utter nonsense. It gave me permission to never look back. Family was nothing to me. My daughter was nothing to me."

"Aren't you being a little hard on yourself?"

"Aren't you being a little naïve? A, you don't know anything about me. And B, you're not my therapist."

I kept quiet. This was the third time she pulled a verbal blade on me.

She folded her arms and looked out the passenger-side window.

"Don't try to be nice to me, Will. I don't want it to cloud your judgment, okay? I'm aware that I'm dragging you into something bad."

"Must be Tuesday."

"Fine," she said. "Don't say I didn't warn you."

"So…then what happened?"

She shrugged. "A couple marriages. That car accident in Nevada. A string of bad choices, and a lot of 'she's washed up' press, then the second Oscar. Miracle comeback. Blah blah blah."

"I meant with the child."

"Oh. Rilling's fortunes went to hell. He moved his business and Gloria to South America for a while. Then he dropped off the radar. Nobody really seemed to know what happened. He popped up in Mexico City about five years ago."

"You didn't keep track of her?"

"No. I'm not a good person, Will. I couldn't be bothered with her. Other people—my people—tried to tell me, but I shut them down. When my manager heard Rilling drank himself to death she reached out—against my wishes. My daughter told my manager to fuck off. She was right to hate me."

I didn't comment. I checked my watch. Four-forty. The sky had lightened. The drizzle that had required occasional application of windshield wipers tapered off. Beyond the far end of the Walmart parking lot, I spotted a set of farm buildings a couple miles away. I used them to gauge the visibility. If we left now…

My phone rang. Andy.

"Hi."

"I don't think your information is accurate."

"Hang on. I'm going to put you on speaker with Earl's client. I promised Earl I would keep her identity confidential, Dee. Here she is."

I touched the speaker icon and laid the phone on the console between the front seats of the van.

"Hello, Detective," Lonnie said.

"Hello."

"This is ridiculous. My name is Lonnie Penn, and yes, I am *that* Lonnie Penn. I'm pleased to meet you, Detective. Your husband has been helpful. I'm grateful."

"He has his moments. May I ask, what's your interest in the child?"

"He's my grandson."

"Oh. Um…and the child's mother?"

"My daughter."

"I see. I would tell you that I'm sorry for your loss but there's no record of a death in custody. When did it allegedly take place?"

"I'm not sure."

"It's popular to condemn Immigration and Customs Enforcement these days, but they are an important federal enforcement agency with a lot of good people doing a difficult job. Like all agencies in our business, they are subject to strict guidelines."

"What are you telling me, Detective?"

"ICE has a rigid protocol for a death in custody. The matter is reported to the Immigration Health Services Corps for an investigation. They review the case to ensure that the subject received proper medical care, determine if there were pre-existing conditions, that sort of thing. They also engage the ICE Office of Professional Responsibility to investigate."

"Sounds like a lot of ass covering to me, Detective."

"Ass covering is the inherent purpose of all such protocols. But there's more. If there is a detainee death, ICE Enforcement and Removal Operations submits official notification to Congress, to NGO officials *and* issues a media release—on a rigid timetable. Two days for the notifications. And within three days, ERO schedules a briefing for senior officials. It's popular to accuse government agencies of misconduct and coverups, but these are a lot of turning wheels with serious *non-political* professionals meeting tough standards and requirements. People lose their jobs for breaking the chain. Most career law enforcement professionals are unwilling to risk that—contrary to all the conspiracy theories."

"What are you saying?"

"Ms. Penn, there's been no report of a death in custody at the Eastern State Detention Center, or at any other ICE detention center nationwide since July. There's no report of a detainee death under the name Gloria Rilling or Mira Apalacio."

"None?"

"Not that I can find in available records."

"Dee, what about custody? Is either name listed as being in ICE custody?"

"That, I can't get. Not without an official inquiry. And to open an official inquiry, I need a reason. I'm sorry. Looking her up would have to be part of an active investigation."

"What about some of our friends in the federal government?"

She didn't answer right away, which told me she didn't like this line of inquiry in front of a civilian.

"I don't think they would be in any better position."

Lonnie rotated in her seat, pressing her back to the door. "What the hell does this mean?"

"I don't know what to tell you. If you believe the child and your daughter are in ICE custody, and if they've been apprehended as illegal aliens, your relationship to them does not have much standing. They are still in custody as a criminal matter under federal law. I think your best move would be to make your relationship known, make contact, and engage legal counsel. Do what you can to assure them and the authorities that you know their status and location and see that they have representation."

"They'll be deported."

"Possibly. But that's only after an immigration court issues an order. You're in a good position to, at the very least, follow that process and render legal aid. It's a clogged mess being made far worse than it needs to be, but it's all we have. You can certainly act as an advocate. And if they're deported, forgive me for being blunt, but so what? Meet them at the border. You have the resources to set them on a path to obtaining a visa and from there, citizenship if that's what they want."

"Dee," I said, "I think we might have some bad actors involved here. A couple of guys tried to shake down Ms. Penn. They told her that for half a million, they could get the child out of detention, otherwise he was going to be deported, and they were going to ensure he disappeared in the system."

"Well, at this point, we can't be sure he's even in the system. I would report them. And definitely don't pay them."

Lonnie grimaced, then knit her brow. "Wait! I can prove he's in the system. That they both are. No one knew my connection to the child except my daughter. They had to obtain the information from her."

"It makes no difference. Ms. Penn, hiring a lawyer to advocate for your daughter is the best path."

"Detective, my daughter hates me. The people who contacted me said she only revealed her relationship to me because she was dying, and she wanted her son cared for. And those people also said that tomorrow morning, the child will disappear into the system with no name, no family, no records."

"What do you think, Dee? Bad apples in the detention center?"

Andy hesitated. At length, she said, "More likely a scam."

"We still need to know if Gloria and Oscar Rilling are behind those walls. And if they are, whether or not they're being transported in the next eighteen hours."

Andy let the line fall silent. I held up a hand when Lonnie opened her mouth to speak. I know when to let Andy think.

"Can I call you back?"

I picked up the phone, touched off the speaker function and pressed it to my ear. I opened the door and stepped out, closing it behind me, ignoring a glare from Lonnie.

I said, "It's just us."

"Will, what are you getting pulled into?"

"The usual crap, I guess. Two guys showed up for her meet this afternoon. Big guys. They assaulted her and took the half a million."

"Oh, lord."

"Yeah."

"Well, that's her mistake. Don't go playing white knight for the stupid money, for God's sake. She spends more than that on hair styling. I mean it. Don't do anything crazy, okay? You have to be seeing the problems here."

"I am. But think about it. Either the girl is dead, and they have the child, and they're dumping the kid in the system and covering up the death in custody…"

"That is not as easy as it sounds."

"Or the girl has a co-conspirator in the system and she's shaking rich Mommy down for half a million. Do you see what I'm saying?"

"Do you have anything else?"

"I got a name. Mallorin. Can you see if there's anyone on staff at the jail by that name?"

She heaved a loud sigh. "Fine. And…I think I might know how to find out if they're transporting any detainees out of that facility. One question…"

"What?"

"Lonnie Penn…so what's she like?"

LONNIE SAID nothing when I climbed back in the van. I expected recriminations for abruptly taking the call private but she sat lost in thought. Finding out your lost daughter was dead had to have been a blow. Finding out she might not be dead had to flip an emotional switch.

I prepped myself to take up Andy's argument that Lonnie hire a lawyer and fight this battle with her ample checkbook. Points and counterpoints lined up in my head.

She twisted in her seat and looked across the parking lot.

She spoke softly.

"I've never been in a Walmart…"

12

"That's it? That's all the guy does?"

She turned around several times to look at the greeter. He hadn't taken his eyes from her. She waved. He waved.

"That's it."

"He's so cute! He's got to be a hundred years old!"

I couldn't argue, but the man at the door surely felt younger at this moment.

"Are you going to tell me what we're doing here?" I asked.

"Your wife was right," she said. "She sounds lovely, by the way."

"Lovely hardly covers it."

"My! Aren't you the smitten one! Lemme see a picture." She poked her elbow into my side and held out her hand, spicing the command with a bright smile. "Come on!"

I dug for my phone. She leaned over to peek, but I turned the screen away. I scrolled through the photo gallery.

I keep a candid photo of Andy I snapped a little over a year ago, a few weeks after the accident, during her I-won't-let-you-out-of-my-sight phase. She'd been sitting beside me on our porch steps in the pinkish light of a brilliant sunset. Fresh off her duty tour as a patrol sergeant, out of uniform and into an old Metallica t-shirt, her hair still kinked after release from the day's French braid. I had just obtained a replacement phone and had been holding it on my knee, angling for a selfie of the two of us. I must have been yammering on about something. Her head was turned toward me. I had the lens on zoom, so only Andy filled the frame.

Her eyes held me. The expression on her face said she wasn't hearing a word I said, yet her look said she had never heard anything so wonderful. Nothing in the vows we exchanged came close to the ironclad assurance I saw in my wife in that photo—in that instant—that we would share our last breaths together.

I found the image and handed Lonnie the phone.

She mugged a haughty *let's see what you've got* look, but it evaporated the instant she focused on the image. She stopped cold in the Walmart aisle.

I wasn't sure what to say. Thankfully, I said nothing.

Lonnie stared.

"Is she looking at you?"

"Uh-huh."

She fixed her eyes on the screen. "If I ever can learn to look at someone like that on a movie set, I'll make room for a third little gold statue on the shelf."

She handed me the phone. I detected a hint of something—sadness? Loss? Envy? I wasn't certain I could trust any emotion coming from a woman capable of slipping them on and off like a laundered t-shirt.

I put away the phone. We resumed our march through Walmart.

"What are we doing here?"

"Wardrobe."

"Meaning?"

"Your wife was right. I need a lawyer to go in there and raise a little legal hell. But we can't call in Lonnie Penn's usual sharks, so we're going with someone far more dangerous."

"You?"

"Killer lawyer. Did you see me in 'Depth of Defense' last year? I knocked that role out of the park."

She spotted racks of women's clothing on hangers between posters showing perfect models in perfect attire with familiar brand names imprinted on the images.

"Here we go," she said.

"When my wife suggested a lawyer, I can guarantee you she didn't mean for you to con a law enforcement agency into thinking you're a lawyer. For one thing, you can't show ID. And then there's that pesky issue of a law degree."

Lonnie stopped and jabbed her hand in the hip pocket of her jeans. She flashed a California driver's license in my face.

"Who's that?" I asked.

"Marie Catalaine. My assistant."

"The assistant you were pretending to be when I picked you up?" I looked over the photo. "Lonnie, if she looked anything like you, she'd be the one with the shelf full of statues. You don't resemble this photo. It's not going to fly."

She laughed and plucked the plastic card from my fingers. "If you ever compare what I look like when I crawl out of bed against what I look like on the screen, you'd realize how wrong you are."

She whirled and began pulling items off the hanger bars. With an armful, she examined her surroundings.

"Where are the changing rooms?"

LONNIE PENN'S transformation from leather jacketed jeans-wearing assistant in a ball cap to buttoned-down lawyer in a suit and a tight hair bun took a little over an hour and a half. She spent the bulk of her shopping time at the makeup counter after settling on a plain white blouse under a black blazer and black pencil skirt. Using a constant stream of products suggested to her by a bewildered counter girl, Lonnie covered the bruise on the side of her cheek, then worked on her eyes and cheekbones. I had to admit, she somehow toned down the natural glamour of her Lonnie Penn face, to a point where the girl behind the counter seemed less likely to ask, "Don't I know you?"

I thought shopping for shoes would kill a lot of time, but she snagged a pair of flats quickly. Then she spent fifteen minutes looking at jewelry before settling on a thin nine-dollar necklace dangling a tiny gold cross. She picked a pair of black-rimmed glasses from a spinning rack at the end of an aisle in the pharmacy section. The round frames accented her tight bun hairstyle. I thought they were perfect, but she kept switching them and looking at herself in the tiny mirror on the rack.

"What was wrong with those?" I finally asked as she swapped a pair for an identical pair.

"Not enough power," she said. She put on a new pair and turned to me. Her crystal blue eyes were huge. "See?"

"I do." The disproportionate size of her eyes further distorted the famous face. "You're going to trip over your own feet wearing those."

She spent ten minutes choosing a leather briefcase from the school supplies section.

I carried her jeans and jacket through the checkout while the clerk took barcode reader shots of the tags still dangling from the new outfit she wore. The clerk offered to cut off the tags, then rang up the case and the collection of cosmetics.

"That's two-twenty-one fifty."

Lonnie turned to me.

"What?"

"I don't carry money," she said as if it made perfect sense.

I blew out a long sigh and pulled out my wallet. From it, I produced a credit card while the clerk smiled at me out of pity.

A few minutes later, I walked out of the Prince Henry Walmart beside a severe-looking woman in a business suit thinking that if I saw her coming at me with a briefcase, I'd run in the opposite direction.

13

"The idea is to gather intelligence," I told her after turning off the ignition.

"Who died and made you commander-in-chief?"

"Commander-in-chief is elected, and I got your vote when you dragged me into this," I told her. "I can't go in there with you. I don't have a reason to be there."

"You can be my assistant."

"They're going to want ID. I can't put mine on the record. As it is, you're running a risk using your assistant's. I'm pretty sure she's not a member of the bar." The makeup transformation brought Lonnie Penn surprisingly closer to the image of Marie Catalaine on the driver's license. I'd never seen makeup applied for the purpose of removing glamour. "Just get in. See if you can confirm that either Gloria or Oscar Rilling are in custody, and then get out."

"What if I can get in to see her?" The plea within the question exposed Lonnie Penn again.

"That's the last thing you want. If she recognizes you it causes all kinds of problems. Remember. Someone in there knows you're here, in Prince Henry. If they see you poking around, they'll take it as a direct threat. Don't engage anyone you don't have to. Try to handle everything with the uniform at the front desk."

She stared at the public entrance to the jail.

"Fine."

"One more thing. We don't know anything at this point. Nothing. Which means don't get your hopes up either way. Hope seeds poor judgment."

She frowned at my attempted philosophy.

A moment later I watched her stalk to the double glass doors, the image of impatient authority. She disappeared inside.

"Hey," I said pressing my phone to my ear.

"There's an ICE ERO transport scheduled for the Eastern State Detention Center at nineteen hundred hours today."

I looked at my watch. "Dee, that's twenty minutes from now."

"Am I on speaker?"

"No. I'm in the van. I'm alone."

"Where's Lonnie?"

I explained. Cold silence at the other end of the call told me how Andy felt about the actor pretending to be a lawyer involved in a federal case.

"What's an ERO?" I asked.

"Enforcement Removal Operation."

"Are you sure about this?"

"I got it from a certain federal source who told me if it ever came back to him, he would kick your ass."

"*My* ass?"

"I'm not taking the fall, dear. But here's the thing. An ERO only comes after issuance of a final removal order by the immigration court, or after an administrative removability review. There's no record of either for a Gloria Rilling with a minor child. There wouldn't be for someone recently taken into custody. Those things take time. Lots of time. Something is not right."

I could not take my eyes off the building.

"Gremlins."

"Will, you can't get mixed up in whatever she's doing. You and I are about to work with one of the highest law enforcement officers in the country. We can't show up dragging an ugly mess behind us."

"I know," I said. "I gotta get her out of there."

"Get her out of there and take her back to La Crosse. Then come home."

"Yeah."

"No, I mean it. Get her out of there *now*."

"Right."

. . .

I JOGGED to the doors and pulled my way through the first set. A second set of doors presented, but three of the four were blocked with signs on portable stands that said *Enter At Right*.

The single remaining door opened on a security station with a metal detector. A deputy sat on a stool, alerted to new business.

I dropped my phone into a plastic tray. Then the van keys. Then my wallet. Thankfully, I left my portable power units in the flight bag behind the driver's seat of the van. They would have prompted questions. I found my Bluetooth earpiece in a pocket and dropped it in the tray.

"Belt?"

"Uh-huh." The belt came off.

"What about the boots?" I lifted my western-style boots to show him. "They have nails."

"Leave 'em on."

I stepped through the metal detector. It chirped a warning that I was dangerous. The deputy picked up a wand and ran it up and down my body, doubling passes over my boots.

"Lift your pants cuffs."

I did. He looked in the tops of my boots and patted the sides.

"Thank you, sir."

I fumbled to get all my possessions back in my pockets, then hurried to the information desk facing the security station across a small, barren lobby. A second deputy who had been watching my entrance lifted his eyebrows.

"How can I help you?"

I held up my phone. "I need to get this call to Attorney Catalaine. She came in here a few minutes ago."

He nodded. "She's down the hall waiting for the duty sergeant." He tipped his head to the left.

"Thanks!" I hopped away, then called backward to him as I hurried. "Is that Sergeant Mallorin?"

The desk officer screwed up his face like I'd just spoken in tongues.

"No. It's Sergeant Hayes." He shook his head. I thought it was worth a try and kept going. He called after me. "Mallorin is in Central Detention." Like I should know.

Bingo!

I found the first door on the left. Lonnie held her brief case across her hips, tapping a toe impatiently and staring bullets at a third deputy behind another counter who worked hard to ignore her.

"Attorney Catalaine? Ma'am?" I leaned my head in the door. "There's a call for you. It's Judge Bean. You have to take this." I held my phone out toward her. "I think they have a verdict."

The deputy looked up. Lonnie, without missing a beat, pointed at him. "I'll be back."

She marched to me and snatched the phone.

"Yes, your honor?" She continued her march out the door. I hurried after her. "Yes, your honor…*ex parte*?…uh-huh…uh-huh…"

She carried on the conversation until the glass front door closed behind us, at which point she handed back the phone to me.

"What the hell? I had them looking up her name!"

I pointed at the van and hurried her away from the building. I went to the driver's door of the van. She climbed in beside me. I turned the key in the ignition and pulled the column shifter into Reverse.

"Andy called. There's an ICE transport—an Enforcement Removal Operation—it's happening…" I checked my watch "…in about five minutes."

I backed up, then put the van in gear and accelerated across the parking lot, across the front of the building. At the end, instead of turning left toward the highway, I turned right. A service lane followed the perimeter of the building.

"Is she on it? The boy?"

"Unknown." I drove along the side of the building until it came to an end. The service road turned right and entered a back lot filled with a handful of employee cars. Several loading docks passed on my right.

A white van sat in a short lane backed up against an overhead door.

"That's it."

"How can you tell? There's no sign on it."

"It has a federal DOT number on the driver's door. That's it."

I looked around. An opening to my left offered entry to the employee lot. I took it and wheeled into a space facing the building.

"Okay. This is going to get a little nutty from here on out." I scrambled to pull my flight bag from behind the seat. From it, I pulled a pair of BLASTER power units and companion props. She gave them a curious look as I slipped them into my pocket. I pulled out the Bluetooth earpiece. I slid it into place. "What's your phone number?"

"Huh?"

"Your phone. Your mobile. What's the number?"

I tapped the icons on my phone as she rattled off the number. A moment later her phone chirped.

"Okay. That's me. After I get out, slide over here and wait. Wait for the van to pull out *but don't follow it.* Understand? Do NOT follow the van. They'll spot you from a mile away. After they pull out of sight, call me. Got it?"

"What are you going to do?"

"Beats the hell out of me, but I can tell you for certain, whatever it is, it will not work if you ignore my instructions. We only get one shot at this."

I grabbed her hat from the floor by her seat. I tried it on. Too tight. I expanded the band and tried again. With a snug fit, I pulled the brim down as far as I could.

"Wait until they're well out of sight. Then call me." I said. "I mean it. Promise me."

"Promise." Like pulling teeth.

I double-checked my pockets. Reaching for the door, I remembered one more item. I pulled my flight bag forward again and rummaged through the outermost pocket.

"Will?"

"What?"

"Judge Bean? Seriously?"

"It was that or Dredd."

I found my emergency knife and slipped it into a pocket. I gave her one last look, then opened the door and jumped out. Without looking back, I hurried across the lot, between parked cars, across the service road to the front of the parked federal transport van. A wall-mounted security camera watched, but I didn't look up to feed it a facial image. I hurried past the van, putting it between me and Lonnie, then hurried up against the building wall, directly beneath the camera.

Fwooomp! I vanished and immediately pushed off the wall on a line for the van. I connected with the vehicle at the rear left corner and converted my forward trajectory to an upward vector. At the top of the van I grabbed the luggage rack.

I pulled myself to a horizontal position over the center of a large numeral 17 painted on the van roof.

I waited. From my vantage point, I saw Lonnie behind the wheel of the airport crew van. She had switched her lawyer glasses for her aviator sunglasses and lowered herself in the driver's seat, creating the perfect image of someone engaged in suspicious surveillance.

I wished I had checked my watch before vanishing. Experience with Andy told me that a law enforcement prisoner transport scheduled for nineteen hundred hours would launch at precisely seven p.m. I knew we were close to the hour but had no idea how close.

The wait seemed to take hours.

A door adjacent to the overhead door opened. An armed officer in a black uniform, ball cap and ballistic vest stepped out. Behind me, the overhead door clattered, rising.

Excellent! I rotated to gain a better view of the detainees about to be loaded.

My hopes shattered when the loading bay door stopped just inches above the roof rack. Worse, the transport officer had climbed behind the wheel and slowly backed the van into the loading bay. The door would soon scrape me off my roof rack perch.

I swung around and prepared to release the roof rack. The officer slowly rolled the van into the bay but stopped when only a few feet of the vehicle had passed under the open door.

The driver remained at his post. Someone opened the rear doors of the van. Commands were issued in Spanish. I felt the van tremble as passengers boarded. The overhead door obscured my view and the open rear doors did the same at each side. This was a well-orchestrated loading procedure designed to deny observers a look.

A moment later, the rear doors slammed shut. The driver dropped the van in gear. The vehicle lurched forward. I gripped the roof rack. The overhead door dropped, but not before I spotted the lower two thirds of a deputy. His face was hidden by the door, but the lava flow belly spilling over his belt looked familiar.

The man who rammed me as he exited the motel room with half a million Lonnie Penn dollars clutched to his chest.

Mallorin wasn't the only man on the inside.

The van rolled past Lonnie. She ducked beneath the rim of the steering wheel. I counted us lucky that she had not advanced beyond front desk gatekeepers in the jail. Had she encountered the deputy who assaulted her, she might not have had the good sense to hold her tongue. On his turf, and faced with exposure, the inside man may have acted rashly, given the possibility that he was covering up a death in custody and was about to face an assault charge.

The van rolled around the low building, turned, and made for the driveway.

I tapped the Bluetooth earpiece in response to the ring tone in my ear.

"It's me."

"I did what you told me. Now what? And what's all that noise?"

"Wind. I'm with the van."

"What?"

"Never mind. Drive. Go out the driveway and turn left. Then go back to the highway we were on when we came into town. Highway H. Make a right and head east out of town. If you see the van, don't catch up! Got it?"

"How are you—?"

"Just do it! Put me on speaker, put down the phone and drive. Keep the line open, even if you don't hear anything. When I want you to catch up, I'll tell you. Stay on the line because I can't call you."

"Okay. I got it."

The transport driver exhibited no sense of urgency. Starts from stop signs were smooth. He held to the posted speed limit, which thankfully remained at 45 as the town thinned out and gave way to rolling farm countryside. High summer painted the landscape brown and gold. The trees were a month away from coloring their leaves, but they looked thirsty in this part of the country. The steady run of summer fronts and storms watering my lawn in Wisconsin appeared to have bypassed the Dakotas. Or maybe it was always this dry by the end of summer. The drizzle and mist in the air did not satisfy the thirsty-looking scrub and dry fields.

I gripped the roof rack cross bar against a steady, forty-five mile per hour wind. Soon the speed limit would increase, making movement more difficult. I pulled myself to the passenger side of the vehicle. I reached down and grabbed the mirror on the passenger-side door. Releasing the roof rack, I lowered myself until I trailed the mirror frame like a banner in the wind.

With one hand, I pulled my emergency knife from my pocket. I didn't unfold the knife. It wasn't the blade I was after.

"Are you still there?" Lonnie asked.

"Yup."

"What's going on?"

"Not a good time."

I closed my right fist around the knife and reached down to the right front fender.

I slammed the butt of the knife against sheet metal.

Bang!

Behind the wheel, the driver glanced to his right, alerting to the sound.

Bang! I counted to three. *Bang!* Counted to two. *Bang!*

Then I began pounding a steady beat.

Bang! Bang! Bang!

I held it steady. The driver released the accelerator. The van lost speed. I increased the beat count against the sheet metal. The driver hit the brakes and edged to the side of the road.

I changed the cadence as the van rolled to a stop on the shoulder.

Counting off the last few beats slowly, suggesting that whatever had gone wrong with the vehicle had to do with the vehicle's speed.

He stopped and threw the gearshift in Park.

I lowered myself below the window line.

Fwooomp!

I reappeared and dropped to the road shoulder. My knees and elbows bit into the rough gravel and I kicked out an involuntary grunt.

The driver opened the door. Looking beneath the van, I saw the driver's boots land on the pavement. I had only seconds.

The knife appeared with me. I flicked open the razor-sharp emergency blade and jabbed it into the front tire. A satisfying whoosh of cool air shot over my hand. I pried the knife free, folded it and stuffed it back in my pocket.

The driver walked around the front fender and across the van's grille.

Fwooomp! I vanished and pushed off the gravel, rising quickly to the level of the mirror, which I grabbed with both hands. I levered myself to a vertical, inverted position, to ensure that the driver would not bump into me.

He spotted the flat tire.

"Son of a bitch," he muttered.

I crossed my fingers. He stared at the tire for a moment, and my hopes faded, but then he crouched beside the fender to examine the slash.

This was the part I hated doing. This was the part Andy would reject out of hand. I had no idea whether this officer was just a driver assigned to a transport, or if he shared a role in the extortion scheme.

If this went bad, I planned to abandon the whole thing.

Lonnie spoke excitedly in my earpiece.

"I see the van! I see it!"

I said nothing. I gripped the mirror mount and rotated my legs until my feet contacted the gravel behind the officer. I pulled a power unit from my pocket and reversed it, extending the small round end from my hand. Gripping the mirror frame for leverage, I leaned down and pressed the power unit against the back of his neck.

"Do—not—move." I pushed the unit harder against his skin.

He froze. He instinctively lifted his hands to show no intent to resist.

Fwooomp! I dropped on my feet.

"Eyes down. You do not want to look at me. Understand?"

"Understood. Just don't do anything. Please. I have a family."

I moved around to stand directly behind him. I switched the power unit to my left hand. Reaching down, I unsnapped the flap on his holster. Using fingernails, I slid his weapon free and flipped it backward across the ditch into tall grass beside a field of already-cut wheat.

"Keys!"

"Christ! Will! What are you doing?" Lonnie demanded.

"They're in the ignition."

"Get down on your belly. Flat. Face down. Don't look at me. As long as you don't look, you're fine. Do it."

He moved quickly to comply.

"Now scoot forward. Crawl under the van. Go. As far in as you can."

He squirmed under the front door. It was a tight fit. He kicked at the gravel shoulder.

"More."

His bulky vest caught the bottom of the van body. I reached down and shoved it under. He inched forward.

"That's all I can, man! That's it!"

"Don't move. And don't look. Eyes closed."

I pulled open the passenger door and spotted the keys dangling from the column. I leaned in and jerked them free.

"Stay put. This will be over in a minute and you can go home to your family tonight. No harm."

Andy's going to kill me.

I hurried to the back of the van. A quarter of a mile away the face of the old airport crew van grew larger. I waved for Lonnie to pull up.

Keys in hand, I found a match for the rear door lock. The latch turned. I pulled the door open and looked inside.

No child.

No girl.

Two men looked out at me. One old and weathered. One young and marred with blue-ink tattoos boiling up from the neck of his t-shirt. The younger wore wrist and ankle shackles.

No three-year-old boy named Oscar Rilling.

Lonnie skidded to a halt on the highway behind me and jumped out. She saw what I saw. Her face fell.

"*Donde está el niño?*" I mustered what little Spanish I had.

"What kid?" the young man asked.

"There was a boy. And his mother. Where are they?"

"Let me loose and I'll tell you!" He held out his hands. I noted that the old man's hands and feet were free. "I know where they went, dude! Let me go and I'll tell you! I'll take you to them!"

The old man spat words I could not understand at the younger man, who answered in kind. An argument erupted.

"Don't listen to him!" the young man snapped at me. "Let me go and I'll take you to the kid!"

I turned to the old man. He sat back and looked at me calmly.

"He lies. He will kill you and take your truck," the old man said. He looked at Lonnie and recognition bloomed in his eyes. "You are her mother."

"Yes! Yes, I am! Is she alive? Is she okay?"

He nodded.

"SHUT UP OLD MAN!" The young man tried to kick across the back of the van. Chains held his feet at bay. "I'll kill you!"

The old man shrugged and said to me, "You see? He makes my point for me."

"We don't have much time. The girl and the child—what happened to them?"

"The coyote," he said sadly. "They gave her back to the coyote. She told them you would pay. I guess you did."

"What coyote?" I asked.

He shrugged. "The one who is taking them."

"Where?" Lonnie demanded.

"To Canada."

The young man spit out a new stream of Spanish invective. The old man reached across the space between them and slapped his face, which only increased the venom. He turned back to Lonnie.

"That is all I can tell you. I'm sorry." He shrugged. "I love your movies."

14

"We go back to the jail! We go back and find Mallorin and rat him out to his superiors. No more screwing around. I know people. We go back in there and raise hell and make him tell us." She reached for the necklace with the cross and jerked it free. "I'm seriously done screwing around."

"No."

I drove at the speed limit. My fingers were tighter on the wheel than they had been on the control yoke of the Arrow scud running our way into Prince Henry airport. I watched the rearview mirror for signs of trouble. I scanned side roads and the highway ahead for sheriff's cars.

"He knows! And he's complicit. He's—"

"We're done here, Lonnie. We're leaving."

That is, if we can get to the airport without being stopped.

I decided that if a phalanx of squad cars suddenly blocked the road ahead, I would pull over and grab Lonnie and vanish. Let them find an empty van. I didn't care. I would explain it all to Lonnie and extract a promise of silence—the price of staying out of jail.

I factored my flight bag into whatever escape move I might make.

"Will, we can't leave! We have to find out who has her!"

"Has her?"

"You heard the man."

"Nobody 'has her,' Lonnie."

"What are you talking about?"

I rolled self-consciously through the small town. Past pizza joints and a hardware store. Past a strip mall and a section of the old town center where storefronts advertised hair styling, or tattoos, or a law office or empty space for lease. Each intersection and alley offered cover for a patrol car to sit in ambush.

The transport driver would have had trouble seeing much from under the van. But once we drove off, he could have moved fast. He could have slid from under the van, caught sight of us, identified make and model, and noted the color.

Crap! What if he saw the license plate!

I fought off the urge to stomp the accelerator and roar out of town.

"What the hell are you talking about?" Lonnie demanded.

"Nobody 'has her.' She wasn't abducted. She isn't in custody." The last stoplight gave us a green and opened the road ahead. The small hill hiding the White Bluff Motel approached and the highway curved. I pushed the van speed to five over the thirty-mile-per-hour limit. "She's on her way to Canada. That was her plan all along."

"You can't know that."

The White Bluff Motel passed on my right.

"Lonnie, she got picked up. She took stock of a couple of deputies and lured them into a scheme to shake you down. They scored half a million and she's on her way. Maybe they even gave her a cut. Or she gave them a cut. That's the only thing I can think of that makes sense."

The highway opened a straight shot to the airport. I glanced at the sky, which hung over us like a gray veil. I estimated the cloud bases to be high enough to get us safely out of the area.

Lonnie said nothing.

She stared at the two-lane blacktop ahead. More effectively than the Walmart makeup, dark hair and plain clothes, the expression of cold realization on her face removed all the trappings of glamour and stardom.

She looked defeated.

Ordinary.

We didn't speak until I landed in LaCrosse and taxied to park beside the shining Gulfstream G650 that would return her—empty-handed—to her world.

PART II

15

"There. See it?"

I pointed over the instrument panel of the Beechcraft Baron. Andy lifted herself in the passenger seat and squinted into the bright eastern sky. A puff of cloud slid under us. The towers of the Mackinac Bridge rose from the platinum surface of the Great Lakes.

I had hoped sight of the mighty bridge would break the last of the ice in Andy's mood. She stared at it for a moment, then sat back.

"It's big."

I looked at her. After a moment, she felt my stare and returned it.

"What do you want me to say? It's big."

I went back to flying the airplane. She went back to watching Lake Michigan flow beneath the right wing.

I sat in flying doghouse at 200 miles per hour.

Andy infrequently plays a game I call *Guess What's Wrong Now*. The purpose of the game is to cause me to reflect on my bad behavior, dissect my failure and determine an adequate punishment or public humiliation for myself—after figuring out what it was that I did wrong, hence the *Guess* in the title.

The guessing portion of the game can span a wide range of transgressions. On one occasion, we spent the better part of a weekend playing the game—me offering up my soul, her responding with sullen rejection. It turned out that what was wrong was that we had been at a party where I failed to recognize the hostess belittling Andy's decision to be a cop instead of a soccer mom. I missed the diss entirely. Worse, I apparently found the hostess funny all evening, although I contend it was the rum punch. The weekend that followed was a four- or five-apology journey through a long, slow reveal of my crime.

This time, the quiz question at hand had an easy answer.

AFTER UNLOADING Lonnie Penn and refueling the Piper Arrow in LaCrosse, I filed an instrument flight plan under the airplane's registered N-number and flew back to Essex County Airport. Before leaving, I sent a text to Andy that the child was not recovered, and Lonnie Penn was probably on her way to meet her lawyers. I may have over-simplified and I purposely communicated by text to avoid probing questions. My long day ended when I finally entered our lightless and silent home after midnight.

Andy did not wait up for me. That's not unusual, but it was the first glimmer of warning from my marital bliss alert system.

Morning shed a blinding light on trouble ahead. I found my wife at our kitchen table. Steam rose from a fresh coffee in her hands and, I swear, from her ears.

"Morning," I said, heading for the cabinet to get a mug, only to realize that the pot was off and empty. She had made a single cup.

"Uh-huh."

Having no coffee service to occupy my hands, I grabbed a glass from the cabinet and filled it with orange juice from the refrigerator. I joined her at the table.

"What's up?" I asked, signaling the start of the game.

"Why didn't you tell me the whole story last night?"

"Oh," I stalled. "Well, it was late. I didn't want to wake you."

She rotated her coffee mug. The fresh-brewed scent joined her side of the interrogation by torturing me.

"Are you going to fill me in now?" she asked. I knew this technique. Asking for details she already had. I did some quick thinking and decided she had heard from someone about the disrupted prisoner transport. It had to have been Special Agent Donaldson.

"Okay, I had to improvise." I took the only path open to me at times like this. I confessed. I laid out the whole story. On the plus side, it was precisely what she wanted. On the minus side, what she also wanted was my head on a pike.

"Will! How could you! You used that *thing* to attack a law enforcement officer. You put a weapon to the head of an officer doing his duty. I don't even know what to say."

"It wasn't a weapon. It was—"

"You don't get it! That's what *I* do. That could have been me out there. How would you feel if someone did that to me?"

"Dee, I tried—"

"We had a long discussion about the future when we went to New York. We took stock of what has happened since this change in you. It hasn't been easy on me, but I support you. Just like I have with your flying." I fought off the impulse to remind her that my aviation career choice accounted for the fact that we met. "I thought we both made an honest assessment of how this was going to impact our lives. How we wanted to handle things going forward. I thought it was *our* decision to go to the FBI, and that we were going to do it on *our* terms rather than wait for them or someone worse to force it."

"We did."

"Yes! But then you go running off and getting all starry-eyed over some Hollywood type—"

I made a note to avoid mentioning Lonnie Penn.

"—and you throw away all the fundamental beliefs we shared! How am I supposed to take that? How am I supposed to trust that the framework *we* established for making this work means anything to you?"

I bit my tongue. In the game of *Guess What's Wrong Now* a question is generally not a question, but a trap into which only the uninitiated venture.

She stood up and moved her coffee to the kitchen counter. I recognized the determined swing of her hips. We had reached the part where she declares—

"I'm going to work." She drove the stake into my heart by dumping her nearly untouched coffee into the sink. Without a hug or kiss, which we always share when parting, she said, "I want you to think this through, because if we aren't on the same page—well then, I just don't know."

She marched out the back door.

It wasn't a fight. In four years of marriage, I honestly don't remember a fight. Or a heated argument. Games of *Guess* pop up from time to time, but they're always my fault, even when they're not. They're always exercises in recalibrating my point of view—even when they end with Andy realizing that it was her point of view at the heart of the problem. And they always end when I gloriously leap onto my own sword.

What made this different was that I had to agree with her assessment of the seriousness of my transgression.

If someone put a gun to her head, I would go nuts. It's happened. The rage it ignited in me had been blinding. Her point about the driver of the ICE transport dug deep.

It didn't matter that my "gun" was just a power unit battery pack, or that I made sure the encounter would not escalate by throwing the driver's duty weapon into the weeds. It didn't matter that I would have vanished the instant the officer offered any resistance.

As Andy saw it, all that mattered was that I had attacked an officer of the law.

And in that sense, her.

That evening, when she climbed the back steps to our kitchen door, I met her at the door and heaved myself onto my sword. I spent the rest of the night tugging said sword deeper and deeper into my chest. We alternated between long, intimate discussions punctuated with my heartfelt apologies, and deeper examination of where we were headed. The New York decision to take me and *the other thing* to the second highest officer in the FBI got a thorough rehashing. She thawed slowly and we wound up in each other's arms. But the sting lingered and resurfaced on Thursday morning in the form of a sullen mood.

I HAVE FLOWN charters to the island's one-runway airport, but I never left the airport. Neither Andy nor I have ever visited as tourists. I once investigated surprising her with a romantic stay at the iconic Grand Hotel. The notion did not survive learning the hotel's room rate. We settled for a B&B stay in Door County that didn't require taking out a personal loan.

We were both pleased and surprised when FBI Deputy Director Mitchell Lindsay chose the island for our first official meeting. His instructions had been simple. Fly to the island. Call a taxi. Have it deliver us to an address he provided.

Ten miles from the bridge that joined upper and lower Michigan, I tuned the radio to the island airport's automated weather advisory. West winds dictated the use of runway 26. The recording asked for a higher-than-normal traffic pattern altitude as a noise abatement measure.

I descended to the stated traffic pattern altitude well before we passed over the big suspension bridge. The view of the 500-foot towers was impressive. Oddly, even though we flew five times higher, I looked at the four lanes of traffic arching across the straits and felt a twinge of fear. It seemed silly. Here I was two-and-a-half thousand feet up thinking it would scare me to drive across the bridge.

Andy's interest stirred as we flew over the north tower. She pulled out her phone to snap pictures. I worked the throttles and focused on a mental map of our flight path to the runway.

"Gas is on the mains," I said, reciting my landing checklist aloud and checking the fuel selector valve, "no fuel pumps required. Undercarriage is..." I checked my speed, then flipped the landing gear handle to the down position. "...down. Mixtures are rich. Props set. Got your seatbelt on?" I looked at Andy.

She tapped the belt joined around her waist and gave me a thumbs-up. Then she gave me a warm look that melted the last frost between us. In that instant, I was forgiven.

I reached for and squeezed her hand. She squeezed back.

"Hey," I said a moment later. "There's the Grand Hotel."

I banked slightly, keeping an eye on my flight path and maintaining a watch for any traffic. She leaned toward me and looked over the left engine nacelle. The huge white building with its pillared façade spread against a green bluff.

"It's magnificent," she said. "I would love to stay there sometime."

"Then I promise we will."

WE TOUCHED down smoothly and taxied back to a central parking ramp tucked against the unbroken green woodland surrounding the airport. Summer traffic filled a majority of tiedown slots, but ample capacity offered easy parking. I shut down the engines and opened the cabin door.

No one hurried to assist with unloading. The airport offers no fuel service, or services of any kind. I unloaded our luggage, then locked and tied down the airplane. The neatly painted airport office, looking like a vintage train station, hosts an airport manager whose job centers around collecting the state park landing fee from visiting pilots. The manager, however, was absent and his inner office was locked. I filled out a form with the aircraft registration number, put the form and cash fee in an envelope and slid it through a slot in a quaint split door.

I called for a taxi. A cheery voice took our order, asked our destination and promised a cab would arrive in about an hour.

Life moves at a slower pace on an island without motor vehicles.

Andy and I waited alone on a bench beside the airport office. Birds issued urgent territorial claims to break the silence. Andy made no further mention of the transport driver incident. I measured my wife's mood and determined that the remnants of her anger were gone, replaced by a slight uptick in nervous anticipation. She gets that way around senior law enforcement officers. I tested the waters by bringing up Lindsay and asking what she knew about him. She launched into a rapid monologue on his career, his record of major cases and his trajectory to becoming director, something all but assured with a change in administration at the national level. For the most part Lindsay had avoided the political fallout from recent national news stories. Lindsay, she said, was the senior official overseeing the senior official who oversaw the General Pemmick investigation. I found that interesting, given Andy's role in revealing Pemmick's involvement with Russian money.

I did not interrupt with questions. Andy's energetic chatter both revealed and relieved her tension. She kept it up until the passive clop of horse hooves on pavement caused her to pause.

"That's our taxi." I pointed at a canopied wagon drawn by a pair of hard-working horses.

She beamed a smile.

"My lord, they're beautiful!" she said as the driver steered the team into the airport driveway loop and stopped under an open roof.

"Thank you!" The driver looked barely sixteen. I wondered if she needed a license to drive horses. "I'm going to give them a rest. You can load your bags in the back."

The driver made no move to assist. I laid our bags on the flat tailgate of the wagon and snapped a canvas cover in place, then joined Andy on the bench seat at the back of the cab.

Andy slid close to me on the seat and scooped up my hand as she engaged the girl with the reigns in a conversation centered around the horses.

I settled in for the ride.

16

"Welcome to Lindsay Cottage."

Lee Donaldson stood at the top of a set of stone steps set into a rising lawn. Meeting my expectations, he wore a black polo shirt over khaki pants. The shoulder holster he favors held his forty caliber Beretta. I noticed it dangled beneath his right arm, meaning he had changed to shooting leftie. He leaned on a cane gripped by his right hand. Behind him, a breathtaking wooden mansion dipped in gingerbread accents rose above manicured gardens. I hopped down and offered Andy a hand.

"Cottage?" The white wooden building with lavender trim shouldered three stories above high ground. The top sprouted turrets and gables. Colorful striped awnings shaded every window. A porch spanned the front of the house and extended to the rear on one side. From hanging baskets and window boxes, pink and white flowers collected summer sunlight.

Donaldson shrugged. "I'd offer to lend a hand but…" He tapped the cane against his leg. "Still working out the kinks."

Lee Donaldson had taken a blow to his skull from a baseball bat after lunging into a melee to prevent the blow from striking Andy. The cranial damage impaired his speech and right hemisphere motion. I repaired the damage inadvertently when I used *the other thing* on him. Apparently, when I made him vanish, his disrupted neural connections reconnected. I have no idea how or why. One minute he had trouble finding the word for roof, the next he spoke like a game show announcer.

The cane served as a reminder that the repair job didn't fix everything.

Andy stood in awe of the so-called cottage and its commanding view of the Straits of Mackinac. I asked the cab driver for the fare and paid it along with a generous tip while Andy stared.

"He lives here?"

"I wouldn't say lives here," Donaldson answered.

I retrieved the bags, then snapped the canvas cover back in place. The driver signaled the horses to pull away on the narrow blacktop road.

Andy and I entered the property through a small gate and climbed the first of two sets of steps to the porch.

"I can take that," Donaldson reached for Andy's bag.

"Absolutely not!" She pulled him into a hug. "How are you?"

"Better and better," he replied, gesturing for us to follow.

"You look a little less like Frankenstein's monster." I pointed to where stitches lined his skull when last I saw him. "Growing your hair out?"

"Trying not to scare little children."

We climbed the second set of steps and mounted the wide porch. Neither Andy nor I could help but stop and check out the view. The broad blue Straits of Mackinac spread from left to right. Five miles away, the big bridge joined Michigan to Upper Michigan. Busy ferries hurried tourists between the island harbor and St. Ignace to the west and Mackinaw City to the south. Some of the ferries threw rooster tails of water high in their wake. The midday sunlight made everything sparkle.

"Helluva view, isn't it?"

"It is." Andy put her arm around my waist and squeezed.

"Plenty of time to gawk at that later," Donaldson said. "The Director thought we could meet over lunch. I'll have your bags taken up. Would you like to hit the head and wash up?"

"Please," Andy said.

We followed Donaldson inside where a young woman in a white blouse and khaki shorts hustled to take our bags. Boldly taking all three in hand, she climbed a broad wooden staircase.

Andy and I took turns in an elegantly fixtured bathroom, then followed Donaldson into a beautiful wood-trimmed dining room. The table had been laid out with four place settings. An array of fruits and sandwiches waited for us. A light breeze found its way through window screens.

Urgent footfalls pounded the big staircase. A moment later, Mitchell Lindsay appeared. Sixtyish and silver-haired, he moved like a much younger man. The physique under a light sweater and the grip he closed on my handshake suggested a religiously maintained fitness regimen. His handsome face wore a few deep lines, but no sign of excessive wear or fatigue.

"Good to see you both again," he said. "Please, have a seat. I hope you don't mind. It's just a light lunch."

Lindsay took the chair at the head of the table. Andy seated herself to his right, facing Donaldson. I sat to Andy's right.

"You have a beautiful home," Andy said.

"Thank you. It's both that and a monstrous money pit. But it's been in the family for over ninety years and if we can, we will hold onto it for another ninety. Life on the island is a challenge. Everything comes by boat, then by horse and wagon. You can imagine what that means when you need to replace a furnace or rebuild a section of roof. The elements can be brutal on these old wooden cottages. But it's remote and quiet and can be wonderfully solitary despite the summer tourist crush."

"Hardly a cottage," I said.

"A local term," he replied. "It was a cottage to the lumber and railroad magnates who built these homes."

"Is that why we're meeting here?" I asked. "It's solitary?"

Lindsay gave me a shrewd glance. "Partly. It took me all of thirty seconds after you did your magic trick in my office for me to realize that my world would never be the same. Detective, you would surely agree with a fellow law enforcement officer that once you've been trained in our profession, you never again see through innocent eyes."

"Well, I…" Andy hesitated.

"Oh, I don't mean that we become jaded. I just mean that we see the world for its potential, both good and evil. We walk into a room and count the exits. Doesn't that ring true?"

"Yes, sir, it does."

"Then you will understand. Will, the moment you appeared the way you did, I became aware that nothing I ever said or did in my office could be considered absolutely secure."

"I don't—"

"Please, relax," he said, raising his hands. "I'm not accusing you of anything. We have our offices swept for electronic surveillance daily. We monitor signals coming and going from the Javits Federal building. The sensors are built in, as is the paranoia. Just when we think we have all the angles covered, there you were, out of thin air. It was a shock to my system, as you may recall."

"If it was a shock, you hid it well, Director." I remembered the calm way he looked at me, then Donaldson and Andy. The first words out of his mouth were equally calm.

17

"Do that again," the Director said, frozen behind his office desk. *Fwooomp!* I vanished, counted off three seconds, then *Fwooomp!* I reappeared. His eyes, which stayed on the empty air I left behind when I disappeared, fixed quickly on me when I reappeared.

"Is that—are you able to do that at will?" he asked.

"Affirmative."

He looked at Donaldson. "And you know about this?"

"Affirmative."

He looked at Andy. "And you, of course?"

"Yes, sir. This is my husband, Will."

I reached for and received a hesitant handshake. Lindsay glanced at his hand after we shook.

Andy said, "We've been aware of it for a little over a year. You mentioned my arrest record. I can't claim to have done it all without help from my husband. And that's why we're here to see you."

"You came here to show me...*that?*"

"We thought—"

"Stop," he said. He held up a hand like a crossing guard. "This meeting —*here, for now*—is over. Special Agent, can I assume that you have close contact with Detective Stewart and her husband?"

"Yes, sir."

"Good." Lindsay opened his desk drawer and extracted two cards. He handed one to Donaldson and one to Andy. "My private number is on that. Don't use it. I will reach out to you. Understood?"

"Don't call us, we'll call you? Is that it?" I asked, ready to argue. Andy put her hand on my arm.

Lindsay smiled. "Something like that, only not what you think. Not by a long shot. Can I assume that until I meet with you again, you will say nothing of this?"

"We haven't so far," Andy said.

"Good." He looked at the three of us, with special emphasis on me. "This may not be the response you were expecting but trust me when I say it is for the best. I will be in touch. Soon. Now get out of my office." He touched the intercom button on his phone.

His gatekeeper ushered us out moments later. I found it bewildering. Andy less so. Donaldson seemed positively ecstatic. Two days later he called Andy and told her to mark off the second-to-last weekend in August.

18

Lindsay handed a bowl of fruit to Andy. He sat back in his chair.

"I apologize for the brusque sendoff in New York. My movements are closely monitored by diverse interests within the bureau. It's nothing nefarious. People stay on the lookout for the boss in anticipation of me interrupting their investigations or pushing for results when things are lagging. They want me available to field inquiries from DOJ. My calendar is fought over by departments wanting more funding, bureau offices wanting more personnel. That woman you blew past when you came to see me has held off Members of Congress and Senators—I'll be honest, I'm surprised you made it past her. Point is…when you came through my door, regardless of the significance, I had to temper my response. As it was, the fact that you did it, and I didn't fire you," he said to Donaldson, "raised eyebrows and stirred rumors."

"Sorry, sir."

"Don't be. Coming to me with Will's…skill…well, the worst thing I could have done would have been to clear my calendar and hold all my calls. Before quitting time that day, the janitors in the basement would have been asking who Special Agent Donaldson and Detective Stewart were. Please," he gestured at the table, "eat."

I did not need to be told twice. The summer-accented spread called to me. The young woman in shorts appeared with a pitcher of iced tea and poured all around. Lindsay described it as a special homebrewed recipe. The refreshment proved worthy of his comment. He asked the young woman to close the dining room doors on her way out.

"That's my granddaughter. She's doing her college junior summer here as caretaker. Cheap help. Be nice to her because she's in way over her head." He sipped his iced tea and focused on me. "Will, I can't say I've ever been as stunned by anything as I was by seeing you appear and disappear like that. We have a lot to discuss. But I hope I've made my point. It could not be discussed in the Javits Federal Building. There would be no explaining why I'm suddenly spending my time with a Special Agent from Sioux City, Iowa —no offense to your station, Lee."

"None taken, sir."

"—and a municipal detective and her husband. People would talk."

"I get it," I said between bites of a ridiculously good ham sandwich. "And I appreciate your caution."

"I've had this weekend blocked out for a visit to the island for months. A chance to deal with personal and household matters. I apologize for the last-minute delay—but as a meeting place, nothing is better suited. This setting is secure, of course, but more importantly, I avoid raising questions internally. My staff knows the drill. I am simply 'on the island,' time I believe they cherish as much as I do."

"Then we can assume that you haven't discussed this with anyone?" Andy asked. She hadn't touched a bite of food.

"Unless I imagined it, and Lee has assured me I didn't, I can't think of a secret that is more important to the Bureau, and perhaps to our national security. We'll dive into everything this afternoon. Depending on our discussions, we may make dinner plans for later. That remains to be decided. Right now, if you don't mind, Will, tell me everything. To put it bluntly…what the hell?"

He caught me with a mouthful of tuna salad sandwich. I held up one hand and chewed quickly. I chased the bite down with a slug of iced tea.

"I don't know, sir," I said at last. "The truth is, I have no idea."

19

I spent the lunch describing the sequence of events that unfolded after I crashed on approach to the Essex County Airport a little over a year ago. I explained how a fall from 500 feet up at over a 140 miles per hour should have killed me, yet I was found alive in the pilot's seat in a marsh—my sole injury being a broken pelvis. I recounted waking up in a hospital room floating just below the ceiling tiles, unable to see my body, and how over the next week I experimented with controlling what I came to refer to as *the other thing*.

Telling the story to Lindsay felt refreshing. Secrecy, like gravity, had a weight I did not notice until I made it disappear. Andy chimed in with important details, in part to be thorough and in part to emphasize that we had come as a team.

I explained to Lindsay that I lacked memory of the crash. I told him how the NTSB and FAA investigated the incident in detail, and how the preliminary report—lacking an explanation—tried to pin the blame on me, the pilot, which resulted in a temporary suspension of my pilot's license—the equivalent of cutting my heart out. He asked if I thought the cause of the crash contributed to my ability to vanish. I said it seemed obvious to me. He interrogated me about what I'd seen, about the moments before impact, about my first memories after waking. He asked what had become of the federal investigation and raised pointed questions about the radar recordings and transcripts of my radio exchanges with air traffic control. The more detailed his questions, the more I became certain that he had already conducted his own inquiry.

Andy picked up the narrative and filled in my role in some of her recent investigations, crediting me with more success than I deserved. I denied being anything more than an assist to her skilled work.

Lunch concluded. Lindsay suggested we continue the discussion in his study. He opened the doors to the dining room and ushered us out as his granddaughter swept in to clear the meal. We adjourned to a large turret at the corner of the second floor. The round room oozed robber baron money, from the expensive-looking Persian rug to the ornate tin ceiling. Floor to ceiling bookshelves lined the inner wall, jammed with antique volumes. Windows spanned the outer wall.

"I can't get over the view, sir," Andy said, taking a seat on a leather sofa that faced the director's desk. She gazed through the bank of windows spanning half the round room's circumference.

Lindsay slid into a leather chair behind his desk. "It's a terrible distraction. I never bring work here. Can't get a thing done." He fixed an interrogating stare on me. "What the hell am I going to do with you?"

I got the feeling he wasn't asking me the question.

"Well, sir, we were hoping—"

Lindsay lifted a hand to cut off Donaldson's suggestion.

"Didn't mean it literally, Lee. We'll get to that question. For now, I need to know more. Aside from you three, who knows about this?"

Andy named Lane Franklin and briefly covered the story of her abduction and rescue. She listed Pidge and Dr. Doug Stephenson. "He's Will's neurologist. He helped Will get recertified after the accident."

"He may have isolated some of whatever is making this possible," I pointed at my head.

"I'd like to talk to him, with your permission, of course. Who else?"

"There's Kaitlyn Aberdene."

Lindsay's furrowed brow plucked at a memory. "Abduction case?"

"She was a victim of human sex trafficking in the O'Bannon case. She swore herself to secrecy and she's a good kid. I trust her—but then who would believe her even if she did say something?"

"Seavers," Lindsay corrected me. "You mean Seavers. I read the file. Who else knows?" Lindsay didn't take notes, but something told me every detail etched itself in a perfect memory.

Andy shifted in her seat.

"Well, sir, there are three others, but with all due respect, we're not sharing that information."

She had been nervous about this part.

We reached the decision together. We elected not to share the unexplained curative effect of *the other thing* on children afflicted with leukemia, which eliminated mentioning a nurse by the name of Christie Watkins. We also elected not to tell the FBI director about Dr. Lillian Farris, whom Andy considered to be half scientist and half certifiable UFO nut. Or that the billionaire Spiro Lewko not only knew about me but had been promised a crack at examining me. Conversely, we didn't tell Farris or Lewko of our plans to meet with the FBI. Lillian, for one, would have freaked out, changed her identity and moved into a yurt in Nepal.

"I don't understand."

"Director, there are parts of this that belong to me, and me alone," I said. "That's the deal. I can't predict if we're going to make something work with you and the FBI, or if I will be happy with the arrangement. We're holding back a few cards. Take it or leave it."

Lindsay's squint told me he was not accustomed to having terms dictated.

"I'm certain our decision will not diminish Will's value to the FBI," Andy offered.

Lindsay said nothing.

Andy swallowed.

"Plus, I want a badge," I jumped in. "An FBI badge."

Donaldson smirked.

"Excuse me?" Lindsay asked.

"I want to be able to appear out of nowhere and flash a badge."

"Will, no." Andy squirmed beside me. "Sir, that's not something we discussed."

"Come on! You get a badge!" I protested to Andy. Her eyes flared at me and her cheeks flushed.

Donaldson chuckled, reading me better than my wife. Lindsay laughed. Andy caught on, leaned back, and punched me on the arm.

"I carry the badge in the family," she announced.

"Yes, dear."

The tension in the moment evaporated.

"Detective, you have the upper hand here. I will work with you and your husband in any way possible. But I agree with you. No badge. This is uncharted territory for the Bureau. Can I assume you have an opinion, Special Agent?"

Donaldson spread his arms and shrugged. "It's like working with Fred and Ethel."

I had no idea who he meant, but Lindsay smiled. He settled a long, appraising gaze on me.

"May I see it again?"

Fwooomp! I vanished. I admit, I get a kick out of the look on someone's face when they see it happen. Lindsay didn't disappoint.

"Why do your clothes disappear with you?"

"I don't know," I said. "I'm not like the guy in the old movies, thank God."

Fwooomp! I reappeared and stood up.

"Then there's this," I said. I walked over to his desk.

Fwooomp! I vanished and reached for a small brass cube on his desk, a paper weight with an inscription. I lifted it. Lindsay watched it levitate.

"Now you see it." I folded my hands over the cube. It snapped out of view. "Now you don't." I gave it a beat while Lindsay studied the trick, then I lowered the object to the desk and released it. My fingertips absorbed an electric snap as it reappeared.

As did I a second later.

"There's one more thing, sir," I said, stepping around his desk. He rotated his chair to face me. I held out my hand for him to grasp.

He took it reluctantly. Out of the corner of my eye I saw Donaldson grinning.

FWOOOMP! I gave it an extra push. He vanished with me.

"Motherfu—!"

I didn't let him finish the sentiment. I flexed my ankles and lifted us vertically. His chair shot back. He kicked me as he awkwardly dealt with the double sensation of vanishing and of going weightless. I felt him flail and wiggle.

We rose until I had to touch the high ceiling to avoid hitting my head.

"Oh...my...God!"

20

Lindsay struggled to regain his dignified persona. He could not stop shifting in his chair.

"Okay," he said, pressing his palms to his desktop, as if to suppress it and his excitement. "Okay, there are issues here. Legal issues. Oversight issues. But at the same time, people, *do you understand the possibilities?*"

I held up one hand. "Before you go all comic book on me, you need to know the limits. Your first thought when you saw this was that I could easily infiltrate your offices, right?"

"Nothing to stop you," he said.

"A door stops me. Bumping into people stops me. I can't walk. I have no way of getting around other than pulling on railings and pushing off walls. Think astronaut at the space station. And if I don't have a map or good signage, I have no idea where the bad guys hang out. And even if I had a map, I can't read it because it vanishes with me. I can't carry a tablet or look at my phone. I can't propel myself without a BLASTER."

The look on his face prompted me.

"Basic Linear Aerial System for—."

"Will's kidding," Andy interrupted. "That's not what they're called." Andy quickly explained the propeller and battery propulsion system.

"Clever," Lindsay mused.

"With a—power unit—I can propel myself, but they make noise. People think they're drones."

"Do they work?"

"I reach around sixty miles an hour, I think, but the wind resistance is ferocious. I need to wear goggles to see. If it's raining, the pressure of the falling water droplets drives me down. A strong wind will blow me all over hell."

"Can you walk through walls?" Lindsay asked.

"Uh, no. And I strongly doubt I'm bulletproof. I just seem to be immune to gravity, but that raises another concern. Without a power unit, I can't alter my trajectory. One wrong move and I could shoot into the upper atmosphere, or space. I'd be dead long before I got to become an astronaut."

"Can't you just reappear?" he asked.

"And drop like a rock. I haven't tested the theory, but my guess is that it won't matter if I hit the earth visible or vanished—either way, at terminal velocity I'm jellied." I pointed at the ceiling. "Would you want to fall from that height?"

He glanced up.

"Sir," Donaldson spoke up, "despite the limits, in terms of infiltration, this is a game-changer."

I made a flat-handed gesture of equivocation. "Maybe. But if you're thinking of sending me into some Al Qaeda hideout to spy on the next terrorist attack, forget it. I don't speak Arabic. Or Russian. Or Chinese. Best I can offer is a little high school Spanish."

"So, we work domestically," Donaldson replied. "Consider the possibilities in a hostage situation."

"I'm no good in a fight. When I disappear, I can't put any weight into a punch."

Andy slid to the edge of her seat. "There's something else to address, sir. Suppose Will witnesses something. He can't testify. And, as I'm sure you may be thinking, there's the question of a warrant. Within the confines of any legal argument, Will is the equivalent of a wiretap. And this, I'm afraid, is where we may have to draw another line. We don't mean to tie your hands, but we can't expose him to courts or congressional oversight committees."

"Detective, I can't even share this with my own people. And don't get me wrong. I don't think I should. But if you look at it from my perspective —suppose we have a task force working on a domestic terrorist group. That's dozens of agents. That's massive surveillance using traditional methods..." Lindsay furrowed his brow. "If we deploy Will for surveillance and he comes up with something material, something actionable, how do we convey that to conventional resources? We can't exactly have him fill out an FD-302."

"Exactly," Andy said.

"Come on," Donaldson protested. "We get creative! We filter it through me. I cite anonymous sources. Cleverly placed intel. We work around it."

"Then there's the moral question," Lindsay said.

"Sir?" Andy asked.

Lindsay looked at me. "Let's say you're out there, doing this thing. Let's say you see someone preparing to plant a bomb on a plane or deploy nerve gas in a subway. The threat is immediate, and no help is readily available. Do you kill them?"

Andy's head began to shake. She leaned forward to give the quick answer, but Lindsay lifted his hand to stop her.

"Let's go a step further. Why not send you to North Korea to take out that lunatic and plant a bomb in his nuke factory? Why not have you slip some digitalis into that Venezuelan dictator's tea? I can think of people who would give up their first born for a chance to send you into Iran's Natanz fuel enrichment plant with some C-4."

"I'm not an assassin. I won't be."

"If it meant saving thousands, maybe millions of lives? Would you do it then?"

"Who makes that call?" I asked. "You? Some committee? Who decides when I become the next 'drone strike' on someone? Central Command? No. If it ever comes to that, nobody makes that call but me. I'm the one who will have to live with it. Or live with the lives lost if I don't do it. But I won't be a tool for someone else's politics. Oh, and for the record, I can't fire a gun. I can carry one hidden but discharging a firearm in the vanished state creates some sort of energy feedback. It kicks the hell out of me. Trust me on that one."

"Well," Lindsay said. He sat back in his chair. "This is a lot to absorb. I need to think. Will…Andrea…I respect and appreciate your decision to come to me. Your terms will be given all due consideration."

"No, sir," I said. "Our terms are absolute. They get accepted here and now or I walk—or maybe float—outta here."

"Will—" Andy protested.

"It's alright, Detective. I agree. No questions asked."

"Sir, we didn't mean to dictate."

"I did," I said.

"And I respect that, Will. I'd like to talk more about some of your case work, Detective, so that I might get a better handle on what this all means." He looked at his watch. "Why don't we take a break? Your room is ready upstairs. If you want to take a stroll, feel free. Technically, if you go down to the Grand Hotel you're not allowed on the grounds unless you pay a small charge. Well worth it if you've never seen the place. On the other hand—what am I saying? You can certainly get on the grounds without anyone stopping you with…you know…"

"That's not how we use it, sir," Andy said quickly.

We stood, having been dismissed.

"Lee, would you hang back, please?"

21

"Did we just get the bum's rush?" I asked.
"A little," Andy replied.
"You still feeling comfortable about this?"

We sat at a small table at Sadie's Ice Cream Parlor in the lower level of the Grand Hotel. Andy insisted on paying the toll for a visit to the hotel grounds. We made our first stop in the period treat shop and ordered single-scoop cups of Rocky Road and Chocolate.

"Are you?"

I shrugged. "I guess. It's funny, but every day that I still have this *thing*, I wonder if it's the last. If it might run out. Or count down like a postage meter until it just doesn't work anymore."

"Don't say that! What if you're on the *other* side when it runs out?"

"Huh. Then you'll know I'm in the shower with you if the soap is flying around."

"That's not funny."

"What's your take on Lindsay?"

Andy slid a spoonful of chocolate between her lips. She savored it thoughtfully. "I think he will respect our terms. But can I confess something? I pictured working with the FBI as part of a team. When they were all over Essex last month, it was heady. They play off each other. They rely on each other. I want to be part of something like that. Not in the dark. Undercover. I guess I'll be a little disappointed if we're kept isolated."

"Someone's got to be a liaison. Someone's got to translate whatever I do into meaningful intel. And it can't just be Donaldson. He does not play well with others."

Andy smiled. "I didn't think you were going to take Lindsay for a ride. Did you see his face when he reappeared?"

I laughed, recalling the crack in Lindsay's polished composure.

"What do you make of his mention of dinner plans for later? I thought we made it clear this went no further than Donaldson and Lindsay."

"I asked Lee about it. He said it's not like that. He doesn't know who it is, but it's not another orientation session. He swears Lindsay is determined to keep this among the four of us."

"Maybe it's our first case. Or a test."

"I hope not," Andy said. "There's too much yet to be worked out."

"Like what?"

"Oh, like *the law*, dear. Breaking and entering? Theft? Assassination? We touched on some of it, but we need to establish rules of engagement. Don't think I came here without thinking all that through. There's a lot to agree on before we attempt field operations. I won't have the FBI put you in danger—"

I made a face at her. She returned it in kind, recognizing that ship had already sailed.

"It's probably what Lindsay wanted to talk to Lee about."

"We've already bent a few rules, Dee."

"Right, but if we are to become part of a legitimate law enforcement effort, or at least the equivalent of a confidential informant, we can't develop leads no one can act on. More importantly, we can't have you vulnerable to criminal prosecution for actions you take on behalf of the FBI."

I worked on the ice cream and left her to ponder the details. Doubt never entered my mind that she would keep us between the lines. Massive doubt, however, had leased space in my head regarding what good I could be to the FBI.

After scraping the bowls clean, I said, "This place is amazing. Let's take the rest of the tour."

She checked her watch. "Well, then we better hurry. There's a dress code after 4 p.m. and you didn't bring a suit."

WE ACTED LIKE LITTLE KIDS—PEEKING into ornate spaces, marveling at photos documenting the hotel's history, dazzled by the size and airy beauty of the massive old structure. We stole a look at the dining room, which spanned one third the length of the building, and agreed that dinner there would feel like being seated in first-class elegance on the *Titanic*. We climbed to the Cupola Bar at the top of the hotel and promised ourselves we would one day see a sunset from its cushioned window seats. We strolled the 800-foot long front porch admiring the idea of long lazy afternoons on the porch, sitting in a pair of white rocking chairs sipping expensive drinks. The Grand Hotel belongs to a different age.

Moments before the hour at which ladies are advised to wear dresses and gentlemen are required to wear coats and neckties, we slipped away from the hotel grounds, hiking the short distance up the bluff road to Lindsay Cottage.

We picked out a pair of wicker chairs on the majestic porch and sat down to take in the view. We'd scarcely settled when Lindsay's granddaughter appeared carrying a tray and two cold Coronas garnished with lime wedges.

"Agent Donaldson told me to have these ready when you returned," she said, placing them on a small table between us. "Papa—er, Director Lindsay asked you to join him in his study at 5 p.m."

I saw the family resemblance in the girl, softened dramatically by a bright, coed overlay and a healthy tan.

"You can call him Papa," Andy said warmly. "I'm Andy and this is Will."

"Gwen. Pleased to meet you."

"Tell Agent Donaldson thank you."

"Tell Agent Donaldson he's a suck up," I said.

Gwen laughed.

"Tell him yourself," Donaldson said, appearing as Gwen departed. He pulled up a wicker chair and lifted his own beer in toast. "New roads."

"New roads," Andy and I said, touching bottles.

"What did Lindsay want to discuss with you?" I asked.

Donaldson took a drink from his beer. Instead of answering my question, he settled a long look at Andy.

"What?" she asked.

"Act surprised when he does it."

"Does what?"

"He's going to offer you a slot in the next training class at Quantico."

I looked at my wife. Her green and gold eyes flared. She tried to hide it, but her breath hitched.

"That's a big deal," I said, watching every nuance of Andy's reaction. She struggled against rippling excitement.

"A mother huge deal," Donaldson confirmed. "Do you have any idea how hard it is to make the cut?"

"He's not going to bump someone on my account," Andy said, horrified.

"No. They keep one or two add-on slots in their pocket." She breathed sharp relief. "Don't tell him I said anything. You going to take it?"

Andy attempted a nonchalant shrug. Badly. "It's certainly something Will and I will discuss."

"Hell, yes, she's going to take it!" I said. She broke out a smile for me. "Hell, yes. Andrea Stewart, FBI. I like it."

"I have to think about it."

"I'm pretty sure it's all you'll be thinking about," I said. "What about me? Did he say anything about me?"

"He asked me if I thought you were mentally unbalanced."

"If I had a dollar for every time someone asked me that."

"Everybody who's ever been able to do what you do goes insane."

"Yeah. In Hollywood movies."

Donaldson shrugged. "All we have to go on. Lindsay wanted to know if I saw any cracks in your psych profile that would spell trouble. You may read that as 'turn around and bite the Bureau in the ass.'"

I started to wisecrack, but Andy interrupted. "Does he feel a need for testing?"

Donaldson shrugged. "Nah. I don't think he wants to. Testing is problematic. He's certainly not going to read in some Bureau shrink. When we get this train a little farther down the line, he'll want a chat with your doc… Stephenson. For now, he's got a task in mind."

"What's the task?"

"He wouldn't say. Whatever it is, I warn you not to be too much of a smartass, Will. You're being watched."

22

I carried a BLASTER to Lindsay's study. The Director looked it over. Andy and I returned to the sofa. Donaldson took one of the wingback chairs. Lindsay had the windows open. A sultry afternoon breeze made my eyelids heavy.

"This thing really gets you moving?" He slid the control forward. The prop spun up from a low growl to a high-pitched whine.

"Like a bat outta hell."

"It doesn't seem like it would have enough power." He held it out at arm's length.

"Not for a person under full gravity. But I have no weight. No inertia. It has no load—not even its own weight. The only load is wind resistance generated by my body."

He let it spin to a halt and handed it back to me. "Someone should tell NASA. I bet the crew on the ISS could use something like this."

He nudged his chair close to his desk and opened a folder. Andy squared herself to him attentively.

Lindsay extracted a photo from the folder and held it up.

"Aaron McCauley. Lawyer. Political consultant. Lobbyist. Registered with DOJ under the Foreign Agents Registration Act. He's a partner in McCauley, Burnham and Doud, a Washington firm that caters to international clients. He and his firm have represented former Soviet republics, oligarchs, African heads of state, and sometimes the rebels that overthrow them. They're well connected. One former partner is the number two man at Justice. Another is on the SEC."

The man in the photo wore a golf shirt, an expensive haircut, and a blinding smile against an outdoor background. Landscaping hints suggested a golf resort with palm trees. I guessed him to be in his forties, but he could have been older, the beneficiary of money's ability to camouflage age. He had leading man good looks and his expression said he knew it. A woman's bare shoulder intruded on the photo frame, but the fingers of McCauley's left hand, wrapped around a bottled water, carried no rings.

Lindsay returned the photo to the folder. He pulled open a desk drawer and deposited the folder, then closed the drawer and locked it with a key that he pocketed.

"McCauley approached the Bureau—me, specifically—and asked for a meeting. Off the clock and off the record."

"Time out," I said. "How? People don't just call you, Director. They don't just blow into your office—present company excepted. You have a connection to this guy."

Lindsay tipped me a respectful nod. A point for me.

"McCauley's father and I served in the Army in Desert Storm. I was military police. He was JAG Corps. McCauley played that card to reach out to me."

"He wants to rat out his clients to you. So much for client confidentiality."

"That's for lawyers," Donaldson said. "For lobbyists it's a slow day if they don't stab someone in the back."

"To be clear, I don't know McCauley. Never met him. I knew his dad to be a good man, but his dad never made it home from the Middle East. Helicopter crash in Kuwait."

"Did he say what he wanted to discuss?" Andy asked, guiding us back onto the rails.

"A matter of national security. He told me he planned to bring his boat to the island and suggested meeting here. What does that tell you?"

Donaldson and I traded blank glances.

"That he knew you have this property and knew you would be here," Andy said.

"Which in itself is a matter for consideration." Lindsay tapped the drawer containing the folder. "I had staff work up a dossier. People in McCauley's business hardly tiptoe around. They're paid to sell their clients, which means pounding the Washington pavement. Which makes for a lot of publicly available intel. We have a good idea who he represents."

"I'm guessing it ain't Mother Teresa's Missionaries of Charity," Donaldson muttered.

"There are two salient clients in his portfolio. The first might be the most interesting—one that is already on Bureau radar. Last year, his firm was approached by a pair of ex-pat Russians with ties to organized crime in Moscow, which translates to us as ties to the Russian government. We'd already been following the two men, so in a sense they took us to McCauley. The Russians work for Yevgheniy Solochak, a former money man for the pro-Russian president of Ukraine. Solochak helped said past president walk away with over forty billion dollars of the government's money. Today, he is part of a group of investors who put a new twist on the concept of a hostile takeover. The Group, as they are known, with Solochak being the only visible member, conducted a buyout of a Mexican drug cartel."

"I didn't know cartels were traded on the stock exchange," I said.

"If the price is right," Lindsay said. "And it was. Somewhere in the B's. Cash. It's the first time we've seen anything like it. The Méndez cartel dominates Juárez, trafficking in heroin, a declining marijuana business, and in humans. They have the busiest cross-border pipelines between Mexico and the U.S. Their network was built by either pushing out or consolidating the smaller, independent human traffickers and one-off coyotes. The Group saw something they liked about the Méndez portfolio and made them an offer."

"I bet the offer included a few incentives such as not seeing their children burned alive," Donaldson said.

"Non-violent," Lindsay corrected him.

"I'm not sure I understand," Andy said. "I mean, it's not unusual to see takeovers. One cartel taking over another. Climbers within taking over from old guard management. It happens all the time. But this was conducted as a non-violent buyout?"

"That's the way we see it."

"Does that mean the Russian mob is consolidating Mexican crime syndicates? Setting up a new frontier?"

"That's what we thought at first. But the buy seems to be a one off—not part of any pattern. On the ground, operations by the Méndez cartel have not significantly changed. Some of the top management stayed on, although the namesake has disappeared along with the cash he got out of the deal. But the day-to-day operations don't seem to have been altered by the change in ownership."

"Corporate raiders buy for the purpose of acquiring cash or assets that can be turned into cash. Are you saying Solochak and The Group bought Méndez as an investment? A business to grow?"

"Jury is still out. The public face of it has been that the cartel's new owners want to convert the operations from criminal to legitimate."

"Is anybody buying that bullshit?" Donaldson asked.

Lindsay shrugged. "Both our government and the Mexican government say they are guardedly optimistic. They're being watched closely by DEA, Customs and us. And no doubt by Langley."

"Which explains McCauley..." Donaldson prompted.

"Yes. McCauley. His firm was approached by the two Russians—acting on behalf of Solochak—who hired them to clean up the international image of the cartel. Project a new face."

Lindsay let the point settle.

"Seriously?" I asked. "Isn't a drug cartel universally down as 'the bad guys?' I mean, don't they actively engage in making themselves scarier? Theatrical murders. Gruesome torture. You don't hear of them sponsoring river cleanups and ten K runs for charity."

"Not true," Donaldson said. "The Cali Cartel organized social cleansing. They murdered prostitutes, street children and homeless by the hundreds in a campaign to clean up the streets. They dumped so many bodies in the Cauca River that the local municipality went bankrupt handling all the autopsies. Talk about river cleanups."

"Did McCauley take the job?" Andy asked.

"His firm did. Money talks."

"Director, if they're being paid by the Russian mob to promote a positive image for a Mexican drug cartel, isn't it a bit antithetical for a partner in the firm to be chatting with the FBI? Isn't that a good way to wind up in the center of a stack of burning tires?"

Lindsay lifted his eyebrows. "Yes. It's antithetical. But that may not be where McCauley is coming from. He could have any number of reasons to discuss the cartel. Or it could be something else entirely. McCauley's other major client is a coalition of what he labels 'Progressive Reformers' in Ghana."

"As in Gold Coast Ghana?" I asked.

"Very good, Will. Better than you might imagine, in fact."

"What's the translation for 'Progressive Reformers,' Director?" Donaldson asked. Lindsay put the question on hold with a wave.

"Ghana, as you probably know, is a democracy with a duly elected president as its head of state—a model we Americans have promoted all over the globe. I won't go into the history, but as of today, Ghana enjoys a stable government with a robust economy. And one of its primary national resources is—as you hinted, Will—gold. Ghana is eighth in production of gold worldwide. Gold mining stimulates economic growth. The current government has done a creditable job of translating that resource into infrastructure and the uplifting of what was otherwise a poor and disadvantaged population. Lee, to your question…the translation for 'Progressive Reformers' is a cabal of ruthless military officers who are one itchy trigger finger away from a coup d`etat."

"Same old same old for the dark continent."

"And they're represented by McCauley's lobbying firm in Washington, D.C.?" I asked.

"They are. A lobbying effort that is gaining traction, particularly with this administration."

"Doesn't that undermine the democratic government that we support?" Andy asked.

Lindsay chuckled. "The democratic, constitutional government that we have promoted in foreign policy for decades? The one that is now falling out of favor in the White House, and by extension with the administration's mouthpieces in Congress—putting at risk tens of millions in foreign aid? That one?"

"I don't get it," I said. "Forgive the high school education, but what's the justification for shifting favor from a democracy to another military coup and dictatorship?"

"Flavor of the day," Lindsay said. "The generals say that the country's leadership is soft on a left-wing rebel movement. That the president is failing to respond to the 'terrorist' threat. The head of that rebel movement—which by the way doesn't so much as blip the radar for our terrorist watch people—is already in prison. The generals want him executed—they say to cut the head off the snake. Human rights activists have been fighting them off. The generals also want the U.S. to extradite his sister, who lives here, so they can put her on trial."

"And you say this narrative is gaining traction with U.S. policymakers?" Andy asked.

Lindsay raised a single finger. "One. One policymaker. McCauley's firm has been placing stories on cable news for the White House to see. The President has begun tweeting, picking up the narrative. Particularly about the sister…she doesn't belong here…send her back…she's tied to terrorists… that sort of thing. Calling the current government ineffective against terror."

"This can't be comfortable for the president of Ghana," Andy said.

"He's positively frantic. The government of Ghana sees the generals as a legitimate threat to democracy. The legislative body wants the president to fire the whole lot of them. He refuses, saying that summary dismissals make him as much a dictator as they seek to be. Frankly, he's right. But remember—none of this had any staying power until the generals hired McCauley. Up to that point, the whole thing was less a coup than a lot of muttering by a few guys who spend most of their time designing their own uniforms. Thanks to McCauley's firm, they're getting play on American cable news and it's challenging established policy in the region."

"Do you think that's what McCauley means by 'national security?'" Andy asked.

"If it is, McCauley is either betraying his client or he grew a conscience. I highly doubt either. This administration—and I don't know or care to know your political affiliations except to say that if we're going to work together, you leave them at the door—has shown that it's enamored with strong men. McCauley sees what a thousand ruthless opportunists in D.C. see—a U.S. president with no foreign policy compass who is easily swayed by his favorite cable news channel. Throw in a few recent stories about atrocities by the rebels—which we know to be social media fakes—and McCauley cashes checks from the generals for a job well done."

I nudged Andy. "See? This is way better than chasing hot VINs at Al Raymond's used car lot."

She ignored me.

"What's the connection to Mexico?" she asked. "Between the two?"

Lindsay shrugged. "Other than the fact that McCauley represents both? I don't know, but my gut tells me there is one."

Andy stood abruptly, giving release to the electric excitement I sensed building inside her.

"Sir, you mentioned a dinner this evening. I take it you have plans to sit down with McCauley?"

"I do."

She paced to the window and back. "And agreeing to this meeting...does that have anything to do with being 'on the island' as far as your staff is concerned?"

"You're living up to your reputation, Detective. This situation has a political stink. Half of my job is avoiding political stink. I need to find out what this is about, but at the same time, stay clear of flying shit—which means keeping this off my official agenda. McCauley wants the meeting to be private—"

"For obvious reasons," Donaldson said. "He doesn't want the Russian mob or a drug cartel finding out he's selling them out."

Lindsay shook his head. "Don't underestimate him. Don't take the obvious at face value, and for God's sake, don't attribute moral norms to him. No one builds the kind of business he has with the kind of clients he lists without having a superb sense of self-preservation. If he wants a meeting with the Deputy Director of the FBI, it's more than likely about leveraging something to his own agenda than about public service. I have no intention of becoming a body thrown in the path of whatever is chasing him. I want to know what he wants, but then I want to know what he really wants."

"And that's where I come in," I said.

"Yes."

"No," Andy said. "That's where *we* come in."

23

"That's what you're wearing?"

I checked myself in the full-length mirror mounted on the closet door. Black jeans. Black t-shirt. Black western-style boots. I didn't think I needed a jacket. The evening air retained most of the day's summer warmth.

"I thought it was. Why? What's wrong with it?"

Andy stepped beside me. She wore tan shorts and a bare-shoulder top with red and white stripes. Clever strapped white sandals wrapped her feet. I noticed she had painted her toenails crimson. She draped a light sweater over one arm.

"You look like you're about to drop out of a helicopter on a special ops mission."

"So?"

"Will, this is a summer island playground. Nobody's walking around here in black. You'll stand out like a ninja at a girls' soccer game. Put on some shorts. And you can't wear those boots. We'll be on a boat."

"Nobody's going to *see* us, Dee."

"Unless circumstances call for us to be seen." She slapped my butt. "Go. Change. I'll meet you downstairs."

I SWITCHED TO SNEAKERS, olive drab cargo pants (with ample pockets for BLASTERs) and a gray Green Bay Packers t-shirt. Andy rolled her eyes at me when I came down the stairs but accepted my selections without further criticism.

We gathered in Lindsay's foyer.

"Dinner on a boat makes it private, and hard for eavesdropping."

"Not for me," I said.

"Us. I'll be with Will," Andy said.

"Nobody's eavesdropping on a conversation that I will hear firsthand. That makes no sense. I want you to watch from a distance until you see me getting ready to leave. Then move in. Your assignment is to find out who he calls after I'm gone. What he says. I want to know if there's anyone on the boat with him that didn't make their presence known while I was there. I want to know if he shares an opinion about our meeting with anyone."

"How big is this boat?" I asked, imagining a typical cabin cruiser. I wondered where someone hides during a dinner, which I pictured as sub sandwiches and beer from a cooler.

"Ninety feet."

"Holy crap! That's a damned destroyer!"

Donaldson chuckled at me. "You haven't spent much time in south Florida, have you?"

"Only at the airports."

"The marina is east of downtown. If we had known, we might have scored a surveillance room at one of the inns facing the harbor. There isn't much in the way of restaurants or waterfront bars to establish a watch station. Lee, you hang back. You two, I'm guessing you can set up anywhere."

"Pretty much," I said.

"Why am I not going in with you, sir? As a bodyguard?"

Lindsay shook his head at Donaldson. "Not that kind of meeting. McCauley went out of his way to catch me 'on the island.' I want him to believe I'm off the clock. Having a bodyguard suggests otherwise. Will, Andrea, how do you want to play this?"

I let Andy take the lead.

"You say you don't want us up close while you're with McCauley?"

"Affirmative. Don't take it personally. We have a few more steps to get through to establish your clearance levels. If he shares something that I have to classify, bringing you in puts me in a difficult position. Let's take this one step at a time. I'll do the dinner and hear what he has to say. You set up a watch at a distance. I'm assuming you can do it from the roof of a building or just about anywhere, right?"

I nodded.

"When you see me leaving, pull up close and monitor him however you are able. I want to know anything that gives me a reading on whatever he shared with me. Got it?"

"How long do we stay on him?" I asked.

"Your call. If he puts on his jammies and goes to bed, call it a night."

"There is a way for us to communicate, sir," Andy said. She lifted her palm to me. "Will, give me your Bluetooth earpiece."

I dug it out of a pocket. She plucked a tissue from her shoulder bag and wiped it down, then slipped it into her ear.

"Phone." She held out her hand. I surrendered my phone. "We can work out something more sophisticated later, but all you have to do is call Will's phone when you're clear, I'll open a connection. If I can talk, I will. Either way, I can hear you, in case you want to give us any special instructions. Like if you see something and want us to look closer."

"Not bad," he said. Andy held up my phone with my number onscreen. He tapped the number into his phone and let mine ring until Andy touched the earpiece to open the connection.

"Alright." Lindsay tucked away his phone and checked his watch. "Time to go. It's a fifteen-minute walk down to the marina."

"We'll take the shortcut," I said. I pulled a BLASTER from my pants pocket and snapped a prop in place. "We'll get there ahead of you so we can see where you go."

Donaldson slipped on a nylon windbreaker to conceal his duty weapon. "I'll find someplace to set up."

"You're not exactly inconspicuous, Lee," Lindsay said, looking over his agent. "Hang back as far as you can."

"Yes, sir."

"Um..." he addressed Andy and me, "...Gwen doesn't know about you, okay? Make sure you do this discretely."

"Yes, sir," Andy said.

Lindsay leaned on the stair railing and called upstairs. "Gwen! Gwen, we're going out. We'll be back late. Don't wait up."

The girl appeared at the top of the stairs. "If you don't need me tonight, then I'm turning in early. G'night!"

Lindsay watched her slip out of sight, betraying a hint of pride. "She's up before five every day taking care of the horses."

"Horses?" Andy's face lit up.

"In the barn out back. I'll have her saddle a pair for you tomorrow if you like. Are we ready?"

All hands nodded.

"You look like an FBI agent, Lee. Give me a wide berth. And you two… I guess I won't see you there." He turned to me. "Will, a word?"

He gestured toward the front door. I followed him through, leaving Andy and Donaldson to watch us curiously. He paused at the top of the porch steps.

"When I get back tonight, we'll talk."

I figured as much but simply said, "Yes, sir."

He narrowed sharp appraisal on my face.

"About Prince Henry. South Dakota."

Without another word, he turned and descended the steps.

Crap.

24

Andy and I returned to the wicker furniture on the porch and watched Lindsay walk down the bluff road. He disappeared around the west end of the Grand Hotel. A few minutes later Donaldson appeared at the side of the house pushing a bicycle. He caught us watching him as he worked it through the front gate and mounted up, gripping his cane across the handlebars.

"What? It's a goddamned island with no motor vehicles. I'm not going to walk all the way down there."

I wondered if his leg would cooperate with the pedals, but with Lindsay Cottage at the peak of the bluff, the road into town sloped in his favor. He rolled quickly out of sight.

"You ready?" I asked Andy.

She glanced into the house for any sign of Gwen, then checked the road in front of the house for pedestrians. A few of the hotel guests had strolled up the hill earlier to look at the cottages. They had since retreated, leaving the narrow road empty.

"I suppose. Are you going to tell me?"

"What?" Except for pursing her lips slightly, she did not grace me with a response. "Fine." I told her what Lindsay said. "I suppose it shouldn't come as a surprise that he's been watching me—us—since New York."

Andy's pursed lips grew tighter. The lower extended slightly. She squinted in the direction of the road where Lindsay had gone, as if she might find a clue in the path he walked.

"Do you suppose he found out about me hijacking that van?" I asked.

"I guess we'll find out later."

I thought she might say more. She didn't.

"Facing me? Or side by side?" I drew a BLASTER from my pants pocket and snapped a propeller on the power shaft. She shifted her shoulder bag to her left, moved to my side and slipped her arm under my arm, then closed a grip on my left hand.

"No funny stuff. Got it?"

"At Divisible Man airways, passenger pleasure is our priority."

Fwooomp!

We vanished. The cool sensation closed over my body. Andy tightened her grip and squeezed her arm against mine. Our feet lost contact with the wooden porch boards.

I thumbed the slide control on the power unit. The prop hummed and pushed a column of air up my arm. We surged forward. The porch steps fell away, then the lawn. We crossed the gate twenty feet in the air. I turned left to follow the road. The bluff fell away sharply on the far side of the pavement. I stayed over the road knowing Andy wouldn't appreciate soaring out over a hundred-foot drop.

A sunset dome of pastel pinks, purples and blues arched overhead with thin cirrus clouds adding fluff and color. To our right, the Straits of Mackinac sparkled, smooth under windless evening air, the surface broken only by the wakes of the last ferries running between the island and the two Michigans.

I maintained a height of roughly twenty feet, following the downslope of the road to where the Grand Hotel dominated the bluff. At the hotel, I surprised Andy by swinging in under the three-story-high porch. The wooden façade of the hotel passed on our left. White pillars the size of tree trunks marched by on our right.

Half of the porch had been closed for a private party. A string quartet played something by one of the famous dead composers I can never seem to identify. Men in suits and bejeweled women in fine evening gowns milled around several portable bars spaced along the porch rail. I envied them the sparkling drinks in their hands, the evening light and the time-travel setting.

A bride in shimmering white posed with a row of guests for a photographer. We passed quietly over their heads, unseen.

"Can you imagine having a wedding here?" Andy said with gentle awe in her voice. I wasn't sure if she envied the romantic setting or had calculated a rough estimate of the bill.

I chose the safe response and squeezed her hand. We left the wedding party behind and passed the hotel entrance. Lush red carpeted steps descended to an elegant horse-drawn carriage bearing the hotel's name. A footman in full uniform assisted boarding passengers.

A short distance down the emptier half of the porch, I swung to the right between two pillars. I lined up on the road in front of the hotel and increased the speed.

We followed the tree-lined road to the harborside town.

BICYCLE AND HORSE-DRAWN traffic gave the main street a lively feel in the descending twilight. The sidewalks carried a steady flow of tourists between twinkling shop lights. The scent of fudge, popcorn and hamburgers oozed from storefronts to mingle with a hint of horse manure. Music radiated from establishments crowded with drinkers. I looked for but did not see Lindsay or Donaldson.

A few wires angled across the main street and forced us higher. We sailed along at rooftop level. The ferry docks passed on our right, looking empty. Bicycle rental stations had closed for the night, their racks jammed with two-wheelers waiting for the next day's tourists to unload from arriving ferries.

On our right, the harbor tucked itself in against the island. On our left, a park sprawled to where the bluff rose sharply. The fort built by the British kept watch over the park, the town, the harbor and the straits. I had heard a canon fired earlier during the day.

Well before we reached the marina, our target stood out. McCauley's boat left no doubt. The white yacht dominated the harbor. Sleek sweeping lines suggested a vessel under full speed even as it swung at anchor on the glass-smooth water. Too large to nudge up against one of the piers serving a fleet of smaller boats, it floated beyond the last harbor marker on its own.

"Let's have a look," I said.

"Not too close," Andy ordered.

I aimed us over the water, careful to avoid sailboat masts. All available slips were occupied. Half a dozen sailboats lay at anchor beyond the last pier. We passed between them and flew a half circle around the yacht.

Within a shell of immaculate white steel and Fiberglas, a warmly lit wood-appointed interior promised lavish comfort. Two open levels offered million-dollar views off the back of the vessel. Additional accommodations hid deeper inside, beneath a command bridge hidden by tinted glass. A table had been set in the upper salon near the stern. Glassware and silverware sparkled, waiting for Lindsay to arrive. I counted two place settings. I noted also that the ship faced the island, which put the secluded stern table away from watchful eyes.

A davit at the back of the yacht hung over the water, empty. I searched the docks and found a sleek motorboat tied at the end of the pier. A deckhand in white waited. Lindsay's ride.

The Director had not yet arrived when we completed our circuit.

"Will, do you see that coffee shop? At the dock? How about there?"

"On the roof or in the shop?"

"He could be out there for hours. Why don't we see if we can get a table with a view?"

It meant appearing. Easier said than done. An alley leading from the dock to the street offered relative privacy. I piloted us up the dock to the small café. I slipped into the alley between a building containing small shops and a bicycle rental business. Steady pedestrian traffic moved continuously past the mouth of the alley, forcing us to hang silently beside the building and wait.

"Now," Andy said urgently when a family pushing a stroller cleared the corner of the building.

I lowered us until our feet touched the pavement.

Fwooomp!

Andy steadied herself against me. She checked both directions to ensure that we hadn't been seen. I tucked away the power unit.

We walked back down the alley to the waterfront coffee shop like a pair of tourists.

"Closed," Andy announced. She pointed at a door sign. "There's outdoor seating. I don't think they'd mind." Scattered empty tables under blue umbrellas waited for the next day's trade. Andy picked a chair with a view of the harbor and the yacht. I sat beside her.

We settled in. Lindsay arrived ten minutes later. He strolled past the shop without looking in our direction. At the end of the dock he was greeted by the attending yacht crewman. In short order, they motored away from the pier, crossing several hundred feet of open water beyond the last anchored sailboat. We watched Lindsay board the yacht. A man greeted him. The distance made it impossible to tell if it was McCauley.

Thirty seconds in, I felt restless.

"You want anything? I could run up the street and get something. A couple beers?"

"Right. Beer on our first assignment from the Deputy Director of the FBI."

I took that as a no.

She crossed a leg and settled in the chair. She watched the white yacht float above a near-perfect reflection rendered on glassy water.

I watched her.

"You're pretty excited," I said, noting a lock of hair that had fallen beside one eye.

"I've been on stakeouts before," she brushed the hair back unconsciously.

"Not that. I mean about Quantico. Want to talk about it?"

She pressed her lips together for a moment. "No matter what silliness you see on TV, no matter what brainless reporting you see in the press, the FBI is the elite, Will. They're professionals. They take only the best. They have the best tools, cutting-edge science, the sharpest people in law enforcement."

"Donaldson notwithstanding."

She ignored the jab. She reached for my hand, taking it in both of hers. She began stroking and rearranging my fingers as if counting them. It's a move she makes when she's thinking. "Yes. I imagined the possibility. I'll even admit I hoped for it. You know? As part of the decision to do this."

"But?"

She hesitated.

"I don't want it to be on your coattails."

"I understand. Makes sense. The hick cop from a small town gets a coveted slot—"

"Do you have any idea how exceptional you have to be to get in, Will?"

"Clearly. And then you come along. A lowly patrol sergeant. I get it."

She made a face at me. "Um, you're not exactly suppressing my insecurities."

"I know. But I also know something you don't. Something you will never know about yourself, no matter how many people tell you. No matter how many times I tell you."

"What?"

"You think you're cheating your way in. And maybe you will have to prove yourself to the Ivy League graduates and top cops from big city departments, but I know that when that class graduates, you will rank in the top three, if not number one."

She shook her head.

"Look," I said. "Take me out of the picture and you may be right. On a conventional path, you might not have gotten your application past the first review, because you're a technical college grad and you don't come with a law degree. If you approach from that angle, the established process is stacked against you. But if they give you a shot, head to head with the best, my money is on you to come out on top. No contest. And I think Lindsay knows that, too."

She skipped past false modesty. "I want it, Will. I do. I just don't want it to be on a handicap."

"Me being the handicap."

She laughed. "Oh, you are totally a handicap."

"Your cross to bear, love." We settled the question with a few minutes of silence, which I found difficult to maintain. "PT-109."

"What?"

I pointed. "PT-109. There."

She followed my outstretched arm and finger to the end of one of the other piers. In a span of open water between moored motor- and sailboats, a large model of a military craft circled slowly in the water. A boy stood on the dock with a remote control in his hands. Two adults leaned over his shoulder. One of the adults instructed him on the operation of the craft, which performed slow figure eights on the glassy surface.

"What's PT-109?" Andy asked.

"President Kennedy's navy patrol boat in World War II. A Patrol Torpedo—hence PT—boat stationed in the Solomon Islands. That's a pretty cool model of it." The model appeared to be around three feet long. I estimated the kid to be eight or nine. A lot of toy for a kid that age. I felt a little jealous. "It's quite a story. Want to hear it?"

Andy shifted her gaze away from the father and son moment. She looked at McCauley's yacht.

"Not particularly. We have a job to do here."

"Right. So, in 1943 the Navy ran these patrol boats, basically oversized motorboats, up and down The Slot, which is a stretch of water between islands in the Solomons. They looked for Japanese barges and troop movements. The PT boats were armed with torpedoes for attacking ships and heavy machine guns for attacking Japanese landing craft or supporting our own troop landings."

"Is this going to be a long story?"

"There's a pretty good movie."

"Let's watch the movie sometime."

"You'll just fall asleep. It has explosions." I tugged my attention away from the model in the water and shifted in my seat to prove my dedication to watching the yacht. "I would do that with our son."

"What?"

"Make models."

She chuckled. "You'd make models. Whether you'd allow our son to touch them, I have my doubts."

"What's the point of having kids if you can't play with their toys?"

She let that one hang. Discussions about having a family had become more frequent. The pace may have been glacial, but lately I sensed a shift in Andy when the topic came up. A little less rush to declare the idea insane. A hesitation before she laughed and declared having one child in the family was taxing her already. Now, knowing her thoughts lingered on Donaldson's revelation about Quantico and her future law enforcement career, I wondered if the question of children would drop from the agenda.

Or if the agenda itself had been challenged.

The yacht sat where it had five minutes ago. Gulls overhead added their customary note to the waterfront tableau. The pinks in the sky shifted slightly toward purple. I pictured Lindsay settling in for a multi-course dinner and tangled political double-talk.

"I don't know if I'm cut out for this surveillance thing," I said. "You sure you don't want a beer? Or a coffee?"

"Coffee at this hour will keep me up all night. I'm fine. But if you want to run up the street for something, go ahead. He's going to be there a while. But no beer."

I tried not to rise too quickly but felt an urge to move before she changed her mind.

"I'll bring you some ice cream."

"No. Don't. I'm fine."

I TROTTED up the alley and struck out on the sidewalk. I searched for Donaldson but picked up no sign of him. No doubt he planned to stick it in my face that he had painted himself like bark and was standing next to a tree or had paid a small family to hide him in their stroller in the park across the street.

I wondered if this surveillance thing would be the degree to which the FBI planned to employ my talents. If it was, I might go back to persuading Andy we should use *the other thing* to visit jewelry stores and casinos until we have enough loot to buy our own island.

An island.

My mind wandered.

John Kennedy's PT boat was rammed by a Japanese destroyer on a pitch-black night in The Slot. He and the surviving crewmen swam to an island. They were ultimately rescued after Kennedy sent a note and a message carved on a coconut shell to an Australian coast watcher. It's a story I grew up admiring. The kid and his dad made me jealous of their radio-controlled replica of Kennedy's famous patrol boat.

Maybe I would build one for my son.

And spend time with him like the father on the dock did.

The same father who now strolled the sidewalk ahead of me with his hand on his son's shoulder.

I stopped.

Twenty feet ahead of me the father and son duo that had been operating the model boat walked toward the center of town, perhaps heading for an evening ice cream or late burger.

Without the boat.

Or the remote control.

That's a lot of expensive toy to just leave on the dock, I thought.

The model PT boat had been circling in the harbor when I left Andy, only minutes ago. It would have taken time for them to bring the boat to the dock, to retrieve and stow it. They couldn't have done all that and reached the street ahead of me.

Maybe it wasn't theirs. There had been another man on the dock, watching the boy operate the boat. Maybe it was his.

Something about that bothered me.

I reversed course and hurried back to the marina. Instead of continuing to the coffee shop, I descended a set of steps to the first pier where the father and son had been standing. A chain across the pier hung a sign warning me that only authorized persons were allowed. I hopped the chain and trotted forward on the wooden planks. At a T-intersection I turned left.

No one stood on the end of the pier with a remote control in hand.

I pulled out my phone and stroked the screen, jabbing at Andy's number in the Recents list.

Across the marina she pulled her phone from her bag.

"Hey," she answered.

"Do you see the guy with the toy boat?"

"What?"

"Look to where we saw the guy with the toy boat." She looked. The instant she saw me, I waved. "Do you see where he went? I just saw the father and kid up on the street. It wasn't their boat."

She lifted her arm and pointed.

"They're still playing with it. Look."

I followed the line drawn by Andy's outstretched arm to the water beyond the anchored sailboats. At the head of a broad vee of wake, the model of John Kennedy's patrol torpedo boat motored across the glassy water.

"No. They're not. The dad and kid weren't operating it. It was the other guy. Do you see him anywhere?"

Andy searched. I pictured him in my mind. Ball cap pulled down. Sunglasses.

Like someone who didn't want to be recognized.

"Isn't he near you?"

I would have looked, but my eyes locked on something I didn't want to see.

"Andy. It's headed straight for the yacht. It's not making circles or figure eights. It's headed out of the harbor on a straight line."

"What?"

"The boat. Look."

Andy stood up.

"Dee, it's not turning."

"Find the operator! Will!"

She bolted from her station under the umbrella. She sprinted the length of the dock, stuffing her phone in her pocket and working the flap on her shoulder bag. Across the water, she shouted at me.

"Find him, Will!"

I searched. I scanned each moored boat, looking for someone seated on a deck bench, remote control in hand. I looked up and down the pier.

Nothing.

I checked the shore, the buildings beside the marina.

Nothing.

The model PT boat hummed on a perfect line toward the yacht.

Andy reached the end of the dock and drew herself to a stop at the edge less than thirty yards from me. She swung both arms up and took a stance, knees bent slightly, a gentle lean forward. Hands joined in a grip on her Glock 17.

No hesitation.

Her first shot cracked twilight's serenity. Fifty yards away, a gout of water splashed up just ahead of the model plowing toward the yacht. Her second shot splashed in the boats wake. Andy's an expert shot, but her chances with a handgun at that distance were slim.

With the target bracketed, she fired for effect. Thirteen more gunshots rang out. Water splashed all around the motoring model boat. I thought I saw plastic pieces fly in the air. I thought I saw the boat shudder from a hit.

When the splashes subsided, the boat motored on. The wake spread behind it, pointing like an arrow at the white yacht.

"Will!" She shouted across the water. "Your phone! Call Lindsay!"

My phone remained in my hand. My screen said the connection to Andy had ended. I poked the Recents caption. An unfamiliar number took the second position from the top. I touched it.

"C'mon! C'mon!" I said, holding the phone to my ear.

The model boat held a steady course for the yacht. I estimated the distance at less than two hundred feet.

Lindsay's voice came on the line, telling me to leave a number.

"No answer!" I shouted.

Andy waved her arms frantically at me. "Pick me up!"

I jammed my phone in my pocket and took five steps back up the dock. Pulling a BLASTER free of another pocket, I snapped a prop on the shaft and broke into a run. Clearing the lip of the pier like someone planning a cannonball landing in the water, I shoved the levers in my head forward—

Fwooomp!

—and disappeared on the move. Andy braced herself. I goosed the power unit and crossed the short expanse of harbor between us.

"Coming in!" I warned her.

I spread my arms and hit her and pushed the levers again.

FWOOOMP!

The sound reverberated in my head. For a moment, the collision brought me to a halt. She vanished in my arms. The question of what someone watching might think flashed through my mind. There could be no doubt that firing a weapon from the dock drew attention.

No time to worry about it. I pushed the power unit control fully forward.

"We have to get to Lindsay," she said breathlessly.

I figured as much. But if this meant what I feared, being anywhere near the yacht when the model reached it was a bad idea.

I mapped out a flight path that would approach from the other side and immediately knew it would take too long.

At full throttle, the prop whined. I twisted my wrist and brought us around, fixing a course for the stern of the yacht. If nothing else, we might have time to shout a warning.

The model in the water made no sound, at least none I could hear over the shrill whine of the BLASTER. We picked up speed rapidly, but so did the model. Andy peppering it with gunshots had ended all pretense. The model surged forward. The bow lifted from the water and the hull skimmed the glassy surface, throwing up a rooster tail of spray.

Forty feet lay between the model and the yacht.

Twenty.

I saw no chance.

"Dee! We ca—!"

Fixated on the model, I looked directly at the explosion. Blast pressure landed twin punches on my eyeballs. Harder punches hit my chest and my belly, expelling all the air I had.

My vision scrambled. Blurry sky and water changed places, over and over.

Any sense of location disappeared. My arms flailed. A second punch followed the first, this one larger and made of light and heat. Spinning, I saw fire leap skyward in a mushroom cloud.

I realized my BLASTER was gone.

Andy, too.

25

I hit trees across the street from the coffee shop stakeout. A wall of thick branches clawed me to a stop. Heat lingered on the skin of my face, telling me I'd been facing forward when the second blast hit.

Andy!

She had been in my arms. Then gone. The blast that threw me backward, tumbled me, end over end. Heat and dull pain inflicted by the blast wave added to my confusion. My ears rang.

I fought tree branches that maliciously snapped back into place or else sent me heaving back and forth. Sharp sticks jabbed me on the outside. Panic gripped me on the inside.

I found a reasonably solid branch and closed a grip on it. I stabilized long enough to heave myself upward into the darkening sky. As I broke free of the tree, I pawed my pocket for my spare BLASTER. Finding both the power unit and prop, I froze and took a sharp breath—held it for a four-count—then let it go slowly on another four-count. The technique calmed me enough to steady my hands for assembly of the power unit. The instant the prop snapped on the shaft, I thumbed the slide control and accelerated.

I'd been blown out of the harbor, over the coffee shop, across the road and halfway up the bluff. I gave the BLASTER full power to regain ground.

The harbor resembled wartime. Black smoke roiled from great clouds of flame. Debris littered choppy water that had been glass smooth moments ago. Two smaller boats, anchored not far from where the yacht had been, burned brightly. Two sailboats lay on their sides in the water, half of their hulls exposed.

The pristine yacht was gone. Burning structure stuck out of the water where the bow had been. Pieces drifted, engulfed in the fire and smoke.

I searched the harbor surface. Flame mixed with unidentifiable chunks of debris. Burning pieces rained down from the black cloud and fell back into the flames or extinguished in the water. Boats moored against the fixed dock shuddered and heaved on incoming waves like a spooked herd of wild stallions.

"ANDY!" I shouted. It came out breathless and hoarse. My mouth had gone dry from heaving air back into my lungs. I tried again. "ANDY!"

Shooting the length of the dock, I raced over the disturbed water. On the dock and on the shore, people materialized out of nowhere, lifting their arms against the heat and squinting at the flames.

I searched the rippling surface. She'd been torn from my grip when the blast hit. We were over the water halfway between the dock and the yacht. Any closer and we would have been consumed.

Something splashed the water below me. I saw a tight French braid disappear beneath a surface full of debris and burning fuel.

She swam under water, trapped below the flames.

I heaved to a halt. Fuel burned in patches on the surface. I followed her white and red striped blouse, rippling and surging away from the flames.

Finding open water, she popped up gasping. She threw her arms forward and pounded a wild stroke away from the floating fire.

I rotated and swept across her path, timing her stroke. As her arm came forward, I grabbed. I felt her stiffen, startled.

FWOOOMP! I pushed *the other thing* over her. She vanished. Sudden buoyancy popped her out of the water. I heard her cough and gasp. We rose against a backdrop of black smoke and heat. She drew in air. I pulled her against me and felt her hands frantically fix a grip on me.

I shoved the slide control to full power. The unit screamed. We maneuvered away from the heat, toward the shore. Cooler air met us. We crossed the dock and sailed over the coffee shop. A skirt of broken glass littered the perimeter of the shop where its windows had blown in.

"Will!" she gasped. I pulled her tighter.

We crossed the road. I cut the power, then reversed it to bring us to a stop. We clutched each other tightly and hung in the air high over the park with the slumbering fort to our backs. The park had emptied. Everyone surged to the water's edge.

I rotated us until we faced the mayhem in the marina.

"What happened?"

"Bomb," she said breathlessly.

"Impossible! It was a lousy little model boat." The scene below us looked like the aftermath at Pearl Harbor.

"Probably packed—" she gasped "—with explosives."

"Enough to do that?"

"No—not that—enough to hit—the fuel tanks."

We watched and held each other.

"Will! My God! Lindsay!"

I saw no reason to believe anyone on that yacht had survived the blast or the fire that followed.

People emerged from the moored boats in the harbor and ran from the heat. They congregated at a safe distance along the shore. Dozens emerged from shops and restaurants in the town center, filling the street, moving to vantage points to try and see what had caused the pillar of black smoke.

Andy's breathing evened out.

"My phone. My bag. They're gone."

"I'm sorry, Dee. The blast tore you out of my hands."

I tightened my embrace as if it might happen again.

"We need to call someone! Do you have your phone?"

"I think the call has already gone out. The whole town is watching this."

We hung in the air at least a hundred feet up, almost even with the canon that fires daily from the fortress on the bluff. More and more people gathered on the waterfront below us, arms extended, phones raised high. I saw damage beyond the marina. Broken windows. Boats adrift. A sign on the roof of one of the ferry companies had toppled and hung on the side of the building.

Andy squirmed against me.

"I don't suppose you see Donaldson down there," I said.

She didn't answer. I felt her hand on my chest. Her fingers moved up my neck. She grabbed my chin from below and turned my head.

"What's that?"

She pointed my face in the direction of the Grand Hotel. Beyond it, a glow blossomed against the dark silhouette of the high bluff and the trees.

"Will! Is that—?"

"Oh, Christ...Gwen!"

26

I held the BLASTER upright and produced a shot of reverse power. We dropped sharply toward the empty park beneath us.

"What are you doing!?" Andy demanded. "No! We have to get to her!"

The ground came up to meet us. The instant we touched, I let her go. She staggered into sight, soaked and glistening.

"Will! What are you doing?"

"Take my phone!" I pulled it from my pocket and pressed it into her hand. It snapped into view. "Call whatever emergency number they have here and tell them that Lindsay Cottage is on fire. Tell them there's nothing they can do for the boat in the harbor, but that—"

"I get it! I get it! Go!"

I kicked off under full power and launched, then angled toward the Grand Hotel and the glow in the darkness beyond. The town slid away behind me. My speed increased. Wind tore at my clothes, my skin. My eyes watered.

As I accelerated, I gained altitude. The huge white hotel dropped away and exposed the bluff road beyond.

Lindsay cottage burned. The ground floor belched yellow flames from blown-out windows. Smoke poured from beneath the porch roof. Cloth awnings caught fire. Flaming fabric joined the rising smoke.

I tracked a direct line as if to a burning beacon. The hotel passed rapidly beneath me. Hotel guests streamed from the west end of the porch onto the bluff road.

Whatever had set the building ablaze, it had been efficient. Flame engulfed the first floor.

I aimed a mad dive at the second-floor windows, which mercifully remained dark. A section of the porch roof offered a landing spot outside of Lindsay's office turret. I dropped hard.

Fwooomp!

I stumbled and planted knees and hands on the roof. Gritty shingles tore at my knuckles where I gripped the BLASTER, holding it firm, knowing I needed it. Knowing it was the only one I had.

I scrambled to my feet and found the nearest window. Heat rose around me, warning of fire below. Air swept past me, drawn by the hungry flames. In a matter of seconds, the porch roof would go.

I smashed the window with the heel of the power unit. An edge caught my palm, stinging it. Glass fell away and slid off the roof. I pounded at the remnants to make the opening safe. I heaved myself through and flopped into Lindsay's office. Sharp corners and boxy shapes jabbed me. Lindsay's desk drawers were strewn across his expensive Persian rug. Finding my feet, I raced to the door and felt the knob. Still cool to the touch.

I pulled the door open, ready to slam it if a wall of smoke and toxic fumes greeted me.

The second-floor landing had wisps of smoke, but they raced away from where I stood. I realized that the well formed by the building's internal stairway acted as a chimney, but in reverse. Air was being pulled down by the consuming fire below.

This would not last.

"GWEN!" I shouted.

No reply.

Andy and I had been given a room on the second floor. Donaldson as well. His had been near the back of the house. Lindsay's master suite was also on the second floor. I guessed that Gwen, caretaker, occupied a room higher up.

I dashed to the stairs, taking the steps by threes.

She smacked into me midway up the stairs, hell bent on descending the stairs. We hit and dropped onto the steps. She scrambled to get past me.

I felt a sudden shift in the air around us.

"Gwen! Stop! Don't go down!" I grabbed her hand and pulled her to her feet.

"We have to get out! The house is on fire!"

"We can't go down. The first floor is gone!"

The air around us stopped moving. I looked over my shoulder and saw death coming. Instead of drawing air down the stairs, the fire now fed a black ball of smoke into the stairway. It boiled toward us.

"COME ON!" I gripped her arm.

I knew only too well what waited for us in that smoke. Toxins might poison us, but the temperature in that black cloud soared into the hundreds. Our lungs would be seared meat long before toxic gasses killed us.

We scrambled up the steps and found the third-floor hallway clear.

"Is there a back stairway?" I shouted over the growing roar that chased us like an animal.

"Yes!"

Hand in hand, we darted forward. Halfway down the hall I jerked her to a stop. I pointed.

Smoke swept around the corner at the end of the hall. The back stairwell offered no exit.

"In here!" I grabbed a doorknob, yanked open the door and pulled her in. I slammed the door behind us. I tried a light switch. Nothing happened.

An outside glow cast illumination through the bedroom window. I hurried to the window and flipped the latch. The sash refused to budge.

She came to my side and helped.

"It's painted shut!"

"Step back." I pulled a flower-printed bedspread off the mattress and balled it up. Gwen moved aside and I threw my wrapped forearms at the glass. Mutton-barred panes shattered. Chunks of glass fell to my feet. Others hung up in the frame. I used the bedspread for protection and pulled the pieces away. Halfway there. A screen formed a second barrier. I kicked. The screen split. I pulled the mesh apart to form an opening.

I stuck my head through the opening to assess our options. A second-floor turret on the side of the house formed a peaked cone beneath the window. It offered little or no footing and sheer drops on all sides. Bright glow on a garden directly below us told me the first floor on this side of the house was well aflame.

Just as I ducked back inside, a muffled blast shook the house. Then a second. The scene outside changed dramatically. A boiling wall of flame rose outside the window. It threw heat at us as it flashed past, followed by black smoke and rushing embers.

Gwen stumbled backward. She turned for the door.

"NO!" I grabbed her by the arm as she reached for the doorknob. Black smoke coiled up from the bottom of the door. If she opened the door we would be enveloped in seconds. Worse, the oxygen remaining in our small sanctuary would mix with the superheated smoke. There was an excellent chance the mixture would ignite, filling this room with a blast of flame as had just happened to the room below us.

She fought me for a second. "We can't go that way! We have to go back!"

"No! Open that door and we die. We're going out the window."

"It's forty feet down!"

"Trust me! I got this! Help me push this bed out of the way."

I let her go, stuffed my BLASTER in a pocket and grabbed the baseboard of the bed. She hesitated, then pitched in. We shoved the heavy bed across the hardwood floor.

"That dressing table. Grab the end." I took the end near the door, just to be sure she wouldn't try to get out. She took the other end. "Tip it over!"

I heaved. She followed suit. The dressing table dropped to the hardwood floor. As soon as it hit, I kicked the spindle legs off my end of the table. They snapped and clattered to the floor. She saw what I was doing and duplicated the effort on her end. With all four legs free the table tipped over flat.

"Help me pick it up. We're going to ram it out the window."

"Why?"

"Just do it!"

She dropped and grabbed her side of the table. We lifted it off the floor and positioned ourselves near the window with the end of the table aimed at the center sash.

"On three. One! Two! Three!"

Using the table as a battering ram, we charged the window. As we charged, I lifted. The heavy hardwood table hit the sash and smashed through, taking sash, glass, screen and most of the frame with it. It clattered out of our grip, hit the window frame and fell, bouncing off the turret roof below.

Just yards away, a wall of smoke blanketed the side of the building, racing for the sky.

Gwen stared at it in horror.

"Come on! We're leaving!"

"How?"

"As fast as possible!" I threw my arms around her and lifted her off the floor. She screamed. I pinned her arms against her sides and gave her no chance to fight. Three steps to the window and I ducked, aiming us both through the opening. It was a less than perfect shot. I scraped one arm. Our legs hit the bottom edge of the frame before following us out.

FWOOOMP!

Gwen screamed. I kicked the window frame.

"Hold your breath!" I shouted at her. Her screaming stopped. My kicks shoved us away from the house and into the smoke.

I anticipated a blast of heat, but the cool sensation that enveloped us held it at bay. We emerged from the smoke high over the side lawn of the house. Rippling bright firelight painted the neighboring cottage, which presented the next obstacle. Our trajectory promised a collision with a wooden wall.

Gwen jerked her arms free and threw them around me as if she meant to climb me. I rotated us to a vertical position, squirmed to free my right hand and found my BLASTER in the cargo pocket of my pants. It took a moment to get the right grip on it. Just ahead of a collision with the side wall of the house next door, I found the power slide.

We pulled away from the inferno, cutting an arc through the air above the neighboring lawn. Gwen sank her fingers into my skin, pressed her head against my neck and became rigid. I aimed for the bluff road. A mob of people lined the road. They streamed up from the hotel below, drawn by the spectacle.

I couldn't appear in front of all these people. At the top of the road's incline, the narrow pavement turned into the woods. A small overlook sat outside the turn, behind the line of onlookers. I aimed for it, confident that every face lining the road was locked on the fire.

I maneuvered and eased down until my feet touched the ground beside a stone bench.

Fwooomp!

Gwen's face appeared inches from mine framing two nearly bursting eyes. Her mouth hung open. She gasped for air.

I peeled her arms from my neck and shoulders.

She tried to speak. I lifted a finger to my lips.

"Shhhhhh…"

We turned to watch a ninety-year-old monument to wealth and tradition go up in flames.

27

Andy never reached the fire department. Calls reporting the harbor explosion flooded the island's 9-1-1 system. Calls eventually reported the Lindsay Cottage fire, but the dispatcher's initial response was to mistakenly tell each caller that they had already received a report of fire in the harbor. Only the beacon of flame on top of the bluff eventually alerted a quick-thinking fire chief that a second fire had broken out.

It hardly mattered. Flames engulfed Lindsay Cottage long before the town fire engine arrived. Gwen and I watched from the overlook. Bystanders ran to help neighbors on both sides of the burning house deploy garden hoses and aim streams at their own wooden tinderboxes. Their action combined with luck and a breathlessly still evening to prevent the fire from spreading.

Several minutes after landing, Gwen snapped out of her shock.

"The horses!" she cried. She spun but I caught her by the arm. She tried to pull free. "We have to get the horses!"

"Fine! My way."

Before she could protest, I threw my left arm around her shoulder.

Fwooomp!

"Whaa—!" she gasped.

"I'll explain later."

I kicked off the ground and aimed the BLASTER at the road leading into the woods. We accelerated rapidly just above the pavement, skimming beneath overhanging tree branches.

Fifty feet from the inferno that now owned the back of the house, the barn remained mercifully untouched. I didn't think it would last.

I landed outside a corral attached to the barn and released Gwen. Gravity's grip caught her feet by surprise. She tumbled to the dirt.

"Sorry!" I reappeared and pulled her to her feet.

Four frenzied horses trotted and snorted in a circular corral. The heat from the burning house radiated into my face and skin. The horses' eyes were white rings of terror.

Gwen threw over the latch on the gate and heaved it open. I followed her into the corral and mimicked her moves as she waved her arms, working the panicked animals around until they found escape. They darted across the dirt yard to the pavement where one slipped and nearly lost its footing. They raced into the darkness and cool air of the woods.

"Let's get away from here," I called to Gwen, shielding my face against the heat with my hand.

She stood frozen. Tears streamed from eyes glittering with the reflection of the burning house.

"Papa! He'll be—it's—"

"Come on. We've got to move."

Bewildered, she accepted my hand. I closed a firm grip and forced the levers in my head forward again.

We vanished. I kicked us off the ground and began a slow flight back to the bluff overlook. This time when we reappeared, she confronted me.

"*How did you—what is—what did we just—?*" Her chin quivered but she fought it. I saw the bloodline to her grandfather. "Tell me what just happened because my house is on fire and I am *this close* to losing my shit!"

I suddenly wished Andy was here.

"I completely understand."

"Oh, I don't fucking think you do! What—*just*—*happened? What did you do?*"

"Gwen, just—"

"God! If you tell me to calm down, I will throw you off this bluff!" She laughed suddenly, a little harshly. "Oh. I guess that wouldn't matter much."

"Not really."

What would Andy do?

I gripped her shoulders and looked her in the eye. "We're going to do this the way your Papa would do it, okay? By the book. I promise to explain what I did, but first I need to know what happened. How did that fire start?"

"You tell me! I heard you come home and—"

"Wait! You heard someone come home?"

"Yes! It wasn't you?"

I shook my head.

"Ohmigod! Was it Papa? Was Papa in the house?" Panic welled up.

I couldn't tell her.

"No! He wasn't in the house! No one was in the house when I got there." At least not that I detected. "Did you hear someone? Gwen, calmly, tell me everything up to the moment we ran into each other on the stairs."

She swallowed down her panic. I felt a jab of guilt for implying that her grandfather was okay.

"I—I thought I heard you come back. Or someone. I assumed it was you or your wife or Agent Donaldson or Papa. I heard someone downstairs—and then I got in the shower—and I thought I heard a loud boom. Like fireworks. I finished my shower and went to the room across the hall and looked out the side window and saw the light in town. I didn't know what it was, so I got dressed. When I looked outside again, I saw light in the yard. Then I smelled smoke. And I got really scared and that's when I ran for the stairs and…you know…into you."

"Did you see anyone? In the house? In the yard?"

She shook her head.

A fire engine wailed in the distance. I glanced at the house, fully engulfed. Volunteers aimed garden hoses at the houses on either side, holding up coats and jackets to shield themselves from the heat.

Paint peeled on the sides of the neighboring homes. The best anyone could hope for was that the fire engine would arrive in time to limit the blaze to Lindsay Cottage.

"Did someone break in? Did someone *do this*?"

"I think so," I said.

"Ohmigod! Why?"

I had an idea but didn't say. I was about to offer a lie when she pointed past me at the harbor.

"What is that?"

Smoke from the blast in the harbor rose like a thunderhead above the town.

A lie would only make it worse.

I really wished Andy would show up.

She would tell me to tell the truth.

"Gwen." I took a breath. Her eyes flared one beat ahead of my words. "Your grandfather was on a boat tonight. Someone blew it up, probably the same people who broke into the house and burned it."

Nope. A lie would have been better.

28

Donaldson caught up to Andy on the bluff road above the hotel where the fire department sealed the road and pushed back the crowd. A flashed badge permitted the two of them to continue to where a single firetruck sent a high arc of water into the night air. Most of the water landed on the walls of the homes on either side of the inferno. There was no saving Lindsay Cottage. When a side wall collapsed, sending flaming debris across the neighboring lawn, the fire crew doused embers and burning pieces that knocked against the wooden walls of the house next door.

Andy and Donaldson skirted the firetruck and hiked up the hill shielding their faces from the heat.

"C'mon!" I took Gwen by the hand and weaved through the spectators. I called out as we emerged into the open. "Andy!"

I waved. Andy tapped Donaldson on the shoulder and broke into a run. He limped after her.

"Thank God you're okay!" Andy cried. She threw her arms around the girl. I stood back as they embraced.

"No problem," I said. "I'm fine."

Gwen sobbed and buried her face in my wife's shoulder. Andy stroked her hair. When the girl came up for air, she asked, "Is it true?"

Andy whispered something to the girl.

It must have been the truth because it made matters worse. Gwen shuddered and wept.

Donaldson hobbled to join us. He studied the crowd, the location and our options. He gestured at me and tapped Andy on the shoulder.

"This way," he said. The spectators parted for us. Some of them, neighbors perhaps, knew the girl. A woman pressed a hand on her shoulder as we passed. A man patted her back. Many fought tears of their own.

Donaldson led us to where the road turned and entered the woods. I wasn't sure what he had in mind other than to escape listening ears. Andy held Gwen against her shoulder. The girl cried. We walked down a road lined with trees. Firelight shadows trembled all around us. No one spoke until we stopped far from the crowd at the overlook.

"Kiddo," Donaldson touched Gwen's shoulder. "What happened?"

Gwen tried to sniffle and wipe her face. Andy reflexively reached for a tissue from her missing shoulder bag.

"I got this," I told Gwen. I explained what she'd told me.

Donaldson pulled out his phone and swiped the screen until the keypad for dialing appeared. "Here. Call your folks and let them know you're okay. This will be on the news or on social media really fast—if it isn't already. But—listen to me—*this is important—say nothing about us, okay?* I'll explain later."

"What about Papa? What do I tell them?"

"Might be best not to say anything...yet."

"Lee! She's family!"

Donaldson ignored Andy. "Gwen, we don't know anything for certain. I understand it's a lot to ask. It's just—"

"Don't be ridiculous," Andy argued. "This is going to get out."

"She won't be able to explain how she knows," he protested. To Gwen, he said, "At this point, no one knows."

The girl shot glances from Donaldson to Andy.

Donaldson said, "Gwen, if you can you give us a little time it might help us find out who did this."

Andy frowned at the lie.

Gwen took the phone and nodded. She tapped out a number and stepped away from us. Against the roar and crackle of a fire several hundred feet away, we heard the connection ring, then a woman's voice answer.

"Mom?" Gwen spoke, her voice high and tight. "It's me. Um...something happened. I'm okay." She looked away from Donaldson. "No. He—he—"

Andy gestured for Donaldson and me to stroll away from the girl as she broke down crying anew. We put twenty paces between us and her.

"That was unnecessary," Andy scolded Donaldson.

"Really? At this moment she's telling her mother that her grandfather is dead. How did she come by that information? You're not thinking ahead, Detective."

I interrupted. "What the hell just happened?"

"A hit," Donaldson said firmly. "They hit the Director and McCauley in the harbor. Then they torched the Director's house."

"They were looking for something," I said. "In his office."

"That girl is lucky they didn't know she was in the house."

"Or they knew and tried to burn her alive."

"What were they after?" Andy asked.

"Something from his office," I said. I described the drawers strewn across the floor.

Donaldson's face gained hard angles of light and darkness in the firelight.

"What if this is about us being here?" Andy asked. "About Will?"

Donaldson shook his head. "I don't think so. In fact, I don't think whoever did this expected or knew that you were here. Or if they did, they saw all of us as incidental. Somebody didn't like McCauley asking for a meeting with Lindsay. They also thought the Director had something in the house."

"What?"

"That folder? Something he didn't show us? Take your pick. Maybe they found it. If not, maybe they torched the place to make sure it was destroyed."

"They're still on the island," Andy said. "They have to be."

"Possible. Or they could have a boat waiting. Or they came in by airplane like you two. Or they have a time share rented out for the week and they're sitting on a deck sipping cold beer. How the hell should I know?"

"There was a guy with a kid—on the dock."

"I know. I saw them."

"They might have been a part of this," I suggested.

"The dad and kid? More likely they provided accidental cover for whoever launched that toy boat full of explosives. Dad and the kid see the guy launching it and strike up a conversation. He lets the kid take a turn, making it all look innocent. He's not going to say, 'Buzz off, I got a ship to blow up.' He's going to play along for a few minutes."

Andy said, "So we find them, and they help ID the guy."

"Needle in a tourist haystack. But we have two bigger and more immediate concerns."

He looked at both of us, then looked pointedly at Gwen, still caught up in an emotional exchange with her mother.

"A top FBI official was murdered tonight in what will play as a full-blown terrorist attack. This island is about to sink under the weight of the law enforcement agencies descending on it. And you two can't be here."

"What?" Andy squared herself to him.

Donaldson shook his head. "You can't be here. As it is, someone's likely to step forward and tell the authorities they saw a woman firing a gun at the yacht seconds before it blew up."

"I wasn't firing at the—"

"Are you suggesting we run for it?" I asked.

"No," Andy declared. "No. I was a witness. I was practically on top of the thing. I know what happened and how. I can't walk away from this."

"I was there, too. I saw everything you saw," Donaldson said. "Look, I can explain why I was here. But trying to explain why you were here is a bad idea."

"Leaving the scene of a crime is a bad idea!"

"Andrea, he was the *Deputy Director!* This will be top of the hour on every cable news outlet in the country. The Director himself will probably take charge. How *exactly* do you explain why you're here? Why *he's* here." He jabbed an accusing finger at me. "We went to Lindsay for discretion. That's out the goddamned window now. Cameras and spotlights from here on out. You two can't be here. Period."

"This is not right, Lee! I'm a police officer!"

"Who can't answer hard questions!" he snapped. "And you know it." He turned to me. "Can you take off at night?"

"That's going to look ridiculously suspicious."

"It might. But it's going to look a lot worse when law enforcement gets the full handle on what happened here and shuts down the airport, which I expect to happen as soon as they can muster the manpower."

Andy shook her head and planted her feet. I saw the war flag—a lock of hair—fall to her eyebrow. I held my breath for a barrage of argument.

Donaldson faced her.

The argument didn't come. At least not with Donaldson. She stood and stared at him for a long moment. She had the argument with herself. And lost.

"Dammit." She said. She looked at Gwen. "What about her?"

"I'll take care of her," Donaldson said.

"You'll have to deal with something else, then." I said. I explained how Gwen had survived the fire. Donaldson rolled his eyes.

"I'll figure it out."

"Wait!" Andy said. "We can't leave. Will, your flight bag. It's in the fire. We don't have keys to the airplane!"

I unzipped a pocket in my cargo pants.

"Oh, hell no. On me at all times." I dangled a set of keys between us. They glittered in the firelight.

"Go," Donaldson said. "I'll reach out as soon as I can."

Andy didn't move.

"Go."

ANDY EXCHANGED A PARTING EMBRACE with the girl and spoke to her softly, sharing understanding, trading secrets, offering emotional strength. Her words staunched the flow of tears. They hugged and held it. When they separated, Gwen stood in stunned silence, staring at the flames.

Andy closed a grip on my arm. I took her hand and we vanished. I kicked us straight up to clear the trees, then used the BLASTER to navigate to the dark and deserted airport at the center of the island. We stopped briefly in the small empty office, then hurried to the plane. I untied the airplane. Andy kept watch for anyone in a hurry to stop us.

No one appeared.

We boarded. I started the Baron's engines and taxied without lights. At the cottage, against the dominating firelight, the night sky had gone black, but once we got away from the flames and out of the woods, faint twilight lingered in the sky—enough to illuminate the taxiway and runway. Flaunting regulations, I operated without lights. We took off to the west. I lifted the nose against the city glow of St. Ignace.

With the gear up and power set for climb, I banked left and flew a circuit around the island. Andy leaned forward in her seat to watch.

Emergency lights flashed on the bluff road where Lindsay Cottage burned between its neighboring cottages like an ancient coastal signal fire.

More emergency lights winked along the waterfront. For an island without motor vehicles, the emergency had quickly produced a small fleet of firetrucks and ambulances. Boats moved slowly around the harbor, circling wreckage where the yacht had been. Clusters of debris burned in the harbor. As I flew two thousand feet overhead, I smelled smoke.

Neither Andy nor I spoke. I completed a circuit around the scene, then set a course for Essex County Airport.

PART III

29

"Turn on your TV."

"Hello to you, too," I said to Donaldson.

"Turn on your goddamned TV, Will. MSNBC."

"Hang on," I said. "I'm at the hangar. Arun has a TV in the office."

"Arun?"

"Arun Dewar. Works for the foundation, remember?"

"Oh, yeah, yeah. The Brit."

"Where are you?" I hurried across the empty hangar floor.

"Still on the island along with every other FBI agent in North America. Hurry up, it'll be on in a minute."

I jogged into Arun's office. A wall-mounted flatscreen broadcast endless financial news without sound. I grabbed the remote from his desk.

"What channel is MSNBC?" I asked him.

"Forty-six."

I thumbed the two digits. The channel flashed to video of McCauley's yacht, broken and burning. The footage, shot with a phone in vertical format, jiggled accordingly.

"I already saw this," I told Donaldson. The scene cut to another angle; someone was smart enough to shoot the chaos in widescreen. "I saw it this morning with Andy."

"Not all of it. Wait for it."

I waited. The image changed to a talking-head split screen. The morning anchor occupied the box on the left.

A familiar face appeared in the box on the right.

"What the—?"

"Uh-huh." Donaldson answered. "It's him."

Aaron McCauley filled a frame with Mackinac harbor in the background. I stared for a moment before I realized he was talking. I found the volume control.

"...am so grateful to be alive—it's devastating, just devastating..."

McCauley explained to the announcer that he'd been interviewed extensively by the FBI. He explained that he told the authorities how he met Director Lindsay by chance on the island—how he planned to dine with the FBI Deputy Director because the Director had served in the Army with McCauley's father, who had been killed when McCauley was a boy—how he looked forward to learning more about a father he barely knew—how a mix-up in timing sent the Director to McCauley's boat while McCauley was still ashore.

"Bullshit," I said.

"Uh-huh."

"What's going on?" Arun asked. I held up a finger signaling for him to hold his question. I muted the TV and wandered back into the empty hangar.

"Did you tell them this is all BS?"

"Yeah...as much as I could. Technically, I'm still on medical leave."

"What are you talking about? You just worked the DeSantorini case."

"Paperwork. My formal reinstatement hasn't come through."

"That's stupid."

"It's not all bad. I used it to explain why I was here. I told the acting SAC that I jumped chain of command to speak to Lindsay directly—that I came here to plead my case."

"You lied to the FBI."

"Everybody lies to the FBI. I couldn't tell them the truth—about you and Andy."

"This is insane. Did you at least fill 'em in on what Lindsay was doing?"

"Which is what, exactly?"

"He told us! He had that dossier!"

"Relax, Will. I covered it. I told the SAC that Lindsay mentioned McCauley, a meeting, and a dossier he had his people put together. I told them McCauley is a lyin' sack of shit."

"And?"

"They don't believe McCauley any more than I do. But the sonofabitch is sticking to his story. He also has some juice in D.C. My guess is it's the ex-partner at DOJ because the shit is rolling downhill."

"Are you back in? Reinstated?"

"Oh, hell no. It's worse than before. Now I'm a witness. If I hear the word 'pending' one more time. Screw it. Doesn't matter. Oh, hey—they found the dad and the kid—from the boat dock."

"How?"

"I told you. Every FBI agent in North America is here. You were right—the boy and his father were on the dock when they saw a man launch the model boat. A nice man, they said. He invited the kid to have a turn."

"I don't suppose they could provide a description."

"Yeah. White male tourist. Wore a Mercury Marine hat. Sunglasses. Looked like every third guy on this island."

"How's Gwen?"

"She's a tough kid. I had a long talk with her. Got her story straight. She's saying she made it down the back stairs before it went up in flames. She said to say thanks—for herself and for your help with the horses. She'll be fine. She won't say anything about people staying at the cottage or about you doing you-know-what."

"Great. Now she's lying to the FBI."

"Everything she said is true—up to the point where you Tinkerbelled her out the window. They're going easy on her. She's family. Gwen's mother is Lindsay's daughter. Her parents arrive this afternoon with the Director himself."

"Did they find Lindsay?"

"Yeah." Donaldson's tone said he didn't plan to elaborate.

"You think McCauley invited Lindsay out to his boat, then blew him up?"

"What do you think?"

"Well, that makes McCauley a pretty obvious suspect."

"The arrogant prick doesn't care that we're looking at him. He thinks his D.C. connections make him bulletproof—and he may be right. Which makes him more dangerous. Keep in mind that McCauley had inside information that Lindsay would be on the island."

"You think there's a leak in the Bureau?"

"Yeah. The numbnuts kind. Everybody knew about his place on the island. Lots of people knew he was coming here. There's another problem."

"Of course, there is."

"My colleagues are sharp, Will. They're all over that airport. It'll take them no time to track down the plane you flew in, and the fact you were the pilot."

"Not necessarily. The office was unattended when we departed last night." I explained the honor system for registering and paying the state park landing fee. "On the way out, my envelope was still sitting in the slot. I took it with me. There's no record that we were ever there."

"But what about a flight plan? We look up that shit all the time."

"Yesterday was severe clear. We launched out of Essex without filing. I thought I might air file, but I ended up calling for flight following instead."

"What does that mean?"

"It means no flight plan. It means a random airplane talked to Chicago Center while flying over Lake Michigan, but they have no record of the destination or the landing."

"What about the tower on the island?"

"There is no tower. I didn't talk to anybody."

"What about last night? Can't they track you on radar?"

"Not the way you think. On the return trip, I flew as far as Escanaba at low altitude with the transponder off. Radar coverage over Upper Michigan is spotty. Trust me."

"Okay. But we're not out of the woods yet. The Bureau will pull Lindsay's phone records."

"So?"

"So, one of the last calls he made was to your phone, remember? At the house? Just before we left."

"Wrong number. I killed the call and he didn't leave a message." I said. "Oh, crap."

"What?"

"I called him back. I tried to reach him when we were on the dock, just before the explosion."

"That's not good."

"I can just say I got curious, called the unidentified number back, but no one answered on his end, which is true."

"Except both calls would have pinged towers in the area. And there's more. I had to tell them the part about a woman shooting from the dock."

"What? What the hell!"

"Will, they already know. There were a dozen witnesses. How would it look if I left that part out? They picked up Andy's shell casings. That's one of the reasons I'm calling. To warn her."

"Jesus." I told Donaldson about Andy's shoulder bag, phone, weapon, wallet and badge at the bottom of the harbor.

"They haven't brought in divers. Yet. But they will."

I stopped pacing the hangar floor.

"Great." I said. "Now what?"

"Look, eventually, and to the right ears, I had every intention of telling them we were there. Just not until the dust settled."

"And what do we do until then?"

"Stay a step ahead of them."

"Really? How does that work?"

"Go tell your wife about this conversation. Tell her to call me."

"My wife is pissed at you."

"Why?"

"Because she's a cop and you convinced her to walk away from a crime. One that she not only witnessed but tried to prevent. And now all this—it makes her look even worse."

"It was still the right call."

"Bullshit."

"I'll make it up to her. Might take a few days but I have a plan."

Oh, great.

ARUN CORRECTLY READ the black cloud in my expression when I returned to the office. He elected not to ask questions. The story continued to play out on his television. A banner blazed *Breaking News: Boat Bombing Kills FBI Top Cop*. I picked up the remote and killed the screen.

"I need to leave."

"You weren't supposed to be here today, anyway," he said. "But since you are..." he picked up a pink message slip and handed it to me, "...the inspectors in San Diego called. The new tires came in early. The airplane is ready. Do you want me to book airline reservations for you?"

Plans to pick up the new Navajo seemed remote and a little meaningless in the moment.

"Don't do anything yet," I said.

30

I drove and speed-dialed my phone. It's dangerous, I know, but like everyone else doing it, I told myself it was important.

The number I dialed picked up after four rings.

"City of Essex Police, how can I help you?" The voice wasn't Mae Earnhardt, the regular dispatcher. I glanced at the dash clock on my car. Too early for Mae, who preferred second shift.

"This is Will Stewart. I'm calling for my wife, Detective Stewart."

"Hi, Mr. Stewart." The new dispatch trainee. I could not think of her name.

"Is my wife there?"

"I have her listed as not available today."

"Yeah, she had yesterday and today off. She said she was stopping at the office this morning."

"Hold on, please." The line went quiet. I drove on.

Andy spoke little on the return flight from Mackinac. It was not a reprise of *Guess What's Wrong Now*. I knew too well what was wrong.

We parked the Baron outside the Essex County Air Service hangar just after eleven. Andy and I drove home worlds apart in the same car. Her mind never left the island. I knew better than to interrupt her train of thought or derail said train with questions she could not answer.

In bed she apologized for the mental separation, then slipped under my arm. I asked if she wanted to talk about it. She said no. She fell asleep with her head on my shoulder.

In the morning, she made a full pot of coffee, but excused herself from breakfast, claiming an immediate need to go to the office. She moved quickly and with purpose, as if a resolution had been reached. Feeling a little lost after she rolled out of the driveway, I elected to drop by the Education Foundation's hangar, where Donaldson's call found me.

"Mr. Stewart?"

"Yes?"

"Detective Stewart isn't here. She was here earlier, looking for Chief Ceeves, but he's off today."

"Did she say where she was going?" The dispatcher hesitated. Department policy prohibited her from disclosing officer movements. "Erin," I said when her name popped into my head, "never mind. I'll catch up with her at home."

"That's a good idea. I'm sorry I wasn't more helpful." She sounded relieved.

We ended the call.

That's a good idea.

I checked my mirrors and the highway ahead. Taking advantage of a gap in traffic, I wheeled my car into a tight U-turn and headed back out of town.

ANDY'S CAR occupied her usual parking space by the garage. Chief Tom Ceeves' SUV sat on the driveway beside the house. I drove on the lawn to get around the Chief's vehicle.

"This can't be good," I muttered, walking across the gravel to the back door.

I found them in the kitchen.

Tom Ceeves stands six and a half feet tall and tips the scales north of two-seventy. His oversized boxy head has a square jaw line and flat-top haircut. Each of his hands can grip a watermelon. He rarely carries a weapon, but when he does, he favors a revolver—an old school Smith and Wesson .38 Special. In his hand it looks like a child's toy. Although he commands a medium-sized municipal police department, he almost never wears a uniform.

Our counter-height kitchen table may have been the only piece of furniture in the house designed to look normal beside Chief Ceeves. He rested his elbows on the table and folded his hands around an oversized coffee mug Andy sometimes uses as a bowl when she makes soup.

Andy sat across from him. I did not like the darkness in her eyes or the heavy mood hanging in the air.

"Will," Andy said. "What are you doing here?"
"Interrupting, apparently. Hi, Tom."
"Will."
"Can you give us some time?" Andy asked. Strain tightened her voice.
"Sure. Is that coffee?"
"It's fresh. We won't be long." Her way of telling me to hurry up and go away.

I pulled a mug from the cabinet, feeling the press of their paused conversation. I poured and replaced the pot, then started to make my exit, running through a list of the things I could pretend to be doing in the backyard or garage.

At the door to the mudroom, I stopped in my tracks.

"On second thought, I think I'll join you." I turned and swung a leg over a stool that centered me between them. I planted my mug on the table.

Andy's eyes flared. "Will, this is police business."

"Which apparently couldn't be conducted at the office."

"Making it all the more confidential," she said, sharpening her tone.

"Hold up, there, Andy," Tom said. Tom's deep voice can silence a room without raising the volume. "It occurs to me that Will may have something to say about all this."

"What are we talking about?"

Andy opened her mouth to renew her objection, but Tom cut her off. "You don't know?"

"I can guess."

"I bet you can," he said. "I got a call from the FBI this morning. And by morning, I mean well before the unholy butt crack of dawn. Seems they fast-tracked some shell casings from a shooting—casings that matched Andy's duty weapon. They wanted to know if I knew anything about that."

Donaldson's warning came a little late.

"I assumed it was a mistake," Tom continued. "I could not imagine a circumstance in which one of my officers, a detective, engaged in a shooting without launching the mighty clusterfuck that is an officer-involved shooting investigation. A mistake by the *federales* is not hard to imagine. I said so to the caller, some pencil pusher from Quantico, Virginia. I told him I recently hosted a rather large contingent of his brother *federales* here in Essex and felt entitled to an explanation. Imagine my surprise when I was simply told to have my officer contact the Federal Bureau of Investigation *toot sweet*."

"Sir, I—"

Tom's big hand came up, cutting Andy off. "Given the hour of the call and the tickle it sent up my ass, I turned on the TV to find out that somebody blew up the Deputy Director of the FBI on Mackinac Island last night. Which seems like it should have nothing to do with us folks here in Essex until I thought about you, Will—and I got to remembering that my officer was off the clock yesterday and today—and getting up to that island isn't all that hard when you have a pilot in the family. Which I confirmed with a call to Earl. And let me tell you, that man knows all of George Carlin's cuss words if you roll him out of bed before dawn."

"Oh," I said, "I am familiar."

"Sir, can I just—?"

"No, you may not, Detective. So…Will…been flying lately?"

"Matter of fact, yes I have. With my lovely wife."

"Will!"

"And did you by chance take my detective to that very special island where it smells like horse shit everywhere you go?" I glanced at Andy. She wore a pained expression on her face. He said, "I've asked your wife the same question, but she is not inclined to answer me."

"Given that my wife would never want me to lie to you, and it is a beautiful island, horse manure notwithstanding, I'd be happy to answer your question." I pointed at a folded paper on the table in front of the Chief. "But first, can you tell me what that is?"

Tom looked down at the paper, then at Andy, who crossed her arms and sat back, accurately assessing that she was outnumbered. "That, Will, is what your wife submitted in lieu of answering."

Tom slid the paper to me.

I picked it up and read it.

I returned it to Tom. "I see she backdated it to yesterday."

"A kindly attempt to cover my department's ass, but she's not doing much to cover her own. As resignations go, though, it is short and sweet."

Andy said nothing.

"Your turn," Tom said to me.

"We flew up yesterday. We were guests of Mitchell Lindsay."

Andy glared at me.

"The same Deputy Director Mitchell Lindsay who got himself blown to smithereens last night?"

"The same."

Tom blew a low whistle without looking at my wife.

"Your detective does not want to lie to you, Tom. Your detective was at the scene when it happened. She was on surveillance at the request of the Director, who went out to that yacht for a meeting with a D.C. fixer named McCauley."

"The asshat on the news. He looks pretty healthy for a guy at a meeting that got blown up."

"He apparently didn't attend his own meeting. It's a good bet that he set up the Director. Andy tried to stop it. That's why she left shell casings all over the dock. They used a radio-controlled model boat with explosives."

"To blow up a yacht? That doesn't seem—oh. They hit the fuel tanks."

"Yeah," I said. "Like they knew the ship inside and out. Makes you wonder. Anyway, Andy did her best to stop it. She even wound up in the water herself. Lost her weapon and her badge. I'm pretty sure she didn't want to tell you that, either."

"No, that hasn't been mentioned."

"Will! What are you doing?"

"He's talking to me, Detective," Tom growled, silencing her. "Go on."

"Whoever hit the boat simultaneously hit the Director's cottage—one of those historic mansions up on the bluff road, past the Grand Hotel. You know them?"

"I seen pictures."

"They broke in, looking for something, then torched the place. Lindsay's granddaughter was in the house. College kid. She was caretaking for him over summer break. She managed to escape."

"God bless. What were they looking for?"

I shrugged.

Tom looked at Andy, who fumed in silence. He looked at me.

"Is that all of it?"

"No. There's more. Can I ask a question first?"

"Shoot."

"How did the feds know it was her?"

Andy answered sullenly. "From the casings. Ballistic records are made of all law enforcement weapons. For comparison at shooting scenes, for tracking if a weapon is stolen, or if a duty weapon is used in a crime." She pushed her fingers through her hair. "I never should have left the island last night."

"My turn," Tom said. "What's the 'there's more' part?"

"Will, don't!" Andy interrupted. "Sir, just take this. I don't want to lie to you."

She pushed the resignation letter back at him.

"Well, this goddamned thing is a lie," he tapped the paper, "so why stop there? You know, I used a few choice words to tell that fed he was full of shit."

"Exactly my point, sir. I don't want this to blow back on you or the department."

"Screw that." He looked at me. "I'm gonna ask you again, Will, what are you not telling me?"

I reached across the table and pressed a finger on the resignation letter. I slid it toward me, picked it up, and tore it into small pieces.

They both looked at me.

"She was there because of me."

"Will, no."

"Tom," I said, "are you sitting down?"

He blinked, looked down at his body, and said, "What does it look like?"

"It's a little hard to tell sometimes."

"Will, no!"

"Detective! Let him speak. That's an order. Since your husband just tore up your resignation, you still work for me."

Andy glared at me. "Sir, I cannot let my husband speak for me. He's—"

"Dee, stop. This is something we should have done a year ago."

"You can't!"

"What's she talking about, Will?"

Tom looked at me for an explanation.

"This."

Fwooomp! I vanished under his steady gaze.

He squeaked.

His mouth fell open and a childish squeak escaped. The sound and the comical expression on his face forced me to suppress a chuckle.

Fwooomp! I returned.

He stared at me. I grinned at him.

"Sonofabitch."

Andy may have been angry at me. She may have been bent on making a career-ending sacrifice. She may have felt her world collapsing, but the look on her boss's face upended her anger. She quickly suppressed an escaped smile with one hand.

"Sonofabitch."

"Do you want a shot of whiskey in that coffee?" I asked.

"Sonofabitch."

31

"Do that again."

I did. Then reappeared.

"Sonofabitch."

I stood and went to the cabinet where we keep the hard liquor. I poured a shot of Jack Daniels into the chief's coffee. He downed a deep gulp without taking his eyes off me.

For the next ten minutes he struggled with a one-word vocabulary.

Andy and I alternated explaining *the other thing* to Chief Ceeves, starting with the crash, my time in the hospital and the rescue of Lane Franklin. We explained the effect, the immunity to gravity and the power units. I pulled a BLASTER from the mudroom cabinet to show him. He stared at it blankly.

As the explanation unfolded, Andy's tension unwound.

"We made the decision in New York to take it to the FBI," she said. "The idea was to get Will to someone we could trust before someone we didn't trust found him. Special Agent Donaldson believed Lindsay was the right man to read in."

Tom couldn't pull his eyes off me. I grew mildly uncomfortable.

"That's why I was on that dock last night." Andy explained the briefing in Director Lindsay's office.

"Sonofabitch."

"Honey, I think we broke your boss," I said.

Tom slapped one hand on the table, startling both Andy and me.

"That's how you did it!"

"Did what?"

He leaned back and took a deep drink of coffee-tinged whiskey. He looked at Andy and squinted. "I never figured out how Will went out that window with Mannis Rahn at your sister's place and wound up going through the ice forty feet out on the lake. There were no tracks. Sonofabitch."

"Yeah," I said.

Tom's eyes grew wider. "And that business in Chicago! You went out the window on the thirty-eighth floor, didn't you!"

"Technically, I went in the window first."

"And Andrea's sister, Lydia, when she went through the ice! That's how you got her to the hospital so fast!"

"Guilty." The Chief had been tangential to more than a few of our past adventures.

"Sonofabitch."

"We can fill in all the gaps for you, sir, but we need to talk about this situation on Mackinac. It isn't just the casings. My gun, badge and ID are at the bottom of that harbor."

Tom reeled in his incredulity. He sipped his whiskey. "Tell 'em the blast knocked you off the dock."

"They're two hundred feet out." I explained.

"That's why we were so close to the blast," Andy added.

"Oh."

"I know. There's no explanation for being there that doesn't end with me going public about Will—or lying to the FBI." She stood up abruptly and scooped up the shredded pieces of her resignation letter. "Now do you understand?"

He shook his head. "If Will hadn't torn it up, I would have."

Andy frowned at both of us.

Tom pointed at the bottle of Jack and gestured for a hit. I obliged.

He drank.

"Sir, you have to let me resign. Coming forward with the truth about Will right now—it's a bad idea."

"I get that," Tom said. He looked me over. "The feds will view you with more suspicion than appreciation. You can't read them in. You'll get taken off the board, Andrea. And you, Will, you'll get taken off somewhere…God knows where."

"The Island of Doctor Moreau would be my guess."

"I don't know any Doctor Monroe, but it sounds like that guy Lindsay had the right instincts. Paranoia powers politics. Someone able to do what you seem able to do, holy shit Will, you're as much a threat as an asset."

Andy planted her elbows on the table. "Either way, they're coming. They've reached out to you, and they're coming for me. I have to resign, sir. To keep you clear when you-know-what hits the fan. Now more than ever."

"Appreciated. But the wrong move to make, Detective. You need department resources and you need me watching your back. His, too." Tom pointed a thumb in my direction. "I don't know what stacked up against Lindsay to get him killed like that, but you can bet all that gold you mentioned in Ghana that it's messy and political and it will steamroll you if you don't get out of the way."

"What do you mean, 'get out of the way?' I told you, I'm not letting this go. Even if I wanted to—and I don't. It's not right. I shouldn't have to hide from the FBI."

Tom finished his whiskey-laced coffee. "No. Not hide. But maybe we can make it hard to squeeze them into your busy schedule…"

I raised my hand.

"I might have an answer to that. How do you feel about giving your best detective some vacation time?"

"Again?" Tom snorted. "Christ, I might as well sublet her office cubicle."

32

"This is insane."

Andy whispered it for the fourth time. I pulled her closer. She squeezed my waist.

"Shhhhh...."

We glided from beam to beam above the winding security line at General Mitchell International Airport. Despite the hubbub and rattle of plastic trays at the security station, I worried that the power unit's noise might generate unwarranted alarm. I stowed it in a pants pocket and switched to working us forward by gripping the open lattice overhead beams.

As we cleared the top of the body scanner, I gave the beam above it an extra shove. We floated toward the concourse, passing over travelers busy reassembling their clothing, sliding on shoes, repacking laptops and pocketing phones.

"Flying Divisible Man Airways eliminates TSA wait time," I said in a low voice. She jabbed me in the ribs with her elbow. "Careful. The money belt—bust it open and it rains Benjamins."

Making an untraceable trip meant leaving our personal credit cards and my phone at home. I carried the Education Foundation credit card for aviation fuel, figuring that if the FBI traced an aviation fuel purchase the result would only tell them where we'd been, not where we were going.

Andy enforced the move by collecting the credit cards from my wallet. "We rely on cash."

A good plan, I told her, if we had any cash. The Stewart family lives from paycheck to paycheck.

She surprised me. She disappeared upstairs and returned with two rolls of hundred-dollar bills extracted from a pillowcase hidden in our upstairs guestroom closet—cash stolen from a pedophile who operated an opioid drug empire. The cash ended up in our closet after I stole it when the son of a bitch abducted Lane Franklin. After her rescue, we decided to funnel the money—sixty-three thousand dollars—into an EdVest Account in Lane's name. It took time. Many of the rolled one-hundred-dollar bills remained in our upstairs closet.

Three thousand dollars lined a money belt under my t-shirt. It chaffed.

The money belt wasn't our only contraband. Andy's shoulder bag hid her Beretta M.92, a suppressor, and a box of 9mm ammunition.

"We need a place to get down," Andy stated the obvious.

Concourse D offered the usual selection of gift shops, restaurants, and bars. I looked for and found security cameras mounted in the ceiling. Even the empty gates contained scattered people waiting for flights or using wall outlets to charge their laptops and phones. Friday afternoon was not the ideal time for what we were doing.

"Let's see if we can find a restroom that isn't busy," I said.

"Really? Yours or mine?"

I pulled the BLASTER from my pocket for a slow, powered flight along the ceiling of the concourse. Passengers pulling roller bags hurried in both directions below us.

My pocket vibrated.

"I got a call coming in," I told Andy. We had stopped on our way out of Essex at a strip mall to purchase burner phones and two new Bluetooth earpieces. I touched mine to take a call I expected to be from Donaldson.

"This is a security alert regarding your credit card—"

I cut off the call.

"Goddamned robocall," I told Andy. "How is that even possible?"

"I thought it might be Lee," she replied. She and I had texted him the new numbers.

I maneuvered us into a side hallway. A sign on the door at the end warned that access was restricted to Authorized Personnel Only. A keypad beside the door emphasized the point. Two lesser doors on the side of the hallway gave no hint as to their purpose.

I rotated us to an upright position and lowered us to the carpeted floor.

"See any cameras?" Andy asked.

"Nope."

Fwooomp! Gravity claimed us. We settled onto the soles of our shoes. I maintained my hold on my wife's slender waist. I pulled her closer. She looked up at me. I leaned down and found her lips for a kiss, which she endorsed with a tender grip on the back of my neck.

"Nice landing, captain," she said.

We traded a second kiss, then she pulled away. "Let's go find a ride."

BEFORE LEAVING HOME, Andy had used her laptop to visit the Delta Airlines website and search flights to San Diego from Milwaukee.

"They all hub through Minneapolis or Detroit."

She made note of three flights from Milwaukee to Minneapolis. We found each gate and waited until the ticket agent began shuffling papers and preparing for boarding, at which point one of us would wander up to the gate and quietly ask if "our" flight was full. The first two attempts brought affirmative responses. I began to worry about our plan. On the third attempt, a 7:45 p.m. flight, the agent replied that the flight was only half full. Perfect.

We returned to our empty hall, vanished, and navigated back to the gate. After the agent announced that boarding for those requiring assistance would begin soon, we eased past the gate agent and performed a slow glide down the empty jetway.

Luck stayed with us. The cabin crew had finished prep for the flight and was nowhere to be seen. I shifted us to an upright position and pulled us through the open cabin door. Both pilots sat up front completing preflight checklists. I used seatbacks to propel us through the empty cabin to the last row. We pulled ourselves down into the window and middle seat.

"We'll pop back when they start boarding," I said.

It worked perfectly. The cabin attendants boarded first, but none moved to the rear of the plane. As the first passengers struggled down the aisle and claimed overhead bin space, we ducked down and reappeared. The plane filled slowly and sparsely.

A man with a boarding pass in hand walked the full length of the aisle, finally settling on our row and looking at us, then at the seat numbers, then at his boarding pass.

"Are we in your seat?" Andy asked sweetly.

"Uh…yeah, that one's mine." He pointed.

"The thing is," Andy said, "we just got married and we sat back here so we could have a little privacy." She leaned onto my shoulder.

It took him a second.

"Oh. Oh, yeah. I guess. That's okay. Flight's half empty. I'll…sit up a few rows." He shuffled back up the aisle, which was good because we had one more trick to pull. Andy giggled.

I watched for the flight attendants to complete boarding. When one of them started down the aisle doing a head count, I grabbed Andy's hand.

Fwooomp! We vanished. I gripped the armrest to keep from floating. The flight attendant finished her count with the man ahead of us and turned back up the aisle.

Fwooomp! Andy leaned in.

"You're such a bad girl."

WE FLEW to Minneapolis without incident and disembarked by conventional means. Our arrival after 9 p.m. left only one possible flight to San Diego. A check at the gate revealed that the flight that was full. We caught a cab to the nearest Holiday Inn.

At 8:55 a.m. on Saturday morning we huddled in the last row of a half-filled nonstop flight from Minneapolis to San Diego. A little after eleven Pacific Time, we strolled off the plane, thanking the attendant for a lovely airplane ride.

33

"She's beautiful," Andy said, warming my heart by using the correct pronoun. Her comment hinted at a release of the tension dogging her since Mackinac.

The Piper Navajo bathed in Southern California sunshine. Perfect paint kicked glittering reflections into my eyes. Her long engine nacelles stretched like runners crouched at a starting gate. The tall landing gear anchored her to the earth, but her sleek shape begged to fly. I felt a pang of regret for the airplane she replaced and hoped the soul of that plane had migrated into this one. I couldn't take my eyes from her.

The keys jangled electric in my fingers.

Dewey Larmond, the foundation's accountant, handled the purchase paperwork. After spending a few minutes in the FBO verifying my identity, I signed receipts and picked up a box full of aircraft logs, certifications and registration documents. A friendly chief pilot offered a cockpit orientation, which I accepted. He handed me the keys, told me and Andy to give it a walkaround, and promised to join us shortly.

At the airstair, I gestured for Andy to board first.

"Don't be silly." She stepped back. "She's your new girlfriend. You go first."

The cabin warmed in the sun, but it had not become unbearable. I found my way up the aisle between plush leather seats. The airplane's service as a corporate transport produced less wear than air charter work. The seat leather remained healthy and smooth. The carpet looked new. Polished wood accents lined the sides of the cabin.

"Arun and Sandy are going to love this," I said. Andy followed me aboard. She slipped into one of the cabin seats and squirmed on the leather.

"Mmmmm, this is nice."

I slid past a panel dividing the cabin from the cockpit. The pilot's seat fit as if it had been molded for me. My fingers stroked the contours of the control yoke. I scanned the instrument panel.

"Does it have all the bells and whistles?" Andy asked.

"And more."

Something chirped in the cabin behind me. Andy pulled out her phone.

"Lee?" She tapped my shoulder to draw my attention away from the instrument panel. "Let me put you on speaker," she said. "Okay, go ahead."

"Where are you?"

"San Diego," she replied.

"Jesus, when I said lay low, I didn't mean go to the end of the continent."

"Will's picking up a new airplane. Am I still on the ten most wanted list?"

"They think you're just being rude. Might'a got that impression from your boss, who actually was."

"How's it going there?"

"I'm not on the island anymore. I'm on the road. It's why I'm calling."

"What's going on?" I asked.

"For starters, the bombing has been claimed. Ever hear of the United Workers Liberation Front?"

I shook my head. Andy said, "I have."

"Then you know it's not the name of a terrorist group."

"It's the name of a labor organization. From Ghana."

"They murdered Director Lindsay. Sounds like terrorism to me," I said. "Did they give a reason?"

"They didn't say. They issued a communique to the military in Ghana, who passed it on to the FBI."

Andy frowned. "That's convenient. Isn't this the same group that the generals have been pointing fingers at?"

"They're past pointing fingers. The military raided the union headquarters. Dozens of people are under military arrest. CNN is calling it a coup. President Nkufo begs to differ but the fear is that if he draws a line in the sand it will become a coup."

"Don't they have the leader of this outfit in prison?" I asked.

"Yup."

"Lee," Andy said, "this doesn't track. They're a labor union—a worker's rights group. Miners trying to organize for better working conditions, better safety standards. They ran a couple strikes, which got violent but there are conflicting stories about who started what."

"You've been digging, Detective."

"Does a bombing on U.S. soil seem right to you? What could they possibly gain by killing a top U.S. law enforcement official?"

"Good question."

I asked, "What about the sister—the one here in the U.S.? Anybody ask her?"

"In Chicago. She's a preschool teacher. I asked. They tell me she's in the wind. They're making it sound sinister. I think they just can't find her. She's probably on a river boat casino with a bunch of girlfriends."

"I thought they were keeping you away from the investigation," I said.

"Well, there's that, too."

"Let's get back to Andy," I said. "Do they still have their undies in a bundle about her shell casings?"

"They'd love to have a chat, but now they have shinier objects to chase after. Nothing musters resources like terrorists. I slipped in the theory that Andy was just a law enforcement officer who spotted trouble. Your chief of police told our guys you both are on vacation, but he didn't know where. He promised the SAC you would be disciplined for not reporting the shooting."

I looked at Andy. A devious dimple peeked from the corner of her mouth.

"Lee," she said, "where is he?"

"On the move. I want you two to meet me."

"Where?"

"El Paso."

34

You don't just hop in an unfamiliar airplane and fly off. Even with several thousand hours in similar aircraft, I needed a checkout in the new Navajo.

Donaldson asked Andy how soon we could meet him in the border city of El Paso. "I'll be there late this afternoon," he said, setting the bar.

"We'll be there tomorrow night," I said. Andy looked disappointed.

"Can't make it sooner?"

I shook my head.

"No," Andy backed me up.

Donaldson said that might be too late, then gave Andy the name of a motel just outside El Paso. He added a room number.

"Meet me there when you show up." The call ended.

"Who?"

"Who what?"

"Who's on the move?"

Andy tucked away her phone and answered without looking at me. "McCauley."

"And the light blinks on," I said. "Here, I thought spiriting you away from Essex was my idea."

The dimple reappeared. She looked up at me. The magic gold in her green eyes cast its spell. "Oh, that's cute. I love it when you think you're in charge."

"Knock, knock," a voice interrupted from the back of the cabin. The chief pilot who had offered the cockpit orientation poked his head into the cabin.

"You boys go ahead and play," Andy said. "I'll wait in the air conditioning."

I looked at my watch.

"Dee," I said. "Call him back. Tell him we'll be there tonight."

AFTER SPENDING an hour with the Navajo's former pilot, I loaded our bags and filed an IFR flight plan from El Cajon to Flagstaff, Arizona—scribing a line aimed at Wisconsin. I used the aircraft's registered call sign, listed my name as pilot and dutifully listed two souls on board.

Forty-three miles from El Cajon, I pressed the push-to-talk switch on the yoke.

"Center, Navajo One Tango Whiskey, cancel IFR at this time."

The busy controller was only too happy to have one less flight on his hands. "One Tango Whiskey, cancellation received, frequency change approved, squawk VFR."

"So long." I switched the transponder code to 1200. Next, I configured the airplane for a descent. I rolled to the right and we dropped. I set a course that skirted the Phoenix Class B airspace.

"Okay," I told Andy. "We just left a dead end for the FBI."

She looked over the nose at the low mountains ahead. Turbulence rocked us. We dropped to a height at which our radar signature would be lost. I switched off the transponder.

"Good," she said.

35

We took a cab from Doña Ana International Jetport to the El Paso motel Donaldson described. The ride took us back and forth across the Texas-New Mexico border several times where the line wanders randomly through fields and small towns. After passing the third crossing marked by a faded roadside sign, I commented to Andy that the original surveyor was either drunk or had one hell of a sense of humor.

Our path took us north, away from Mexico, through a sparse settlement called The Village of Rio Valley. A grid of streets offered dusty, empty lots for a housing boom that never materialized.

Ten minutes later the cab turned into a two-pump gas station sharing a gravel lot with the Starlight Motel. A sun-faded sign offered Free HBO and a pool. The pool nestled inside an oval of leaning Century fence. At some point in the motel's history the pool had been filled with gravel.

"There," Andy pointed for the driver's benefit.

Two sedans sat side-by-side in front of a one-story structure. Numbered doors and curtained windows alternated on a long, low façade of faded siding over a brown brick half wall.

The driver stopped behind a Nissan rental and a government-issue Crown Vic. I paid the fare in cash and told him to keep the change. He motored away ahead of his own dust. A yellow sunset intensified the tan hue left hanging in the air.

The door marked 12 opened. Donaldson appeared in his black polo and khakis. He squinted in both directions and studied the sprawl of empty lots across the road from the motel.

"Classy," I said. I pointed at peeling paint and signs of wood rot in the window frames. "That's going on my Yelp rating."

"Let's get inside. You sure you weren't tracked?"

We hustled into a dim motel room. Heavy curtains blocked the sunset. The room smelled like an old gym bag.

I considered explaining the limitations of the airspace system and radar technology designed to sequence and safely separate flights, not detect intruders. Instead I replied, "Positive."

Donaldson closed the door behind us.

"Detective Andrea Stewart, meet Special Agent Mike Horowitz, DEA."

A man looking nothing like my image of a DEA agent stood beside a small desk. A head shorter than me, he had a round body that easily exceeded my weight. Male pattern baldness pushed his dark hairline past his ears. A fleshy face wore black-rimmed glasses. The way the lenses magnified his eyes made me wonder how he passed the DEA's physical/medical requirements. Brown irises bulged at the sight of Andy. He extended a hesitant hand.

"Pleased—really, um—pleased to meet you." A red tint flooded his cheeks as she shook with him and replied likewise. He was not the first man I'd seen trip over himself in Andy's presence.

"Mike and I go back," Donaldson said. "This is Will, Andrea's husband. He's the pilot."

I shook with Horowitz. His hand was soft and clammy, his grip tender. He nodded at me but could not resist swinging his eyes back onto Andy.

"Call me Andy," she said warmly.

"Andy. Sure. Okay." The red in his cheeks deepened. "Sorry for the accommodations. Don't get too close to that bedspread."

"We won't be here long," Donaldson said. "Mike can't be seen consorting with us rogues, but he's the best field agent in the El Paso office. I'm grateful for his unofficial assist."

"Lee is full of shit. I would know. I've put up with him for—well, for longer than I should admit."

"I told Mike we want to track Aaron McCauley," Donaldson explained. "On the other side."

"And I told Lee he's out of his damned mind. Which is nothing new. I don't know what he proposed to you, Detective, but under no circumstances should you—any of you—go over the bridge to Juárez."

"Is he here?" Andy asked.

"Coming in tonight."

Andy lifted her eyebrows at Donaldson.

"I have a few friendlies in the Lindsay investigation. McCauley is crossing over in the morning to confer—he says—with his clients."

"He just up and said that?" I asked. "Jesus, why isn't he locked up and being interrogated about Lindsay?"

"I told you. Friends in high places. And he's Mister Cooperation. His office emailed his schedule to the team. He even offered to consult with his clients in Ghana on behalf of the FBI."

"Are they buying that 'people's liberation army' crap?" Horowitz asked.

"I sure as hell ain't," Donaldson said. "That's why we're here. My money's on the cartel."

"How does that play for you?" Andy asked Horowitz.

"McCauley? We see his game in Juárez for what it is," Horowitz said. "My counterparts on the Mexican side are circumspect. The public face of the Méndez purchase is that the new owners are looking to reform the organization. They say they will shift the resources of the cartel into legitimate enterprises. Transportation interests. Manufacturing. Mining. Trucking. Oil and gas exploration. It promises new jobs which redirects previously illicit cash flow into the local population. The tradeoff is that the government backs off. They say they want to end the war."

"War?" I asked. Nobody mentioned a war to me.

"Juárez and Sinaloa have been butchering each other for close to two decades."

"Just what does McCauley do for Méndez—or whatever they call themselves now?" Andy asked.

Horowitz said, "Not what he does. What he sells on their behalf. A new day. Conversion, not destruction. Investment, not interdiction. Contracts, not contract killings."

"Bullshit," Donaldson muttered.

"The Federales publicly say they'll believe it when they see it, but back channels say they're all in. Hard to blame them. It's the first time in forty years that there's a glimmer of hope of ending the cartel wars down here. Over a hundred and fifty thousand dead."

"What do you think?" Andy asked.

"Legalized marijuana may have crimped their drug trade, but Juárez is still the main channel for cocaine and heroin into the U.S. and nobody turns their backs on the millions they make in human trafficking. The anti-immigrant stance taken by the U.S. created a whole new Prohibition. Mules and coyotes are the new bootleggers. Méndez was-slash-is up to their hair plugs in it. They've been consolidating the coyotes for years—either assimilating or killing off the independents. Trafficking is big business with low overhead. There's nowhere near that much profit in mining."

"This purchase—did they really let a Russian step in?"

"Some say it takes the iron hand of the Russian mob to gain control." Horowitz pushed his glasses back up his nose. "Look...the Russians are pragmatists. They don't give a rat's ass whose brother killed whose cousin. They focus on financial gain, although some of their political motives are cloudier. They never miss a chance to stick it to the U.S. The one thing they are not is emotional. Remember, their criminal organizations are deeply entangled with Putin's government. His policy of screwing over the U.S. is long-standing. That said, whether real or an illusion, they are shifting millions into legitimate enterprises."

Andy said, "They can't possibly think that a PR campaign is going to wipe up the blood in the streets down here."

"No. They can't."

"Then why bring McCauley in?"

"We live in the post-truth world, Detective. Reality down here doesn't have to match whatever truth McCauley sells in D.C. The DEA doesn't have a letter of marque for someone like him, even if we don't believe a word he spins."

"But you have to ask yourself why he's spinning it."

"We wondered if he was being duped or if he was doing the duping. We even considered recruiting him. Or turning him. Is that what Lindsay was doing?"

Donaldson shrugged. "Nobody knows. The office pool is still on the cartel taking out Lindsay, not this 'power to the people' baloney out of Ghana." He turned to Andy. "Mike knows the local territory like nobody else. He knows the Méndez organization down to the kids they send out for pizza. He knows the local street gangs they farm out enforcement work to. He knows which banks are in their pocket and which taco trucks they own."

"What I don't know is what you're thinking. You can't put a tail on McCauley and you can't just set up a spotter's nest in a hotel across the street from their offices."

"They have offices?" I asked.

"Like fucking CitiBank," Horowitz said. "Even if you talk me into helping you into a hotel over there, the maid bringing in fresh towels would have you bugged before you drop the room key on the dresser. Hell, you won't even clear the bridge without being spotted. They keep photo libraries on every fed, every county cop, every city cop on this side. They know who belongs over there—and who doesn't. Anyone new stands out like a hooker in a convent—sorry." The blush briefly returned.

"Mike," Donaldson said. "You gonna trust me on this?"

Horowitz hesitated. He looked at Andy.

"Lee tells me you have another angle with McCauley." Horowitz said. I glanced at Donaldson who did not return the gesture. "My old pal isn't sharing—"

"My way of staying pals with you, Mike."

"—which tells me it's got something to do with you, Detective."

Andy shrugged. He shook his head. "Believe me when I tell you. It's worse than Beirut over there."

"We get it," Donaldson said.

Horowitz looked us over.

"Right. I tried." He gestured at a tablet on the desk. The screen displayed a map. "So, let's take the tour. Maybe I can talk you out of letting Lee get you killed."

36

Horowitz meant what he said about the bedspread. He confessed that the DEA owned this dump and didn't waste government funds on cleaning. We ended up sitting on the floor in a semi-circle around Horowitz, who used the single room chair like a kindergarten teacher during story time. For about an hour, he explained the culture of Juárez, the relationship between the criminal class and the struggling population and the government. He explained the complex history of the warring cartels, the role of the Mexican federal government, and the bedfellows created by intertwined criminal and legitimate enterprises. He told of the area's descent into kidnapping, death and anarchy, including details about a notorious Death House where a mass grave was found. He described property the cartel owned. People they controlled. Streets and whole neighborhoods under their influence—which regulated street crime. He explained that in areas under cartel control, the police and the army were neither needed nor effective. He used maps to show vast tracts of land owned by the cartel. Their property included countless brothels populated by victims of their trafficking business, but also a library and a medical clinic. He described the unusual and unexpected foreign purchase of the cartel and leafed through screen after screen of photographs showing the former owners—most of whom had disappeared—and the men who remained in charge of operations in Juárez.

On one image, he paused.

"Is that him?" Donaldson asked.

"Yes. Garcia Roane." The image portrayed a middle-aged man with handsome Latin features and dark hair. He wore a precisely tailored suit. Eyeglasses in designer frames gave his face an academic accent, but a dark shade of brown in his eyes suggested sinister intent. A hint of smile in the photo bore no warmth; it was the smile of a man who knew something likely to hurt you.

"The Russians installed him. He cleaned house quickly. Bodies piled up," Horowitz explained. "But at the same time, Roane is the public face of the legitimizing process. He meets with local officials, international banks, even the Federales. He carries a portfolio of lavish plans for all sorts of public works and talks to the press. He plays a populist card but is also rumored to have said, 'There's no point in being a king if you have no kingdom.' The Federales, including the Mexican Army, used to pursue cartel leaders for apprehension or assassination. Now they have brunch with him. Your man McCauley works directly with Roane. He has a home in Virginia and regularly entertains Members of Congress."

"Is he Russian?" Andy asked.

"Brazilian. Married to a Russian woman, who happens to be the daughter of Yevgheniy Solochak who—"

"That's the oligarch Lindsay named," Andy reminded us. "Ukrainian money man, now in Russia."

"That's him. Roane has always been a person of interest to our CIA brethren because of his marital ties. He built a small broadcasting empire in Brazil—a Latin Murdock—but then moved here from Rio to take over Méndez. These are his two sons." Horowitz swiped the screen to show two young men leaning together in private conversation. "Sergei and Lev. Sergei, the older brother, is the enforcer. He's a certifiable sociopath. Lev is the younger brother. He's the college grad, an MBA brought in to run the new legitimate enterprises."

My butt hurt from sitting too long. I stood and stretched.

"Almost done," Horowitz said, reading my move. He switched back to a map. "Here. This entire city block—every building on this block—belongs to Méndez. Forget the Hollywood cartel compound. You know…guys patrolling some walled hacienda with AKs. This sits smack in the middle of downtown. Shops. Office buildings. Even a bank. A small city within the city. They have their own maintenance services, trash collection, and security officers. In uniform. Tech up the wazoo. Cameras everywhere. Motion sensors. They also have their own server farm and industrial-sized generators. It's been nonstop construction and remodeling since the buyout." Horowitz nodded and switched to a satellite image. "The central office tower is a combination of luxury apartments for upper management and offices where they work. That's where McCauley will go tomorrow for his meetings. You won't get within a block of it. We can't. And remote surveillance is out. They have interrupters mounted on the window glass to generate vibrations that disrupt laser microphones. They use their own cell tower and encrypt signals for all calls. They shoot drones out of the sky. I don't want to call it impregnable, but it's a nut we haven't cracked. Nor do we have much cooperation from the Federales. Especially as more and more of the cartel's money is flowing into local economic interests."

Horowitz folded up his tablet. He looked at Donaldson.

"You're not going to tell me, are you."

"Nope."

"Fair enough. But a word..." He spoke to Andy, "Detective, all due respect, a woman who looks like you—you won't get ten feet across the border without drawing attention. And Lee, they'll smell the badge on you. In fact, unless you plan to stay here tonight—and I cannot emphasize strongly enough what a bad idea that is—no matter what hotel you choose, chances are good your presence will be reported across the border before you even get to your room. They're that good. Hell, they've got facial-rec software better than ours."

"Detective Stewart doesn't plan to be seen anywhere near the border," Lee said.

Horowitz fired a sharp look at his friend. "You better mean that. Because this block is protected by a paramilitary force that's better trained and better armed than the army. Ten blocks around that you've got mid-level foot soldiers. Beyond that local gangs like *Barrio Azteca* and *La Linea* own the turf. They know every face in their territory—and every face that doesn't belong. And don't get me started on your face, Lee."

"What?"

"I've never seen a face that said 'FBI' more than yours."

Donaldson chuckled. "Truth is, Mike, I'm counting on it."

37

"Here he comes." Andy slid closer on the red leather bench seat.

Donaldson hurried through the hotel diner, zigzagging past busy wait staff working the breakfast rush. He tucked away his phone and dropped into the semi-circular booth. A waitress laid a menu on the table and poured him coffee.

"McCauley is jamming his transparency down the FBI's throat. He gave them ten a.m. for departure from his hotel and provided his route across the border. He knows they have a team on him. Bastard's treating it like a game."

"Hey," I said, "your friend wasn't gilding the lily. Juárez might be one of the most dangerous places on earth. You get that, right?"

I hadn't slept well. Mike Horowitz's apocalyptic description of Juárez intruded dreams and waking thoughts all night. Phantom arguments with Andy in which I convinced her to let me go alone played out in my head. I wondered well into the dawn if putting Andy in danger made sense.

As always with such a restless night, I managed to slip into deep sleep just before the morning alarm. Andy popped off the Holiday Inn mattress, showered and dressed quickly. She moved with an energy that told me my phantom arguments against her going across the border with me would not survive the light of day.

"Look and listen only. Period. No exceptions," Donaldson warned. "Where do you want to do this?"

"Let's find a parking lot near the river," Andy answered.

He pushed the menu aside and tasted the coffee.

"Lemme see if I can get this to go."

DONALDSON CHOSE the public lot beside the Chamizal National Memorial Cultural Center. Few cars occupied the lot. Fewer visitors walked the greenspace trails between sparse trees.

Andy stepped out into the bright sunlight and checked the cloudless blue through her Ray Ban Aviators. She had sculpted her hair into a tight French braid, a sign of serious business ahead. She wore a white top over jeans and the tight calf-height boots she favored, she once told me, because the solid toes deliver a nasty kick. I checked the pockets of my dark gray cargo pants. Three power units, fully charged, plus propellers, fit snugly in a thigh pocket. The hip pocket above it contained my folding aluminum aviation survival knife. The opposite pocket contained my phone and two rolls of Velcro which I extracted.

Andy watched me wind a Velcro band around my left forearm above my wristwatch, then another on my right wrist.

"Those are new," she said.

"I'm tired of dropping these things." I looped a leather strap through the right wristband and clipped both ends to a ring attached to the BLASTER power unit. "And here..." I pulled the prop off and flipped the power unit around. A Velcro patch on the unit gripped the wrist band. "It stows out of the way without having to use a pocket. The props kept catching on my pants."

"Nice."

"You know what this means." I pointed at the new power unit strap.

"What?"

"New name. I have a list."

"Well, you just hang on to it." She slipped her shoulder bag free and opened it. She removed her Beretta, checked the magazine, and pulled the slide to confirm a round in the chamber. She confirmed the load in each of two additional 15-shot magazines.

"Top of the list is—"

"Seriously, Will. I have a gun." She zipped the bag.

I took the bag and slid the strap over my head and right arm. "Ready?"

"Never." She pressed her hands to my face and kissed me. "Got your earpiece in?"

I pointed. "You?" She pointed.

"I'll call you on the hour," Donaldson said. The look on his face said he wanted to reopen his argument for going in Andy's place. That argument had been short and sweet. I don't want to say it came down to which of them could withhold sex from me, but Donaldson never had a chance.

Donaldson surveyed the parking lot. His rental was one of only half a dozen cars slotted near the visitor center. A slab-sided minivan beside it provided cover.

"Looks clear."

Andy and I crouched.

Fwooomp! We vanished.

"Goddamned amazing," I heard Donaldson say as Andy and I kicked off the asphalt.

38

The contrast between El Paso and Juárez surprised me. El Paso, while infused with the culture of her neighbor and its people, bore the familiar trappings of most American cities. Broad highways. Concrete and steel. Large buildings and inevitable suburban sprawl spawning car dealerships and big box stores. Juárez struck me as shrunken. Smaller buildings. Smaller blocks. Narrower streets. The Rio Grande came as a surprise to my eye. While the river is allotted a broad expanse commensurate with its significance, we crossed little more than a trickle on stained concrete.

The twin cities share a ring of small, gray-brown hills beyond the point where construction and sprawl ran out of steam. The landscape outside the demarcation line of civilization made the density of the two cities seem like an island in a dry empty sea.

The border wall looked less formidable than I expected, razor wire notwithstanding. More daunting were the six lanes of traffic on the César E. Chávez Border Highway. Heavy trucks and scores of commuters raced within stone throwing distance of the national border. I wouldn't try to cross it.

Directly to our left, the Bridge of the Americas spanned the Chávez Highway and the river. A glittering river of vehicles extended north of the U.S. Customs and Border Patrol Center, queued up for passage south. Horowitz told us that the cartel uses high-definition cameras on all vehicles coming across. Plate readers and facial recognition tech alert them to law enforcement officers crossing over, as well as rival cartel members attempting to use Méndez's proprietary transport routes. Encroachment on the Juárez routes was one of the root causes of the war with the Sinaloa cartel. That and the occasional internecine murder. The DEA agent made his point by saying that we could easily expect to be stopped within a mile of the border by low- and mid-level enforcers, if not by the police.

The power unit pulled us over Juárez streets set at confusing angles near the river, then over a more organized residential grid pattern. Glints of harsh sunlight bounced up from automobiles lining the streets. An occasional abandoned car, sometimes burned out, hinted at the violence suffered by the city.

The city block Horowitz described rose into view quickly.

"See it?" I asked Andy, who had snugged herself against my left side. I felt her head turn.

"Uh-huh."

I fixed a direct course on the glass tower at the center.

The city streets grew wider, the buildings taller. The city center of Juárez boasted defiant beauty in boulevards lined with trees and small parks. It might have been any other city full of people wrapped up in the rush and purpose of daily life—if not for military Hummers parked at street corners or camo-clad soldiers armed with automatic weapons strolling the sidewalks.

Andy suggested a slow reconnaissance of the Méndez block. I aimed us down a broad boulevard. Smaller buildings, four and five stories tall, fronted the block. A broad plaza created a gap that set the main building back from the street. A simple glass rectangle. Without counting I guessed it to be twelve stories. Blue tinted glass mirrored the sky. A fountain in the plaza sprayed arcs of water into the morning sunshine, creating fleeting rainbows in a mist that darkened the concrete around the fountain. A bronze duplicate of the classic headless and armless Winged Victory dominated the fountain. Rows of heavy round concrete planters containing thin trees dotted the plaza. The trees provided shade and a greenspace accent. The planters made it impossible for a car bomb to reach the building. The same could be said for what was essentially a moat around the building, a reflecting pool set behind a low concrete wall. Foot bridges connected the plaza to the building lobby. A few people hustled across the plaza, but no one lingered on any of the benches set around the fountain. The plaza and the streets around it seemed overly quiet, even for a Sunday.

"Cameras," Andy said.

Individual light poles mounted black glass balls housing cameras capable of rotating through 360 degrees.

We passed in front of the building, then turned right. Shops lined the sidewalk. Stacked chairs marked a closed sidewalk café. More cameras. More planters. Right again across the back side, we surveyed a utility courtyard. Trucks in a gated and guarded lot lined up beside trash containers. A fenced area surrounded what looked like two parked railroad freight cars.

"Generators," I said.

Another right took us over the main vehicle entrance. A broad driveway curved in off the street. Two guard stations manned by uniformed officers flanked the midpoint between the street and the glass high-rise. One lane descended to underground parking. Another lane emerged. Heavy gates and pop-up posts restricted both.

"This is where he'll come in," Andy said. "This is where we'll watch, but I want a closer look at the building."

"Your wish…"

I steered us at the wall of glass rising at the center, choosing the west side of the building. The rising eastern sun caused most of the blinds to be closed. Pulsing the power unit, I brought us to a halt level with the first floor.

"Up. Slowly," Andy said.

I gave us a shot of power, then killed it. We rose in silence thirty feet from the glass.

The first two floors contained office space with cubicles from wall to wall. The third floor separated the space into executive offices. The fourth floor sprawled, relatively open. Leather furniture and a substantial bar took up most of the floor on our side of the building. Above that, blinds were closed. The few that were open suggested residential space. In one, a pair of small children played near the window.

"I gotta say, this isn't what I was expecting," I said.

"Which was?"

"Swarthy characters with AKs and machetes. Piles of cocaine. Pallets of cash. Hookers. You know. The usual décor de cartel."

The second from top floor had blinds. Through the blinds we saw banks of servers and rows of workstations. The top floor had a higher ceiling than the rest. Rooms with residential furniture and open space with dining and kitchen areas occupied what we were able to see.

"My guess," Andy said, "is that Roane and his sons get the penthouse."

"Where to?"

"Let's park down on that roof."

"Are you pointing?"

"Oh. Yeah. Sorry. The one with the black border around the top, overlooking the entrance."

"I see it."

I gave us a blast of power, swung around, and swooped down across the roof of a lower building. I eased to a stop over an edge above the driveway entrance. The roof had a gravel surface. Patio furniture meant the roof saw casual use, although I suspected that the only users allowed on it were uniformed guards with weapons. Nevertheless, the edge of the roof had a one-bar railing set in a parapet. The steel railing had enough space between it and the concrete lip for us to slip our legs through. We fixed ourselves in place.

"Perfect," I said as Andy adjusted her position beside me. She twined her fingers with mine to maintain contact.

"Now we wait."

"We could make out."

She didn't answer.

39

"That's him."

The time and trio of identical silver Chevy Suburbans rolling off the street gave her assessment high probability.

We detached from our perch. Uniformed security guards carrying automatic weapons stepped from their guard huts but made no move to stop the caravan of vehicles. The SUV's big V-8s pulled the Suburbans past the huts and down the sloped driveway into the underground parking. The rising steel gate managed to barely clear the first vehicle, which never slowed.

I goosed the power unit and aimed for the back of the last SUV in line. Even as we closed the gap, it cleared the gate, which reversed and dropped immediately. I reluctantly killed the power as we shot past the guard huts to avoid drawing attention but was then forced to rotate us to a horizontal position to slip under the rapidly descending gate.

Too close. My heart picked up a few beats.

I pulled off and stowed my sunglasses. I heard the faint snap of Andy's bag as she did the same. My eyes adjusted to the underground garage. A large black Hummer, a pair of Porsches, a white Cadillac Escalade and a utility van occupied parking slots off to the side. The silver Suburbans pulled forward and parked nose to tail in front of a broad glass entrance. Behind the glass, uniformed security guards divided their attention between the action out front and monitors mounted in a marble counter. One of the guards slipped around the end of the counter and took up station by the doors.

The doors of the Suburbans opened as if choreographed. Dark men in dark clothing wearing dark glasses emerged. I wondered which Hollywood action film had inspired their boss to dress them up like cartel thugs.

I reduced power to quiet the BLASTER and steered toward the entrance, staying close to naked concrete beams in the ceiling. I timed it, watching the security guard who watched the disembarking SUV passengers. He extended his arm as we passed over the SUVs. He swiped his card in a reader, and the glass doors parted. Andy and I glided through just over his head. Perfect timing.

Aaron McCauley hustled through behind us. He pulled a roller bag that clicked across the seams of the concrete, then changed its tune on the tile floor of the lobby.

Without a word, the security guard hurried ahead of McCauley to swipe his card on a reader between two elevator doors. The door to the right opened.

Andy squeezed me, signaling her wishes. I let the glide carry us to the elevator as McCauley stepped in and turned to face the door. The security guard stepped in with him and swiped his card on the control panel. I cut the power and flipped the BLASTER back onto my forearm. The Velcro gripped it. With my hand free, I closed a grip on the top of the elevator door.

Not soon enough. The door began to close. Andy shifted. The door closed partially, then stopped and reversed itself. Her doing.

McCauley glanced down at the control panel. The guard swiped his card again. I pulled us in above their heads.

Elevators are tricky. This one was about to launch upward, but when it did, we wouldn't. Not unless I could fix a hold on something.

The stainless steel and dark wood interior offered nothing but smooth walls above a gold-finished handrail. Overhead panels of polished wood offered no seams.

I rotated quickly and extended my legs. My feet touched the wall. I reached up and pressed a hand to the ceiling. My toes wedged on the handrail. Pressure on my hand above locked us in place.

The car rose.

Neither man spoke. LED numbers above a buttonless control panel blinked, B to L to 1 and all that followed until it stopped at 4. The doors parted.

"Señor." The security guard stepped aside and nodded at McCauley, who rolled his bag out of the car onto a plush maroon carpet. Andy pulled herself tightly against me.

I pulled my legs up and repositioned to push off the back wall, but the door closed too quickly. I reached out. The doors hit my hand and reversed, arousing the security guard's curiosity. He leaned forward to look for a cause. I pushed with my legs and we coasted clear of the car. The guard swiped his card again. This time the doors closed.

We floated into a space with the feel of a private club, accented by a rich mahogany bar. Plush carpeting stretched from the central elevator bank to the windows in three directions. Leather furniture had been arranged in small groupings around coffee tables with fanned copies of *Fortune* and—I had to look twice—*Yachting* magazines.

"Jesus Christ," I whispered.

I rotated us and applied a small amount of power to bring us to a stop.

McCauley wheeled his roller bag to a concierge desk. An attractive young woman with a charming smile greeted him in his native English. Distance and a low undertone of classical music broadcast from ceiling-mounted speakers interfered with eavesdropping.

The woman did not pick up a phone to announce McCauley. Instead, she extracted a small envelope from the top center drawer of her ornate wooden desk. She held it up and spoke instructions to McCauley.

"I'm quite familiar." He reached for the envelope, which she relinquished with a smile and a parting word.

"You, too," he said. He turned and marched for the elevator. She touched something on a small panel on her desk. The elevator doors parted, allowing him to board without pausing.

Crap. Key cards and security controlled the elevators.

We were caught unprepared. Not even a hard and noisy blast of power could have carried us to the elevator before the doors closed behind him. Andy's grip on my arm tightened.

"Look," she whispered.

The digital panel above the call button ticked off the car's ascent. It stopped on 6.

"Stairs," I whispered.

We performed a slow glide around the central elevator block until we found a door bilingually marked *Salida* and *Exit*. The woman at the front desk had no line of sight on the door, but a ceiling-mounted camera surveyed this area.

"They'll see it open," I warned Andy.

"If they're watching. Make it look, I don't know, random."

I wasn't sure what my wife thought a door opening randomly looked like.

"Press the wall."

I felt her shift. I grabbed the knob, turned it slowly, then pulled.

Thanks to Andy's pressure on the wall, I had leverage. The door eased open. I stopped, started, let it swing back and forth as if pushed by a breeze. I was just getting the hang of random when Andy whispered in my ear.

"For heaven's sake, just open it!"

So much for random. I pulled it wide enough for us to slip through. A pneumatic arm on the door pulled it shut behind us. I grabbed the interior knob and turned it to avoid a loud latch click.

Stairwells I can handle. Naked concrete flights of steps angled back and forth with a narrow gap at the center. I noted a camera pod above the door.

I pushed off the door and grabbed the railing. Andy gasped as I heaved us over the railing above five stories of descending stairway that ended at a concrete floor below us.

"Sorry," she said. "I can't get used to that."

I looked up. The M.C. Escher geometry of the stairs ran all the way to the roof. Her grip tightened. "I don't know how you do this. It's freaking me out."

I pulled and we rose. I used handrails to climb from one flight to the next.

"It's weirder around structure for some reason," I said. "Out in the open it's more like flying. Structure makes the height more real."

"That was four."

"Does it seem strange that no one met him?"

"Five. A little. It's like he was checking in to a hotel."

"Wouldn't surprise me if they run this like a hotel. I gotta say, this is not what I was expecting from a murdering drug cartel. Horowitz called it. CitiBank."

"Six. This is it."

I pulled us over the railing. Andy's grip loosened incrementally.

A small window in the door offered a limited view of a hallway. Opening this door was harder; it required pushing, which is easy when gravity plants your feet on the floor, and entirely different when floating free. Andy twisted around and placed her feet on the railing. I turned the knob and opened the door just far enough to close my hand on the jamb.

"Got it."

We worked our way through. Anyone watching would now see a second door strangely swing open on its own, then close.

"If they're monitoring these cameras, that had to set off alarm bells. One door…weird. Two?"

"Right," I said. "But put yourself in their shoes. Even if they investigate, what are they going to say? A breeze? Air pressure changes? Even if security guards rush—"

Andy shushed me.

A door halfway down the hallway opened. A man in business slacks and an open collared shirt stepped out. He closed the door behind him and pocketed a key card. He set off toward us. I pushed my toes on the carpet and rotated. We rose and bumped against the ceiling. He passed under us, humming to himself. A moment later he rounded the corner and disappeared into the elevator lobby.

"So which room is McCauley's? And what do we do when we find it?"

"*If* we find it."

WE DIDN'T FIND IT. The sixth-floor layout matched that of most hotels I've seen. The central elevator opened on a small lobby. A hallway extended in two directions off that lobby. Numbered room doors spaced out on either side to the end of each hall. McCauley occupied one of them, but we had no clue which. We had no choice but to anchor ourselves in the elevator lobby.

"Okay," I whispered. "We can't spy on him in his room."

"We have to be ready when he comes out. This is the best place to be."

We hung in the air above a small sofa no one ever sat on. I felt Andy squirm and flex.

"I can't get comfortable with this weightlessness. I don't know how those space station astronauts do this for a year at a time."

"You have to consciously relax your muscles. Your natural impulse is to tense up. You gotta let go."

"This wasn't what I expected."

Me either. For the second time, I began to wonder if a career in stealth surveillance might prove the world's biggest bore.

My earpiece buzzed.

"Hang on," I said. "I got a call."

"Me, too."

We both shifted and touched our Bluetooth earpieces. I heard her speak first.

"It's Andy."

"And Will."

"Good," Donaldson said. "I conference called you. Where are you?"

I let Andy explain.

"Any sign of Roane?"

"Nothing," she said. She described our situation.

"What time is it?" I asked.

"Eleven. Are you sure you haven't lost him?"

"Reasonably," Andy replied. "Hold on."

The elevator door opened. A waiter carrying a tray appeared. A tall, thin man in a black suit stood beside him. His gaunt face and thin black hair, slicked directly back across his skull, contributed to an undertaker appearance. The tall man marched out of the elevator leading the waiter out of the small lobby and left, down the hall.

"Call back at noon!" Andy cut off her call. I followed suit.

I pulled the power unit free of the Velcro, wincing at the tearing noise.

I snapped a prop in place and powered after the duo. Andy and I floated across the carpet, around the corner and down the hall. As we moved, I rotated us to a horizontal position and aimed higher until we skimmed just below the ceiling. I cut the power as we drew close.

The tall man stopped at the third door onf the left. He rapped on the door.

The door opened as we arrived.

Aaron McCauley had removed his suit jacket and loosened his tie. Recognition bloomed on McCauley's face.

"Anton, where the fuck is Sergei?"

The tall man's head dipped slightly. "Señor Sergei sends his apologies. He has been detained. He begs your indulgence and asks if you will meet him for dinner this evening in the penthouse."

"Tell me he found her," McCauley demanded.

"I have not been informed, Señor." The head dipped again, showing deference.

"Christ."

"I brought you a light brunch, sir." The tall man stepped aside, signaling the waiter to perform his duties. Andy and I coasted directly above the tall man. I could have rearranged the combed lines of his greasy hair without fully extending my arm. The ceiling offered nothing to grip, and I didn't dare use the power unit to stop. We passed overhead.

"I didn't come all this way with the FBI on my ass just to dick around, Anton. Make that clear to your boss. I'll take this to Garcia if I have to. None of this should have happened."

The tall man flicked his eyes to the waiter setting his tray somewhere in a room I could not see. McCauley took the hint and glanced back at the servant. He leaned closer to the tall man and spoke softly.

"Tell Sergei. This wraps up tonight."

"Of course."

The waiter hustled out. McCauley closed the door on his visitor. Andy and I continued down the hall as the duo made their exit. When the hall cleared, I used the power unit to stop. I rotated our legs to hang beneath us.

Andy pulled herself close. Her lips touched my ear, sending an unintended shiver down my neck. I turned us around, anticipating an urgent command to follow the tall man.

"We need to find a bathroom."

40

I suggested the floor with all the cubicles. Andy nixed the idea. Too many people. She called for a return to the fourth-floor lobby and reception desk. It seemed like a low-traffic public space, and as such might offer a public restroom.

We found a unisex bathroom halfway down a hallway extending away from the lobby area. The door displayed the international symbols for man and woman. With fingers gripping the jamb, I turned the knob and pushed the door open.

We slipped inside and turned the lock behind us. I shifted to let Andy slide off my arm when she suddenly froze.

"Camera."

I looked up. She wasn't wrong. "Jesus, wait until HR hears about this."

"HR is a bullet to the back of a brain in this outfit. Now what? I really have to go."

"So, go." I used the power unit to maneuver into position.

"You can't be serious."

"It's actually kinda funny to see it when you—."

"Oh, you are *not* watching this."

"Fine. But you can't appear, and I have to hold your arm to maintain contact. Use that bar to get in position." I was glad she could not see the smirk on my face.

We had a clumsy moment while she figured out how to put the seat down.

"Men," she muttered. "Turn around."

"I am."

She reached up and probed my neck, then face to make sure. "Told you."

I heard her unsnap her jeans and a rustle as she slid them down.

Nothing happened.

"I can't do this with you here." Andy and I have always kept personal hygiene private. The occasional shower together is purely amorous.

"Ocean waves. Babbling brooks. Cool, refreshing beer. Rain falling on—"

"What are you doing?"

"Trying to help."

"Well, stop. You're making it worse."

I twisted slightly and reached for the nearby sink. I grabbed the edge, then worked my grip up to the faucet and twisted it. Water rushed into the bowl.

"Does that help?"

"Just—be quiet! God." Her arm came up and closed a grip on mine. "Let go of me and cover your ears."

That seemed to do the trick, although it took a while.

41

"Where are you now?" Donaldson asked.

I checked my watch. Our earpieces had chirped to announce another conference call at noon on the dot. The man was nothing if not prompt.

"A little café a few blocks over," she said. "Café Roma, for some reason, although it's not Italian."

"Authentic Mexican," I said. "Who knew?" Our order for tamales, placed at a small window, had not yet arrived. We sat under an umbrella in a courtyard off the street. Most tables were filled. Embattled or not, Juárez's citizens working in the shops and banks and markets still found time for lunch. I rotated my cold Corona on a cardboard coaster. Beads of condensation ran down the glass bottle. Andy frowned at my choice and drank bottled water.

After the bathroom adventure, we departed the building. Our first attempt to leave the way we came in stalled at the basement level where magnetic door locks requiring key cards stymied us. *The other thing* trick fails against a magnetic lock.

From the basement, we ascended the stairwell to the roof where we not only found a door, but found it unlocked. The presence of four armed sentries on the roof explained the unlocked door.

"Why lock a door when you have men with M-16s wandering around?" I commented. The four sentries patrolled the rim of the building. Luck and timing let us open the door and slip through unnoticed.

Andy selected the Café Roma after a brief reconnaissance of the streets and blocks surrounding the glass tower.

Donaldson's call jangled our earpieces soon after we sat down.

"Okay…" Donaldson said. "I did not expect that."

Andy explained the non-events of the morning, leaving out mention of the relief stop. "We'll go back after lunch. There's an easy in."

"McCauley is seeing Roane this evening?"

"Junior. In the penthouse," Andy said. "Curious dynamic. McCauley threw his weight around with the messenger they sent."

"What's your take?"

She mulled it over. "I don't know. He's either stupidly arrogant, or he has more power here than we thought."

"Any sign of what we're looking for?"

"As in Director Lindsay's murderer? Not yet. What I heard sounded like Sergei has a mess to cleanup. It could be Lindsay. Or something else."

"It's Lindsay," Donaldson said. Andy shot me a glance laden with doubt.

"Um…I don't know…it didn't feel like that. They're looking for someone. A woman."

"Gwen?"

"Jesus, do you think so?" A chill coursed my spine.

"Where is she?" Andy asked. "Can you get someone to her?"

"I'll get on it."

"Do you really think so?" I asked again. "I mean, why her?"

"If they're after her, it would be for something she knows," Andy said.

"Or something she doesn't know she knows. Or something she has. The people who burned the house were searching."

"The horses," I said.

"What about them?"

"Just a thought. She was attentive to the horses, which means the barn was her domain. Did the barn burn?"

"No. The fire department saved it."

"Get someone to go through it," Andy said.

"I'm sure the team did, but I'll check." If Andy issuing commands irked Donaldson, he didn't say.

Andy nervously twirled a strand of hair at her ear. "I'm worried now. For Gwen. I feel like we missed an obvious threat."

"I'm texting them as we speak. What's your plan?"

"Lunch," I replied.

A young man in an apron swept up to our table with a tray of tamales. Andy thanked him with a smile.

"We're going back in," Andy said after the waiter departed. "I want to take an in-depth tour, then set up for the dinner meeting. We may be in there for a while. Lee, it is not at all what I expected. It's an office building, a hotel, and I don't know what. Security is over the top. Cameras everywhere, including the bathrooms. And there are scores of people working there. A whole floor of office cubicles. I got a look at a directory. Insurance companies, trucking companies, a law firm, even a florist. There's a whole floor of I.T. Looks like they have their own server farm. And something else. It all feels new."

I had not put my finger on that, but now that Andy mentioned it, I remembered the new look and feel of everything inside, even a hint of fresh paint.

"Mike said they remodeled. Fits with the whole 'we're going legit' legend," Donaldson said.

"You know what I haven't seen?" Andy asked. "Counting rooms. Drug labs. Cutting tables. Chemical storage. Vehicles being converted for transport."

"I'd really like a look around in there."

"When we go back in this afternoon, I'll try to get pictures."

"Does that work?"

"It's awkward, but yes," she said.

"I did the floating thing with your husband in New Mexico. That's some weird shit."

"It works," I said.

"It is weird," she said. I made a pouty face at her. She squeezed my hand. "Will's a good pilot, though. He takes care of me."

"Don't get over-confident. You're in the murder capital of Mexico."

"That's Tijuana," Andy said.

"Whatever. They catch you—I don't even want to think about it."

WE ENJOYED the tamales and beer a little less as worry about Gwen percolated to the surface. The midday heat grew oppressive. I found myself anxious to slip back into *the other thing* which provides its own climate control system.

As we finished our meal, I casually scanned the tables around us. Diners chatted in Spanish I could not understand. A few ate alone in silence. Some thumbed devices. Most of the male eyes strayed in our direction—in Andy's to be specific. Men overtly looked her over. I expected that and it did not concern me. The eyes that concerned me were the ones that darted to us, then quickly away. Two men at separate tables worked hard not to notice us. When one of them casually held up his phone at an odd angle, I knew we'd been photographed.

"Somebody is getting curious," Andy said, watching from behind her Ray Bans.

"You saw that?"

"Uh-huh."

"They didn't get our pictures at the border, but they have them now."

"Maybe we should…disappear?"

"Want to hit the restroom first?" I grinned at her.

"Not a word from you." She stood. "And yes. I'll be right back."

"Might just do the same," I said.

I followed her across the patio to a narrow hallway that ran behind the kitchen. Signs on a pair of doors at the end of the dead-end hall directed us. I hurried. When finished, I grabbed the doorknob and—

Fwooomp!

—I vanished and leaned out to survey the hall.

The man who shot our photo loitered at the end of the hallway, leaning against the entrance with one hand tucked in his belt at the small of his back. Young and lean, he had long hair and the look of a beach volleyball player. The black butt of a weapon peeked from under a Hawaiian shirt. His companion, still seated, watched from across the courtyard.

I pulled myself out of the restroom and reached across the narrow hallway for the doorknob to the women's room. Behind the door, a toilet flushed, water ran, a towel dispenser sang its mechanical tune.

The doorknob turned under my hand. Andy pulled the door open and me with it. Before she could step forward, I grabbed her arm. She jolted. I held tight.

"It's me."

FWOOOMP! She winked out of sight with a gasp.

"*Lord, Will! What are you—?*"

"End of the hall. One with a gun. Another watching."

She let me pull her close. I eased us back into the hall.

The door action drew our stalker's attention. He watched for Andy to emerge. When she failed to appear, he slid sideways out of the sunlight and walked toward us. His hand came up holding a gun.

I pushed with my toes and rotated to a horizontal position. We ascended until we bumped the glossy paint of a low ceiling. Marginal clearance separated us from our stalker.

He stopped beneath us. He listened at the men's room door while examining the slightly ajar women's room door. We held our breath above him. In such close quarters, I could not draw the BLASTER stowed in my pocket. Nor could I shift enough to grip the narrow walls and propel us. We waited.

After a moment of listening, the man threw open the door to the women's room, weapon held high. The door bumped against an interior wall. He waved his gun back and forth, searching.

The empty room bewildered him. He turned and grabbed the doorknob to the men's room and repeated the move.

I assumed that the Spanish expression he uttered contained an expletive.

He jogged to the hallway entrance, looked around, then jogged back again to search a second time. That the dead-end passage ended with a wall caused him to dart back and forth between the two small, windowless rooms. Nothing in either small restroom offered an answer.

His companion joined him. A short argument followed, then both men hurried out and away through the courtyard.

"They know we're here," Andy said. "For whatever that's worth."

THE INCIDENT SAVED us the trouble of finding a place to vanish. I pressed my hands against the narrow walls and propelled us into the open courtyard. We drifted above umbrella tables until I deployed a power unit for the trip up and away.

The glass tower's rooftop contained utility features attendant to building ventilation, heating and air conditioning systems. A block at the center housed the elevator motors and support structure. Attached to the block, a short stairwell joined the interior stairwell we had used earlier. The unlocked metal door gave us access.

We circled for a landing. I counted five men on the roof. Four of them patrolled the square perimeter. They wore blue uniform shirts over black cargo pants and carried M-16 rifles. Sunglasses and ball caps completed the uniform. The fifth man wore the same uniform with a sidearm belted against one leg. He sat at a small table under a canvas canopy. He made notes in a binder, occasionally speaking into a handheld radio.

He sat with a perfect frontal view of the door.

"We need to distract him," I told Andy.

"Wait," she said. "Take us back down. Behind the building. By the generators."

I twisted my wrist and altered course. We descended directly over the two large diesel motors.

"Stop."

I obeyed. After a moment, I asked, "What are we doing here?"

"Thinking."

I left her to it.

"What would it take to disable them?" Andy asked.

"Let's see." I lowered us between the two generators and quickly found the answer. "See that blue cylinder hanging from the motor? That's an oil filter. Loosen that, or remove it, and when this thing fires up, the oil pressure will blow all the oil out. Engines don't run for long without oil."

"Can you do it?"

"Not without a tool…unless…" I eased us down until our feet touched the ground. "Keep a grip on me. I need my hands."

Andy obliged with a grasp of my upper arm. I worked my belt out of my pants loops. I wrapped the belt around the oil filter and cinched it tight, then propped myself against the engine and pulled. I felt the cylinder give, then turn. After a few quarter turns using the belt, the oil filter turned freely. I removed the belt and rotated the cylinder by hand. Black oil oozed out of the top seal. I continued turning until the filter wobbled. I left it hanging loose. Oil dripped on the ground. Anyone walking by would notice immediately, but the fence around the generator prohibited casual strollers.

We worked our way around the engine and repeated the task on the second generator.

"Are you thinking they might have a power outage?"

"You never know," she said.

"Well, if they do, these things won't last long. A few minutes. Maybe five."

"Good enough."

I threaded my belt back in my pants and launched.

A HANDFUL of gravel scooped from the rooftop and tossed into one of the aluminum air vents created a distraction. The gravel hit a fan and caused a racket inside the shaft. Rattling and pinging continued for a few minutes. The two nearest riflemen hurried to the source of the sound, joined by their supervisor, who left the door unguarded. Andy and I slipped in.

"Now what?" I asked.

"Let's get some pictures."

WE SPENT THE AFTERNOON EXPLORING. Andy commanded me to navigate from floor to floor. She pulled her burner phone from her satchel and deftly released it from one hand, catching it in the other, which caused it to appear, enabling her to activate the camera. She then closed both hands around the phone and it vanished. From that point on she snapped pictures. Directories. Names of companies on office doors. Workers at computer workstations. Documents on desktops.

At one point, I commented on how mundane it all seemed.

"You're kidding. This is a goldmine. Banking, transportation, logistics," she whispered. "The DEA is going to love this."

Donaldson's dire warnings seemed incongruous as we passed over cubicles decorated with family photos, postcards, house plants and personal toys. Office workers tapped keyboards, chased screen documents with wireless mice and spoke in official-sounding tones into phone headsets. I wondered how many of the workers knew the true nature of their employer.

After a while, my arms and hands grew sore from maintaining a grip on Andy. I shifted hands and we changed positions, but the need to keep physical contact and pilot us with the slow, low fan of the power unit limited my options. This was the longest we had flown together. My mind wandered. Close contact with her—her soft skin, her scent—made me want even closer contact.

When we reached the floor with the server farm, I saw an opportunity. In a large space occupying one corner of the building, three aisles of server racks stretched away behind a glass wall. Ubiquitous cameras monitored the entrance, but the ceiling inside the server room showed no sign of watchful eyes.

The sliding glass door required a key card for entrance. Passing a workstation, I spotted a key card sitting on a desk. The technician seated at the workstation hunched in front of three screens full of code, open windows, and scrolling data. I slipped the card off the desk and into my pocket where it vanished.

"Nice," Andy whispered.

We flew to the glass wall. Server cooling systems hummed steadily and covered the sound of the BLASTER.

I stopped at the sliding door, pulled the card out and dropped it between hands. An electric snap tickled my fingers as it reappeared. As small as it was, the weight of the card affected us immediately. We touched the floor. I swiped the card through the reader. The glass door slid aside.

I made the card vanish in my pocket and pulled us through the opening.

We performed a long slow glide between two server racks. At the end, a right turn took us down another channel, this one hidden from the glass wall at the front. Checking once more for cameras and finding none—

Fwooomp!

—we dropped into the embrace of gravity. I let go of my wife and flexed my fingers. I was about to reach for a more personal embrace when Andy quickly held up her phone and scrolled through the photos she had taken blindly.

"Any good?"

"They'll do."

"What about all this?" I gestured at the tech around us—wires, plugs, blinking lights on black boxes slotted into metal racks. "Souvenirs?"

She shrugged. "I wouldn't know where to begin, what to take, what to copy. Speaking of souvenirs, let me have that key card."

I handed it over. She dropped it on the floor and pushed it partway under a server rack. "It will be missed. This way, it's not a security breach, it's just clumsy."

I looked over the server rack. "Why don't we yank out one of these drives?"

Andy shook her head. "Who knows…this might be the internet hub for the whole city. Or a co-location for half the businesses in Juárez. Will, they're mixing crime with business here. I mean—I came in here thinking in terms of raiding the place."

"Solo?"

"Not me. Not by myself, silly. But picturing the DEA and Federales swooping in and taking the head off the serpent. But now? I don't know. It's all mingled together. If you raid this place it would have to be with accountants and programmers as much as armed officers."

"I guess that explains McCauley."

"Maybe."

42

We killed time in the server room until a couple of techs entered and set up camp at a workstation in one of the aisles. Andy suggested we get back to work. We slipped out and spent another hour cruising the floor while Andy took photos. A rhythm developed. I assessed each new space, hallway or office and positioned her. She snapped photos and nudged me when it was time to move on.

The battery charge in the BLASTER eventually ran down. I swapped it for a fresh one, reminding Andy that the third unit I carried should stay in reserve to guarantee passage back across the border.

"Let's head up to the penthouse," she said. A wall clock said six-fifteen, surprising me that the afternoon had passed so quickly.

We returned to the stairwell and used it to ascend to the top floor of the building. I pulled us over the steel railing. I tested the doorknob.

"It's locked." I looked through a small window at the top of the steel door.

The penthouse elevator lobby had a marble security station directly across from the twin elevator doors. Two uniformed guards occupied the position.

"Now what?" she whispered.

"We get them to come and open the door for us. Reach in your bag and eject one round from your magazine."

"Okay..." I felt her movement. "Got it."

"Slide around and piggyback me. Keep a grip on me. I need both hands."

She moved. Her legs clamped my hips. "When he comes out here, toss it down the stairs. Make sure it makes noise."

I repositioned so that I had one hand on the doorknob and one on the railing.

"Ready?"

"Ready."

I rattled the doorknob. A little at first. Stopping. Starting. Through the glass, I watched the guards. They alerted to the sound instantly, recognized the source and locked their attention on the door. First one stood, then the other. Hands went to their sidearms. I stopped and let them stare and wonder. Then I hit it again, shaking the knob more urgently.

Guns came up. They moved.

I moved, too. I let go of the door and used my grip on the railing to swing my legs over and out until I pointed us at the door like a torpedo. Andy lowered her profile, snuggling against my head.

The door opened swiftly. Guard One poked his weapon through. He swept the stairwell. He did not enter, but instead moved from one side of the frame to the other, searching every dimension of the stairwell.

I pushed lightly and released the railing, rising.

Holding the door open, Guard One let his partner pass through. The second guard stepped across the landing and leaned over to look down at the zigzagging railings below—exactly where we had been a moment ago.

I fixed a light grip on the top edge of the door, now held open by the second guard who swept his own weapon across the descending steps.

Andy shifted on my back. I heard a *click-click-click*. The bullet she ejected from her magazine hit the wall, ricocheted and tapped its way down. It hit the landing below, then the tapping continued, growing more and more distant until I heard a *ping* far below—the bullet hitting a steel railing.

Nice shot.

Both men alerted to the sound. Guard Two gestured for his partner to remain at the door. He hurried down the flight of stairs. The first guard used one foot to hold the door open while he leaned over the railing to watch.

I reached for the door frame, grabbed it, and pulled carefully through, mindful of Andy on my back. She squeezed against me. We eased into the lobby and coasted to the reception desk.

The guard working his way down the stairs used a loud whisper to say something. The guard at the top moved out of sight. The door closed behind him.

"Nice," Andy whispered in my ear. I got a kiss. "What happens when they find the bullet?"

"I give up. What?"

A light jab signaled disapproval of my response.

We hit the security station and stopped. I studied our surroundings. A white and gray marble floor spanned the broad open space, reflecting recessed canister lights above. Warm, dark wood lined the walls. To our left and right, arched passages opened to more spaces decorated with low leather furniture, full-sized house plants and tasteful sculptures tucked in corners. At intervals around us, tall hardwood doors marked entrances to the penthouse apartments we had seen from the outside. All of it looked new and expensive.

Aaron McCauley's dinner appointment would be in one of these apartments. The security and reception area offered ample spaces for us to await his arrival.

"Take us around the desk," Andy said.

It wouldn't have been my first choice. I expected the security duo to return quickly to their post.

I pulled us over the countertop. Andy's interest became apparent. An array of four wide flatscreens filled with tiled windows displayed dozens of security camera shots.

"Stop," Andy commanded.

I rotated us to face the screens and froze us in place with a handhold on the countertop. Many of the camera shots looked familiar, showing spaces Andy and I had toured.

"What are you looking for?"

"The floor where McCauley is staying. I want to see him coming."

"We can't stay here."

The instant I said it the stairwell door opened. Guard One held a radio to his lips and spoke urgently. He hurried across the marble floor and around the end of the counter.

I reached for the counter surface and pushed us upward. The room had a high ceiling. We ascended vertically over the row of monitors until I gently touched the ceiling to stop.

The security guard spoke in Spanish. A voice answering his radio call matched his pace.

Guard Two returned through the stairwell door. He said something and shook his head.

His partner pulled a stool from under the counter, sat down, and drew a keyboard from a hidden space beneath the monitors. He touch-typed commands that changed the presentation. He worked a wireless mouse. Individual frames leaped to full-screen size high-resolution full-color shots.

The second guard joined the first. They leaned over the monitors and studied image after image. Many were stairwell shots. When those provided no satisfaction, they looked farther afield. Hallways. Open spaces. Elevator interiors.

They exchanged a few words tinged with mounting frustration. After a few minutes, Guard One reported his findings to someone on the radio who did not sound pleased.

I looked for a clock—a wall clock, a clear view of a wristwatch, anything—then realized that the timestamp on the video feed told me what I wanted to know. 18:55 plus a relentless roll of seconds. Almost seven p.m. Time for McCauley to appear.

With no idea which of the penthouse apartment doors opened on Roane senior or his sons, or where the planned dinner would take place, I decided this was as good a place as any to wait.

The guards searched. Chatter diminished between them.

Away to our right, one of the penthouse doors opened. The tall man, Anton, slipped through and closed the door quietly behind him. As soon as the latch caught, he stretched long legs on a rapid march into the lobby space, calling out commands to the two security guards who snapped to attention.

My high school Spanish teacher would kill me—I had no idea what he said.

Something something something Señor Sergei *something something* Señor McCauley *something.* He projected urgency. The second guard jabbed one of a series of buttons on a control panel. The right-hand elevator door silently opened. The tall man did not slow his pace to enter. As he turned back to face the doors, he threw commands at the security guards who acknowledged while the doors closed.

The digital readout on the panel at the elevator counted down from P to 6 and stopped. Onscreen below us, the tall man appeared in the familiar elevator lobby on McCauley's floor. Another camera showed him hurrying to McCauley's door. He rapped. Then rapped again. When the door opened, his commanding urgency turned to subservient respect. His head dipped. He explained something. The camera angle did not show McCauley, but a moment later he emerged sliding his arms into his tailored jacket sleeves. Andy squeezed my arm.

Here he comes.

I started to pull my BLASTER from the Velcro mount and instantly realized that the signature sound of peeling apart Velcro screamed for the guards' attention.

Dammit. I tried doing it slowly. Just as bad. Andy's grip tightened, signaling me to stop.

On the monitor, the tall man led McCauley back to the elevator lobby. He pulled a key card from his trouser pocket and swiped it. The elevator car opened. Both men boarded.

The first guard tapped his keyboard. The screens broke up into dozens of smaller windows again. In one of the small frames, the two men in the elevator adopted standard elevator posture, facing the door, not speaking. Andy moved again. Her urgent grip signaled trouble. Her lips found my ear.

"Going down," she whispered at a level so low it might have been mistaken for breathing. I saw what she saw. Instead of increasing, the numbers on the digital readout showed the elevator car descending. Past 1. Past L. It stopped on B.

A camera in the parking garage watched the tall man and McCauley emerge from the elevator. They took up a waiting posture near the glass wall facing the garage.

Dammit. We had it wrong. Flashcard possibilities ran through my head, none of them satisfying. None suggested waiting above the security station and watching. Andy tapped my arm.

I ripped the BLASTER free of the Velcro.

"*Qué es?*" Guard One alerted to the sound. Both men looked around. Guard Two looked up, correctly locating the source of the noise.

I snapped a prop in place and thumbed the slide. In the hollow marble-lined acoustic space of this security lobby, no level of power would have gone unheard. The BLASTER sounded like an angry insect. Both men startled. Guard One leaped to his feet and instinctively waved his hands over his head. He spun away, ducking and searching.

The power shot took us across the lobby space to the door. I rotated us as we floated so that we met the door in a relatively standard posture.

"Do it," Andy whispered.

I propped my right fist against the wall and pulled the door open wide and fast. It slammed the wall. I pulled on the frame and heaved us through. We shot to the railing. Footsteps and startled words behind us said the guards were coming.

My right hand held the BLASTER. I grabbed the railing with my left. I felt additional leverage from Andy. We pulled ourselves over—headfirst—something I never expected from her. The move was dizzying—twelve floors up. We shot down the center channel between descending flights of stairs.

Shouts followed us. Both guards, guns drawn, once again searched the empty stairwell.

Flights of concrete steps angled past us. I didn't bother counting floors. Andy spoke breathlessly.

"McCauley's meeting Sergei in the parking garage. They must be leaving."

The concrete floor rose quickly to meet us.

I reversed thrust. We halted. I rotated us to right side up. The power unit pulled us to the steel stairwell door. Andy and I bumped heads trying to look through the tiny glass in the door.

The tall man and McCauley stood at the glass wall, not speaking, staring out at the well-lit underground garage. Two security guards stood at attention behind a counter lined with a twin to the panel of monitors we'd seen on the penthouse level.

"How do you want to do this?" I asked.

"Try the door when something happens. Maybe we can do it without drawing attention."

We did not wait long. The steel door over the entrance to the parking garage rattled to life. It rose emitting a mix of metallic and motor sounds. Headlights appeared on the ramp. The first arriving vehicle sustained the silver Suburban theme. Close behind came a black Mercedes utility van. A Toyota sedan tailgated the van. All three pulled up in front of the glass wall.

Both security guards hurried forward. One card-swiped the glass wall to open it, the other hurried to open the right rear door of the silver Suburban.

Our moment arrived.

I clawed the door jamb to gain leverage and push the steel stairwell door open. We slipped through, although I instantly wondered if we had been too hasty. This looked less like McCauley leaving and more like a reception committee. We might have raced to the basement only to face a return trip to the penthouse.

Sergei Roane stepped out of the Suburban. He wore knife-edge creased black trousers and a yellow polo shirt. I recognized the older brother from Horowitz's photo. Handsome, mahogany-skinned with short black hair, he sported the popular stubble of beard men use to cast themselves as rugged. His eyes were cold, his physique solid, and his arms corded and etched with threatening tattoos. Gawdy gold rings adorned the central fingers of both hands. A gold bracelet dangled on one wrist.

The opposite door of the Suburban thudded shut. A man walked around the vehicle. Slightly taller than Roane, he had the same capable physique under blue-black skin that glistened in the fluorescent lights. His hair was cut short and revealed no gray. A pale scar, an apostrophe, ran down one cheek below his left eye. The palms of his hands were fair and flashed as he walked with a military bearing enhanced by a tan shirt with dual pockets and epaulets.

Roane and the dark stranger stepped up to McCauley. I studied them to assign a pecking order. McCauley had been authoritative with the tall manservant, speaking harshly of Sergei.

Andy and I maneuvered closer. The acoustics of the parking garage, with engines running, masked my power unit noise.

I positioned us above and to one side of the conversation, close enough to hear them speak.

"Do you have her?" McCauley asked without greeting or preamble. He clearly knew both men.

A cold chill hit my gut. *Gwen.*

"No." Sergei's clipped answer betrayed anger and impatience. He avoided McCauley's disapproving glare by glancing at the Mercedes van behind the Suburban. "We will."

Two men stepped out of the van. Both wore all black tactical clothing and carried holstered sidearms. They looked at Sergei for a signal. He nodded. They stepped to the rear of the van. Dual doors opened. A third man in black jumped down.

With some shuffling, coercion and a dash of cruel manhandling, the three men extracted a young man, a young woman and two children from the back of the van. The woman clutched a toddler to her chest with one hand and held an iron grip on the hand of a small boy. A swollen red cheek distorted the young man's face. He winced as he moved. Bent posture and a torn shirt said his beating went beyond his face.

All four wore rings of white terror in their eyes.

On seeing Sergei, the young woman called out, *"Señor Sergei! Señor Sergei! Por favor! Por favor!"*

That much Spanish, I knew.

The young man reached for the woman but one of the men in black jerked him away.

The men pulled and pushed the small family toward Sergei, McCauley and the third man. The woman's pleading increased until Sergei's hand shot out and slapped her, nearly knocking her off her feet. The toddler screamed. The small boy, no more than six or seven, cried out, *"Mami!"* He clutched his mother's skirt.

Sergei spoke to the men in black, then turned and gestured for McCauley and the third man to follow him. Instead of entering the building or the vehicle, they set out across the asphalt parking garage surface. The paramilitary men followed, dragging and prodding their victims.

The young father begged in English. "Please, sir! She doesn't know. I don't know more than I have told you. *We don't know.*"

The prisoner's pleas did nothing to change the trajectory of the group.

I pushed the power unit slide and we surged after them. Andy shifted and moved beside me.

"I need my hands."

I hooked her arm with my left arm to maintain contact while I drove us forward with the power unit in my right. She moved. I heard her open the flap of her shoulder bag, then felt her manipulate the contents. A moment later, I read her repetitious motion as twisting the suppressor onto the muzzle of her Beretta.

"You can't fire that like this," I whispered urgently.

"I know."

Twice I'd been in the vanished state with a fired handgun. Once I fired it. The second time someone else fired. Both times, the energy of the discharge resulted in what I can only describe as electrocution while hitting a brick wall. Both times I'd been jolted out of *the other thing* and immobilized.

Andy had been present each time.

The group crossed the parking garage and headed into a square concrete tunnel. One of the men found a light switch, activating fluorescent ceiling lighting. Except for electrical conduits and a pair of pipes, the gray tunnel walls were featureless. The tunnel ran for roughly ninety feet before a junction offered a choice of left or right. The group went left. More lights came on.

Andy and I followed twenty to thirty feet behind them. I mentally mapped the tunnel in relation to the surface above us. The glass tower occupied the center of the block behind a plaza. Smaller buildings formed a perimeter around the glass tower, excluding the plaza and the generator lot. The first tunnel ran parallel to the parking garage driveway. I guessed the junction to be near or even with the east side of the block. The new leg of the tunnel ran either behind or under street-side buildings. In distant darkness ahead I detected a wall, confirming my suspicion that the tunnel circumnavigated the entire block, probably granting access to the basement of every building on the perimeter.

I thought the small parade might enter one of those basements, but Sergei turned and led us into a black space on the interior side of the tunnel. The sound of his footsteps changed. Something crinkled underfoot. One of the men found a light switch. Florescent lights winked on, revealing a square, featureless bunker.

Industrial plastic spanned the floor. Chains and manacles hung from bolts in the ceiling. The sight of both renewed desperate pleas from the young man and woman. They pulled the children close between them. They chattered desperately, begging in Spanish and English.

McCauley and the man in the military shirt fanned out to one side to watch. Sergei strolled forward and gripped the young man's chin.

"Let me explain, Milo, what I will do to your children while you and your wife watch. Then to your wife while your children watch." He leaned close and muttered in the young man's ear. The words brought pain and tears to Milo's distraught face.

"Please! We don't know!"

"You do know. It is your business to know. I made you wealthy and let you build a future and a family on what you know. You used all that I gave you to cut out my heart." Sergei's low voice carried above the mewling of the children, which their mother attempted to mute by pressing their faces against her body. Sergei pulled a paper from his back pocket and unfolded it. He held it up.

"Look!" He shoved the paper into the young man's face and pushed his head back. "You would take this from me and then lie to me about it?" Sergei shoved the wrinkled sheet down into Milo's shirt.

"I have never lied to you! I swear!"

Sergei gestured at the men in black. "Chain them up."

New mayhem ensued as the young man threw his arms around his wife and children. The men in black waded in to peel them apart.

Andy twisted. She pressed her lips to my ear. I felt her drawn weapon between us, solid and ominous.

"Drop me. Then get them."

I started to object but she pushed away from me.

Fwooomp!

Andy appeared, dropped to her feet, landed in a feline crouch and brought her gun to bear.

"Back off!" she shouted. Her voice cut the air and reverberated in the concrete chamber.

All heads turned toward her. As if choreographed, all three men in black jabbed their hands to their hips for their weapons. A red laser dot landed on the chest of the man on Andy's right.

Snick! Click!

Andy's silenced Beretta fired. The man on the right doubled over and sat back on his butt, clutching his chest. He emitted a coarse rasping gasp and began to moan.

Body armor. The 9-millimeter round hit him in the diaphragm and kicked the air from his lungs but did not penetrate.

"DROP THEM!" Andy swung the dot to the next man, this time dancing it on his face. She made her point. The armed men slowly extracted their weapons and dropped them to the plastic. To her right, McCauley and the third man edged sideways, away from Andy.

Sergei turned a murderous look on Andy.

I had momentarily frozen. Shaking myself loose, I shoved the power unit slide forward and carved an arc through the air that took me around Sergei and behind the small family. Their fear did some of my work for me. They clutched each other in a tight group. I came up behind them as the men in black stepped away. I spread my arms and prayed.

"Hold tight!" I called out. Out of the corner of my eye, I saw Andy lunge for the wall near the entrance.

She slapped the light switch. The chamber went black.

I slammed into the cluster of prisoners.

FWOOOMP!

I felt an electric snap up and down my arms. The tunnel spilled just enough light into the bunker to show me that the small family vanished the instant I clamped my arms around them. I heard a gasp, then screams.

Twin flashes and sharp snaps told me that Andy fired again. Sergei Roane's silhouette dropped to the floor and slapped against the plastic. The men on either side of me dove for their weapons. Framed in the light of the chamber entrance, Andy broke into a run and disappeared into the tunnel.

"Stay quiet! *Por favor! Silencio!*" I rotated my passengers and rolled until they were above me, a tight mass of shivering arms and legs. "Hold each other and stay silent!"

I heard Milo and the woman repeat the order in Spanish to the children. I didn't think we had a prayer of keeping the children from crying out, or the adults from gasping, but shock did the trick. I heard nothing.

Their silence changed my plan.

I had intended to shoot out of the chamber and race after Andy. I had no idea if we could add one more to this floating mass, but the thought of her running, alone, visible, trapped in this underground fortress, fueled the impulse to try.

It was the wrong move. When this room full of assholes woke up and charged after my wife, she would be ready. She would want a clear shot at them. If they fired at her, if she fired back, chasing her would put us in a deadly crossfire.

I goosed the power unit. Reverse thrust sent us away from the entrance. We floated to the back wall of the black chamber. We bumped and stopped.

"Shhhhhhhh…" I felt the family pull each other tightly together. The mother stroked and rubbed the children.

The lights snapped on. McCauley stood at the entrance. Sergei lay on the floor with bloody hands wrapped around his right knee, gritting his teeth and moaning.

McCauley pointed at the men in black still standing. "Go after them!"

Both men scooped up their weapons and charged the door. The third gasped on the floor, clawing open his shirt and squinting in pain. Sergei lay writhing on the plastic, smearing blood and swearing.

Someone screamed in the tunnel. Andy had ambushed them and scored silent hits. Half a dozen thunderous shots rang out. Rapid fire. Desperate. I prayed their bullets found only empty air.

Between curses in Spanish, Sergei cried out, "Help me up!"

"Help him," McCauley commanded the tall dark man. He poked his head into the tunnel, then pulled back quickly. "They're down. Your men are both down. The woman shot them! *What the fuck!*"

McCauley and the military man heaved Sergei to his feet. His right knee oozed blood. He snarled and cursed. Had I been Andy, I might have aimed higher.

Sergei hobbled out with his arms on the shoulders of both other men. I heard relieved breathing after the three men disappeared into the tunnel.

"*Dios mio,*" the young woman uttered. She trembled and began to weep.

"*Silencio, por favor,*" I repeated. Nothing guaranteed help wasn't coming for Sergei, or that there wouldn't be men searching these corridors.

My heart raced. I desperately wanted to get to Andy.

"Who are you?" the young man whispered. "*What are you?*"

"The hand of God," I said. Why not? It worked once before. "Stay silent, don't move. Hold each other tight. If you let go, you will fall and they will see you." Then I added, "I command you."

Yeah…that was too much.

The young man translated to his wife and children.

"Si, Papa!" a small voice answered.

"Okay," I said. "We're leaving."

43

At the bunker entrance, I steered left toward the dark end of the tunnel. Doorless openings to black spaces on our right offered possible exits. I glanced back to see if reinforcements had arrived. Far up the tunnel the two men who had pursued Andy lay on the floor. Both moved, dealing with wounds I could not see. McCauley, Sergei and the military man had vanished around the corner that would take them back to the parking garage.

My mind raced through possibilities. Return to the parking garage and try to escape (the damned steel doors were down). Try getting to the elevators (blocked by two guards plus Sergei's driver plus the driver of the van and the sedan—and I had no key card). Try reaching the stairwell and ascending to escape via the roof (the five of us were too bulky to rise in the space between flights of stairs).

That left the tunnel.

I took the second opening on the right. My sense of direction said the opening led to a basement beneath a building at the street. Rotating to an upright position for better orientation, we entered a dark room cluttered with boxes and furniture. Musty odor joined the air. The vague outline of a stairs revealed itself as my eyes adjusted.

Four people was three more than I've ever carried before. I didn't know if I was straining *the other thing* or if it might fail me at any moment. Reappearing was not an option. Being seen on a security camera or setting off an alarm would rain trouble down on us.

We bumped our way through the clutter in the basement space. I turned us and reduced my hold to a single hand clamped on the man's upper arm. I aimed the power unit up a too-narrow stairway. My passengers bumped the wall and railing. I quickly collided with what proved to be a locked door.

I flipped the BLASTER body back against the Velcro. I wrapped the palm of my free hand around the doorknob and pictured the levers in my head that make me vanish. They were pushed to the limit. I closed a mental hand on them, drew them back slightly and pushed them forward. Around my right hand, *the other thing* spread into the door. Light seeped through where wood and metal vanished.

The other thing spread to the edge of the door where the lock's bolt extended into the jamb. I pressed on the door. A soft snap transmitted up my arm. The door swung free and the severed end of the bolt tumbled to the floor.

Twilight had fallen. Streetlights cast long shadows into a closed retail shop filled with clothing racks. I grabbed the door jamb and pulled us through. On the ceiling a black camera bulb watched.

"Do not let go." No one answered. Fear, shock or utter disbelief silenced my passengers. I didn't care which, as long as they held together.

The Velcro that snagged my BLASTER now rendered it awkwardly out of reach. I kicked the floor and sent us soaring over the clothing racks. As the ceiling came up, I reached overhead and grabbed a track light bar. Using it for leverage, I sent us sailing.

We landed at the locked front door. I performed the same trick of severing the lock bolt. In short order the door swung open. If it set off an alarm, it was a silent alarm.

"Stay close. Hold tight," I said. I felt my charges renew their embrace.

I twisted around and positioned my right wrist against my left thumb, which freed the BLASTER from the Velcro. Powered up once more, I aimed for the open street.

Sunday evening. Few vehicles and only a handful of pedestrians moved on the street and sidewalk. A golden sunset sky hung overhead.

I applied power. We rose over the nearly empty street.

A gnawing sensation dug at my guts. My nerves sang like tight wires in a high wind. I needed to dump these people and get back to Andy. Yet I could not leave them just anywhere. They would be picked up in minutes.

I aimed skyward and we climbed. Building façades fell away. A row of three- and four-story structures lined both sidewalks. I shot up and scanned the rooftops across the street from the plaza and glass tower. A few had patios and furniture. That meant easy access. The tallest had a peaked roof and above that, a large cylinder on a lattice structure. Thirty feet up, a catwalk skirted the base of a rusty water tower. A narrow ladder traversing the roof and disappearing over the side of the building offered the only access. It would do.

I chose a landing approach that brought us in alongside the round steel reservoir. Reverse thrust stopped us and pressed us down until my feet found the steel catwalk. I misjudged.

FWOOOMP!

An electric snap coursed my arms. I let my charges go not realizing that they had not touched down. The little family crashed and clattered onto the catwalk. The woman fell against the water tower. The boy fell against a flimsy railing—and for a moment teetered on the edge. His father threw an arm around him.

"Sorry!" I said. "*Lo siento!*"

The woman scrambled against the steel tower. She clutched her toddler and pulled her older child to her shoulder. Her eyes blazed, wide and wild. She examined the deadly slope of the roof, then searched in vain for the sound of my voice.

The father dropped beside the mother. He threw his arms around her.

"Stay here!" I ordered them. "Do you understand?"

He looked up at empty air.

"If you move from here, you will be caught. Do you understand me?"

He nodded.

"I will come back for you. I have to find the woman who saved you."

They shivered in the warm yellow sunset light.

"Gotta go."

44

I kicked off the water tower and shoved the power unit slide control to the stop. The prop howled. I accelerated and aimed for the glass tower with no idea what to do next. My heart hammered against my chest wall. How far could she get? Cameras everywhere. Guards on alert. I had a clear view of the driveway entrance, guard stations and lanes descending into the parking garage. Both steel doors remained down.

Plan B.

I angled for the roof. At intervals across all four sides of the roof parapet, armed guards took up stations with their rifles aimed outward. Additional men with binoculars scanned the streets below. Men exited the rooftop door I had hoped to use. Worse, the last man in line stationed himself at the door gripping his rifle at the ready.

I widened my orbit. Figures ran from the office building entrances. They jogged to the streets on all four sides of the block. At the edge of the plaza, a cluster of men broke left toward the clothing shop.

Silent alarm.

Vehicle tires screeched at the back of the building. Two SUVs roared out of the utility lot. The gate, attended by armed guards, closed quickly behind them. The vehicles split directions and joined what little traffic moved around the block perimeter. More vehicles approached from surrounding blocks. The reserves had been called in. Armed young men spilled from sedans and SUVs that parked at the intersections on all four corners. The few civilian vehicles on the streets accelerated away.

Deep below, in the middle of all this, Andy either hid, had been trapped, captured or worse.

My pulse thundered in my ears, nearly drowning out the persistent twitter of an incoming call. I tapped the earpiece hard enough to hurt.

"Dee!"

"No, it's me," Donaldson said calmly.

I heard the click of a conference call. "I'm here," Andy said, barely audible.

"What's going on?" Donaldson asked.

"Shut up! Dee, where are you?" I realized I was talking too loudly. Faces on the roof tilted upward.

I aimed the BLASTER at the yellow sky and climbed higher. The twilight lights of Juárez fell away in all directions.

She whispered, "Tunnel. Basement room. Exit's locked. Got company."

"Don't move. The cameras."

"Didn't see me," she whispered. "In the dark."

I wasn't sure Sergei's system didn't use infrared but kept the idea to myself.

"Break out to the street. I can get you. Which side are you on?"

"I can't move. Lights in the tunnel."

Donaldson said, "What the hell is going on?"

"Not now!" I snapped.

"Will, I need a blackout."

The fog closing in on my mind snapped clear. *Of course!*

"Stay put!" I rotated and looked down at the generator engines. Power lines ran from the building to the street. A line of marching poles extended into the distance. Near the corner of the block, on a pole, I found what I was looking for. "This'll take me a few minutes. Be ready."

"Hurry."

"What side are you on? Which side of the block? I need to know where you will come out."

Nothing.

"Her connection is gone," Donaldson said. "What the hell happened?"

I GAVE Donaldson the movie pitch version, then told him to hang up and try us again in five minutes.

"I gotta make a call." He killed the connection.

I searched the scene below. Men now moved in all the open spaces. The block took on the appearance of an ant colony awakened by a stick stabbed into its tunnels. Cars rolled slowly down the streets on all four sides. More cars blocked the streets farther out. Men with weapons loitered on street corners. Windows in the perimeter buildings darkened. Lights went out. Shades fell.

I searched the plaza, the sidewalks, the streets for a weapon.

I saw benches. Trash bins. A boxy old-style newspaper vending box.

Nothing met my need. A chunk of concrete would work, but the immediate area had no demolition or construction. A bench might be too big to vanish. Or too light for my needs. The same for a trash bin.

I needed weight. Several hundred pounds.

She stood at the center of the plaza fountain.

Winged Victory.

I dove for the fountain in the plaza. The power unit buzzed. Heads turned, but I didn't care. What could they do? Shoot at me?

I reversed thrust sharply as I passed over the edge of the fountain. The BLASTER buzzed. Men jogging to their stations stopped and searched the sky. A few shouted out and pointed.

The statue came up fast. My approach was lousy. I shot through the fountain spray and slammed into the bronze body. She was larger than I expected. I wrapped my arms around her.

Once again, I pictured the throttle-like levers. I pictured my hand on the round knobs. I closed a grip and pulled them back slightly—then pushed. Hard. *Harder.*

I expected a struggle, but it happened instantly.

FWOOOMP!

The statue vanished. I planted my feet on the statue's base and tried lifting. It remained rigid. I heaved upward. It gave. Minutely. I heaved again. This time it gave way. A soft snap transmitted through my arms. *The other thing* severed the metal bolts at the base of the statue.

We shot upward.

She had no weight and no inertia, but she had bulk. My arms fit only halfway around her. I repositioned and wrapped my legs around her waist, freeing my right hand to use the power unit.

I aimed high and away from the plaza. The glass face of the building fell away. City lights spread a twinkling carpet in all directions.

I steered away from the building toward the rows of power line poles connected by aligned strands of charged wire. The pole I wanted stood above one corner of an intersection guarded by tattooed young men in t-shirts and sneakers, brandishing a chilling array of automatic weapons.

A flat gray metal transformer hung near the top of the pole. Wire lines angled toward the glass tower.

I established a stabilized approach to the top of the pole. The knot in my chest, squeezed tight by the thought of Andy trapped underground, shortened my breath. I focused on flying.

Live wires reminded me not to descend below the top of the pole. I steadied myself and tweaked the power until I floated directly above the flat wooden top of the pole.

My earpiece buzzed. I cut the power and hit the button with the heel of my hand.

"Dee?"

"Here," she whispered.

"Me, too. She's all yours." Donaldson had initiated the conference call.

"You okay?"

"I hear them in the tunnel."

"Hang on. Taking the power out shortly."

I hope.

I used reverse thrust to press my feet on the top of the pole. I bent my knees and then slowly pushed off, straight up—I prayed.

The pole fell away. The street changed perspective. Below me, the gray transformer, a unit the size of a kitchen refrigerator, dropped. Too high, and the chances of a miss increased. Too low, and the chances of the result consuming me increased.

Roughly one hundred feet above the transformer, I released my grip on Winged Victory.

The bronze statue, easily five hundred pounds, snapped into view and dropped. Silent.

I held my breath, thinking that if I missed, I would pick her up and do it again.

I didn't miss.

The flash blinded me. The statue hit the transformer squarely. Statue and transformer disappeared in a ball of white light. The blast punched my ears and stunned me. A shock wave shot skyward around me.

I forced the power unit thumb slide to the max. Arcs of sparks climbed past me like tracer fire. Lightning raced up the lines in both directions. Sparks leaped from the next pole, and the next.

Against flashes of calamitous light, this section of the city went dark. Seconds later I heard diesel engines roar to life and the lights of the Méndez block flicked back on. The generators, on cue, took up the electrical strain and powered the building—the lights, the elevators and the cameras that would expose Andy to relentless searchers.

"Emergency power just came on," she said calmly into my ear.

"Stay still. Just a few minutes. Can you find your way out in the dark?"

"Yes."

I gathered my senses and steered to the rear of the block, to a spot above the utility lot and the generators. In my haste to escape the snapping and sparking transformer, I had risen to more than double the roughly one hundred and fifty-foot height of the building.

I watched the twin generators. Exhaust plumes belched from the formidable engines. Black oil sprayed from each dislodged oil filter. Oil coated the security fence and fuel tank. Oil coated the companion engine. I spotted a surprising bonus. Oil from the first engine hit the exhaust manifold of the second engine. In less than a minute the manifold heated to the point of vaporizing the oil. White smoke boiled and swirled.

"Get ready," I said to Andy. "It's going to happen faster than I—"

The oil vapor ignited. A yellow bulb of flame leaped forty feet into the air.

I went to full power knowing what would come next. I dove toward the building, hoping it would shield me when the fuel tanks blew.

The explosion overwhelmed my senses.

A thundering cloud of fire skyrocketed. Half a dozen windows facing the utility lot shattered. Glittering shards rained down the face of the building.

The emergency power died. The tower went black.

Beneath ringing in my ear Andy said, "On the move!"

In the plaza and on the streets, men pointed and shouted and ran. Vehicles performed screaming U-turns and raced to the back and side of the block where the flames roared. The explosion and fire drew people from all directions.

"Which side?"

I heard her breathing heavily. I heard thumps and a loud slam.

"I'm in a—looks like a coffee shop! South side! South side!"

"I'm coming!"

The rising black cloud of fire and smoke consumed the northwest corner of the block. I powered away from it. My path took me over the plaza, over the street. I sailed over men closing in on the fire from all directions.

I hooked right and then right again, lining up with the street that bordered the south perimeter of the Méndez block.

At the center of the block, Andy walked out the broken front door of a coffee shop like a woman who just picked up a latte on her way to work. She pressed the handgun with its fat suppressor against her side.

She strolled across a nearly empty street.

Men who had been patrolling this block ran toward the end of the block, away from her. The SUV that had, a moment earlier, cruised slowly past the same coffee shop now heaved out of sight at the far corner.

Andy hurried. I aimed for her.

A fresh set of headlights swung into the street from an alley less than a hundred yards from where she crossed the street. A rusted wreck of a pickup truck lunged onto the street, bounding like an old dog on one last hunt. The headlights caught Andy at the centerline.

"Dee! Look out!"

A rattling engine powered the old truck toward her.

"Stand down! Stand down!" Donaldson shouted. "Do not shoot! He sees you! Do not shoot the friendly!"

What the hell?

I dove, too far out to help, but not too far out to see men shout and reverse course. She'd been spotted. Half a block away, a trio of men bolted toward her. They pulled handguns from leg-strapped holsters. One man put a radio to his mouth.

"Hostiles! Dee! Coming at you!"

Caught in the headlights, Andy automatically lifted her weapon at the on-coming vehicle.

"Friendly! Friendly!" Donaldson cried.

"The hell they are!" I watched the men raise their weapons.

Even as the pickup bore down on her, Andy swung her aim and crouched in the street. She fired. The suppressor did not allow the weapon to speak—but the silenced rounds she aimed at the men running toward her said enough. Her rounds either hit or passed close enough to be a warning. The nearest two men dove to the pavement. Their weapons clattered on the concrete.

Still more than a hundred feet away, I dove toward her.

Not fast enough.

The pickup bore down on her. She fired again, but not at the truck. She fired at more men rounding the corner and sprinting toward her. They began firing wildly back. Staccato handgun pops cut the evening calm. Andy's aim was steady, mounted on a practiced, professional stance. Her attackers fired one-handed, on the run, without training or discipline.

The BLASTER screamed. Wind tore at my clothes.

Too far!

Squealing old brakes clawed the truck to a stop. Through the earpiece I heard someone shout at her.

"Get in!"

She broke and ran for the passenger door. Even as she slid onto the seat the driver slammed the truck in gear and roared forward ahead of a cloud of oily exhaust. The pickup rushed beneath me. Men racing after it fired wildly.

I aimed my arm straight up to climb out of the path of gunfire. I heard rounds strike the pickup's tailgate.

The truck hooked right at the intersection, bouncing and leaning out of sight.

"Dee!"

"Will, I'm okay," Andy said breathlessly.

"Lee! Is that you?" I called out.

"Not me, man. I been sitting in Mexi-custody all the livelong day."

Andy spoke to someone. "Hola, Señor Miguel."

"Who?" I raised the power unit and climbed until I could see the pickup's taillights over the rim of the buildings. I watched for vehicles to charge after it. Nothing took up the chase.

Donaldson said, "It's Mike, dude."

45

"Let me come for you."
"Will, no," Andy said. "Those people—where are they?"
I explained about the water tower.
"You can't leave them there. You need to get them out of Juárez."
"Who?" Donaldson asked. Andy ignored him.
"Can you get them across? Make two trips if you have to. They can't stay. They won't have a chance."
I hung in the air and said nothing. The pickup slipped from view.
"Will?"
"Jesus, Dee…"
My pulse pounded. The nerves in my arms jittered. I swallowed down delayed fear with a dry mouth. It slowly sank in that Andy had escaped—narrowly.
"Are you sure you can get across?"
"Will, I'm fine. I'll be fine. They need you."
"Who are you talking about?" Donaldson interrupted.
"Are you really okay?"
"I'm really okay."
"I love you."
"I love you, too," Donaldson said.
"Shut up, asshole." To Andy, I said, "Fine. See you on the other side."
"Love you, too," she replied.
I tapped the earpiece before Donaldson poisoned the moment again.

46

Burning diesel fuel cast a hot yellow glow across the tops of the buildings. The fire's light grew stronger with the sun below the tops of the low western mountains and the city lights extinguished.

"Jesus," I muttered to myself. Firelight caught the water tower and the small family as if in a spotlight.

It had been a lousy place to leave them. They should have moved to the back of the catwalk. They simply sat where I dropped them, too shell-shocked to realize how visible they were.

Andy was asking a lot.

Flying two adults and two children miles across the border scared me. Beyond the blackout area, a sea of Juárez and El Paso lights glimmered under a blue-black sky—a daunting expanse. What if I failed to hold them? What if one slipped free? Or panicked? The image of a child falling to his death rushed my mind's eye.

Why not simply move them to somewhere nearby, somewhere safe? *And where, in this city owned and operated by Garcia Roane, would that be?*

Shouting broke out on the glass tower roof. Despite the flames and skyrocketing black smoke adjacent to the northwest corner of the roof, the security team showed discipline and remained at their assigned, evenly spaced sentry posts.

Two of the guards pointed at the cluster of people huddled on the water tower catwalk. A third man ran across the roof with binoculars. He fixed the lenses on the escapees, then raised a radio to his face.

Oh crap.

A moment later, armed men emerged from the glass office tower and bolted across the plaza. These were not blue-shirted security guards. These men wore black tactical clothing, web belts and side arms, and they carried semi-automatic rifles.

Whoever Milo and his family were, Sergei Roane wanted them back.

It would take the team a few minutes to charge across the plaza and the street. The rusted metal ladder offered sole access to the water tower catwalk. Reaching the rooftop, and then the ladder, and then climbing it would take time, but not much.

I crossed high above the street separating the two blocks and aimed for the water tower. I cut the power and let myself coast in for a landing. Reaching the catwalk, I grabbed the rickety railing and pulled myself over. I purposely pushed my feet hard against the steel catwalk to cause a metallic tremor. The young man jumped and cried out.

"Easy, Milo" I said. I placed a reassuring hand on his shoulder. My touch made him stiffen, which made him wince in pain. "Relax. It's okay."

"*Mano de Dios!*" the young woman whispered. She searched the empty air for my voice. She pulled her children closer. The poor kids were in danger of being strangled if her grip grew any tighter.

I knelt and shifted my hand to the man's arm. He stared at the indentations in his flesh.

"Sergei's men are coming. We don't have much time."

"Who are you?"

"I told you. The hand of God." I glanced over my shoulder. The man on the glass tower roof watched through his binoculars, holding the radio to his face, calling play by play for his team on the street. "I'm here to save you."

The woman I took to be Milo's wife asked, "Are we to die?"

"Oh, hell no. Not that kind of 'saved.' I'm here to save you from Sergei. But you need to tell me everything."

Milo said, "If you are truly the hand of God—"

"Shouldn't I already know everything? Do you want to bet your salvation that I don't?"

He didn't answer.

"Either way, I wouldn't lie if I were you. But first, do as I say. Move." I fought the impulse to point. "Move to your right. All of you. *A la derecha, por favor.* They're watching."

Milo searched across the street and saw what I saw. "We have to get down from here!" He leaned over the edge and looked at the ladder sloping down the roof.

"They're on their way up. I'm the only way you're getting down," I said. "For now—move!"

He snapped commands in Spanish to his wife and son. The small group slid on their butts to the right.

"Keep going, keep going."

They slid around the outer diameter of the rooftop cistern. Shadow darkened them as they skidded away from the light cast from the fire across the street.

Milo watched the ladder and the rooftop below.

"How is this possible?"

"It's a miracle."

"I don't believe you."

"Milo!" his wife scolded.

"You got a better idea? Then tell me how you got up here. Tell me why you're not hanging from a chain in Sergei's playroom. Tell me how you plan to get your family down that piece of crap ladder."

He said nothing.

"Yeah, I didn't think so. The truth, Milo. Unvarnished. I'm not here to make you die in the name of The Lord, but those guys are more than willing to kill you and your family in the name of the Devil. Time to choose sides."

It amazed me that he had to think about it for a moment.

"Señor Sergei."

"What about him?"

"*Es mi patron.* My employer. My wife's employer. We work for him."

"Then that was one really bad employee review."

He fell silent. His wife watched his face. When he said nothing, she poked him. "Tell the truth, Milo."

"Yeah, Milo. Clock's ticking. And nothing but the truth."

He regained a hint of bravado. "What will happen to us? To *mi familia?*"

"I will take you to a safe place."

A helpless laugh broke from his lips. "Ha! There is no safe place. He will find us. Better I should try to make a deal with him."

"How has that worked for you so far?"

His wife begged, "*Por favor*—can you take us to America? And promise they will not steal our children or send us back here to die?"

"God's word," I said. Lightning did not take me out when the transformer blew. I hoped it would not do so now. "Keep talking, Milo."

"Señor Sergei—it was my job—my work to move people."

"Coyote?"

He shook his head. "I was once. Now I am a manager. I manage many coyotes. I plan. I work in an office. My wife, she worked in the Hacienda." He pointed at the office building. "She worked for La Señora. *Asistente ejecutiva*—ah, secretary."

"And?"

"Maria—*mi esposa*—she knew—she knew that things were not good for La Señora."

"Sergei's *esposa*? Not good? How?"

"You saw," Maria said. "Señor Sergei is cruel."

"So, you helped Sergei's wife escape." *So, it wasn't Gwen they were after.* I felt relief.

"No!" Milo clenched his fist. "No. But I was a fool. I listened to La Señora. She asked me questions and I answered. I told her too much. *But I did not help her!* And I don't know where she is!"

"Sergei thinks you did help."

"He would not listen."

I heaved a long sigh. "What was McCauley doing there? And who was the Black man?"

"I don't know them—the men who were there—on the heads of my children, I don't."

The woman pleaded, "*Por favor, you have to protect us.* He will not stop looking for us, even after he finds La Señora!"

"Señor Sergei does not forget," Milo said. "I did no wrong, but an example must be made."

"Yeah. It's just business," I said sourly. For a split second, I wondered if explaining to Andy that these people were not innocents would give me a pass on leaving them. The wide eyes of the children in Maria's arms killed that thought.

The woman read my tone and my mind. "Please! I beg you!"

"I'll see that you're safe."

She cried, "How can you be sure? They can get to anyone. They killed—"

"Maria!" Milo snapped. She clamped her mouth shut.

"The whole truth, Milo. Let her speak."

Silent argument passed between the husband and wife. She won.

"The American chief of police," she said. "How can God protect us if Señor Sergei can kill such a man?"

I tightened the grip on Milo's arm.

"Are you talking about Director Mitchell Lindsay of the FBI?"

"Maria!"

She ignored him and nodded emphatically.

"What do you know about it?"

"*Nada.* I know nothing about it…but…"

"But what?"

"La Señora predicted it. She knew his plans—worse plans, things she refused to tell me. She made me swear to forget that we spoke. She told me if Señor Sergei learned that we spoke of these things at all it would seal my death." A terrified laugh broke loose, which instantly spilled tears from her eyes. *"But just look at us now!"*

Voices rose from just below the edge of the roof near the ladder. They had come faster than I expected. Milo twisted abruptly and found my hand on his arm. He probed until he closed a grip on my wrist.

"I don't know who or what you are, but you have to help us!" His swollen cheek displayed half the colors of the rainbow. His left eye glinted behind a narrow slit. With his right eye he searched in vain for me. "Leave me if you must. I can persuade Señor Sergei, but *ayuda mi familia! Por favor!*"

Paper crinkled beneath his torn shirt—the crumpled paper that Sergei had jammed into Milo's face to show him what he was about to die for—what he was about to see his children murdered for. It strongly suggested Milo was dreaming.

I peeled his grip free.

"I gave you my promise," I said. Maria's pleading eyes glittered, laden with tears. For her benefit, I added, "God's word."

Her lips quivered. She hugged her children.

I reached down and pulled the paper from Milo's torn shirt. To Milo's astonished eye, it hung in mid-air and uncrumpled itself.

A color photocopy of a family portrait.

The photo had been staged in elegant surroundings to advertise wealth and power. Sergei stood tall with his arm around a beautiful woman and the child she had borne him. Trophies. She gazed down at the small boy in her arms. The love her expression showered on the child contrasted starkly with the dead eyes of the child's father.

Astonished, I locked on the young woman's angelic face.

A face she shared in every detail with Lonnie Penn.

Gloria Rilling.

PART IV

47

We launched off the water tower just ahead of Sergei's men. Milo lifted his older son and gathered Maria with their younger son between them. They pulled together in a tight mass.

I knew from recent experience *the other thing* would envelop them. The worry gnawing my guts was whether they could hold together. Height induces a reaction in primitive parts of the human brain, with thousands of years of good reason. Andy cringes and tightens when we fly, no matter how often we do it or how important the mission.

What I tend to forget is that vanishing in *the other thing* not only makes my body and anyone I carry disappear but makes gravity irrelevant. The fear gripping me, and no doubt terrifying Milo and Maria, was of dropping one of their children. But without the pull of gravity, holding another person, even at a deadly height above ground, requires almost no effort. Strain and strength hardly matter.

I didn't tell them that.

The first of the men pursuing us poked his head over the edge of the roof, forty feet below. Military crew cut. Murder in his dark eyes. He reached for the next segment of ladder and heaved himself up.

"Stay close and hold each other," I instructed them. "If you let go, you will fall. And I can do nothing to stop you."

Maria buried her face in Milo's chest. He stretched his hands around her and the children between them. I wrapped my arms around the human bundle.

I shoved the levers against the stops.

FWOOOMP!

I heard gasps and felt tremors.

"What's your name? Your last name?" I asked, hoping to calm everyone with pedestrian conversation.

"O'Brien," Milo replied.

"You're kidding me."

"*Mi bisabuelo*—my great grandfather—he came from Galway. Everyone thinks it's funny," he said. He added, "I thought you were all-knowing."

"Don't push it. Okay, O'Brien family. Here we go."

Five minutes later the toddler chanted the names of fairies as we followed the steady hum of my BLASTER across the rooftops of Juárez. Behind us, a squad of armed men completed their climb to an empty water tower catwalk.

I STRUCK upon the idea of finding a church, preferably a Catholic church, as a temporary shelter after hearing Maria's nonstop Hail Mary prayer during the flight across the two cities. Her pleas to God were interrupted only briefly when the smaller child cried out several times.

"*Somos hadas! Somos hadas! Como Tinkerbell y Rosetta y Fawn!*"

His parents shushed him, but their admonishment didn't take. Over and over, he called for them to *Mira! Mira!* what he was seeing and then he called out more names. Maria seemed to accept that the miracle of their salvation sprang from the Bible, but their toddler son clearly assumed he sailed over rooftops courtesy of Walt Disney.

I spotted a church near the airport. A neon cross on a steeple that needed paint called out like a landing beacon. The peaked-roofed building sat on a narrow lane beyond the fringe of El Paso suburban sprawl, where lots grew larger, building codes grew lax, and the carcasses of dead or dying vehicles decayed in dry dirt yards guarded by old washing machines, tilted sheds and indispensable junk.

I landed on sagging wooden steps in front of the small white building and was surprised to find a CLOSED sign below another sign that said, *Saint Rupert Design and Arts*. The sign explained the array of metal sculptures, windmills, garden statues and planters in the front yard.

Not a church, then. It would have to do.

I confirmed that my passengers had their feet on the boards before I released them. Even so, the O'Briens wobbled when they reappeared, as if stepping onto ice.

I remained unseen.

The dual front doors were locked. I looked for signs of an alarm or security system; I found no wires, no keypad, no sticker warning of rapid response. I made short work of the deadbolt, which tumbled and clattered on the dry wood. My escapees slipped into the dark vestibule. Inside, distant suburban light poured a weak glow through twin rows of tall windows. Shelves and cabinets stood where pews once seated the pious.

"Wait here," I instructed them. I grabbed Milo's wrist and read the time on his gaudy, bloated watch. Not quite ten on a Sunday night. Saint Rupert probably would not make an appearance for another eight or ten hours. Plenty of time. "The Americans will come for you. Soon. Don't leave."

"Border Patrol?" Worry etched itself in bold on Milo's misshapen face. "No! They have no secrets from Señor Sergei."

"Not Border Patrol. Or ICE. The man who will come for you is with the FBI. Tell him everything you told me. Every detail."

Milo shook his head, doubting, but said nothing. Maria, however, begged to know.

"He will protect us?"

"If you are truthful," I said. "One more thing. The FBI isn't on the same footing with God as you are. Telling them how you came to be here will hurt you more than help you."

Milo seemed to understand the transactional nature of their future.

"I suppose," he said, "I can find a way to tell them how we crossed. It is, after all, my profession."

"Was."

He said nothing.

"He would have killed you," I reminded him. "Sergei."

Milo nodded but held his tongue.

"*Gracias, Mano de Dios!*" Maria said.

"*Y por hadas,*" I said to the little one. "Stay here."

I slipped out and left them to find scant comfort in God's former house.

48

"Let me meet you."

"No," Andy replied.

"Let me at least escort you. Tell me where you are."

"I have no idea where we are. We're off-road and driving without lights. Will, I told you, I'm fine. We'll be there in…what?" I heard Mike Horowitz tell Andy forty minutes. "In forty minutes. What was the name again?"

"Saint Rupert's Art Gallery, er, something like that."

"We can Google it. I love you. Stop calling me."

Andy ended the call.

I stood in fresh silence under an absurdly large, star-packed sky on a patch of what a Wisconsin kid like me would call desert. More likely, it was just an empty dirt lot behind Saint Rupert's junk-filled backyard. As the dimensions of Rupert's collection revealed itself to my night vision, I began to wonder how I ever mistook the place for a church—steeple and neon cross notwithstanding. Hulking metal sculptures and piles of twisted debris surrounded me.

"I'm not calling you," I told my disconnected phone. "Not that much. A couple times." I had called three times to check on her progress.

On my first call, Andy and Mike were still navigating the northwest fringes of Juárez through neighborhoods ruled by street gangs. She told me Mike had her curled up on the passenger-side floorboards with an old jacket over her head. Mike, she said, had no intention of crossing the Bridge of Americas.

On my second call, I gave her the name of the rendezvous point. She reported sitting up in the cab and told me they had gone off-road and would soon cross the border. I asked how they planned to get through the border wall. She relayed the question. Over the unhealthy sound of the pickup's motor I heard Mike laughing as Andy ended the call.

On my third call, she reported that they were on U.S. soil. She gave me the forty-minute estimate.

"Okay, maybe that was a little clingy," I admitted since no one could hear me.

I lowered my phone. The screen cast a blue glow at my feet where something black and hairy the size of my hand crawled past my boot.

"JESUS CHRIST!"

Fwooomp!

I kicked the dirt and shot into the air shaking my arms and legs and slapping myself. Several hundred feet above the church-gallery-junkyard I finally stopped beating away imaginary spiders and pulled out my BLASTER to arrest the ascent.

I decided to float above the building while I waited.

H<small>EADLIGHTS SWEPT</small> the barren landscape half a mile away, then settled on the narrow lane leading to the church. I had just repositioned a few hundred yards south of the building. An annoying southerly breeze kept nudging me in the direction of Canada, calling for adjustment every five or ten minutes, which threatened to use the last of the handheld unit's power. Glad to end the wait, I navigated to the front of the church where I planned to meet Andy. Warmly.

Donaldson piloted his rented Nissan to a gritty halt. I checked the road for a second set of headlights and saw none. I had not expected or wanted him to arrive first. Suppressing my disappointment and expecting that voices outside the church door might be unnerving to Milo and family, I pushed off the porch and performed a short glide to the gate. After twisting myself over the gate, I popped back into sight near the rear fender of the car just as Donaldson stepped out.

"Man, don't do that!" he froze at the sight of me. "Get yourself shot."

I double-checked the dirt and gravel at my feet.

"Drop something?" he asked.

"No. There are goddamned spiders here the size of Volkswagens."

"Tarantulas. Forget about them. They're harmless. So, who are these people? Are they inside?" He gestured at the church.

"How do you know about them? For that matter—how did you know to come here?"

"Your wife called me. She told me we had guests. I gotta say, I'm not pleased that she decided to go Rambo down there."

"And I gotta say—where the hell were you when the shit hit the fan? I thought you were crossing over to have our backs."

"I did. I completely had your backs. I crossed at the bridge and immediately got hauled in by the Mexican authorities."

"You were never there?"

"Hell, no. I've been a guest of my fellow law enforcement professionals all day. So was the team sent to keep an eye on McCauley. Exactly as planned."

"Oh." My anger faded, extinguished by clarity. "I get it. Mike was the backup. You were the clumsy and obvious and easily intercepted FBI investigator who made them think they outsmarted us. You could have said something."

"To be clear, the other team were the clumsy obvious ones. I was the too-clever-for-our-own-good ace in the hole they could feel smug about catching—which let them lower their guard for you. Your turn. What the hell happened over there? What about McCauley? And what in God's name did you blow up?"

I gave him the short version. I explained who Milo and Maria were to Sergei Roane. Donaldson recognized Milo's name.

"O'Brien. No kidding." He seemed impressed.

I explained about Sergei's wife, but said nothing about recognizing her.

"So," Donaldson mused, "Sergei's wife might be able to finger him for Lindsay's murder. I take it back. You did better than I thought."

A new set of headlights turned toward us. I recognized the wheezing sound of Mike Horowitz's pickup truck.

Donaldson asked, "Wait a minute. You brought his whole family over? They know about you?"

"Not really. They never saw me. I told them God sent me."

He chuckled. "How'd they like the ride?"

"They thought it was magical. Listen, I told them they would be safe."

"Might have been a promise you—or God—can't keep."

"Hey, if that's how it is, I'll take them out of here myself. I mean it."

"Relax, cowboy," he said.

"I'm serious. Milo warned me that handing him over to Border Patrol or ICE was a death sentence. I promised him the FBI would protect him and his family. You have to pull strings and get them into protective custody."

Donaldson frowned. "I gotta think about that."

I didn't like the answer and he didn't explain. Several hundred yards away, Horowitz killed the headlights on the pickup. The truck rolled to a stop behind Donaldson's car. Horowitz slid sideways out of the cab and hit the ground dressed in a paint-stained pair of bib overalls that exaggerated his oval shape. Between the truck and the get-up, I understood how he had mastered his own version of vanishing on the streets of Juárez.

I hurried between the two vehicles to meet Andy. We stole a much-needed private moment while the two federal agents exchanged pleasantries and tried to ignore our public display of affection.

I held her tightly. "Let's not do that again," I whispered into her hair.

"I'm okay with that. Where are they?" She looked at the building.

"Inside. Listen," I leaned close. "I need to talk to you. Without Donaldson."

I felt Andy's posture shift.

"Your lady detective refuses to say how she managed to get in," Horowitz said as he and Donaldson joined us, stealing the moment. "Are you going to stonewall me, too?"

"Need to know," Donaldson said.

"Yeah, that's a crock. You're pissing in my backyard here." He pointed at me. "And what the hell is he doing here?"

"Easy, Mike. I called him and asked him to babysit our witnesses," Donaldson lied.

Horowitz glanced at the church. "These are the people you rescued from Sergei?"

"Yes," Andy replied. I wondered what story she had told the DEA agent.

"How the hell did they get here ahead of us?" he asked.

"Mike, c'mon. It's Milo O'Brien."

"No shit? Milo O'Brien?"

"Yeah. The guy's a coyote legend. He probably flew across."

Horowitz ignored Donaldson's grin and considered the news. "O'Brien, huh. Management. Not that Sergei Roane ever needs an excuse, but why was he about to turn one of his trusted lieutenants and his family into human piñatas? Was he one of yours?"

"No. But a few minutes ago, I had a chat with him." Donaldson lied. He sketched what I had told him about Sergei Roane's wife. Horowitz hung on every word.

"Damn," Horowitz said when Donaldson finished. "Mitchell Lindsay. Roane will go out of his mind. Losing his wife *and* O'Brien and coming up as the prime suspect for Lindsay. That's gotta sting. I want a crack at O'Brien. You owe me that much, Lee."

"I'll go you one better. I want you to take them. You always keep a couple safe houses in your back pocket. Off DEA books. I want to turn O'Brien and his family over to you. Just you."

Horowitz hesitated. "Why do I feel like you just asked me to bend over and pick up the soap?" He glanced at Andy. "Sorry. Why do I feel what I'm feeling? You want McCauley for Lindsay's murder. O'Brien's wife—she's the connection to Lindsay you've been after. Why aren't you jumping for joy and hauling them up your chain of command?"

Donaldson scraped a shoe in the gravel and looked in the general direction of Juárez. Against the night sky, a pillar of black smoke reflected city light.

"I told you. McCauley has a guardian angel. Someone who is keeping the heat off him."

"You can't be serious! C'mon, Lee. That's conspiracy theory crap."

"The guys they sent down here to keep an eye on him? I met them. Decent agents, but B team at best. They told me DOJ put McCauley on the backburner. The terrorist angle has everyone wetting their pants."

"But now you have your proof. You can put the investigation on the right track," Horowitz said.

"What I have is second-hand hearsay that the right track exists. If I take this to the investigation now—it gets filed away. Or worse, it gets back to Sergei and puts Milo and his family in serious jeopardy."

Horowitz pointed at Andy. "Are you seriously not gonna tell me how she got in?"

"I posed as a high-priced call girl from a D.C. madam McCauley uses. I came down here on special order."

Horowitz looked at Andy in the dark. If his cheeks reddened, it was impossible to tell.

"Fine. If you're going to BS me, I'd rather you just didn't say anything."

Andy laughed. "Agreed."

"I'll take 'em," he said to Donaldson. "I got a place. But a deal's a deal. I get full access to O'Brien."

"Talk all you want with him. Lemme have a word with him first."

49

Donaldson spent half an hour with Milo. Andy tagged along. Horowitz hung back, not wanting to overwhelm the subjects, he said, or be present in case Donaldson needed to become threatening. I suspected Horowitz had his own interrogation in mind and didn't want Donaldson taking notes.

Horowitz and I made small talk while I watched the ground around my feet. I was surprised, and not surprised at the same time, to discover that Horowitz knew about my accident and the miracle of my survival. He asked a few questions, probing politely. I told him what I could, which is never much. Like most people who bring it up with me, he expressed amazement that I fell from a disintegrated airplane and lived.

Horowitz asked questions about Andy, but not the questions I expected. I thought he might try to probe me about her infiltration of the cartel headquarters. Instead, he asked about her background, about her role in the Clayton Johns arrest, and the Olivia Brogan arrest before that. I searched his unassuming mild mannerisms and polite demeanor for something ulterior beneath the surface. If it existed, I failed to see it. His questions seemed buoyed by genuine respect.

When Andy and Donaldson emerged from the church building, they ushered the small family to Horowitz's truck. Quick introductions were made. I drifted as far away as possible. I didn't wish to be introduced or prompted to speak; I didn't want Milo or Maria to hear the sound of my voice. Milo spared me a suspicious glance, nonetheless.

On parting, Andy received an abrupt hug from Maria who recognized my wife from the bunker. Tears came. I wondered if Maria shed tears out of gratitude or out of regret for the utter destruction of the life she had known. I wondered if Milo, a professional human trafficker, understood the irony of his situation.

Horowitz packed them into the cab of his truck and motored away.

"Are we done?" I asked. "Because I'm beat."

"Let's get back to the hotel. I've got calls to make," Donaldson said.

"OKAY, WHAT'S THE BIG SECRET?" Andy asked the moment I closed the hotel room door behind me.

Donaldson's room being directly beside ours prompted me to put a finger to my lips, which bought me an eye roll. I listened for sounds from the room next door.

"What *are* you doing?"

"Shhhhhh." I heard nothing. I turned to Andy and whispered, "Are you hungry?"

She looked at her watch. "Will, it's after midnight."

"Let's go down to the bar. Maybe the kitchen is still open."

"I really don't want to eat anything heavy at this hour."

"Come on." I took her hand and pulled her toward the door. "I'd rather not talk here."

BLESSED WITH GOOD LUCK, both the bar and kitchen were open. Andy and I settled on a pair of stools well segregated from a thinning bar crowd. Andy took the seat she favors, facing the entrance. We ordered a set of Coronas and asked for menus, which the young bartender quickly produced.

We tapped down our limes and raised the cold bottles.

"Us," she said. I echoed it. We drank. "Darling, you know I love you without the cloak and dagger. Although you would look good in a tux."

I pulled the photocopy from my back pocket, unfolded it, and held it up. She recognized the sheet of paper from Sergei's assault on Milo in the bunker. Now she narrowed her gaze at the family in the photo.

"Is that her? Sergei's wife?"

"Yes," I said. "You know who else that is?"

Andy blinked her negative response at me.

"That's Gloria Rilling."

Oh, if only I could bottle and keep the moments when I genuinely surprise and impress my wife.

"That's Lonnie Penn's daughter."

ANDY NEEDED a minute to send runners of thought in the new directions revealed by this development. She arrived at the conclusion that I had reached several hours ago.

"There is no way under heaven or on earth that this is a coincidence," Andy announced. Detective Andrea Katherine Taylor Stewart would leave sandwiches in our backyard for Bigfoot before she would tolerate coincidence in a police investigation.

"Exactly!" I slugged down some cold beer.

She plucked the photocopy from my fingers and stared deeply into it, as if searching each bleached fiber of the paper.

Her intense gaze shifted to me. She squinted, issuing an unasked question.

"I know," I said. "I need to talk to Earl."

"When he asked you to go and meet Lonnie Penn, did he give you any indication that someone put him up to it?"

"He said the client asked for me." Andy considered this. I hadn't mentioned it at the time, thinking it had to do with my fleeting fame. Now I wondered. "How did she know about me?"

"Lindsay," she said. She sat back on her stool and took a hit from the condensation-coated bottle. "But..." she stopped and thought for a moment. "No. Impossible."

"Not so much. Do you remember just before he left for his meeting with McCauley? Do you remember him taking me out on the porch for a word? You never asked me what he said."

"I expected you would eventually tell me. Of course, I forgot all about it after everything that happened. What did he say to you?"

"He said he wanted to talk later. About Prince Henry. South Dakota."

"What?"

"*He knew.*"

The bartender intruded and asked if we'd made a selection. I ordered enchiladas for both of us.

After the bartender carried off our menus and I finished off the first third of my beer, Andy asked, "How on earth does that connect? We only met Lindsay three weeks ago. How do you connect dots between Sergei Roane's wife, Lonnie Penn, Earl Jackson and then get to you?"

"I give up. How?"

She frowned at me. "We need to talk to Earl."

"Okay." I looked at my watch. "Let's call him. Right now. And by 'let's' I mean you. He won't reach through the phone line and throttle you."

"Just…just…" She held up a hand. Andy's hesitation wasn't fear of Earl Jackson. If anyone could call Earl in the middle of the night without causing him to register on a Richter Scale, it was Andy. Earl loves her.

She took a minute to think. I exploited the opening.

"We have to ask another question here."

"What's that?"

I swallowed. Hesitated. She instantly read the reluctance and fixed a relentless stare on me.

"Donaldson," I said. "What if…?"

The stare grew hard. "Will, not this again. Hasn't the man proven himself enough?"

"Dee, hear me out. It was Donaldson who insisted you—we—run from the FBI on the island. He's the one pushing us off the grid. He's the one that brought us here. I don't know…what if—?"

"What if the good guy is really the bad guy? What if the trusted cop is really the cartel mole? What if the buddy cop partner turns out to be the one on the mobster's payroll? Oh—my—god!"

I shrugged. "Okay. I get it."

"Every bad cop movie you've ever made me watch, dear."

"I know, I know," I conceded. "Then why wasn't he there for us today?"

"Because it was the plan."

"That's what he said."

"Because it was the plan."

"You knew he was going to be detained?"

"Lord, Will, he *planned on it.* I didn't know about Mike, but yes, Lee told me they would grab him the minute he crossed over. So much the better for us."

"Well, I guess you might have mentioned it."

I expected immediate pushback. That it was her profession, not mine. That this was still a criminal investigation. That she might call *Usual Disclaimer* and share details about her work, but it didn't mean she had an obligation to share every detail—because her work was *her* work.

None of it came. Instead she dropped her long lashes and put a hand on my arm.

"I know. I should have," she said, knocking the argument out from under me. "We're a team."

"Well, okay then." I wasn't finished. "Why didn't he take Milo and Maria to the FBI? Why didn't he let you take them in? Think about it, Dee. Walking into the FBI offices with those two completely exonerates your involvement in all this."

"It's not about me."

"No, but it's about the entire investigation hauling ass down the wrong rabbit hole. They're off chasing terrorist gold miners from Africa—which is about as far-fetched as it gets—while McCauley is down here schmoozing with the cartel boss who killed Lindsay."

Her head cocked on an angle that signaled an abrupt change of direction.

"Did they look like they were schmoozing to you?" she asked.

"You mean, like, socializing? Dee, they were about to torture and murder two children in front of their parents. Not exactly game night among friends."

She shook her head. "No. Not that part. I mean, McCauley. He's been...I don't know...bossy."

"Yeah. So?"

"So, that's not the typical dynamic around cartel chiefs. That will get you killed in this company. And speaking of company, did you get a good look at the third man?"

"Tall. Black man. Military type?"

"I got the military vibe from him, too. I also got his picture."

"We need to get someone to examine that photo."

She gave me a feline smile. "I already did. I sent the whole batch to Horowitz."

"Horowitz? Dee, what if he's...?"

"Oh, Lord, stop it. Him, too? Mike is not the friendly, trusted cop who came to the rescue who turns out in the end to be the bad guy, either. Besides, I kept a copy. I sent them to Horowitz because Lee asked me to."

"Why?"

"He wanted it run through an agency that isn't currently fixated on a terrorist attack."

"Why?"

"Because he doesn't believe it. Neither do I. And today we found a witness who can confirm that belief."

I folded the photocopy and delivered it into police custody. Andy pushed it into her bag. She looked up at me.

"Honey, you can't still have doubts about Lee. When would he have had time to become the minion of a Brazilian cartel boss working for a Russian oligarch in Mexico? The man was in a rehabilitation hospital until a few weeks ago and he's been with us practically ever since."

I shrugged.

"Will, if you doubt him, then why don't you do the one thing nobody in your stupid cop movies ever does?" A dimple appeared, warning me.

"What?"

"Ask him, silly." A second dimple appeared.

"Ask me what?" Donaldson's hand dropped on my shoulder and I nearly jumped off the barstool. He looked at Andy's now full-blown smile and at my startled expression. "What?"

"Will wants to know if you're the bad cop in the movie."

"Yup. That's me," he said. He waved at the bartender for a Corona to match ours, then slid onto the stool beside me. "In deep with the bookies. Wife living beyond our means. Bought a seven-figure house on an FBI agent's salary. Addicted to oxy. They took my badge and gun and gave me twenty-four hours to solve the case. Listen, I hate to break up movie trivia night, but I made some calls. Guess who Sergei Roane's wife is."

"Gloria Rilling," Andy and I said together. I added, "Lonnie Penn's daughter."

The look on his face paid dividends. The dividends doubled when I said, "And I know where to pick up her trail."

50

We talked for another hour before leaving the bar. I explained how we had arrived at the identity of Sergei Roane's wife before he did by sharing the story of my trip to South Dakota with one of the Hollywood elite. Donaldson interrupted often, peppering me with questions. The one that seemed to concern him most came at the point in the tale where I met Lonnie Penn in LaCrosse. He clamped a grip on my arm and leaned toward me.

"Don't lie to me," he snapped. "I have to know. Is she as hot as she looks onscreen? Or is it all lights, makeup and CGI?"

Andy turned on her stool to face me. She folded her arms across her chest.

"Yes, Will. Do tell."

"Okay," I said. I took a moment to finish off my beer and consider my words—potentially my last words—carefully. The bartender lifted his eyebrows at me. I waved off a second. "God's honest truth, Lee, I have no idea. I just don't notice other women."

I turned and collected the kiss I had coming.

None of us had a viable theory as to why Gloria Rilling had popped into my life twice within a week, or why FBI Deputy Director Mitchell Lindsay's final words to me warned that he wanted to talk to me about a woman on the run from the man who more than likely murdered him.

"We need to talk to your boss, Jackson," Donaldson agreed. "And we need to talk to Lonnie Penn."

Andy and I agreed but argued that the middle of the night wasn't the time to start ringing phones. We paid the tab and arranged to meet Donaldson in the lobby at ten in the morning. He muttered about being anxious to join the hunt for Gloria Rilling. I told him the hunt wasn't going anywhere until I got some sleep.

51

Earl picked up on the second ring. Andy and I stood in the shade of an air museum hangar at the airport. It was all I could do not to wander off and look at the World War II airplanes parked inside.

"This better not be a goddamned robot call. If it is, I'm coming for you, swear on my mother's grave."

"It's Will."

"Will? What the hell number are you calling me from?"

"Burner phone."

"You're lucky I picked it up. I'm telling you—I get one more of those damn calls I'm going to grind up my phone and jam the shards down the throat of the first telemarketer I can find. What's up?"

"Why did you send me to handle that deal with Lonnie Penn?"

"Told you. She asked for you. I would'a done it, but my knee was all swolled up."

"How's the knee now?"

"Rosemary II drove me to see the doc and get shots. I can walk on it again. Why?"

"Just asking. So, did she say why? Lonnie Penn?"

Earl didn't say anything for a second or two, then lowered his voice. "You ain't getting any ideas, are you son? Because your wife—"

Andy, who could hear Earl despite the call not being on speaker, smirked.

"No! No, nothing like that. It came up in Andy's investigation."

"What investigation?"

Her smirk turned to a grimace and she waved her hands at me.

"She won't say. But no, Earl, I don't have a thing for Lonnie Penn. Lovely woman, I'm sure, but—"

"Because I will kick your ass."

"Andy will be pleased to hear it. That said, do you have Lonnie Penn's personal number?"

"Goddammit, this is what I'm talking about."

"I'm not looking for a date, Earl! Here! Talk to Andy!" I almost threw the phone at her.

"Hi, Earl," she said sweetly. "It's fine. I need to speak to her about something I'm working on...yes, I think so, too...no, I'm keeping an eye on him. He knows how lucky he is...aww...thank you...okay, hold on!" She tucked the phone against her shoulder and pulled out a pen. She grabbed my hand to write on my palm. "Ready..." she wrote down the number and read it back to him. "Uh-huh...I'll tell him. Thank you, so much...Uh-huh...yes, that would probably hurt...okay, bye."

She handed me my phone.

"He's such a sweetheart, offering to murder you like that."

"You forget. I worked for him. I heard that every day."

Lonnie Penn did not answer. After half a dozen rings, a machine voice advised that the person at this number was not available and that I could leave a message at the sound of the tone.

"Miss Penn, this is Will Stewart. We met in LaCrosse. I was the pilot. I need to speak to you. Please call me at this number. I was wrong about your daughter and grandson. There's a chance they are in some...danger..." Andy winced and shook her head at me. "Please call me. I'm heading for Prince Henry now. It's urgent."

I ran out of ideas and ended the call.

"You sounded like you were trying to con her," Andy said.

"Then she definitely won't call. That's already been done."

El Paso to Prince Henry flight-planned at just under nine hundred miles. The new Navajo had the legs to make the trip, but Andy's bladder did not, and fuel consumption would leave less than legal reserves on arrival. I laid out a two-leg trip, with a stop at McCook Regional Airport in McCook, Nebraska. At the midpoint stop I suggested taking the airport courtesy car to get some food, but Andy and Donaldson pressed for a fast turnaround. The fuel truck topped us off and we were on our way quickly.

A little before four p.m. I kissed the wheels to the familiar pavement of Prince Henry's single runway and taxied to the gas pump.

"There's our ride," I said, pointing at the old blue Chevy van.

It still smelled like pizza.

52

"Why are we stopping here?" Andy asked.

"Because I'm starving, and this place makes a great burger." I rolled the van to a stop in front of the White Bluff Motel café, joining a row of parked cars, SUVs and pickups. Business for the early dinner hour looked good. I glanced up at the motel room where Lonnie Penn lost her half million and where I had tossed a large man over the railing onto the windshield of his Dodge Ram pickup. The truck was long gone, and the closed room door upstairs sealed in its secrets.

I took it as a lucky omen to be seated in the same booth I had occupied with Lonnie Penn. Restaurant patrons filled roughly one quarter of the available seating. Two teenaged girls dressed in jeans and t-shirts worked the tables. Their rapid navigation to and from the kitchen distinguished them as staff. I looked through the gap between the front counter and the kitchen to see if the same cook worked the griddle. He did.

We ordered coffee all around to get the neurons firing again after an afternoon of flying. The waitress produced mugs and poured. The brew was decent, though not quite as good as I remembered. We placed a unanimous order for cheeseburgers.

Andy and Donaldson engaged in a low-volume conversation about the best way to locate the ICE officer who handled custody of Gloria Rilling and her son. Donaldson advocated for the FBI to take the lead and go directly to the commander of the ICE unit, being federal siblings. He argued for a full-frontal charge with accusations flying. Andy preferred a quiet approach to the county sheriff, relying on the fellowship of local law enforcement, and not steam rolling him with Donaldson's federal credentials. The verbal contest continued until the food arrived. I looked up to see the cook himself carrying three plates on his wiry forearms.

He slid the plates onto the table, then stood back and examined Andy.

"This fella's been in here twice in one week with two of the most beautiful women I ever laid eyes on," he said to her, earning a smile. "Miss, you blink three times if you're here against your will."

Andy laughed and held up her left hand, displaying her modest diamond. "Strictly voluntary."

"Well, then maybe I shouldn't'a mentioned t'other one," he said. "Folks stayin' at the motel?"

"Just dinner," Donaldson replied.

"Well, 'njoy. Holler if you need anything." He drank in one more appraisal of Andy, then gave me a nod that felt like a blessing.

"Got any mustard?" Donaldson asked.

"No."

THE BURGER WAS BETTER than I remembered. After a couple days of sporadic dining, the meals hit the spot. I finished first and slipped out of the booth while Andy and Donaldson resumed their strategy discussion.

Our teenaged waitress gave me a glance but said nothing when I edged my way through the gap in the counter and slipped into the kitchen. The cook worked at a flattop grille full of sizzling meat. An unlit cigarette dangled from his lips. He didn't seem surprised to see me.

"Thought maybe if you stayed, I'd get to see you toss another fella off the balcony. Maybe that cop you're with out there."

"He's federal."

The cook glanced in Donaldson's direction and nodded. "Yeah. I guess he is."

"You thought it was funny," I said, "when I asked you about law enforcement around here."

"It was. What with you trying to evade two of them."

"Yeah, I figured that out. The one I threw off the balcony. You know him?"

"I know 'em all. Hell, I know ever'body." He took a moment to slap a cooked patty on a bun and spin the plate around for a load of fries. The plate went up to the service window. He tapped a bell and returned to his griddle.

"Found it int'resting you didn't get hauled off in handcuffs. Them boys didn't stick around."

"Deputies?"

"One of 'em. T'other works for the ICE. You wouldn't think you'd find 'em around here, but Prince Henry is some kinda immigration enforcement hub."

"Which one did I toss?"

"Deputy Arvin Tolliver. That was a piece of work. He's a big man."

"He a good man?"

The cook gave it some thought as he plopped fresh meat on the hot steel. "Doesn't hassle the kids who party here on prom weekend, if that counts. Otherwise, I don't bother him, and he doesn't grabass m' girls out front. If that makes a man good."

"I thought I might stop and see how he's doing. You wouldn't happen to know where he lives, would you?"

Something about the cooking process became intensely interesting to the man. He said nothing while meat sizzled. His metal spatula scraped and arranged the fixings. I wondered if I might have asked too much.

"You know," he said, "t'other one, the ICE fella, I think his name is Schiff, er Schultz, er something like that—no, it's Schmidt, yeah, that's it—it sure looked like he left here with a satchel that belonged to Miss Penn. Did you notice that?"

"You don't miss much."

"Might that be summin' you're lookin' to get back?"

"Might be."

He picked up two eggs and with one hand, cracked and spilled them onto the griddle without fracturing the yolks.

"That gal makes some great movies," he said. He pulled a small notebook from an apron pocket and a pen from his shirt pocket. He scribbled a few lines and pocketed the pen.

He tore off the page and handed it to me.

53

"Here. Turn here," Donaldson leaned between the two front seats and pointed at a narrow driveway that rose to a freestanding one-car garage beside a small ranch-style house. The cook's directions gave the name of a county road and said to look for a pink house a mile west of another county road. The house had faded pinkish siding with white trim and sat alone on the side of a narrow, straight county highway. Farm fields sprawled in all four directions in varying states of late summer harvest.

I smelled freshly cut grass as soon as I stepped out of the van. The shaved lawn accounted for the sweet scent.

"He's in back," I told Andy who started up a cement sidewalk toward the front door. I pointed.

A cloud of white smoke rose from the backyard. I smelled steaks on a barbecue.

"You should wait here," she said.

"Agreed," Donaldson added. "We'll put the fear of the federal god in him." He slid past Andy and led the way between the garage and the house, leaving me at the van. Andy glanced back at me and shrugged.

I waited for them to make the corner.

Fwooomp!

I carried a freshly charged power unit in a cargo pocket but opted for hand over hand navigation via the gutter attached to the garage roof. I reached the backyard just as Andy and Donaldson stopped on a brick patio facing a tall man.

It was him. The same man who climbed the side stairs at the motel to find Lonnie Penn waiting. The same man I threw off the balcony. I wondered if his truck was in the garage or the body shop. I also wondered if his hand matched the imprint in Lonnie's bruised skin.

"Deputy Tolliver?" Andy asked.

He turned from his smoldering grille, holding a set of tongs in hand. His overall dark chocolate complexion stood out against a white t-shirt topping gray work pants. A corset-like device over the shirt cinched his ribcage. When he turned, he used his whole body, moving stiffly and carefully, the way someone moves when sharp pain rewards the wrong move. Several days' beard stubble blackened his cheeks and chin, although shaving had to be a challenge. Pockmarks and divots marred his face.

Donaldson held up his badge folder. "Stewart and Donaldson, FBI. She's Stewart."

"Hello, FBI," Tolliver said. "What can I do for you here in my backyard, you showing up uninvited and without a warrant and all?"

"Are you here alone, Deputy?" Andy asked.

"And you two makes three. Gonna tell me what this is about?"

Andy took a fearless step closer to a man easily a foot taller and a hundred pounds heavier. Tolliver's arms bulged with muscles.

"We're here about the incident that led to your injury last week. We—"

Donaldson interrupted. "This afternoon we arrested Schmidt and Mallorin in connection with the extortion of half a million dollars from the film star, Lonnie Penn. They named you as their leader and gave us information that you also kidnapped a woman named Gloria Rilling and her male child. We're here to arrest you, Deputy Tolliver."

The man did not flinch. He ran his eyes up and down Andy in a way I did not appreciate, then glanced at Donaldson who stood with his hand on the butt of his holstered weapon.

"Arrested, you say? This afternoon? Right here in Prince Henry? Did those boys put up a fight?"

Neither Andy nor Donaldson answered. Tolliver knew the game and played it well. He said nothing. The hint of a smile pulled at the corners of his mouth.

"Deputy put down the tongs and place your hands behind your back," Andy said.

He ignored her. "This afternoon? Both of them?"

"Hands behind your back," she repeated.

"Because Tony's fishing up at Red Deer and I just got off the phone with Trace. Maybe you want to polish up your story a bit?" He turned and used the tongs to flip a slab of steak on the grill. A fresh cloud of white smoke boiled up over the sizzle. "Who are you really?"

"Where is Gloria Rilling?" Donaldson asked.

"I don't know any goddamned Gloria Rilling."

"Yes, you do," Andy said. "You know her as Lonnie Penn's daughter."

"Who the hell is Lonnie Penn?"

"Yeah, now I know you're lying," Donaldson said. Tolliver smirked.

"Mallorin told Penn she traveled under the name Mira Apalacio. She had a child with her. A boy about three."

"I remember Mallorin mentioning a kid. Huey. Husty. Something. Kid was all alone, if I recall. Sad. These people come across and don't give a shit what happens to their kids."

Donaldson eased past Andy and approached Tolliver, tapping his cane on the patio blocks. The big man ignored him.

"How'd you get hurt?" Donaldson asked. "On the job?"

"Got hurt over in go fuck yourself."

"Cute," Donaldson said, casually lifting his cane and changing his grip. Almost too quickly to follow, he leveled the cane and jabbed it forward, poking Tolliver in the rib cage.

The big man gasped and dropped to his knees. He gripped the gas grill, but being mounted on wheels, it shot away across the bricks. Tolliver heaved for breath and moaned.

"Lee! No!" Andy grabbed Donaldson's arm as he drew back for another strike.

Between clenched teeth, Tolliver said, "You get that one for free. Now I'm gonna make you eat that stick."

Tolliver heaved himself to his feet, muscles corded against the pain. He turned slowly to face Andy and Donaldson.

"Deputy, you're in serious trouble," Andy said. "I apologize for my partner, but unless you come clean and cooperate, you're only going to make things worse for yourself."

Tolliver winced with each breath. Angry lines embossed his neck and forehead. He took a step toward Andy and towered over her. She stood fast. I formed a grip on the corner of the garage roof and positioned my feet against the wall, ready to launch myself at Tolliver if he lifted a hand against her.

"Like—I—said—go—fuck yourself," he muttered between short sharp breaths. "And if you need help, lemme know."

Donaldson adjusted his cane for another strike.

Andy put her hand out and pressed Donaldson to take a step back. She said, "We're leaving."

Donaldson and Tolliver traded hate-infused stares, then Donaldson broke the connection and turned his back. Andy followed.

I pushed myself down. She passed me. I leaned close and whispered, "Wait for me down the road."

A moment later, she started the van and backed out of the yard with Donaldson riding shotgun.

Tolliver maintained an upright posture until they rolled out of view. The instant the back of the van disappeared from his line of sight he doubled over and cried out in pain. He cursed and staggered to a plastic lawn chair. He leaned over gripping the arms, gasping.

He used his left hand to hold his ribcage. With his right, he fished for a phone in his pants pocket. He thumbed it to life and placed a call.

Someone answered. I pushed off the garage wall and floated slowly closer, drawing a power unit and fixing the blade in place.

"It's me," he wheezed. "Hell, no! I'm hurt! Shut up and listen. I just had two FBI agents here. Lonnie Penn sic'd 'em on my ass...Who else would it be?...They wanted to know what we did with the *chica* and her kid...No, goddammit! What do you think!" He squeezed against the pain and swore. "How the hell should I know? Just keep your head down and make sure nobody can find any of that money. I mean it, Trace. If you got it anywhere in the house, they'll find it...Yeah, that's probably okay...You gotta call Tony. Tell him to call Padd. I can't talk anymore."

He cut the call and dropped the phone to his side.

Padd. I had hoped for something more revealing.

I drifted closer. I tucked the BLASTER in my back pocket and reached out, aiming for his substantial bicep.

The instant I made contact—

FWOOOMP!

—I made him vanish. I heard him gasp for air. I felt his arm muscle turn to stone and jolt. I tightened my grip and lifted.

With both of us detached from gravity, my lifting action resulted in an equal and opposite reaction. He went up and I went down. I planted my feet. With resistance, I shoved him up and away—and released.

Fwooomp!

He reappeared. Shocked. Wide-eyed. Flailing in the air. He dropped, landed awkwardly, and tumbled over backward.

"MOTHERFAAAAH—!" He clutched his ribs and howled.

I used the BLASTER to maneuver to where he now lay on his lawn. Teeth clenched. Eyes clamped shut.

"That had to hurt," I said.

He swore.

I pulsed the power unit and dropped near his feet. With my left hand I closed a grip on his right ankle. He immediately tried to kick, but I was too fast.

FWOOOMP!

He vanished and his kicks became another Newtonian exercise in futility. I pushed off the grass and we rose. I felt him flailing. He cried out in pain. I let go.

Fwooomp!

He reappeared eighteen or twenty inches above the turf and dropped flat on his back.

"GAAAHHH! STOP! MOTHERF—STOP!"

Huge wet tears streaked from his eyes. He clenched both hands around his middle and curled his legs.

"Where did you send the girl and the child?"

"*Who are you? Whaddya want?!*"

"Answer my question or take another ride."

"NO! PLEASE!" he gasped and sputtered for breath, then abruptly turned his head and vomited. Retching ignited fresh jolts of pain up his midsection. He heaved, then groaned in pain, then heaved again. "*For the love of Christ! Stop!*"

"The girl and the child—where did you send them?"

"Mallorin took her! Mall—!" he abruptly heaved again. I waited. His muscles trembled. His skin glittered with sweat. He coughed up saliva that ran down his chin. New dry convulsions tore into his broken ribs and he cried out.

I almost felt bad for him.

It took several minutes for the cycle to stop. He lay on the ground clutching himself. He moaned and shivered. Not that it was easy to tell, but I came to realize he was crying.

I maneuvered closer to his head, curling my legs and powering down until my knees touched the grass. A grip on his head would probably work. I prepared for another round.

"They said you gave her back to the coyote. Who's the coyote?"

He lay with his eyes sealed. Ragged breath shot in and out of his mouth. Spittle and bile ran from the corners of his lips. My stomach turned when I caught a whiff.

"Who's the coyote?"

"Padd!"

"Explain that in detail or we go again, you understand? Don't make me drag it out of you."

He bobbed his head quickly. "*Alright! Alright! Just—gimme a—sec!*" He gasped for air in minimal breaths that stabbed him as his lungs pressed his ribs. "Paddington Trucking—in—Desmond. They run 'em all the way from Missouri—to Canada! Jesus! It was Padd turned her over to us! *That's it! Please! That's—all I know!*"

He sobbed. The man easily weighed two-twenty with most of it toned muscle. He lay on the ground weeping like a child.

"Was the girl in on it? The money! Was she in on it?"

He shook his head.

I said, "Mallorin told Penn her daughter was sick. Was she sick?"

He nodded. He stammered, "I—nuh-nuh-never—touched her! It wuh-wuh-was—Mallorin!"

"Mallorin? You mean he hurt her?"

He shook his head again. "No! Man, no—it was—he just—*you know*—I swear, I never touched her!"

I felt lightning flash down my arms, deep into my hands, into my fingertips. Raw anger.

I leaned closer.

"Do you know who that girl's husband is?"

"*What do I care?*"

I drew close to his ear.

"He's Sergei Roane, the enforcer for the Méndez Cartel. I'm going to make sure he knows who you are. *Who all of you are.*"

He wept. Each sob stabbed him. Agony wrote itself across his face. His mouth tried to make words but the sound coming out was barely human.

I grabbed the crown of his head.

FWOOOMP!

I uncoiled my legs and lifted him. He shrieked.

At eye level, I let him go.

His screams followed me over the sound of the BLASTER as I powered myself over his roof, over his front yard, over the narrow county road in the direction Andy had driven.

54

I used the short flight to the van to quell the murderous impulse charging through my veins. Half a mile down the country road, out of sight over a small hill, the blue van waited at the side of the road.

I dropped out of *the other thing* on the pavement behind the van. The sliding door on the driver's side wouldn't open. I jerked and swore and came close to punching the sheet metal on the old clunker.

Andy opened her window. "Go around to the other side." I made a point of not meeting her eyes.

Inside, I counted out several calming breaths, then relayed the details Tolliver had shared. Donaldson pulled out his phone and stroked the screen while I spoke. When I finished, he said, "Paddington Trucking is a milk hauling outfit. You sure that's what he said?"

I confirmed and described his mention of the name *Padd.*

Donaldson looked at Andy, "They're in Desmond, Minnesota."

"Desmond," Andy said.

"Yeah."

"What?" I asked.

"When we interviewed Milo, we asked him about coyote routes into Canada. They have half a dozen. Practically an underground railroad. Each one has a name, like a person's name," Andy said. "Desmond is one of them. I guess it's a town, not a person."

Andy started the engine and did a U-turn that would take us back to Prince Henry Airport.

55

Lonnie Penn sat beside an overstuffed backpack in fading golden hour light on the flight shack steps. Through Ray Ban Aviators, she watched us park the blue van. The long, dark hair was gone, replaced by her signature short blonde cut. She replicated what she wore when she met me on the ramp in LaCrosse—jeans and a leather jacket over a t-shirt.

"Is that—?" Andy asked, killing the ignition.

"Yup."

We climbed out of the van. I'm accustomed to the silence of small airports, but the sound of our feet on the gravel lot made our approach to her feel oddly self-conscious.

She jumped to her feet and held her phone out.

"You call me to tell me my daughter and grandson are in danger, and then you don't answer my calls?"

Oh crap. I instantly realized that I had set my phone ringer to mute during our escapades in Juárez. I fished the phone from my pocket and found the incriminating evidence, along with half a dozen missed calls.

"I'm sorry—uh, stupid of me—"

"I'm Andrea," Andy stepped ahead of me with a hand extended. "Detective Stewart, but you can call me Andy."

"Call me Lonnie. Please." She shook hands. "Wow. You live up to your photo—and it's an amazing photo."

Andy looked sideways at me, eyebrows raised. I felt blood tinting my cheeks. I pointed at my ear and said, "—without the Bluetooth ear thing—I couldn't hear—"

"This is FBI Special Agent Lee Donaldson," Andy said.

"Pleased to meet you, Miss Penn."

"Lonnie."

"Lee."

"Lee," she said. She turned to me, "What the hell, Will?"

"Good question," I said, regaining a shred of my wits. "And speaking of…you never mentioned that your daughter was married to Sergei Roane, who runs the Méndez Cartel in Juárez. Or that Roane is the boy's father."

Her jaw fell. She stepped back until her heels found the shack steps. She sat down shaking her head. If her surprise was an act, it was worthy of the Oscar on her shelf.

"What?"

"You seriously didn't know?"

"No, I seriously didn't know!"

"You also didn't mention that I was recommended to you by Deputy Director of the FBI, Mitchell Lindsay."

The jaw closed.

"How did you know Director Lindsay?" Andy asked.

"I swear to God I didn't know who the boy's father is. Not until this moment. My god—are you saying my daughter has something to do with the FBI Director being killed?"

"Deputy Director. And yeah, we are!"

"Will." Andy gave me a look.

"I should have known," Lonnie said, shaking her head. "I should have known."

"Known what?" Andy asked.

Lonnie heaved a sigh. "Director Lindsay called me several months ago. He wanted to know if I was in touch with my daughter. Which was a shock of its own. I thought it awfully damned personal of him—bringing up that chapter of my life. I thought someone put him up to it. I got a little angry about it."

"Go on," Andy said.

"He insisted it was an official inquiry, but he refused to explain. He asked me to contact his office if my daughter made contact. I was filming in London at the time—I don't know—I convinced myself it was just one of those blips on the celebrity radar. I get calls from law enforcement more often than you think."

"Then what happened?"

"Nothing. Nothing ever came of it. I mean—I had no connection to Gloria. Until all this happened. When I got the call about Gloria, I got a little frantic. I decided to go to the top. I called the director's office and he said he could help. He told me to call Mr. Jackson."

"I thought you knew Earl," I said.

She shook her head. "No. Director Lindsay told me he was pals with my dad, but I don't remember him. I guess it should have seemed weird to me that the FBI would refer me to a private individual—but look at the position I was in."

"And did he tell you to ask for Will Stewart?"

Lonnie sensed a trap in the question and hesitated, but then nodded.

Andy turned to me. "Lindsay started digging right away, Will—to learn everything he could about you. Right from New York."

"Great." I turned to Lonnie. "You're saying you didn't know Earl and you didn't know me?"

"I didn't know either of you. That's the truth. I thought Lindsay hooked me up with some mercenary, someone off the books. A lot of good it did." She looked up at me with a hint of familiar venom.

"And you swear you knew nothing about this?" Andy asked Donaldson.

He shook his head. "Sounds like the Director was testing you, Will. It also sounds like his interest in McCauley and the Roane family goes back."

Andy asked, "Lonnie, what are you doing here?"

"I can't sit on my ass in Malibu and do nothing."

"How did you get here?" I asked, noting that the Navajo rested alone on the ramp.

"Chartered jet. It dropped me off an hour ago. They told me my plane wouldn't fit on this runway. I've been calling nonstop. When I saw that airplane over there—I ran the tail number on Google and it came up registered to a foundation in Essex, Wisconsin—and what are the chances? The courtesy van was gone—I figured sooner or later you'd be back here."

"I didn't mean for you to come here," I said. "I just wanted to know about Lindsay."

"I don't care. You said she's in danger. I'm not leaving them. Not again. Where she is?"

"We don't know," Andy said.

"Are you trying to find her?"

"We are. But...Miss Penn..."

Donaldson interrupted. "Miss Penn, your daughter is, indeed, the wife of Sergei Roane who is more than likely responsible for the murder of Director Lindsay. She ran away from her husband for reasons of her own, but she took with her knowledge of the crime. For that reason, among others, he wants her back, and not in a good way. We have to find her before he does."

Lonnie stood quickly and heaved her backpack over one shoulder. "I'm coming with you."

"Will, a word?" Andy gestured for me to follow her. "Excuse us, please."

My wife led me away from Lonnie, across the expanse of ramp toward the parked Navajo.

"Don't look at me," I said. "This wasn't my idea."

"Lee knows about you. She doesn't. Taking her along might limit your use of *the other thing*. Or force you to reveal it to her. That's for starters. Then there's the fact that she's an A-list celebrity who is accustomed to having her way. This is not going to work."

"Agreed."

Andy stopped. "Agreed?"

"Yeah. I agree. Boot her out. Go ahead."

"Me? She's your passenger," Andy said. "You got her here."

"Excuse me," Lonnie said, jogging after us. "Andy, can I say something?"

Andy waited.

"I get it. I know what you're thinking. But let me ask you—are you a mother?"

"We don't have children," Andy answered curtly.

"But you hope to, right?"

"What's your point?"

"I'm not a mother either. I mean—physically, yes—but I'm not. I haven't been. But I hope to be. These last few days, the idea of it has been overwhelming. I can't think of anything else. I can hardly breathe. The possibility that I can be—I don't know how to let that go. I don't know how I can."

Andy frowned. Her posture said No.

"I'll do whatever you tell me," Lonnie promised. "Please."

"Oh, Lord," Andy said. Her posture shifted to Yes.

Lonnie lifted her face to the setting sun and closed her eyes. "Thank you."

"I want to gas up," I told Andy.

"Go ahead," Andy said. "I need to talk to Lee."

56

Something went wrong during the preflight. Not with the airplane. I moved the Navajo to the pumps and filled each tank, then performed a thorough walk-around, being only my fourth flight and knowing that problems hidden by a seller might take time to reveal themselves.

Whatever went wrong happened while Andy and Donaldson huddled near the shack. Donaldson spent a long time on the phone while Andy listened. I loaded Lonnie into the cabin and asked her to take the seat directly behind the pilot's seat—Andy's least favorite. I hoped to score a point or two with my wife by putting *the other woman* in this growing equation in a seat Andy did not favor.

Andy and Donaldson remained on the ramp.

While we waited, I worked up the flight plan. Desmond, Minnesota is a small town on the western fringe of the Ten Thousand Lakes region. The town sits within spitting distance of the North Dakota border. It has no airport of its own, but ten miles to the northwest, the town of Wahpeton, on the Dakota side of the border line, has the Harry Stern airport featuring a single concrete runway and a secondary grass runway.

Between glances at my wife and the FBI, I programmed the flight in the Garmin navigation system. A direct flight measured one hundred and forty miles, a short flight for the Navajo. The weather looked good. Southerly winds favored us. The sun was long gone, and the evening sky hung clear above us, promising a starlit flight. I elected to fly the direct route without filing a flight plan.

Lonnie asked what was taking so long. I told her I couldn't begin to guess.

Eventually the ramp conference broke up. Donaldson, looking shocked, dropped into the forward-facing seat on the right side of the plane. He stared blankly at the cabin floor. Andy latched the door and climbed into the copilot's seat.

She radiated *Something Wrong*. I might have concluded that she blamed me for Lonnie Penn's appearance and the woman's pressure to tag along, but this had much more weight. Andy said nothing and slipped her headphones on while I started the engines. She remained silent during the pre-takeoff checks.

A few minutes after leveling off at seven thousand five hundred feet and completing the checklist for cruise flight, Andy reached across the armrests and closed a gentle hand on my arm.

She looked grim.

"Dee, what's going on?"

"Mike Horowitz is dead," she said. The news boomed in my headset.

I bit my lip to hold back an incredulous, *What?*

"Lee called Mike while you were preflighting. Someone—not Mike—picked up Mike's phone. They did some 'Who's this?' back and forth until Lee identified himself. The other person was a sheriff's deputy, but he handed the phone over to an FBI agent on the scene—one of the B team agents who were tailing McCauley."

"What happened?"

"Lee's guess is that Sergei found Mike—his safe house. I don't know how. They hit the safe house—a ranch on the New Mexico side—and—" She swallowed. Her eyes gained wet glitter. "—Mike was killed. They also killed one of—I think—"

Her grip on my arm tightened.

"I think it was the little one," she said.

"*One of the kids?*"

She clenched her lips and nodded.

"*Oh my god.*"

Steady engine drone carried us into a darkening sky. Oblivious to tragedy, the lights of small towns winked on below us and slid beneath our wings. People tuning in television programs. People raiding the 'fridge. People who had not been murdered, or witnesses to murder. I let the autopilot fly. I took Andy's hand and squeezed a message to her. She nodded.

"They have Milo and his wife now. I can't imagine how they found them so fast."

"I can," I said. "Milo."

She quizzed me with a look.

"He thought he could deal his way out of this. I don't think he ever stopped believing he was invaluable to Sergei."

"*Oh, Lord.* If that's true, he killed himself and his family."

We rode in silence for a few minutes. I glanced back at Donaldson. He stared down at his phone.

"Dee, if we know that Paddington Trucking is the Milo O'Brien route Gloria Rilling is using—"

"Sergei knows, too," Andy said.

"Did Lee call in the cavalry? Tell me he's not playing lone wolf at this."

"Oh, everyone's alerted," she said. "But for all the wrong reasons."

"What?"

"They left a message at the scene proclaiming Mike's murder to be the work of the United Workers Liberation Front."

"Please tell me no one believes that crap."

"I think we're at the point of people believing what they want to believe."

I pictured Mike Horowitz. I saw him in his grubby coveralls, piloting the rolling wreck of a pickup truck. I saw him blush at the sight of a beautiful woman. I wondered if he had a woman of his own in his life.

"That proves it, you know," Andy said.

"What?"

"The claim of credit. Sergei used it for Lindsay and used it again for Milo. The pattern proves it was McCauley and Sergei. Circumstantially."

We rode in silence until about ten minutes later when Donaldson poked his head into the cockpit between us. Andy and I each lifted one headphone cup from the ear nearest to him.

"She tell you?" he asked me. I nodded. He said, "I've been checking online. It made the news. Homeland Security is on it like an avalanche. Washington issued a heightened threat level. The media is reporting an imminent terrorist attack. State Department reports are that the situation in Ghana is deteriorating. The President is talking about evacuating Americans and of course rattling his plastic sabre for military action."

"Can't you get on the phone with somebody?"

"And tell them what? The only person who can expose this whole thing for a false flag operation is Gloria Rilling. And right now, an argument to divert resources to a search for Sergei Roane's wayward wife won't get much traction."

I said, "I don't mean this the way it sounds, but this was a DEA agent killed in El Paso. How did it become a national security emergency and panic festival?"

"Terrorists, baby. The big T. That DEA agent was sheltering someone with knowledge of illegal entry routes into the United States—and that someone has just been kidnapped by terrorists. The conclusion is that Milo either has facilitated entry by said terrorists—or he will be. Oh, and *The New York Times* is reporting that the White House put out a new call for closing the southern border."

"That's insane!" I said.

"That's opportunity."

"We're not going to get any help, are we?" Andy asked.

"No." Donaldson shook his head and looked at the blackening landscape beyond the Navajo's nose.

"I'm so sorry about Mike," I said.

"Yeah."

57

Finding the Harry Stern Airport deserted at a little after ten p.m. came as no surprise. Fuel wasn't an issue, since we had topped the tanks in Prince Henry. I parked and secured the Navajo.

A plain brick building at the end of a row of hangars stood the best chance of being an airport office. The door was locked and the gravel lot behind the building lay bare.

"How do we get a car if they don't have a courtesy car?" Andy asked.

"Is there a rental office?" Lonnie asked. She examined the flat empty landscape looking like someone who had been dropped on the moon.

Donaldson set off in the direction from which we had come.

"Where are you going?" I asked.

"I saw a couple cars down the line, parked by those hangars."

"Lee, you can't just—" Andy protested.

"I won't," he replied over his shoulder. "I'll ask nicely."

Ten minutes later headlights approached on the service road behind the row of hangars. A maroon full-sized sedan lunged its way around the corner and skidded to a halt on the gravel lot with Donaldson behind the wheel, his arm resting on the open window.

Andy took one look at the broken plastic ignition cover on the steering column and said, "Oh my god."

"Get in!"

"Shotgun!" I called out.

We piled in a well-worn Eagle Vision. The back wore a blanket over torn upholstery. The leatherette dash peeled to reveal yellowing foam underneath.

"Five-hundred-dollar airport car," I said. "Lots of people keep them at a fly-in destination. The personal equivalent of a courtesy car."

"Well, she sounds good and rolls nice. We'll leave twenty bucks on the seat when we're done." Donaldson stomped the accelerator.

We departed the airport and headed into dark open countryside. In short order, a road sign promised we would find Desmond eight miles ahead.

A debate ignited between Andy and Donaldson. Andy argued that finding Gloria Rilling meant she could be produced as proof that the investigation had been drawn off course. Donaldson countered that Gloria wasn't enough to convince higher authorities that the terrorist threat masked a scheme to murder Lindsay. He proposed using and pursuing what she knew to unravel the scheme. Lonnie chimed in to insist that the girl and her child be protected, hinting that she would not allow the FBI's need for a witness against Lindsay's killers to put her in danger.

After a mile or so, I tuned them out. My mind wandered to Mike Horowitz, and to Milo's terrified family. Images of chains hung from concrete ceilings attacked my imagination. *I had them. I got them out.* How could this happen? Should I have stayed and played the card I threatened and taken them away myself? They would still be alive if I had dropped them in some empty canyon for a day or two to let Milo come to his senses. A little dehydration beats the living hell out of being murdered.

Hateful, horrifying images flooded the cinema screens of my mind. I squirmed in the car seat and cracked the window for air.

"Can somebody tell me what we're doing?" The movie soundtrack voice came from the back seat.

"When you didn't find your daughter in Prince Henry," Andy explained, "it was because she went back into the pipeline. The people who took your money needed to get rid of her. They gave her back to the coyote. In this case, it's not some guy in denim guiding refugees through the desert. It's a sophisticated transport system. We think the hub—at least for this region—is a trucking company in the town of Desmond, just down this road."

"Do you think she'll be there?"

"I'm almost certain she will not," Andy replied. "She's probably in Canada by now. My hope is to get them to tell us if she was transported, how and where. Then we have a chance to track her."

"And what you two were talking about—the terrorists. Is that real?"

"No."—"Yes." Donaldson and Andy answered simultaneously.

"No," Donaldson said. "Sergei is running a false flag operation, using

America's knee-jerk fear of terrorism to cover killing Mitchell Lindsay. The terrorism is a fake."

"Probably cooked up by some African generals looking to overthrow a democracy," I chimed in.

"What? For real?" Lonnie asked.

Andy said. "My colleague overlooks that the perception is real. It's guiding the Lindsay investigation. We *need* your daughter to set the record straight. She knows that Sergei and a man named McCauley were behind Lindsay's killing. She may or may not know why, but she knows who."

"If that's true, he can't let her live," Lonnie said. "That's what I've been trying to tell you. I need to take her somewhere safe."

I glanced back at Andy. She held Lonnie's gaze. "You're right that Sergei will ensure that your daughter is not a threat. But don't forget, she birthed his son, and that's a powerful token in a *machismo* culture. He will want the boy back. He might use the boy as leverage to take her back, too."

Lonnie said nothing.

Streetlights appeared on the horizon, half a mile ahead.

"That's it, ahead on the left," he said.

"Go past it," Andy ordered him. She leaned across the seat and looked out the window on Lonnie's side of the car.

A substantial house sat on a vast lawn. The house shared the property with several large metal sheds. A row of trucks with polished metal tanks filled a lot behind and to one side of the steel sheds.

Huge open doors on the main building exposed a machine shop and maintenance garage. Two trucks occupied the workspace under bright halogen lights. I looked for but did not see movement.

A sign flashed past. Paddington Trucking. The lot marked the fringe of the town of Desmond. In short order the speed limit dropped another 10 MPH and scattered liquor, drug and convenience stores popped up on both sides of the highway.

Donaldson pulled into an asphalt lot fronting a nail salon and dry cleaner. He wheeled around in a circle and pointed the car at the road.

"Stop," Andy said. "Will and I will get out here and walk. You drive back out of town and wait for us to call."

Donaldson looked sideways at me. "Does she always give the orders?"

"Only on the days that end in 'y.'" I hopped out, knowing that Donaldson knew perfectly well why Andy had separated us from him and Lonnie.

"Wait for our call," Andy reminded him.

He saluted and drove away.

58

F*wooomp!*
    I pulled my wife close and pressed my toes to the pavement. The asphalt dropped away.

"That was careless," Andy said.

"What?"

"We're going to wind up on a YouTube video. We should have gone around to the back of the building. How do you know there weren't cameras?"

"Even if there are, nobody looks at security footage unless there's a reason. And if someone saw it, they'd never get anyone to believe it. It's a prank or doctored video. Car pulls up. Two people get out and vanish. Nothing is real on video anymore."

Before launching I had checked for wires. Utility poles lined the edge of the street above a sidewalk. Now they fell away. Surpassing the tops of the poles assured me we were clear of the wires.

I aimed the BLASTER toward the edge of town. Taillights from the borrowed car grew smaller in the distance.

We cruised above the highway, returning the way we had come. The trucking company revealed itself as we approached. Seven polished steel tank trucks lined up on a gravel lot. Five sheet metal buildings dotted the property, varying in size from a two-car garage to an aircraft-hangar-sized maintenance shop. An island containing fuel pumps bordered a small fuel tank farm. This looked like a going concern. I wondered why a thriving business would engage in human trafficking. Perhaps they didn't. Perhaps Tolliver lied and this was a wild goose chase. Or perhaps human trafficking accounted for the fact the business was thriving.

I veered right for a circuit around the property to gain a sense of the layout.

"Body," Andy said suddenly.

"Where?"

"See the yellow Camaro?"

I picked out the car parked behind the main workshop. A dark shape lay on the ground beside it.

"Take me down," she commanded.

The body sprawled beside the driver's door. I was surprised she had seen it; the figure lay in a black shadow. A man. Face down, arms thrown forward. I took us lower.

"This is good enough," Andy whispered. We hovered a few feet above the lifeless figure. I felt Andy turning her head, checking all around us. "He's dead."

"How can you tell?"

"He has a hole at the base of his skull." I had no idea how she could see that in the dark. I chose not to confirm her observation. "Take us around to the front."

I used a low-revolution power setting to ease forward and slightly up until we flew just above typical man height—in case we encountered anyone in the dark. We rounded the corner and moved along the side of the building. A trapezoid of light spilled onto gravel in front of the open doors. We swung around into the light.

"They're all dead," Andy announced. "Take me down."

"Wait, what? How can you tell?"

"In the pit."

Once again, her keen eyes found the corpses before mine. The central service bay had a pit and a lift. One of the trucks had been parked on the lift and raised roughly six feet above the concrete floor. The pit below it provided mechanics with access to the belly of the vehicle.

Two more bodies lay motionless in the pit. One flat on the floor. One as if sitting against the back wall, his head lolled on his shoulder.

"Take me down," Andy repeated.

"How do you know they're not still here?"

"Will, they're long gone. We have to call this in."

I dropped us to the floor.

Fwooomp!

Andy stepped lightly over snaked compressor hoses and peered down into the pit.

"Are they?"

"Yes. Head shots." She pulled her Beretta from her satchel and wrapped both hands around it. Following the muzzle, she moved swiftly to the truck in the second bay, searching beside it, under it, searching the far side of the truck and the dark recesses of the service bay. She returned and hurried across the floor to a door. I followed her as she cleared the doorway and the space beyond, then entered.

We traversed a short hallway into an office. Old metal desks lined two walls under bulletin boards plastered with notices, tool product calendars and at least two pinup girls. Each desk had a PC. Both keyboards were sooty and blackened with grease.

Andy found another door and edged up to it. She cleared the space within, then swung her weapon through the door and followed it. I gingerly trailed her.

The inner office had carpet, albeit filthy. The desk was wooden, once expensive, now scratched and stained. The computer on the desk was a silver laptop mounted in a docking station.

A woman sprawled in a low, armless office chair. Her iron-gray hair showed no sign of coloring. Her body betrayed no hint of concern for a healthy diet. Large fleshy arms hung at her sides. Both hands looked as if they'd been dipped in blood. The gray sweatshirt she wore advertised a college on the front. Red-black blood from a wound across her throat saturated the logo. Copper scent dominated the small office.

She stared up at the ceiling. Her mouth hung open—frozen in the act of gasping or screaming, or both. I forced myself to look away. A wireless mouse lay on the floor beneath her dangling fingertips. The blood soaking into the carpet nearly reached it.

"Lee," Andy said into her phone. "We're too late. There are bodies. Four so far. Come in but make Lonnie stay in the car. I'm calling local PD."

I looked at the laptop screen. A collage of photos. Nearly all were of small children. A few featured the woman behind the desk surrounded by the children.

"This is fresh," Andy said. "They're not far ahead of us."

I leaned over and touched the keyboard space bar.

"Will! Don't!" The screen-saver image flicked off. A complicated page full of listings, boxes and a map appeared. "Go outside."

I did as the detective ordered.

. . .

Lonnie refused to stay in the car. The moment Donaldson stopped the vehicle, she bolted from the back seat.

"Is she here?" She met Andy coming out of the brightly lit maintenance shop. Andy hooked her by the arm and reversed her course.

"No," she said. She pulled her to the back of the car. "Lee! Can you pop the trunk?"

Donaldson, who had climbed out, climbed back in. He searched until he found a release. The trunk lid latch snapped. Andy shoved it open.

"Get in," she ordered Lonnie.

"What? No."

"It's that or have your face all over the internet at the scene of a multiple homicide. Take your pick, but do it quick, because I just called 9-1-1 and the local police will be here any minute."

Lonnie looked at Andy, then at me. I leaned into the trunk and cleared away jumper cables and a box of quart-sized plastic oil bottles.

"I'm sorry, it's the only thing I can think of," Andy said. "We're going to have to give our names and explain why we're here. We can. You can't."

"Unbelievable." Lonnie grabbed the trunk lip and lifted herself in. She wiggled and curled into position.

"Sorry," Andy said again. She pressed the lid down. It failed to latch. She pressed harder. It failed again. She lifted it and slammed it shut.

"OW!" came from inside.

"Sorry!"

Donaldson hobbled into the garage. He stopped and studied the bodies in the pit. Andy told him about the woman inside. He went for a look.

Andy waited in the light for the police to arrive. I didn't want to look at bodies or talk to cops, so I walked out of the light toward the line of trucks parked behind the building, confident that if I ran into trouble I could easily disappear.

The trucks were straight-chassis, double-axle bulk milk haulers. Silver tanks carrying the Paddington name and logo—a bear of dubious trademark legality—backed up red International tractor cabs. I knew from working on a farm as a kid that the milk haulers were more than just truck drivers. At each stop, the driver of this type of truck was tasked with measuring, weighing and testing the milk product that he hauled from the farm to the processing dairy.

These were older trucks, though clean and well-maintained. I knew from weekly breakfasts at the Silver Spoon diner in Essex that local dairy farmers who owned their own trucks, or carriers that served dairy farm routes in the county, favored new triple-axle trucks, or tractor-trailer combinations with greater capacity.

I moved into the line between two of the big trucks. I pulled out my phone and lit the screen, waving the weak light over the sides of the tank, the built-in hose bin, the pump motor and the control panel. The unit looked clean, a sign of recent use. Stainless steel fixtures at the rear glittered in the light. Regular washing prevented a buildup of road grime.

The idea that this outfit used these trucks to move humans instead of bulk milk seemed plausible from a distance, but up close nothing looked amiss. Deeper examination might uncover another story, but I wasn't sure we had that kind of time. Whoever had committed the murders had a solid step ahead of us. If this was Sergei Roane's doing, I saw little chance of Andy and Donaldson finding Gloria Rilling and her son before he did.

I strolled up and down the line, finding each vehicle virtually identical. Clean, polished fixtures. Sealed tanks. No hint of hidden doors that I could see, but I had a feeling access into the tank would be anything but visible to the casual eye. Each tank had a hatch on top. Conceivably, a load of immigrants could be made to climb up and in, but it would be just as easy for an inspector to open the hatch and see them huddling in a stainless-steel tank. There had to be more to it. Only expertise and daylight would expose these trucks as conveyors of humanity. I had neither.

I reached the back of the lot when a whiff of something sour tickled my nostrils. Up to that point, the property mixed the usual aromas of engine oil, diesel fuel and machine shop grease.

This smelled…bad.

Beyond the row of trucks, the lot ended at the edge of a field. Three rusting cargo containers rooted themselves in a sea of weeds along the fence line. Between two of the containers, a leaning blue Fiberglas port-a-potty explained the odor. The temporary toilet reeked of needing emptying.

Which begged a question: Why was there an old, yet decidedly ripe portable toilet sitting at the back of this lot? Surely the garage and office building had a toilet. And why were the weeds in front of its flimsy door beaten down?

The trail of stomped weeds broke like a sunburst, dividing into smaller trails that lead to the cargo containers.

Holy crap.

I switched off the phone light and let my eyes adjust. The cargo containers became black rectangles against the moonlit yard. I chose the nearest one and followed the narrow footpath to its door.

No lock.

I lifted the latch and pulled open the door. A new cloud of odor billowed out. Sweat. Mildewed fabric. Vague hints of food.

The black interior revealed nothing. No one jumped out at me. I hit the phone light again, half expecting it to illuminate a crowd of frightened faces.

The cargo container did not hold a huddled mass of tired or poor, but it gave away their passage. Discarded food wrappers, abandoned clothing items, a single shoe, and other unidentified trash littered the floor of the container. Old blankets hung on ropes across the top of the space created limited privacy. A battery-powered lamp had been duct-taped to the side wall.

This was a way station.

I checked the other two cargo containers. Both were locked. I rapped on the side and called out in English and Spanish. No answer. No sound issued from within. Horror stories of people suffocated in such containers rushed to mind. I forced myself to believe that the containers were simply locked when not in use—at least until a set of bolt cutters could be found.

Or something just as good.

I stepped up to the lock and—

Fwooomp!

—vanished. I wrapped my palm around the padlock body. The lock vanished. *The other thing* seeped up the shank, making the u-shaped steel look blurry and frayed. I jerked and it snapped free. The visible remnant of shank hung in the latch. I pulled it out, tossed the pieces into the weeds and opened the door.

More litter and odor, but no bodies.

I opened the third and last container.

The same. *Thank God!*

All three cargo containers shared the same purpose. All three were empty.

By the time I returned to Andy, a black and white Ford Explorer with a *POLICE* door decal blocked the driveway. A young blonde woman in full uniform and belt stood listening to Andy who gave directions, pointed and explained. I would have bet a lot that the patrol officer, slightly wide-eyed, was about to see her first homicide victims.

Andy left the officer, who lifted her phone and made a call. Andy joined Donaldson and me inside the garage.

"She's one of two Desmond police officers. They're not equipped for this. She's calling in the county sheriff. I told her to reach out for state assistance."

"Did you tell her the FBI is here?" I asked.

"Not yet," Andy replied.

"Well, I found something." I explained.

Donaldson turned around and surveyed the inside of the garage. "So, they're using bulk milk trucks. Hauling people in the tanks."

"Maybe," I said. I stepped closer to the truck on the lift. "Do you see any access other than the top hatch?"

"We could be looking right at it and not see it."

I studied the truck sitting on the concrete floor. The door displayed the same stolen bear logo, along with several decals. Somebody treated the truck like a NASCAR racer. The door had decals for oil products, cleaners, and a US Cellular Fleet Business sticker. I hopped up on the passenger-side running board and looked inside. Nothing about the cab surrendered contraband hauling secrets.

"Will, don't touch everything," Andy scolded me.

I climbed down and rejoined her as the patrol officer approached.

"This is our pilot and my husband, Will. And this is FBI Special Agent Lee Donaldson," Andy said.

"Officer Burns," she introduced herself but did not offer to shake hands, which she had covered with blue latex gloves. "FBI? Is this your case?"

"Yes." Donaldson offered no explanation.

"Officer Burns," Andy said, "Is the woman inside the owner?"

Burns left us and entered the office, then the inner office. She came back drawing deep breaths.

"That's not something I thought I'd ever see," she said. Her face lost color but she showed no sign of losing her lunch. "Any idea who did this?"

"Is she Padd?" Andy asked.

"Yes. She's the owner."

"Is there a Mister Paddington?"

"No." Burns walked over to the pit. She aimed her phone and took pictures. She checked the pictures and rejoined Andy. "We'll wait for county to get here. Then I want to search everything." She looked at Donaldson. "If that's okay with you?"

"My case, your crime scene. You're in charge."

I started to wonder how long we would leave an international film star in the filthy trunk of a twenty-five-year-old beater car.

"Is this connected to that terrorist alert rattling cages at all the alphabet agencies?" Burns asked. "Is that why the FBI is involved?"

"No," Donaldson said. He offered nothing further.

"Tell her what you found in back," Andy said to me. I described the containers.

"You think Padd's running a human trafficking operation? With her trucks?"

"We're sure of it," Andy said.

Burns lifted her eyebrows. "The old bird wasn't doing well. The big operations started using their own trucks. She laid off a bunch of drivers a couple years ago, but then things seemed to pick up again. I guess we know why."

"We're looking for someone she may be transporting," Andy said. "A witness to the murder of FBI Deputy Director Mitchell Lindsay."

"Then this *is* tied to those terrorists," Burns said.

"The people who did this are after the same witness and obviously have the jump on us," Andy said. "I'm afraid they got information from the owner and made sure no one else would."

It hit me.

"Holy crap!" I squeezed between Andy and Burns and bolted for the inner office.

I carefully picked up the wireless mouse and then swiveled the desktop computer to avoid standing in the blood seeping into the carpet.

"Will! Stop!" Andy dashed in after me. "Don't touch that!"

I ignored her. I placed the mouse on the desktop and clicked once.

The screensaver, which had returned, disappeared again. The page full of lists, menus and a map reappeared.

"Ha!" I cried out. I clicked the map. "They use US Cellular GPS tracking, Dee! Look at this!"

I clicked on the map. Andy leaned in at my shoulder.

The map expanded. It showed western Minnesota and the eastern tracts of the Dakotas. The range had been opened to a little over a hundred miles in all directions. A cluster of dots colored the epicenter.

"That's us. Here. Those are all the trucks parked out back. They use GPS fleet tracking." I scrolled the mouse wheel and zoomed out slowly. The map expanded and adjusted. The spinning wait cursor took over and forced us to watch while the map updated. "There! That's what they killed her for!"

A single red dot appeared to the north. It throbbed. Moving.

Donaldson joined us. "You think that's her?"

"If it is, Sergei's people know," I said.

"Where is that?"

Burns crowded in with us. "That looks like I-29, north of Grand Forks."

"It'll take them hours to catch her," Donaldson said.

"They don't have to catch her. They know where she's going," Andy said. Everyone looked at my wife. "I've been trying to understand the 'why' of it. Why did they need Milo? Sergei owns and operates the system—but Milo knew all the specific waypoints. Why not just pick her up wherever she arrived at the end of the line? Why come here—and do this?"

"Because she hadn't reached the end of the line," Donaldson said.

"Yes," Andy said. "They knew she was here. Probably on information from Milo. For whatever reason, when you and Lonnie were told she had moved on, she hadn't. She was delayed. Maybe stuck here, in one of those containers out in back, waiting for the next run. Milo must have told Sergei. But they missed her."

"But why kill everyone here? Aren't these people all working for Sergei?" I asked.

Andy shook her head. "Doubtful they know who they're working for. Either way, Sergei didn't want his wife leaving a trail."

"She's there," Donaldson pointed at the dot. I scrolled in and centered the moving marker, reducing the scale until it throbbed on I-29 in northeast North Dakota where the highway ran just west of the wiggling line that is the Red River.

"The highway goes all the way to Winnipeg," Burns said.

"But their waystation could be anything. A town just over the border. Something along the way. Or Winnipeg itself. Whatever it is, if they don't catch her, they'll be waiting for her."

"We have to get to her first," Andy said. She turned to Burns. "Officer, I need you to stay here, right here. In this room. Don't let anyone touch this computer. Make sure that PC stays plugged in and powered up—and keep this program open. If we lose it and access is password-protected, we may not be able to get back in." Andy pulled out her phone. "What's your number?"

Burns gave it. Andy dialed. Burns's phone chirped.

"What are you going to do?" Burns asked Andy.

"Get to her before they do."

"How on earth do you plan to catch up to someone a hundred miles away? Why not call in an intercept?"

"That does make more sense," I said.

"Let ND State Patrol intercept. They can close the highway," Burns suggested.

Andy frowned. "Nine times out of ten, I'd agree. But what if someone working with Tolliver and Schmidt hear the call?"

"Who?"

"People who can't be trusted," Donaldson said. "If this gets broadcast, the wrong ears might hear about it. All it takes is one call to that driver, and the woman and her child disappear—or wind up dead in a ditch."

"You're never going to catch up."

"At two hundred miles an hour we will," I said.

"Station yourself here and don't let anyone touch this, Officer. And one more thing. The people who did this—they know what we know. They made the woman—Padd—tell them. They're headed up the highway in pursuit of that truck. I want you to call North Dakota Highway patrol and tell them you have possible murder suspects, armed and dangerous, on I-29 moving at high speed. Can you do that?"

"Yes, ma'am."

"Can you do it without mentioning the milk truck?"

Burns hesitated, then said, "All I know is what I saw on that screen."

"That works. Stay here for my call," Andy said.

"Yes, Ma'am."

DONALDSON SKIDDED the stolen car to a halt on the ramp after a highway run that topped ninety at times. I helped an angry Lonnie Penn out of the trunk.

"Didn't you hear me banging on the lid?" she demanded.

"All the way up the highway. Get aboard. We gotta go!"

I cut short a longer discussion Lonnie had planned and told her to take her same seat. I dropped in the pilot's seat. Andy threw money into the borrowed car before slamming the door and running to the airplane behind Donaldson. By the time she secured the door, I had the left engine turning. The right engine fired before she could belt herself into the copilot's seat. She pulled on her headset. I released the brakes and handed her the laminated aircraft checklist card.

"Read it off to me, starting here." I pointed.

She read and I taxied, checking each item as we went. By the time I reached the runway only the engine runup remained. I skipped it and rolled onto the concrete runway, pushing the throttles forward and surging through the turn. As soon as the nose aligned with the runway, I pushed everything to the stops and double-checked power.

The Navajo leaped across the big 15 painted on the runway. I clicked the mic button on the yoke five times. The runway lights woke up.

"Power check...suction's good...airspeed's alive," I chanted, checking each item. I eased back on the yoke until the nose grew light on the nose-wheel. She flew when she was ready. I lifted the gear and rolled into a shallow bank. A climbing left turn carried us across the Red River into Minnesota. We swung around the edge of Breckenridge, Wahpeton's twin across the river.

Half of the moon hung sixty degrees above a cloudless eastern horizon, ghost lighting the landscape. The winding Red River defined itself by glittering with reflected starlight. I followed the river rather than head ten miles west to pick up I-29, knowing that the two eventually converged just south of Fargo.

Andy pulled out her phone and paired it to the Bluetooth in her headset. I leveled us off at three thousand feet, which put us two thousand feet above the ground, a safe height to clear any towers on our path.

Andy's voice carried over the intercom, sharing her side of the phone call she initiated.

"Burns? Where is it?...Okay. This call will probably drop. We're moving fast...Burns?" She turned to me. "I lost her. She said the truck is about ten miles north of Grand Forks."

I set the altitude hold and used the heading bug on the autopilot to lock our course. Hands free, I pulled up the iPad and stroked the screen.

Burns' information posed a multi-part flight intercept problem. Where is she now? How long until we can reach her? Where will she be when we reach her at—I checked groundspeed—two hundred and twenty-one miles per hour?

A hand landed on my shoulder.

"What's the plan, Stan?" Donaldson poked his head between Andy and me.

"Go away," I said. I touched the screen to create a Present Position anchor point, then scrolled up to just short of the U.S. and Canada border and planted another anchor point. Then I located a point roughly ten miles north of Grand Forks and planted an intermediate point.

"Can you land this thing on an interstate highway? In the dark?"

The flight plan calculation for the end point, at our present speed, put us there in just over forty-five minutes.

"My husband can land this thing on top of that truck if he wants to," Andy said. She threw me a flash of pride laced with affection.

Damn! I thought. *She looks good in this red cockpit light.* I'm the poster child for the statistic that says that men think of sex every twenty seconds. In my case, I have an excellent excuse.

"Not now, not now, not now," I muttered to myself. She heard it and suppressed a smile.

From Burns' position report to the border, estimating on the conservative side, the distance came to a little over fifty miles. The milk truck driver would hold to the speed limit, not wanting to draw attention. At seventy miles per hour, that came to…I pulled an old school circular flight computer from a side pocket and worked the numbers…*crap*.

"We have a problem," I said. "Rough guess, we have a two-minute margin to catch them before they make the border."

"What about crossing the border?" Donaldson asked.

"Low-flying aircraft, at night, no flight plan, international border and—oh, yes, there's a heightened threat level. What do you think?"

"Can we go any faster?"

"I'm running at seventy-five percent power now."

"Then run at a hundred percent power."

He had a point. I had set the power out of habit. Typical cruise power rarely exceeds seventy-five percent. Any higher and the fuel consumption isn't worth the small gain in speed.

I shoved the throttles to the stops, reset the props and adjusted the mixture control. The airspeed needle edged upward. The GPS groundspeed readout reported the increase. Two hundred twenty-seven.

"Is that enough?" Donaldson asked.

"I'll let you know when we get there."

LIGHTS CREPT OVER THE HORIZON, a glittering expanse ten miles wide. The river snaked toward it. Morehead and West Fargo. The city wasn't a problem, but our flight path cut directly through the Hector International Airport Class D airspace and the Fargo Terminal Radar Surveillance Area. I released the altitude hold and let the altimeter slide up a few feet at a time. The gentle climb didn't cut into our speed, but the added height offered a potential boost at the other end. Higher altitude also reduced the chances of being asked by the Fargo controller to deviate.

I called Fargo Approach Control and crossed my fingers.

"Navajo One Tango Whiskey turn right heading three six zero, vectors for traffic," the controller requested after identifying me.

"Crap!" I said aloud without the mic button down. I looked at Andy. "If he vectors us it'll cut into our time."

"Can you ask to stay on a direct course?" she suggested.

"Fargo, Navajo One Tango Whiskey, unable that requested deviation. We require a direct course."

Donaldson tapped me on the shoulder. I tried to ignore him, but he tapped again.

I turned my head to find him wearing one of the cabin headsets and holding his FBI badge up in my face. He'd been listening.

"You sure?" I asked him. "Proves you were here."

He shrugged.

"One Tango Whiskey, I need that turn. Right to three six zero."

The controller didn't really need the turn. I knew what he wanted. Traffic at Hector would be departing on to the south. My flight path took me directly over the airport, which meant they would have to hold a departure while I transited the departure path—assuming they had a departure at this hour on a Monday night, which I doubted.

"Fargo, I'm on an urgent mission with a priority FBI passenger, Special Agent Lee Donaldson, badge number..." I grabbed the wallet from Donaldson and read off the number. "We need to maintain direct. Can you help us out?"

If you ask nicely...

"One Tango Whisky, proceed on course." Donaldson gave me a thumbs-up and slid back in his seat.

Less than ten minutes later we transited the dark plot of land representing the airport. As I suspected, we received no traffic alerts. Empty black terrain lay ahead and before too long the Fargo controller authorized a frequency change and wished us a good night.

Grand Forks became a glow on the horizon.

"Burns, what's the update?" Andy asked, holding up her phone with a renewed connection. "Okay...got it. Stay on the line. Will, it's tracking just south of Drayton."

I found Drayton on the map. Either the first estimate had been off, or they were moving faster than I expected.

"This does not look good," I said. I glanced down at the groundspeed readout. Two hundred thirty-three. We picked up a little. My altitude read three thousand seven hundred. "I'm going higher. Maybe get more tail wind."

Andy touched the mute button on her phone.

"Can you really land on the highway?" she asked.

"Piece of cake. It's as wide as most decent runways, has few wires, and in this part of the country runs straight enough to put drivers to sleep. The only problem is the occasional moving hunk of metal in the way."

"We don't have to land right in front of her. Land anywhere ahead of her and it shuts down the highway. They'll have to stop."

"If nobody hits us."

THE TAILWIND ASSISTING us worked against us for landing, adding to our touchdown speed. I wondered if I might have enough time to fly ahead of the truck, turn back and land to the south on the southbound lanes. But a southerly landing opened the possibility that the truck would get past us. Even if I found a place to cross over to the northbound lanes to attempt to block traffic, it would mean taxiing into seventy-mile-per-hour traffic. I ruled that out.

Accounting for the speed of the airplane, which would touch down in the neighborhood of eighty to a hundred miles per hour, and the speed of the traffic, I estimated my chances of finding an ample landing gap to be fairly good.

I-29 ran due north a few miles west of the Red River. I watched it after we emerged from the Fargo area. The northbound lanes were busier than I would have liked.

"What the hell? Where are all these people going?"

Andy didn't comment on the traffic. She said, "I lost her again."

"We're jumping cell towers."

"She's getting some flak from the county sheriff. Gotta hand it to her, she's standing her ground." Her phone lit up. "Go ahead, Burns," I heard Andy say. "Just north of Drayton. Got it." She leaned over to look at the iPad on my lap. "We're coming up on Grand Forks…I think so…yes, on the highway. As soon as we do, I'll call Highway Patrol and report on scene… and… Burns?... Burns?...We lost the connection again."

"Dee, I'm not going to do this if there's a chance of it going to hell. Not with you onboard."

"Then it's good I'm here with you," she said, "because if I wasn't you probably *would* try to land on top of the stupid truck."

She had a point.

GRAND FORKS SLID BEHIND US. The altimeter crept above five thousand feet. The groundspeed rose to two thirty-five. The time came to apply the altitude gain to our advantage. I trimmed the nose down for a steady two-hundred foot per minute descent. The ground speed ticked up to two-forty. Two-forty-four. Two forty-six.

I eased the aircraft heading five degrees left. The Red River shifted to our right. The interstate highway crept closer.

"Traffic's lighter," I said. "Get Burns on the horn again. Tell her we're over Drayton."

"Burns," Andy said a moment later. "I need play by play now. We're closing fast. We're over Drayton." Andy listened and relayed. "They're even with Bowsemont...passing over an overpass...now turning on a dogleg northwest."

I increased the descent rate. Speed picked up to two-fifty. Headlights and taillights traced the interstate highway below and ahead. I positioned the lanes between the nose and the left engine nacelle. Weak silver moonlight defined the highway.

"On the dogleg now, coming up on another interchange."

"I see more than one interchange. Which one?"

Andy relayed the question. "There are three...the second and third have little bodies of water...after the third, the road turns due north again...a few miles up there's a jog to the left..."

"Okay!" I got the geography. "Where's the truck?"

"Where's the truck," Andy asked. "Burns? Burns? Dammit!"

We dropped to less than a thousand feet above the ground. Individual cars and trucks moved beneath us, headlights consuming pavement.

Andy worked her phone. A moment later, I heard her say, "It's okay. Update...They're just south of the third interchange, on a slight curve to the right."

"Dammit!" I jerked the power levers back and plunged the nose. "I see it! I see the truck! Two miles ahead!"

Andy craned her neck and looked over the nose. "We got her... thanks!" She killed the phone connection and stuffed the phone in her bag. I took a last look at the iPad before handing it to Andy.

"Alright. Just past the interchange. That straight stretch. That's our spot. Hell or high water. Take one more look at the map—tell me if there are any unexpected overpasses. Little county roads."

The idling engines thrummed. Windmilling prop drag produced deceleration that pressed us forward against the seat belts. I heaved the airplane into a tight turn to the left, then back again to the right, across the highway path, then left again.

"Looks clear," Andy reported.

"Too high. Too fast," I muttered to myself.

Sharp S-turns slowed us. We shed speed and altitude.

"C'mon! C'mon!" My attention shot between the silver tank truck on the highway and the airspeed indicator. All that speed I wanted earlier became my enemy now. The needle dropped at a glacial rate. I put my hand on the landing gear lever and waited. "C'mon!"

Five knots above maximum gear speed I threw down the lever. The cabin thundered. The nose pitched down. I rolled in trim to take the pressure off the yoke. On the instrument panel, the amber gear-up light turned to three green lights.

"Gear down."

Five hundred feet. Four hundred. With the gear down, the speed dropped wildly. I brought the throttles back up, reawakening the engines. The out-of-synch props throbbed harmonically. The ribbon of pavement became a moonlit gray line against black.

"It's clear ahead of him for about half a mile," Andy called out.

I saw what she saw.

"Gas. Undercarriage. Mixture. Props," I recited, checking each. "Seat-belts on everybody!" I reached for and flicked on the landing lights. Twin beams stretched ahead of the wings, defined by humidity in the night air.

"There's a car moving past him on the left! Fast moving!"

"Yeah, I got him. He's gotta be doing ninety and he's going to get in our way."

The airspeed needle slipped past the top of the white arc that defined flap speed. I grabbed the flap handle and dropped it all the way down. The flaps sank into the slipstream and added to the thunder in the airframe. The aircraft pitch changed. I trimmed to compensate. I added power as the speed decayed. Three hundred feet. Two hundred.

"Final gear check—three green."

The landing lights poured illumination on the highway.

We closed the gap with a truck that matched the Paddington milk haulers. The car passing on its left surged ahead—smack into the opening I needed for landing. The curved and louvred rear boot of a Porsche 911 explained the driver's heavy foot. I inched the throttles forward. Now wasn't the time for more speed, but I had to get past the Porsche. My lights captured the car.

"Oh, Christ," I said, "the sonofabitch is speeding up!"

We passed over the tank truck. I shoved the throttles forward and the nose down. We dove toward the Porsche's roof.

"C'mon, idiot! Go or don't go!"

He paced us.

The twin-lane highway rose to meet us. The Porsche cruised just ahead of my left engine, now fully illuminated by blazing landing lights, more powerful and far-reaching than his headlights.

He has to be seeing this!

I shoved the throttles forward and back, creating an engine roar just above his roof.

The left wing suddenly glowed red.

Brake lights!

We shot over the Porsche and I slammed the throttles to idle. We settled and now paid for the tailwind and the race with the Porsche. I crossed mental fingers that we had cleared the car beneath us. We floated for what seemed like a mile, bleeding off speed, then touched down fast and hard. The landing lights painted the open road ahead. Rough pavement, worse than most runways, jolted up through the landing gear and into the cabin.

I eased on the brakes. The airplane rattled and bumped. We owned the road. If the landing lights weren't enough, our strobe lights, flashing navigation lights and the red rotating beacon on the tail warned traffic behind us. Anyone who didn't understand that an airplane just materialized out of the dark might at least think the flashing lights represented a police emergency.

We rolled. I took my time bringing it to a halt. There was no sense in getting rear-ended. Centered on the highway, the Navajo blocked both lanes with the full span of her wings. Vehicle headlights lit up the airplane from behind.

Andy sank in her seat. Her chest heaved up and down, drawing deep relief.

I pulled the mixture controls. Both engines died. I secured the ignitions but left the master switch that powered the lights.

Donaldson dropped the airstair door. He pulled himself out of the cabin. Lonnie followed quickly. Andy unbuckled and hurried after them.

I brought up the rear.

59

"What the hell, man! You almost killed me!" The Porsche driver slammed his door and stalked toward the tail of the Navajo.

Donaldson limped past him without sparing a glance. He drew his weapon and fixed it on the cab of the milk truck a car length behind the Porsche. Headlights lined up on the highway behind the two vehicles. Both lanes came to a halt.

Andy freed her weapon from her bag.

"Police! Get back in your car! Now!" she snapped at the Porsche driver, who threw his hands up. He caught sight of Lonnie. "Hey! Aren't you—?"

"Back in your car! Now!" Andy ordered. He hurried away, stealing backward glances and fumbling for his phone.

The milk truck idled in the right lane. Donaldson reached the truck cab. He pulled himself up on the running board and jerked the door latch. Locked.

"FBI! Open the door! Now!" he barked at the driver. "Open it!"

The door latch released. The cab light flicked on. Andy took up a flanking position, maintaining a clear shot at the driver.

I caught up to Lonnie, closed my hand around her arm and pulled. "Let them do this."

The driver, a heavy man with a bushy beard and bald head, pushed open the door and raised both hands.

"Get out!" Andy ordered him. "Keep your hands where I can see them."

"Easy, officer. Take it easy," the driver said, swinging himself out of the cab. He climbed down.

"Open it," Donaldson ordered him.

Headlights edge-lit the scene. Traffic on the southbound lanes began to slow.

"Hey, no problem. Just take it easy." The driver walked to the centerline of the tank where a short ladder arched over the left side of the polished steel cylinder. He grunted and pulled himself up the ladder aided by toe holds in the truck frame. He climbed to the top of the tank and released a clip on the center hatch. After a glance back at Donaldson and Andy, he lifted the hinged cover over and laid it on the tank top.

"Get down here," Donaldson commanded.

I jogged forward. "I got this."

The driver reversed down the ladder then dropped to the pavement.

"On the ground, face down, hands behind your head," Andy ordered.

I climbed the curved ladder to the top of the tank and peered into darkness. I pulled out my phone and lit the screen.

Milk. Glossy white ripples defined a white surface just below the rim of the tank hatch.

"Anything?" Donaldson asked.

Lonnie stood beside him, her face upturned, her hands clasped at her chest as if in prayer.

Prone on the ground, the driver turned his head and looked up at me. A trace of smile told me he knew exactly what we would find.

I met his eyes and smiled back.

"Get me his stick. His testing stick." The driver's smirk disappeared.

"Where is it?" Donaldson demanded of the driver.

"Screw you," he replied. "I can't allow you to contaminate—"

"Never mind," I said.

I turned around and plunged my right hand into the cold liquid.

Six inches down I hit steel.

I pulled my arm out and shook off the liquid. I climbed down the ladder and went to the driver. Clamping both hands on his collar, I jerked him to his feet.

"Open it!"

"Screw you," he said, curling a lip.

"Shoot him," I said. "In the left nut."

Donaldson didn't hesitate. He poked his weapon into the driver's crotch.

"WHOA! NO!" the driver danced backward, clamping his hands over himself. "You can't do that!"

"Don't worry. I rarely hit both."

"Okay! Okay!" He lifted his hands to wave Donaldson away. "Please! Okay!"

Donaldson grabbed his fleshy arm and rotated him to face the truck.

"Do it!"

The driver trudged to the truck and slid back the cover on the pump control panel. He showed us his hands and slowly reached in his pocket. Donaldson's weapon touched his cheek.

"Very carefully."

The driver nodded and lifted a small keyring from his pocket. He dangled it in the air for us to see. Donaldson eased his weapon away. The driver inserted the key in a lock and turned it. He flicked two chrome switches from down to up.

The pump motor hummed.

We heard the sucking sound of a seal breaking at the back of the tank. Andy darted past us into the red glow of the tanker's taillights.

"Get your ass back on the ground," Donaldson ordered the driver, pulling him away from the control panel. "Hands on the back of your head."

I joined Andy.

The convex rear end of the tank extended slightly, then swung aside on internally mounted hinges. The hatch cleared, exposing the full circumference of the tank cylinder. At the top, a steel panel had been welded in place, a false tank bottom that created the filled-tank illusion I had seen from above.

Beneath the false upper tank, pale faces hovered in darkness. Glittering eyes squinted into the glare of headlights lined up behind the truck.

"Come out," Andy said gently. "It's okay. It's okay."

A man slid to the back of the tank. Rumpled layers of clothing spoke of the cold inside. He dragged a cloth bag after him. I reached up and gave him a hand. He jumped to the ground, then reached for a woman who followed. We lifted her free. Both wore weary faces etched with fear. A second man slid to the back, pulling a roller bag. Andy joined me and we assisted him to the pavement. His grip felt like ice. His worried eyes darted to each of us in turn.

I strained to see into the darkness.

Movement.

A pale face—Lonnie Penn's face—took form. Wearing a sheen of perspiration beneath sweat-matted black hair, a girl clutched a mass of clothing and blankets to her chest. The mass moved. A small face peeked at us with dark and curious eyes. The resemblance to Sergei Roane leaped from the child, absent the cold stare captured by his family photo. The woman in the portrait radiated beauty and sophistication. The girl clutching her son in this cold steel cylinder was a terrified child. I never thought to do the math, but Gloria Rilling couldn't be more than seventeen.

With a three-year-old son.

Lonnie released a sob and pressed a clenched fist to her lips.

The girl moved swiftly. Steel flashed reflections of the headlights behind us. Her hand came up. Thin, bloodless fingers clutched the hilt of a heavy hunting knife. She raised the knife between us—not in defense. She held the blade in reverse, aimed at herself, at the child in her arms. Her hand shook and her eyes blazed.

Lonnie gasped. She lunged forward. Donaldson clamped a grip on her from behind.

My mind saw the knife flash and bury itself in the child she held.

"Gloria."

Andy's voice, soft and sweet in stark contrast to the deadly edged weapon, rose and echoed in the empty steel tank.

"It's okay. *Esta bien.* We're not federales. We're not ICE."

For a split second I thought Andy had blown it. The words seemed to incite the quivering ghostly face framed in damp black hair. The knife jerked toward the child.

"Gloria, please. We *do not* work for Sergei. Do you understand? *Sergei did not send us.*"

The blade hesitated.

"Please, honey. We're here to protect you from Sergei. He sent men for you. We're here to get you before they do. Please, sweetheart. Put down the knife. You don't want to hurt your child, your baby."

I marveled that Andy could speak so calmly.

Andy's words paved a soft path between her and the girl. Gloria locked her eyes on my wife. Andy stepped to the lip of the tank. Her weapon had disappeared into her bag. She held out both hands.

"Come. Come to me. You're safe.

The knife suddenly seemed too large, out of scale for the delicate hand that held it. It gained weight. The girl's arm trembled as the weight became too much to sustain.

"Gloria, listen to me," Andy said. "Your mother is here. She came for you before but Mallorin lied to her and told her you were dead. She's here now."

The girl's eyes blinked as if the machinery of her coiled self-destruction had short-circuited. A tremor shook her arm.

Andy, without taking her eyes from the girl, reached back for Lonnie. Donaldson released his grip. Lonnie moved to the lip of the tank.

"She's right here," Andy said. "Your mother. She's here."

Lonnie Penn, a woman whose scripted words and manipulated expressions flawlessly served every moment on screen now stood utterly speechless. Her eyes filled with liquid that spilled onto her cheeks. She bit her lower lip to stop it from quivering.

"Honey, please, put down the knife and come to us," Andy said softly. "Please."

Lonnie's arms rose, open.

The blade slowly descended, then slipped from the girl's fingers and clattered on the steel tank floor. She threw the freed arm around the child and shifted her frozen stare to Lonnie. The utter terror in her eyes melted into recognition.

"*Mother?*"

Lonnie released a sharp sob.

"I'm here."

I let myself breathe again. I stepped back and turned to Donaldson. "I'm gonna shut off this damned truck."

"Exhaust stinging your eyes?"

I marched past him. "Something like that."

I climbed into the cab and killed the engine. A quick scan of the truck cab revealed no hint that the operator engaged in anything except hauling milk. The driver kept a neat cab. I found a cell phone mounted on the center console. A swipe of the screen opened the phone to wallpaper of a naked woman, one unlikely to know the driver personally, judging by her porn star looks. I tapped the phone icon and touched Recents. The last call had been more than an hour ago. It might be worth mentioning to Andy, but the absence of an outgoing call meant that he hadn't alerted anyone to being stopped on the highway.

I hopped out and returned to the scene at the back of the tank truck. Andy's stance stopped me. She stared, transfixed, as Lonnie and Gloria, bathed in the truck's red taillights, clutched each other tightly with the small boy between them. The mother and daughter reunion absorbed my wife. Andy's phone jangled. She paid no attention. It rang several times. I opened my mouth to say something when she tore herself free and rejoined the moment. She checked the screen, swiped to take the call, and tapped the speaker button. I joined her to listen.

"We got her, Burns." Andy told the caller.

"Oh, thank God. Detective, that's good news."

Andy stared at Lonnie and her daughter.

"Detective?"

I touched my wife's arm. She startled. She forced herself to turn away. "I'm here. Go ahead."

"ND State Patrol spotted a vehicle moving at high speed, northbound, headed your way. They gave chase and shots were fired from automatic weapons. The patrol unit was disabled with injuries."

The news shattered Andy's distraction. She drew the phone closer. "How bad?"

"Not known. But the suspect vehicle wasn't stopped. All hell is breaking loose and units are responding, but it sounds like there's nobody between them and you. I thought you should know."

Andy looked at the line of cars filling both lanes behind us. Drivers and passengers clustered outside of their vehicles. A few held up cellphone cameras. A white-haired man from one of the stopped vehicles in the truck's lane stepped into the light.

"Excuse me," he said.

"Sir, go back to your vehicle," Andy ordered him. He didn't move. To Burns, Andy asked, "Where?"

"The exchange took place just north of Grand Forks, about ten minutes ago. You called it, Ma'am. They're coming."

"Then we can't stay here. Thank you, Officer Burns," Andy said. "I have to go."

"Good luck!"

Andy looked at me.

"On it," I said. Donaldson heard the call as well. He leaned over the sprawled driver and pointed his gun at the man's head. With his free hand, he pulled the driver's wallet from a back pocket, flipped it open and found the man's photo ID license.

"I'm taking this. We will find you. My advice—you drive to the nearest sheriff's office and turn yourself in. Paddington is dead, along with everyone else in Desmond. Sergei's men are coming. I suggest you don't hang around."

The driver did a quick calculation. "Wait! You can't just—"

"Watch me."

The white-haired man Andy had ordered back to his car ignored her. "Excuse me! Was there an accident? Is anyone hurt?"

"We're fine. Everyone's fine. Go back to your car, sir," Andy told him.

"I'm a doctor." He looked past Andy.

"Just go back to your car."

"Wait!" I hurried to him. He regarded me with sharp features and a thin face that wore no glasses. He looked younger than the head of white hair suggested. I asked, "What's your opinion of the wall?"

"The Pink Floyd album?" I liked him instantly.

"No. The border wall. Mexico. What's your opinion?"

He hesitated, examining me. He looked at the people pulled from the belly of the tank. Despite the harsh light of halogen and LED headlights, the warm tone of their skin showed.

"I think it's the fever dream of xenophobic idiots," the doctor said, squaring himself for an argument.

I pointed at the two men and the woman.

"These people need your help. Do you have room to take them with you?"

"Yes."

"Just don't take them to the border."

I didn't wait for comment or questions.

"Lonnie!" I called out. "We're leaving!"

Less than three minutes later I performed my first takeoff from an interstate highway.

60

We carried enough fuel to reach Ashland, Wisconsin, a town on the edge of Lake Superior. During the one hour and twenty-minute flight, Donaldson sat on the right side of the cabin, Lonnie sat on the left directly behind me. Gloria held Oscar, facing her mother. The child planted wide-eyed wonder against the window. No one spoke. No one except Andy, sitting in the copilot's seat, wore the in-cabin headsets that suppressed the engine noise. Despite my efforts to engage her, Andy remained largely silent, occasionally glancing back at the passengers. Each time she looked over her shoulder, she turned forward again wearing a curiously distant gaze. She saw something I didn't.

I concentrated on flying.

The local time read two-thirty-five when we touched down on Runway 02 at John F. Kennedy Memorial Airport. I chose it for the comfortable log-cabin airport office that offered round-the-clock restrooms and snack vending to pilots. Self-serve fuel would replenish our tanks and take us home to Essex.

I let the plane roll to the taxiway angling onto the deserted main ramp. At the gas pumps I killed the engines. Donaldson, now an old hand at it, popped open the cabin door and helped Lonnie, her daughter and her grandson disembark. Andy watched them go. She made no move to release her seatbelt.

Donaldson limped ahead to scout the FBO office. I found his vigilance comforting, although I could think of no way Sergei Roane's men would find us.

Following Andy's lead, I remained in my seat. I shut down the ignition switches and killed the lights, including the cabin lights. We sat in the dark listening to the gyros unwind.

Andy's hand found mine and squeezed. The pressure felt firm and urgent.

"I want to have a baby."

I stared at the Kollsman barometric pressure window on the altimeter. During the approach to landing I had picked up the airport ASOS broadcast which informed me, among other vital things, that the barometric pressure at Ashland was 30.07—which I set accordingly.

The altimeter displayed the field elevation. Eight twenty-seven.

I like sevens; they feel lucky to me; they pop out of chaos like sweet omens.

I peeled my gaze off the altimeter and shifted it to Andy, a goddess in any light, and no less so at that moment in the semi-darkness of the cockpit. She brimmed with something new, something I'd never seen in her, something mildly terrifying. The veneer of wonder I'd seen on the highway gave her elegant and perfect lines an added glow.

After countless discussions dissecting and rejecting the question of bringing a new life into an ever-turbulent world, after downing cases of Corona in deep debate over an infant's unimaginable impact on our private and perfect union, the thing most astonishing about that vibrating moment was the word that popped out of my mouth.

"Okay."

61

"Burns?" Andy poked her phone screen to put the incoming call on speaker.

"It's me...um..."

We stood on the ramp beside the plane. I had just finished fueling. Donaldson left Lonnie and her daughter alone in the airport office. Fifty yards away, he hovered outside the building entrance in a cone of light with his phone pressed to his ear.

"What's going on?"

"Detective, I...I might be stepping out of line here..." She sounded hesitant. She let the connection hang silent for a moment.

"What's your first name?" Andy asked.

"Lorraine."

"I'm Andrea. Call me Andy. Are you still at the scene?"

"No—I mean, yes."

Andy waited for more. When nothing came, she asked, "What about the trooper? The one they shot at?"

"Oh, he's okay. He got a face full of airbag crashing his unit when they opened fire on him. He put out a description of the car. It's a plain vanilla SUV. Might be rental. Everybody in the world has been alerted, but if they abandon the car—"

"Which they will."

"Yeah, probably." We heard her take and release a breath. "Any chance you can tell me where you are?"

"Ashland. Wisconsin."

"Are you coming back?"

"Not right away, but I will make myself available to your department for a statement. Is that what's on your mind?"

"Well, partly. But…"

"They told you to find me. Who was it? Federals?"

"Right after I called you to tell you about the shooting, after you got off the phone, the county sheriff arrived on the scene here. I filled him in. Everything. He called the FBI, got passed around a bit, but then got an earful from somebody. Your name came up. You and Special Agent Donaldson—they said he's not actually working for the FBI. Next thing I know, he ordered me to evacuate the scene. Right quick. He said he was under orders to lock everything down until a team from DOJ got here."

"Investigators?"

"He didn't say. All he said was that this crime scene was pertinent to a national terrorist threat and Homeland Security wanted me to get my ass out to the highway, pronto."

"You said a team from DOJ, right?"

"The sheriff was explicit. A few minutes ago, he came out to my unit and told me to reach out to you and get your location."

"And now you have it."

"Can I ask you a question, Detective?"

"Anything."

"What's going on here?"

"The young woman we rescued tonight will shed some light on that. I haven't had a chance to speak to her."

More silence on the line.

"Lorraine, finding me isn't the only reason you called. What happened?"

"You remember that computer? The one on the desk?"

"Yes."

"Okay, so… once we were done, I wasn't going to touch it. GPS trackers have a logging function, so I figured whatever is in its memory may be evidence in the investigation."

"Correct."

"I didn't want to shut it down or log out, you know, because of the possible password lockout."

"Good call."

"The thing is…"

"What?"

"Remember the map? How I had the tracking map zoomed in? I mean, I had it *all the way in*. I actually saw the little blip stop when the truck put on the brakes."

"Yes."

"Well, before I left the office, I got to thinking, what if I zoom out? All the way out. So, I did. And I found something. I feel like you should know."

Andy waited.

"I found another truck. It's moving."

62

Andy told Burns she would call her back. She stared at the FBO office. "Mira," she said to herself.

"What?" My question followed the back of her head.

Andy hurried into the pilot's lounge. Lonnie sat upright on a small sofa. Gloria faced her mother, curled up in her arms, cradled like a child, resting her head on Lonnie's shoulder. The boy knelt on the floor, cheerfully munching from a vending machine bag of Cheetos and pushing a plastic airplane back and forth on the coffee table.

Lonnie forced a weak smile at us and wiped water from her eyes. Her lips formed a silent *Thank you*. When she looked down at her daughter, she became the Madonna image of Gloria looking down at her child in Sergei Roane's family portrait.

Andy pulled a chair around to face them and sat down.

"I need to talk to your daughter," she told Lonnie. "It's important."

Gloria lifted her head. Posed beside her mother, the similarities were astounding, yet the differences were equally marked. Gloria's skin was pale, her cheeks gaunt, her eyes sunken and dark. She composed herself and in doing so erased a degree of wear and fear. With a few simple moves she demonstrated her mother's talent; she transformed from a damaged child to a protective young mother. She leaned over and stroked her son's head, then tidied her clothing and brushed her matted dark hair behind her ears.

One ear was swollen. She had a cut on her lower lip and yellow remnants of bruising on her neck.

Mallorin. And Tolliver.

Something cold and black stirred inside me—something restless and angry. I appeased it by recalling Tolliver's shrieks. I wondered if Andy would object if I made a trip back to Prince Henry. Or if I would tell her.

"Gloria, what do you know about your husband and Aaron McCauley?"

The girl's posture shifted. She became guarded, less vulnerable. She studied Andy.

"I need to know," Andy said.

"Who are you?"

Andy explained her position with the City of Essex Police Department. The answer spawned little comfort for someone from Juárez.

"*La policia?*"

"Yes. But not the kind you know. I also worked with Director Mitchell Lindsay of the FBI."

"And him?" She gestured at Donaldson.

Andy gave his name and title.

"He is federal?"

Donaldson nodded.

"Are you turning me over to ICE?"

"No," Lonnie interrupted. "Absolutely not!"

Gloria ignored her mother. She searched for an answer from Andy and Donaldson.

"No, we're not," Andy said.

"You said you do not work for my husband. Do you swear it?"

"I shot your husband. Two days ago," Andy said.

"Did you kill him?"

Andy shook her head. A flicker of excitement in Gloria winked out. She asked, "Why did you stop us? Why did you bring her here?" She gestured at Lonnie, who tried to reply.

"Sweetie, we—"

Andy held up a hand to silence Lonnie. Surprisingly, it worked.

"We pulled you off that truck because your husband sent men to find you. They killed the people in Desmond. They—"

"The woman with the trucks?"

"Yes."

Gloria stared into a memory. "She was kind. She gave Oscar candy."

She also gave you to Tolliver and Mallorin. I checked myself to make sure I hadn't said it out loud.

"Sergei sent men after you. They have men waiting for you at the end of the line. Sergei wants you back because you know what he did."

"Knowing what he did is all I have. If I tell you, I have no protection."

"Little girl, there is no protection," Donaldson said sharply. "I think you know that better than anyone in this room."

Andy glared at him.

"What?" He spread his hands. "You know I'm right. You can't promise her protection. I can't. The FBI can't. DEA can't. Her mother sure can't."

"You're not helping, Lee."

"And you're a fool if you disagree with him," Gloria told Andy. "What he says is the only thing I've heard tonight that I know to be true." Her crisp and precisely pronounced English had just enough accent to sound exotic. She spoke with her mother's voice. Eyes closed I would have hardly known the difference.

Andy sat back.

"You're right. And you knew it when you left, didn't you?"

A secret smile hid just beneath the surface of the girl's lips. With a talent that was clearly genetic, her entire affect shifted again. This time from guarded and defiant to confident and worldly.

"You want to know if my husband killed the FBI Director."

"Your husband and Aaron McCauley. What can you tell me?"

"Only that they did it. I knew as soon as it happened. People in the trucks with us had phones. We saw it in the news."

"How do you know that it was your husband and McCauley?"

"My husband liked to dress me up. For his guests. One of his many possessions for display," she said. "But makeup and plunging necklines didn't make me deaf."

"Something specific?"

"Never. Sergei never let anything specific be said in my presence, but he also thinks the more you see of a woman's breasts, the less you need worry about her brain."

Andy sat still.

"When a husband speaks," Gloria said, "even in the code men use, you come to know the meaning. When he speaks of failed negotiations with the American named Lindsay, and of eliminating the problem, and then one day it is on the news, a wife knows."

Donaldson leaned against the doorway. He maintained a casual pose, but he listened intently.

"Did you hear anything about how? Who did it?"

She shook her head.

"To get away, you enlisted the help of Milo O'Brien—"

"No!" She stiffened. "No, I did not ask for his help and he did not give it. No one knew my plans!"

"Gloria," Andy said softly. "Milo himself told me that he helped you."

"Milo? How—?"

Andy explained the rescue from the bunker. The unfolding story etched new lines in the girl's face.

"Where are they?"

"We had them in a safe house…but…" Andy shook her head sadly. "We think Milo reached out to Sergei to try and reconcile."

Gloria cringed.

"I'm so sorry. Sergei has them."

"No—no—Milo did nothing!"

"We know you tried to protect him."

"*Maria! Dios mio! Pobrecita! Maria was my friend!*" Gloria stared into her hands. "*Dios mio…*"

After a moment, Andy said, "Maria said you knew something more. Something you kept from her. To keep her safe. Something about Sergei,"

Gloria said flatly, "He will kill them. If he hasn't already."

Andy slid closer.

"Gloria, tell me about the names you traveled under. Your alias. Yours and your son's. The names you gave to Mallorin in Prince Henry."

Gloria reached for her son and stroked his head. He smiled up at his mother, but wise three-year-old eyes saw something in his mother's face. I made a bet with myself that he'd seen darkness and sadness and pain in his mother before. He reached over and patted her on the knee.

"*Mami, está bien,*" he told her. Earning a smile from his mother, he returned to flying his coffee table airplane.

"What secret did you keep from Maria?"

The girl's words emerged slowly.

"We were waiting for one of the trucks—that's when the ICE took us. I thought Sergei had found us. I knew what I had to do. I made an oath before God. I swore I would end our lives before I would go back—before I would let him take Oscar. I swore I would give my son to Heaven first." She reached for and stroked her son's thick black hair. The knife she held in the same hand flashed through my mind. "But the ICE didn't send us back. We were treated like all the other illegals. They said we would be deported. It was then that I understood that these men didn't know who I was—didn't know about Sergei."

"That's when you told them you were Lonnie Penn's daughter."

"I had to. We could not go back. I had to buy our way out." To Lonnie, she said, "They took your money. They said so. They told me you came. They said you paid."

"They told me you died," Lonnie whispered, unable to find her voice. *"I'm so sorry I didn't find you."*

"I thought they would let me go with you. But they…they…the men took the money…and then they took what they wanted. And when they were done, they returned us to the coyote to ensure that what they did would never be known."

Lonnie pressed a fist to her lips.

Gloria stared into empty space and black memory.

"I was glad," she said. "When they did it, I was glad. I knew such men would never touch me if they knew who I was to Sergei."

I realized that my fingernails, tucked inside fists, were close to puncturing the skin of my palms.

Andy pressed. "Gloria, the name you gave the ICE officer was Mira Apalacio. And for Oscar?"

"*Justicia.*" The girl looked at Andy and smiled weakly. "You understand, don't you."

"I think I do."

Andy glanced at me. I shrugged, utterly clueless.

"I gave those names when I thought they were giving me up to Sergei. When I made plans to kill myself and my child. A mother and child dying like that—in ICE custody—that would not go unnoticed. There would be an investigation. Our names would be noticed."

I tried hard not to imagine what would make a young woman choose to end her own life and that of her child over going back to Sergei Roane.

Andy sat back. "I do understand."

"I don't," I said.

"It's not a name."

"No," Gloria said. "It was my suicide note. *Mira a Palacio de Justicia.* I wanted someone to know what Sergei is planning."

"*Mira a Palacio de Justicia,*" Andy repeated.

"*Si.* That is what they have paid him for." Gloria reached for her backpack. "My husband showed me a table covered in these."

Taking the padded shoulder strap in both hands, she pulled until the seams split. She clawed the halves apart and poked her fingers inside. Wiggling and pulling, she extracted a small shining wafer.

"He made me lie on it. He didn't see me take one."

She placed the wafer on the coffee table.

A one-ounce bar of solid gold.

63

Andy, Donaldson and I congregated outside the FBO in cool night air. Insects swirled around spotlights that illuminated the building, accurately reflecting the thoughts that swirled in my head. Crickets sustained an urgent symphony.

"We were both wrong, Lee," Andy said. "The terrorist angle isn't a fake. It's real."

I thumbed in the direction of the FBO office. "What exactly was that?"

"*Mira a Palacio de Justicia,*" Andy said. "Look to the Palace of Justice."

"I know the Spanish—er, some of it. What is it?"

Donaldson leaned on his cane and replied, "It's a reference to the M-19 attack on the Palace of Justice—the Colombian Supreme Court—in Bogota in—what? 1984? '85?"

"Is she saying Sergei is planning an attack on the Colombian Supreme Court?"

"I don't think so," Andy said. "Not the Colombian Supreme court."

"Ours?" I asked.

No one wanted to say it. She held the gold bar up in the light. "Do you see what's on it?"

Donaldson lifted it from her fingers and squinted.

"Government stamp for the Republic of Ghana." Donaldson flipped the bar in his palm, then handed it back to Andy who pushed it into her shoulder bag.

"What would you bet that the man we saw with Sergei in Juárez is from Ghana?" Andy asked Donaldson.

"I'd bet that gold bar and all its shiny brethren."

"A table covered in them. Payment," Andy said, "to the biggest human trafficker in North America. What if Sergei isn't just moving drugs, refugees and immigrants? What if he's moving a team of terrorists into the United States?"

"In a milk truck that's half a continent away from where it should be," Donaldson added.

I held out my hand. Andy looked at it, then me. I wiggled my fingers. She pulled the gold bar from her bag and handed it to me. I held it up in the light.

"What does this mean?" I pointed at the .999 engraving on the bar.

"That's the real deal," Donaldson said. "That's twenty-four-carat gold. The number denotes the degree of 'fineness.' Ninety-nine point nine percent pure."

The weight, the engraving and the sheen gave the small bar electric potency. I pictured a table covered in them, and the evil such riches could buy.

"Terrorism doesn't make sense," Donaldson said.

"Unless you're a terrorist," I muttered.

"No." He shook his head vigorously. "Sponsoring terrorism against the United States is a risk no cartel would take. My god, we invaded two countries over 9/11. Can you imagine this administration having proof—real or imagined—that terrorists came across the southern border?"

"They would turn the Rio Grande into the thirty-eighth parallel in short order," I said.

"Yeah…they would…" Donaldson rubbed his scalp where there had been stitches a few weeks ago. "I need to think this through."

"We should go," Andy said, looking at the office. "She needs care and rest. And we need to warn somebody. We can do both better in Essex."

"I'll get ready for takeoff."

64

Lonnie Penn stretched like a cat after planting her feet on the Essex County airport ramp. Hints of dawn tinted the eastern sky. She brushed her fingers through her short blonde hair and shook it. Stretching and preening restored some of her movie star aura.

"I want to take them home," she told Andy. "With me."

"Miss Penn—"

"Andy," she said, "people say 'Miss Penn' to me when they're looking for a way to say no."

"I *am* looking for a way to say no," Andy said. "You can't protect your daughter. Her husband wants to kill her, and our government wants to give her back to him. If what she told us is true a whole new storm is brewing for her. But more than anything, right now she needs food and rest and she needs to see a doctor."

"I appreciate everything you've done. I just—Andy, *I can't let go of her now. I can't.* I never for a minute in my life understood what it would feel like to be her mother…but…now..." Lonnie struggled for the words. "I know she may not need me. In the light of day, away from all *this*, she may even hate me. *But I need her.*"

"Then don't lose her again," Andy said. "Not to Sergei Roane, and not to the U.S. Government. What Gloria told us has serious moving parts. The people moving those parts see her as a threat. They will ruthlessly eliminate that threat."

Lonnie turned and looked back at the plane. Gloria and the boy had been sleeping, curled together in their seat. They remained so even after the lullaby of the engines stopped and the rest of us quietly exited.

"Do you believe it's real? What she said?" Lonnie asked.

"We have to."

"And her?"

"I know a safe place for your daughter. Someplace out of the public eye."

"Out of the public eye. You mean away from me," Lonnie said. Andy started to protest, but Lonnie waved her off. "I know. I'm an attention magnet. But isn't high visibility a kind of insurance? If she stays with me, in the light, wouldn't she be safe?"

"I don't mean to be harsh," Andy said, lowering her voice, "but it won't matter. They'll kill her live on MSNBC if it suits them."

Gloria appeared at the cabin door with the child. Lonnie hurried to scoop the sleeping boy out of her daughter's arms. Oscar stirred and threw his tiny arms around Lonnie's neck and nestled against her. His sleepy embrace squeezed wet drops from the A-list actor's eyes. Lonnie laughed abruptly and wiped them away.

"Works better than a menthol stick!"

I used a phone app and launched the ponderous process of opening the big Foundation hangar door.

"There's a lounge, a kitchen, a 'fridge with some snacks. Help yourselves. Bathroom is to the left. If you run into anyone at this early hour, his name will be Arun."

Lonnie and Gloria followed a line from my outstretched arm across the polished hangar floor toward the office.

Donaldson, who had been on his phone at the edge of the ramp walked back to where I stood beside Andy.

"Any luck?" she asked.

He tucked his phone in his pocket.

"We're screwed," he said. "I spoke to Lindsay's executive assistant."

"Carlisle-Plinkham?" I asked.

"Her name is Carson-Pelham," Andy corrected me. "Why did you call her?"

"I didn't," Donaldson said. "She called me."

Andy looked skeptical. Lindsay's gatekeeper had been chilly toward her on the phone. I sensed a lack of trust.

Donaldson read her expression. "I know. I don't get it either. She called to tell me they want to interview me about Mike Horowitz's murder. In not so many words, she told me to keep my head down—which I did not expect. In any case, it means we're screwed."

"They can't possibly suspect you," I said.

"I doubt they do. But Carson-Pelham suggested that somebody wants to invite me—us—for a week or two of slow and senseless questioning."

"What does she know." Andy dismissed the idea.

"More than you think, Andrea. The only person more powerful or knowledgeable in Lindsay's office than Lindsay was his executive assistant. Don't kid yourself."

"Good," I said. "Did you tell her about the attack?"

"No."

I glared at him. "Why not? For God's sake, man, tell the FBI. The CIA. Call the D.C. Metro police. We know a detective there—Dee, what was his name? The guy that was all hot for you?" She made a face at me. "Call the Capitol Police. The Army. The Navy. Anybody—*everybody!* You can't tell me that someone isn't going to take a terrorist threat seriously. Christ, it's the demon they're already chasing. C'mon, this should be easy. A milk truck from a murder scene in North Dakota on the streets of Washington, D.C.? Pulling up to the Supreme Court? They'd have to be dolts to let that through."

"It might not be a milk truck," Andy said. "I sent a text to Burns to ask her to confirm that all the Paddington trucks are accounted for. I haven't heard back."

"Getting someone to believe isn't the problem," Donaldson said. "*All* of those agencies are already seeing terrorists under every rock."

"Then what's the problem?" I asked.

"The girl's goddamned story doesn't hold water. The Supreme Court —*our Supreme Court*—is not in session. The Court does not resume session until October." Donaldson let his statement hang for a moment. "That means she's wrong about the target, and without that computer we can't figure out what is. We don't even know it is a milk truck."

"The police have the computer, for chrissakes!" I argued.

"Doesn't matter." He leaned on his cane and stared at his feet.

"How could that possibly not matter?" I asked.

"Because," he said, "I keep going back to the island. They made this about terrorism from the start. Jesus, *they advertised it.* But sponsoring terrorists is a lousy move for a cartel paying millions to a D.C. spin artist to polish their image. Only idiots would provoke the United States. Just ask El Chapo. Ask Saddam."

"So, they're idiots. That doesn't make it less real."

"That's not the point. It means Sergei is not worried about irking us. Sergei knows his role in this will not harm him. Which can only mean one thing."

"What? He doesn't think he'll get caught?"

"It means he doesn't care. Politically, he's protected."

"On our side of the fence?" Andy asked.

"Uh-huh."

"That's ridiculous," I said. "McCauley doesn't have that kind of juice. At the end of the day he's just another Washington consultant whoring himself out to international checkbooks."

"It's not McCauley. Remember, since Mackinac he's also been shielded."

"By whom?"

Donaldson ignored me and asked Andy, "How do you suppose DOJ knew about Desmond so fast?"

Andy started to answer, but her words hung up. Donaldson didn't wait.

"Milo told Gloria about the coyote route. Then he told us. We can assume that while he watched his wife and children murdered, Milo spilled it all to Sergei, which is how Sergei knew to send a team of cleaners to Paddington Trucking to find his missing wife. But how did DOJ almost instantly tie a murder in a small-town trucking company in Minnesota to a terrorist threat?"

"Please," Andy said. "Can we not muddy this with conspiracy theories?"

"God dammit, Stewart, it's not a conspiracy theory. They're painting the crime scene to fit a narrative—just like they did on the island."

Andy didn't respond.

"Fine. If you don't want conspiracy theories, then let me muddy this with facts. The current administration is and has been anti-African Union."

"The labor union?" I asked.

"No, the African Union. It's like the United Nations of Africa," Andy explained.

"The U.S. has always had a touchy relationship with the organization, thanks to Cold War influences. But the current White House has been ramping up enemy-talk against them."

"Lee, we don't have time for civics lessons."

"Yes. You do. Guess who the sitting president of the African Union is?"

Andy folded her arms. "The President of Ghana."

"Bingo. Here's another fact. American mining interests have tried for years to take over the gold operations in Ghana. Our biggest mining companies were built on coal, but the coal business is in serious decline—and that's only going to get worse when this country reverses direction on alternative energy. Coal companies desperately want in on the international gold trade. Jay Manning—owner of the biggest coal producer in the country—threw a ton of money behind the President—and, *voilà* —we get a sudden policy swing from The White House that includes verbal attacks *on a democratically-elected leader*. A leader who has roadblocked any international acquisition of his country's gold mining."

"Man, you are really reaching," I said.

"Am I? Lindsay told us most of this. I'm just filling in the blanks."

I threw up my hands. "Okay. Okay. Let's stop there. Because I gotta ask, how does selling everyone the idea of a terrorist attack benefit all this?"

"It's the icing for this shitcake. If they can show that terrorists supported by the now-discredited president of Ghana are planning an attack on the U.S., what do you think will happen? What do you think will happen to the southern border?"

Andy said, "Lee, the workers union is not a terrorist group. They're a labor union."

"*Until someone makes them terrorists.*"

"My god! You exhaust me." I threw up my hands. "You're arguing *for* the very thing *you just argued against!*"

"Come on, Will! Lindsay brought you in to retrieve Gloria Rilling even before you knew you were in. His little surveillance test on the island was no test. He was already knee-deep in this mess. It got him killed."

Andy's lower lip emerged slightly—a warning. I held my tongue. I didn't need to argue with Donaldson. In a moment, Andy would shoot this hot air balloon out of the sky.

I stood back to watch it go down in flames. Donaldson waited for her to speak.

"I think you're right," she told him.

"About what?" I asked, astonished. "That we're screwed or the tin-foil hat part?"

"I think he's right, Will."

"Jesus, Dee! Even if crazy town here is right, we don't know what will happen, where, when or how—and that pretty much *guarantees* no one will listen."

"Why *would* they listen?" Donaldson asked. "They already know. The alarm's already been raised. They've been chasing terrorist boogeymen since Mackinac."

"They don't know about this Palace of Justice thing," I said.

"*That's* the part I disagree with! The girl has it wrong. But even if she didn't, my guess is that DOJ will listen politely and then grab up that little girl in there to send her back to her husband. Plus, I wasn't kidding about us disappearing for a few weeks of questioning. We can scream terrorist attack at the top of our lungs and they'd just ask if we want a cup of coffee and go back to demanding to know why you—" He pointed at Andy. "—were on that dock in Mackinac. And what exactly would you tell them about that?"

"Then we call *The New York Times*," I said, feeling a mix of anger and pure exhaustion coming to a boil.

Donaldson laughed.

"And tell them what? A heightened terrorist threat level is already the front-page story." He pulled out his phone and waved it in the air. "And believe me, they have better sources than we do. We don't have jack to give them. Plus, they'll be the first to confirm that the Supreme Court is not in session. I'm telling you, the girl has it wrong."

Andy's phone rang. She checked the screen, then touched the speaker function.

"Burns, you're on speaker with my husband and Special Agent Donaldson."

"Hi, all. Um, Detective, I have that information you asked for. Paddington has eleven trucks registered with Minnesota DOT. They added a few two years ago, but the fleet has been eleven ever since. All the same. There were seven parked in back, two in the maintenance garage, and the one you stopped going to Canada."

"That's ten. Where's number eleven?"

"Gotta be the one on the road."

"Officer," Donaldson spoke up, "Detective Stewart said you had to turn over the scene to the sheriff. Any chance of getting to that computer?"

"I suppose if I don't mind losing my job," she replied.

None of us spoke.

"Are you serious? You want me to lose my job?"

"I want you to get your hands on it. Did that DOJ team show up yet?"

"The county cars are still here. And the coroner's truck. Nothing else."

"Burns," Andy said, "we can't ask you to do something—"

"Illegal?"

"Risky. But we think the terrorist threat is real and that it involves that truck."

"Isn't that the whole point of the feds showing up? Shouldn't they have it?"

"I don't think they're going to show up anytime soon," Andy said, catching Donaldson's eye and a nod of agreement. "And we don't have time to wait for them."

Burns let the line hang silent for a moment. "Okay. I'll get back to you. Either with the computer or my resumé."

Andy ended the call.

"I get it," I said. "Get the computer. Find the truck. Then call every local law enforcement agency within fifty miles of it and intercept it."

"A good way to get a lot of local LEOs killed," Donaldson said. "The attack in Colombia used explosives and high-powered weapons and killed over a hundred people. It ended with the army storming the Palace of Justice. Plus, we don't know if it's packed full of heavily-armed terrorists or packed full of C-4."

"Or loaded with milk."

Andy started for the hangar. "I'm going to see to Gloria and her boy."

"And then?" I asked.

"And then I'm going to call someone who can help us."

65

"Are you kidding me?" Andy's sister Lydia leaped from her car. She grabbed my arm. "Lonnie Penn? For real Lonnie Penn?"

"For real Lonnie Penn," I said.

"Yes, and for Heaven's sake, calm down," Andy said. "I don't have much time. They're fueling the plane. We have to go."

Lydia didn't calm down. She squealed and clenched herself. There are times when Lydia, the older sister, is nearly a twin to Andy. This moment of girlish exuberance wasn't one of them.

"How long? How long do you think she'll stay with us?"

"I'm not sure. But Liddy, this is absolutely secret. No social media. Nothing. Not even Mom and Dad. Especially not Mom."

"Ever?"

"I mean it, sis. No pictures. No posting. This is as serious as it was back when Mannis Rahn was on the loose. She has her daughter and her daughter's little boy with her, and they are in real danger. If this gets out, you will put them and your own family at risk."

"Okay, okay, okay. But...*Lonnie Penn is a granny?* What?"

"The child's father is a drug lord, Lydia. He's after Lonnie's daughter."

"You just called her 'Lonnie!' OMG!"

"Liddy. Focus. If her location gets out—" Andy stopped. "You know what? This is a bad idea."

"No! No, I can take care of her. Absolute secret. Absolute," Lydia insisted. "I promise, Katie. Cross my heart!" Use of Andy's childhood nickname added weight to Lydia's commitment.

Andy relented.

"I asked Chief Ceeves to put a couple cars on The Lakes. I also called Dr. Morrissey and asked him to meet you at your house, hush-hush. The girl needs to be examined. But for God's sake, Liddy, get back down to earth or we're not doing this."

"*Eeeeee! I can't!*" Lydia forced herself to freeze. She took a deep breath and flexed her fingers. "Okay. I'm fine. Just—what's she like? Will, have you met her?"

"Yup," I said. "She's nice. Just don't get on her bad side. She can bite."

Andy led her sister to the door to the hangar office. "Another thing. This is her story to tell, okay? Don't press her. She needs time with her daughter. She just met her grandson. They need seclusion. And security. No phone, no email, no internet."

Andy stopped. She made Lydia pause and settle herself. "Are you ready?"

"How do I look?" Lydia adjusted her hair.

Andy shook her head, full of fresh doubt.

THE INTRODUCTIONS WENT SMOOTHLY. Lydia managed to breathe and speak coherently. Lonnie employed equal aplomb in making Andy's sister comfortable, deploying flawless celebrity people skills.

While Lydia and Lonnie traded small talk, Andy pulled Gloria aside. She pointed at Oscar, who had purloined the plastic airplane from the lounge in Ashland and now taxied it on the office carpet. I could think of worse things for a boy to steal.

"That's your son, your child, Gloria," Andy said. "Is there anything you wouldn't do to save him?"

The girl, unblinking, said, "I think I've proven how far I would go."

Andy studied her.

"What?"

"Lydia is my sister, my family. Tell me now if you plan to do something stupid."

"What do you mean?"

"Calling Sergei. That's what Milo did. He was safe. His family was safe. But he thought Sergei would take him back. Now at least one of his children is dead. More than likely, the whole family is dead."

"Never."

Andy stepped closer and lowered her voice. "You're a woman, Gloria, but you might also be a girl who would make the terrible mistake of believing a man when he begs her forgiveness, when he promises undying love, when he promises security and wealth and protection. When he swears that he will never raise a hand to you, ever again. I've seen it before. Men lie, especially men like Sergei. I need to know if you will endanger my sister, and her children, by falling for Sergei's lies."

Gloria's lips pulled into a sad smile.

"You think he can beg to be forgiven and just like that—" she snapped her fingers "—I would forgive him? For being beaten? For being raped day after day? For being made numb to his brutality? *For what I know he has done to Maria and Milo? Should I spell out some of his favorite ways of hurting people?*" Fury honed a razor edge to her words. She clenched her teeth and leaned toward Andy. "*I am not a child.* But, yes, one day *I will* return to him. The day I know Oscar is safe. The day I can claw out his eyes and cut his throat."

Andy faced the girl, motionless. She took in the full measure of Gloria Rilling who was, in that instant, as far from a child as any girl I have ever seen.

"Does that satisfy you?"

Andy nodded.

"Be patient with my sister. Having your mother in the house might make her a little crazy."

66

Arun looked up from the computer screen. He whispered, "That's Lonnie Penn!"

"What? Where?" I made a show of searching the office.

"How do you know Lonnie Penn?"

"Her dad knew Earl. Did you find anything?" I had faith. If something could be found on the internet, Arun would find it.

He glanced in the direction of the office door. Andy escorted our guests to her sister's car. Arun grinned helplessly.

"Lonnie Penn!"

"I'll get her autograph for you. What did you find?"

He waved me to his side of the desk.

"Only this. You are quite right. The United States Supreme Court is in recess for the summer. Their session resumes, officially, in October. Opening session is a significant event. Depending on the docket, media coverage can be intense. Sometimes there's organized protesting."

"But nothing now?"

"Nothing. They do not don their black robes until autumn."

"Sounds like someone sacrificing a virgin. You best steer clear."

"I'm not a—!"

"Ha! I knew it! You and Pi—" I stopped myself. Ever since Pidge fell for the dusky Englishman, she has called herself by her given name. "—er, Cassidy! You and Cassidy finally did the deed!"

Arun blushed. "None of your business!"

"Aw, relax. Everyone is rooting for you. I had Seventh Date in the pool. Was it?"

"Pool? What pool?"

"I'm kidding."

He stared daggers at me. "I am a mysterious man with the blood of India in my veins. It is in my power to kill you in your sleep."

"That would only work if I slept. Do me a favor and keep looking. We're missing something."

"If I do not choose to end your life first."

"Here." I used his message pad to write down a name and a phone number I had memorized. I tore it off and handed it to him. "If you hit a wall, ask this woman for help. Not sure if she'll answer—or if she'll trust you. If she asks for proof of ID, tell her you think I act like a twelve-year-old."

Arun leaned back in his office chair and muttered. "You do."

I clapped him on the shoulder. "Fine, mystery man. I leave you to it. Call us the minute you know something."

"I will."

I stopped at the door. "Was it the seventh date?"

"Get out!"

67

Refueled and ready, the Navajo's aura bristled with new energy. The chrome spinners kicked back morning sun rays. The engines strained at their mounts. The landing gear begged to be tucked away.

Andy and I loaded our bags in the long nose compartment. I stashed my flight bag. She loaded an overnight bag she had acquired on a rapid round trip to our home where she changed clothes and brushed out her auburn hair. Before leaving the house, she pushed two boxes of 9mm ammunition into the bag. I put on fresh cargo pants and stuffed several fully charged power units from the mudroom cabinet into the pants pockets.

Pidge arrived first. She parked beside the Foundation hangar and disappeared inside for a visit with Arun before joining us on the ramp.

"Stop teasing my boyfriend," she snapped at me when she approached the airplane. She shoved a backpack into the nose compartment. "Nice ride," she added. "I get to fly."

She conducted a walk-around, then climbed inside and took the pilot's seat.

A black and white SUV pulled up beside Pidge's Honda. Chief Tom Ceeves unwound himself from the seat, opened the back door and pulled out a small bag. He leaned in and extracted a department-issue shotgun. The polar opposite of Pidge's blonde pixie-sized frame, Tom strolled to the airplane, growing larger with each step and making me second-guess my weight and balance calculations.

"Did you get through to her?"

"No sir," Andy replied. "We will."

"Terrorists? For sure?"

"I'll brief you on the way, sir," she replied.

He looked me over as if he expected me to vanish before his eyes.

"You got one more coming," he said before performing the minor miracle of climbing into the cabin.

"One more?" I asked.

Andy formed the same question on her lips when a voice called to us from the other side of the airplane.

"Told you she was a beauty."

Earl Jackson ducked under the horizontal stabilizer carrying a gym bag. He stomped toward us on a bow-legged stride. He led with an expression that fathers wear when they find out the kids just used dad's golf clubs to smash pumpkins. On Earl, it merely said Hello.

"Did you think you could take my best pilot and not me?"

"I heard that," Pidge said loudly from the cockpit.

"How did you...?" I asked.

"Hear about this circus? Rosemary II told me. Figured somebody who can actually kick some ass better go along."

"I heard that," Tom rumbled from within the cabin.

"How did Rosemary II...?" Andy asked.

"The woman is a witch. C'mon. Let's launch ol' Pegasus here. You can explain the rest on the way."

PART V

68

I fell asleep while Pidge prepared for takeoff. Sleeping on an airplane has never been a problem for me. Andy is the opposite. She can't sleep in a vehicle of any kind. During a nighttime car ride, she chats nonstop, largely I think because she believes conversation will keep me awake at the wheel.

We had a five-minute ATC hold at the end of runway 13. The steady thrum of the engines became hypnotic. I sat with my back to the partition behind Pidge. Andy faced me. Tom faced aft in the seat directly behind Earl, who sat in the copilot's seat. Donaldson took the rearmost seat since Tom's knees prohibited placing anyone directly opposite him.

I closed my eyes for the first time in over twenty-four hours. Andy let her knees rub mine while we waited for takeoff.

Knocked me right out.

THE DREAM RODE in on the Navajo's idling engine song.

Instead of Pidge, I sat at the controls, listening to the soft, minimal conversation of air traffic control in my pilot's headset. The controller wanted to know what approach I planned to use at Essex County.

"RNAV 31, please," I requested.

The glistening surface of Lake Michigan flowed below. As I have done before in this dream, I reached down beside the pilot's seat, past the checklists and extra pens in the elastic side pouch, and dragged my fingers through the smooth surface of the lake at two hundred miles per hour. The cold water induced a refreshing shiver. I reminded myself that I would die if I had to spend more than twenty minutes in the water, so I pulled my fingers back, all the way up to ten thousand feet and shook off the drops. The controller cleared me for the approach to runway 31 at Essex County Airport.

My fingers closed on the throttles. I reduced the power, then rolled the trim wheel to lighten the load on the control yoke. The controller, suddenly testy, said to bring the *other* tray and call maintenance, but in a moment of dream clarity I knew that the line came from my time in the hospital when someone vomited and intruding dialogue from the nurses' station stuck to the dream like graffiti on a wall.

The black earth of the shoreline passed under me. No more dragging my fingers in the water. The airport beacon called out to me in alternating flashes of green and white.

Something loomed ahead, dark and empty. A void into which memories were sucked.

The black hole hung against the night sky, distinguished by the way it blotted out the stars. I tried to break hard right. The yoke turned but the airplane remained on course. The emptiness—the thing I could not remember—hit the left wing. Sudden. Explosive. The wing and engine vanished along with the side of the cockpit. Wind ripped at my clothes. The airplane became a trail of debris falling from the sky. A cool sensation wrapped itself around me, penetrating my clothes, my skin. It became a living sheath. I rose against the seat belt.

The other thing.

Deploying like a parachute, *the other thing* freed me from gravity's grasp.

The Navajo's cabin disintegrated, replaced by a never-dark hospital room. Transported by the magic of dreams, I was no longer falling to earth in my pilot's seat. I was in the hospital room where I first woke after the crash. Where I first floated to the ceiling. Where I floated now.

"I don't think you can reach me if you're floating," Andy said. She stood beside the bed. She brushed a lock of hair from one eye. Behind her, a floor-to-ceiling glass window shattered. The shards flew out the rectangular hole.

"Do you want to have a baby?" she asked. Before I could answer, Sergei Roane materialized at her side and shoved her violently out the window. She screamed. Sergei turned a rictus grin on me.

"Now we're even."

My dream heart stopped. I flailed and scrambled, banging into the hospital room ceiling light, smashing my knee against it (again), desperate to get out of *the other thing* because the vanished state left me helpless. I had no propulsion units—in this dream. They did not yet exist.

Twin levers. Right there in front of me. On the power quadrant, just to the right of the red-knobbed mixture controls. My right hand flopped on the levers like numb meat. It refused to close a grip.

This can't be happening! Andy had gone out the window ages ago. This was no longer Essex Memorial Hospital. This was the thirty-eighth floor of a Chicago high-rise office building. She would surely hit the sidewalk long before I could reach her. I tried the levers again. My fingers would not answer.

Lillian Farris sat in a visitor's chair reading a paperback that Andy left behind. "I have nineteen PHD's and it's obvious what you're doing is wrong. I mean, if you have to pull those stupid levers every time you deploy *the other thing*, what good is it?"

"Push," I said. "You pull them to reappear. I'm already gone. I'm trying to reappear."

"As usual, you have it backward, dumbass."

She pointed. I stood at the dizzying edge looking down through the broken window. I had reappeared. My feet pressed the carpet and the weight comforted me. Gravity isn't something you notice until you don't have any.

I saw a chance. Andy had only fallen a few floors. I dove out the window. My wife, just a few floors down, looked up at me with a serenity utterly detached from falling to her death.

"If it's a girl we'll name her Rug Rat."

I dove after her.

Fwooomp!

I vanished. Too soon! She began to accelerate away from me, but not before she reached up and touched me.

Shaking my leg.

"Will."

The Navajo engines hummed at climb power. Andy shook my knee.

"What?" I adjusted in my seat. I idiotically tried to pretend I had not fallen asleep. The window showed me the brilliant white tops of a layer of scattered clouds.

Andy glared in my direction. She darted her eyes to the cockpit and Earl.

"What?" I rubbed my face. "Was I drooling?"

She pointed at me. Across the aisle, Tom also stared. Donaldson, too. I rubbed my face again. Andy reached across to tap my chest.

Except I wasn't there.

Andy glanced again at Earl.

Crap! I felt the cool sensation and I realized my feet were not on the floor.

I struggled for a moment to weed the dream out of my mind and locate the imaginary levers that control *the other thing*.

Fwooomp!

I reappeared and settled in the seat just as Earl glanced over his shoulder at me. Andy smiled at him. Tom continued to stare.

"Okay," I said. "That hasn't happened before."

69

We cruised in and out of clouds and between layers. Glimpses of cobalt blue told me we crossed the southwestern tip of Lake Erie, somewhere between Detroit and Cleveland. Andy stopped making *let's talk about it* faces at me, but Tom couldn't stop glancing across the narrow aisle. I briefly considered vanishing again, just to mess with him.

My old school phone ringer jingled. I wondered who had the burner number, then remembered that Andy and I had swapped the San Diego burners for our own phones.

The memorized number I gave Arun appeared onscreen. I answered it.

"Hang on a sec!" I found my headset. The Bluetooth connection opened the call in my ears.

"—told you not to mess around with the government, dumbass." It came as no surprise that the woman on the line launched into the conversation without me.

"Lillian," I said, responding to Andy's curiosity-laced expression. "Thanks for getting back to me."

"Did you hear what I said?"

Lillian Farris sounded judgmental as usual. Lillian doesn't have the nineteen PHDs she claimed in my dream, but she has a few. Her mind and credentials landed her in the employ of the U.S. government until paranoia and paranormal beliefs put her at odds with her employer—and perhaps reality.

"Did you talk to Arun?" I asked.

"The English Indian? Yes. Bright fellow. Wish I could say the same for you. I warned you about the Federal Bureau of Imbeciles but you—"

The line went silent. "Lillian? Lillian?" The problem with cellular connections in a high-speed aircraft. "Lost her," I told Andy.

Rather than play cross-dial with her, I waited. A minute later my headset signaled her incoming call. I tapped to open the connection.

"I'm in an airplane. The call will drop in a minute, so bitch at me later. Did Arun tell you what we're looking for."

"Black Robe Week," she said. "That's what you're looking for."

"What the hell is Black Robe Week?"

"You already know the Court is not in—"

Gone again. I gave up.

Text me the details.

I hit send.

70

"Do you see her?" I asked Andy. She had a better view out the right side than I did. She searched through the Navajo side windows. I changed my watch to Eastern time and felt the pinch of losing an hour.

"No."

Pidge rolled the Navajo onto the ramp and brought it to a stop facing a small airport office at the end of a row of hangars. She held the brakes and cut the engines. Donaldson opened the airstair door and eased himself out cane first.

The ramp at Warrenton Fauquier Airport in Midland, Virginia, lay quiet. No roaring sedans, flashing lights or men in FBI windbreakers. A handful of light single-engine airplanes occupied tiedown spots. I stretched the kinks out while the chief squeezed himself from the cabin. The plane rocked when his weight left the steps. Andy and I joined him on the ramp.

"Got a text from Lillian." I held up my phone.

"Got a text from Burns," Andy said.

"You first." My news wasn't helpful.

"She wants me to call." Andy poked her phone screen and waited. On speaker, the line rang. Burns picked up immediately. "Lorraine, I have you on speaker with my boss, Chief Ceeves. Did you get it?"

"No," she said. "I'm sorry."

"What happened?"

"I decided to be straight with Sheriff Colgan. He's a decent guy He knew my dad. And he was willing to listen. But right as I'm explaining the situation to him, a lawyer from DOJ shows up and bull-rushes us both."

"Excuse me," Donaldson said, "I want to be clear. A lawyer? Not FBI?"

"No. Seriously, a freakin' lawyer. He started barking at us about federal authority and told us to get out and seal the scene. He ordered the coroner to stop everything he was doing. I went in the office to get the computer and he followed me. It got ugly. He told me to back off. Then he pulled the laptop plug, pulled the ethernet cable and powered it down. I tried to stop him, but he said it had to go to a lab for immediate analysis—and that if I stood in his way all kinds of Homeland Security hell was going to rain down on me."

"Were you able to explain—?"

"Ha! That stink in a suit wouldn't let me get a word in edgewise."

The collapse of our hopes rendered us silent.

"I'm really sorry, Detective. If I had been five minutes faster…"

"That's not on you, Lorraine. You did your best."

"You're sure he was a lawyer from DOJ?" Donaldson asked. "Did he show you any credentials."

"I got his card. Department of Justice—Fargo office. Do you want me to send a photo?"

Andy, never one to dismiss data, said yes.

I leaned in on impulse and asked, "Hey, Burns, can you tell us where that truck was when you saw it on the map? I mean, precisely."

"Hold on. I wrote it down," she said. She came back a moment later. "Five miles east of Willow Springs, Missouri on State 60."

"What time was that?" Andy drew a pen and notepad from her bag.

"Three fifteen."

"Okay, thanks."

The call ended. Andy cleared the screen, then initiated another call. It went directly to voicemail. She waited, identified herself, stated our location and asked for a call back.

"I don't think she's coming," I said.

"What's your news?"

I held up my phone for her to read Lillian's message.

"*Black Robe is a GD government secret. Ask your new best friends dumbass.*" Andy made her I-told-you-so face and said, "So much for Doctor Dark Web."

"What now?" Tom asked.

Earl dropped down the steps and joined us. "You guys look like somebody sacked your quarterback."

"There's a good chance we just made this trip for nothing," I said. I looked at Donaldson. "Got anybody else on speed dial?"

"Chairman of the Joint Chiefs, but he doesn't do domestic law enforcement." I could not determine if he was kidding.

Andy heaved a long sigh. Small airports can be loud and vibrant but are more often vast and deserted. The empty ramp and silent runway amplified her disappointment.

This trip had been her gamble. I recognized the play as a long shot when she suggested it. In Essex, Andy's urgent calls to the one person she thought might help us went through office bureaucracy and dropped into the black hole of voicemail. The decision to fly to Virginia sprang from hope for a response that failed to materialize.

"Dee," I said, "we all signed off on this."

"We're here. We keep trying," Tom said.

Andy acknowledged the moral support and took another stab at her phone. "That was her cell. I'll try her office again."

"Who's this guy?" Earl pointed.

A black GMC crew cab pickup rolled around the terminal building onto the ramp. The windshield reflected the bright mid-afternoon sky, obscuring the driver. The truck steered directly toward us. It stopped in front of the Navajo. The driver stepped out and walked past the rear fender on a purposeful athletic stride.

Andy dropped her phone into her bag.

"I wasn't sure you got my message."

Like the first time we met, the woman wore jeans, riding boots and a denim shirt. I knew if I got close enough, she would smell of horses. She rounded the wingtip of the Navajo and pulled off a ball cap revealing tight curls of red hair. She removed her sunglasses and measured us with steel blue eyes.

"Hello, Andrea. Will."

"Karen," Andy said. "Lee Donaldson, FBI, this is Chief Deputy Karen Whitlock of the U.S. Marshals Service." They shook hands. "This is my boss, Chief Tom Ceeves of the City of Essex Police Department." Tom extended his hand and Whitlock took it, but not after hesitant appraisal of his oversized hand—perhaps wondering if she would get hers back. "And this is Will's former boss, Earl Jackson." Earl clamped his claw-like grip on Whitlock's hand. She winced. "And you remember our pilot, Cassidy Page." Andy pointed at Pidge, who poked her head out of the cabin.

"Hi!"

"Nice to see you again, Miss Page," Whitlock said. "I saw your name on a report out of Nebraska not too long ago."

"That was just a little road rage," I said. Pidge waited for Whitlock to turn back to Andy, then flipped me the finger.

"Detective, this is the second time you've pulled me away from my horses. More to the point, I should be on my way to D.C. My office just put out an all-hands-on-deck call."

"Why?" Andy asked. "Did something happen?"

"The White House went on lockdown twenty minutes ago. Homeland is reporting a credible threat from the same people that hit Mitchell Lindsay," Whitlock tossed a glance at Donaldson. "Every agency with a badge is locking and loading."

"Yet you came here," Donaldson said.

Whitlock sighed, "Detective Stewart said the magic word. I got your voicemail message, Andrea."

"The target isn't the White House," Andy said. "The target is the judiciary. The Supreme Court. The Justices."

"Detective, part of me is here because I owe you. But not enough to chase wild geese while every other agency is lighting up the board based on credible intel. What you're saying can't be. The Court's not in session." Whitlock slowly added, "Unless you know something I don't."

"Black Robe Week," Andy said.

The words landed like molten lead.

"Mother of God," Whitlock whispered.

WE HELD a conference at the trailing edge of the Navajo's left wing. Andy gave Whitlock a bullet point summary. The Chief Deputy listened without comment. Growing alarm on her face spoke for her. At our first meeting last winter, she had reminded me of a middle school physical education teacher. Slightly stocky. Possibly a practitioner of an obscure martial art with an exotic name. Now she layered on the impression of a general finding out that her forces are surrounded.

Andy finished. "Losing the computer cuts us off at the knees. We think we know what's coming, but we don't know where or when."

"Where is it now?"

"The truck?"

"The laptop."

"Last we heard, some paper pusher from DOJ grabbed it. Said it was going to a lab," Donaldson said. "Good way to take it off the board during the critical hours. There's no way we get it back in time, and if we do, it's probably protected by a password only a dead woman knows."

Everyone stared at the Chief Deputy.

Whitlock pulled her phone from her jeans pocket. She tapped to speed dial. A voice answered.

"Paula, it's me. Who's on Black Robe?" She stared at her feet until the answer came back. "Thanks." She cut the connection and opened a new one. After three rings, someone answered.

"Karen Whitlock here. Are you on Black Robe?...Is it at The Plantation?" Whitlock stood still through a longer-than-necessary response. Finally, she interrupted. "Lock it down...That's what I said. Lock it down. Full alert...No, I heard, too, but it's not D.C., it's The Plantation...Because I know...No. Listen, to me. Get a team down from D.C. and get everyone ready for transport...Goddamit, on *my* authority, okay? I'm driving down myself, but don't wait for me. Seal the road. No traffic...No, I think the best bet is secure in place until the cavalry arrives. You don't want to get caught in the open...The possible tango vehicle is a milk tanker truck fitted out to carry bad actors inside the tank. May have a company name. Paddington. Get word out to local PD, too. Tell them to notify you, but make it clear, *do not approach*. If this reads the way I think it does, we're looking at multiple offenders with heavy weapons and high explosives. The intel says they're modeling this after the Colombian Palace of Justice attack...Look it up. Go."

She ended the call.

Andy blinked, summing up the reaction of the rest of us. "Ma'am, I...uh..."

"Detective, I just put my head on the rails."

"What the hell was that?" Donaldson asked.

Whitlock tucked away her phone. "The Supreme Court of the United States has its own police force, about a hundred and fifty officers. They're already on high alert and the Supreme Court building in D.C. is sealed off, same as almost every other federal building. But the court is not in session. You knew that."

"We did," Andy said.

"You also knew about Black Robe Week."

"We just found out."

"I'd love to know how. We try to keep that quiet," Whitlock said.

"What the hell is Black Robe Week," Earl asked.

"Once a year, the justices convene, informally. Not to discuss cases. They take up office matters, housekeeping, talk about who's stealing whose yogurt from the 'fridge, that sort of thing. They brag about their grandchildren and connect to each other as people and not just conservative or liberal figureheads. Been going on for over a century."

"It's this week..." Donaldson said.

"Yes. You called me, Detective. Why?"

"We called everyone," Donaldson interrupted. Whitlock waved him off.

"Why me?"

"I called you because I thought you might listen."

Whitlock frowned. She planted her hands on her hips and carried on a ten second debate with herself.

"But you knew about the protection chain, right?"

Andy said yes.

Whitlock nodded.

"Somebody wanna explain?" Earl demanded.

Whitlock obliged. "When the justices are off premises, away from the court, their protection transfers from the Supreme Court Police to the U.S. Marshals."

"Does that mean you have a detail on them? Right now?" Donaldson asked.

"It's not my detail, but yes, that's who I spoke to. Our service has nine Justices of the United States Supreme Court under U.S. Marshals' protection at the Siddley Plantation," she said. "It's a glorified bed and breakfast most of the year, but this week, it's all ours. If what you say is true, then your theoretical attack very definitely has a target. I need to get there."

"We're coming with you," Andy said. "Extra hands. Extra eyes. At least until you can get reinforcements and evacuate."

Whitlock started for her truck.

"Wait!" I stopped her. I hurried to the cabin and returned with the iPad from my flight bag. "Where is this place?"

I held out the device. Whitlock pointed at the screen. "Here. Off Albermarle Bay."

"Jesus, that's the coast of North Carolina. That's gotta be a three-hour drive."

"Closer to four with Richmond traffic. It will take at least four for a team from D.C. to get there."

"Right. But there's an airport five minutes from this plantation. We can get you there in forty minutes." I turned to Pidge and Earl. "We need gas in this thing as fast as you can. Topped."

"Why topped?" Pidge asked. "We've got enough to—"

"Because after we drop her off, we're going to hunt down that truck."

Earl didn't wait for a committee decision. "Fire it up and haul it over to the pumps." Pidge ran for the cabin door.

"Dee, give me your note. The note you took—the location that Burns gave you."

Andy pulled out her notebook and peeled off the page. I took it and looked at Whitlock. "I think I know how we can track the vehicle. Maybe locate it before it ever gets near this plantation."

The Chief Deputy hesitated. She read the faces around her, then focused on Andy.

"If anyone can..." Andy said.

"Okay. Let me park my truck and make a couple more calls."

71

Whitlock leaned across the aisle and looked at my iPad. Pidge ran at full throttle. Light low-level chop rocked the cabin. None of us wore headsets.

"Point of origin, we think, is Missouri," Andy explained over the engine noise.

"Which you know, how?"

"I picked it up from a deputy sheriff in Prince Henry, South Dakota," I said. Whitlock shot me a skeptical look. "Long story. But more relevant is that at three-fifteen this morning, the truck was here." I pointed at the map.

"How do we know the thing isn't simply being delivered somewhere? Or carrying a load of milk? Did anyone check the manifests at the trucking company?"

"We'd love to, but the laptop…" Andy lifted her hands, empty palms up.

"Best guess, the truck left somewhere in Missouri around midnight," Donaldson said. "Based on timing out the murders at the trucking company."

"By itself, this location information is useless," I said, "because we didn't know the destination."

Andy said, "But we guessed D.C."

"Homeland thinks it is D.C.," Whitlock said. "Homeland says the same social media that claimed responsibility for Lindsay put out a claim they were going to hit our capital. DHS also said police in Juárez shot it out with the leader of the human trafficking ring that likely smuggled the tangos through the border."

Andy startled. "What? When?"

"I don't know. Sometime in the night. Why?"

"Did you get a name?"

"Irish. O'Brien. Notorious smuggler, trafficker. The report said the locals found evidence on him suggesting an attack on the capital. The finger's pointing at some terrorist group out of western Africa. Government authorities there are reluctantly admitting that the leader of the outfit escaped their custody some time ago, and his trail points this way."

"Wait!" Andy placed her elbows on her knees and pressed her palms against her eyes. Whitlock looked at Donaldson and me and read our faces.

"What am I missing here?"

Donaldson summarized the briefing Lindsay had delivered.

"This terrorist—he has a sister here? In the states?" Whitlock asked.

"Apparently in the wind. Unless they found her."

"But they're not hitting the capital," Andy declared.

"Your intel comes from this girl? Sergei Roane's teenaged bride?"

"She's not wrong."

"Which is how," I redirected Whitlock to the map, "we know the real target. If you connect those two dots using Google Maps, you not only get a route, but you get a time." I showed her the line on the map. "From Willow Springs, Missouri it's fifteen hours and forty-five minutes to your plantation."

Whitlock checked her watch. "With no traffic and no stops, that puts them there at … lemme see…" she stared at her watch. "Any time after six p.m."

"Seven p.m.," I corrected her. "Eastern Time. That's if they drive straight through. At the very least they need gas. I've seen the inside of that tank. It will be tight for a squad of armed men. I should think that they'd want time to get the blood flowing again before launching an attack."

"We can't count on that," Whitlock said.

Andy asked, "How formal is this Black Robe thing? Are we talking about meetings? Seminars? Agendas?"

"No," Whitlock replied. "Nothing like that. Casual. A few justices play golf. One of them knits. They pair up for walks. First half of the morning, half of them have fitness routines."

"But they get together—all together—at some point. If you wanted to hit this Black Robe thing, when do you think you would have the best chance of having all nine justices together?"

Whitlock mulled. "Dinner. Dinner is always congregate. Around seven p.m."

"Then we may have time."

"Tell me about the venue," Andy said.

"Siddley Plantation, a few miles from Edenton, North Carolina, on the bay. It's an antebellum plantation turned bed and breakfast. Big house on a big lawn. The outbuildings are long gone. There's a golf clubhouse on the course. The big house overlooks the bay."

"Not exactly great optics," Tom squeezed his knees to one side and leaned into the conversation. "The Supreme Court hanging out at an icon of slavery?"

Whitlock shook her head. "First off, Black Robe doesn't do optics. Second, Siddley is famous because when the Brits abolished slavery in 1833, the plantation owners freed all their slaves and hired them on as farm hands. It's one of the only plantations in the Confederacy that wasn't operating on slavery at the time the war broke out. And for that honor, Confederate soldiers partially burned it ahead of Union forces arriving. Most of the land was sold off in the late 1800s, but the old house was rebuilt in the early 1900s. Some New York millionaire's winter home. He went down with the crash in '29. It changed hands a few times, was made a National Registry landmark, and was rebuilt again twenty or so years ago with a nine-hole golf course."

Pidge turned her head from the pilot's seat. "Landing in ten, people!"

"You have someone meeting you?" I asked Whitlock. She nodded.

"How many deputies on the security detail?" Andy asked.

"Four. I have a full tactical team coming down by chopper from D.C., but they will not be there when we arrive."

"We'll go with you," Andy said. "Chief Ceeves and Special Agent Donaldson and me."

I said, "As soon as we drop you off, we'll launch and start backtracking the Google map route. I know what the truck looks like. They could be anywhere in the last two hundred miles of the route. Or holed up somewhere waiting for the dinner hour."

"Or headed somewhere else. Or not a threat at all," Whitlock said, "let's hope."

"Hope kills," Tom said darkly.

72

Whitlock's ride rolled onto the ramp in the form of a police SUV with a decal for Edenton, Virginia on the side doors. While the marshal had a rapid conference with the officer behind the wheel, Chief Ceeves unloaded his bag and pulled his shotgun from the baggage compartment. Andy went around the Navajo's wing to the nose and deftly opened the nose baggage door. I followed her.

"Hey," I said, sliding up close and slipping one hand around her slender waist. She moved the nine-millimeter ammunition from her overnight bag into her shoulder bag. She looked up at me. Her eyes caught early evening sunlight and warmed it.

"You going to tell me to be careful?" she asked.

"I'm going to tell you to run and hide if anyone so much as sneezes at those judges."

She reached up and stroked the side of my face. "Five U.S. Marshals, the FBI, my own chief, and it looks like local PD is joining. Plus, that tactical team should be here before seven. I think there's even a military base around here somewhere. We'll call in the army. I think I'm good."

I caught a whiff of her scent, sweet and stimulating. Strands of her hair danced in the light breeze. I fought an urge to run my fingers through it. "I had a dream you wanted to name our child Rug Rat."

"Mmmmm," she lifted her eyebrows. "Nice alliteration."

"We could call the kid *the* other *other thing*."

"You're really bad at names." She glanced up at the cockpit to determine if we had an audience. The coast was clear. She turned to me and slid her hands down to my pants. "Like this propeller thingy."

"You mean my BLASTERs?"

"We're not calling them that."

"And that's not what you have in your hand right now," I said a little breathlessly.

She drew closer. Our lips touched.

"I know."

Every twenty seconds.

I WATCHED her slide into the back of the police SUV between Whitlock and Donaldson. Chief Ceeves took the front seat and all the legroom it could spare.

Andy conjured a dimpled smile at me just before the black and white rolled forward. My feet refused to move for a few minutes. My eyes refused to leave the tinted glass hiding her from me until the vehicle made the turn at a hangar and slipped out of sight.

I found myself replaying her touch, recalling her whispered, "I love you," and tasting her scent in my senses.

"Hey! Stewart!" Pidge called to me. "I'm lighting her up."

"Yeah."

It should have been easier to break my feet loose and board the plane.

73

We launched from Northeastern Regional Airport on its sole operational runway, taking off into a light south wind. I told Pidge to go left, east, along the shore. We passed over a golf course and open fields.

Siddley Plantation stood out on the North Carolina coast. Springing from green lawns and a second, smaller golf course, the antebellum mansion faced the calm waters of Albemarle Bay a few miles from where the bay drank from the Chowan River. White pillars lined the double-deck porch façade of a building set among tall old-growth trees. A circular driveway delivered visitors to the front of the building but offered no parking. Some distance from the building, separated by an arm of the golf course, a small parking lot on the edge of a wooded area hosted a handful of vehicles. The police SUV had not reached the plantation yet. Several black SUVs suggested the presence of the U.S. Marshals. Our overflight passed quickly before Pidge turned us out over the bay to loop back and pick up the highway trail suggested by the gods on Mount Google. I took a last look at the plantation as we passed and found myself searching for people in black robes wandering the grounds.

Dumb.

Pidge intercepted Highway 17 where it bridged the Chowan River, settling us in for a flight over the North Carolina countryside.

. . .

"Stay over the road. Ain't no goddamned towers in the road," Earl said.

"I can't see if you're over the road," I said. I had moved to the rear seat on Earl's copilot side of the plane. My window offered a clear view beneath the right wing. "Pidge, fly to the left of the highway. Boss, you watch the road. Eastbound lanes."

Pidge adjusted our flight path. "A little more. Gimme a little more," I said. Pidge side-slipped, expanding the space between us and the highway. "And take us down."

"We're at five hundred," Pidge announced, making a point of the minimum legal altitude.

"Take us down to three hundred."

"Okay," she said, "you're officially pilot-in-command. If the feds ask, I was taking a nap in the back."

She plunged the nose to make her point.

"Uh-oh," Earl said. "Looks like the transponder just took a dump. I guess nobody will be able to get an altitude readout on us. Lucky for us I can swear we never got within five hundred feet of any person, vehicle or structure."

"This is good," I said. With my head against the Plexiglas, I had a clear view of the road. "Slow us down. Gimme one-twenty." I figured a hundred and twenty knots left Pidge enough speed to maneuver if she needed it and still give me time to scan the traffic. I estimated that I only had about a mile of pavement within my view. The combined speed of traffic and the Navajo gave me around ten seconds to spot the truck.

"Wish I had a helicopter," I said.

"Twenty-thousand parts moving in loose formation," Earl muttered. "What's this thing look like again?"

I described the Paddington tank truck down to the bear logo on the tank. "That eliminates tractor-trailers and three-axles. I suppose we can't be sure they didn't paint it, but frankly a milk truck is a pretty benign cover."

"Got one," Earl announced.

"Good," I said. "Call 'em out so I know they're coming."

"Abeam...now."

The truck appeared below. A silver tank mounted behind a blue cab. I counted three axles and apparatus for fuel oil. The tank was an oval, not circular.

"Nope."

Pidge chimed in. "Is anyone going to look at the map and warn me about any fucking towers?"

"Hell no," Earl answered.

"We wouldn't want to scare you."

"Thanks a bunch."

"Got another one. Nope. Trailer."

We banked to follow the curves in the highway. Cars and trucks streamed by. Trucks pulled trailers over eighteen-wheels. Gravel trucks plowed by with and without loads. Lowboy trailers carried equipment. We spotted only a few silver tankers, and of those, none rode on two rear axles.

"Got a two-axle," Earl said when he spotted one. "Not silver. Abeam…now."

I looked it over.

"Firetruck."

Ladders and apparatus hung alongside the red water tank. A light bar rode on the cab roof. I tried but could not read the quaintly styled engine company name on the door. It passed quickly out of sight.

"What if we don't see it," Pidge asked.

"Fine by me," I replied. "It means they're moving slower than our worst-case guess and there's time for the cavalry to arrive." I wanted heavily armed men in black Kevlar between my wife and Sergei Roane's band of terrorists. I wanted Andy evacuated with America's Supreme Court Justices. I wanted, with a new ache of worry sprouting out of nowhere, my wife out of harm's way.

"Two more," Earl called out.

One was a city water truck with the wrong kind of tank. The other was indeed a milk truck, but a tractor-trailer combination.

"Negative."

THE INITIAL STRETCH of four-lane highway narrowed to two lanes. Earl called out potential suspects, casting a wider net than I would have, calling out anything with a cylinder behind the cab. In one case, he alerted to a lowboy trailer literally hauling giant industrial cylinders.

I let him err on the side of caution.

I calculated a turnaround point. Sixty miles put any potential suspect more than an hour from the plantation, which allowed more than enough time for Andy and Whitlock to secure the site and prepare the justices for evacuation. I felt no overwhelming urge to find the truck. Eliminating their target seemed good enough to me. Whitlock and the weight of the U.S. government could manage the rest.

About the time I designated Rocky Mount, a small city roughly sixty miles east of Raleigh, a reasonable turnaround point, my phone vibrated.

A text from Andy.
You're not answering. Fire at the plantation.
I gaped at it.
"Turn it around!"
"What?" Pidge didn't move the controls.
"Turn! Turn it around!"
Son of a bitch! How did I not see it?
Pidge didn't question a second time. She added power and rolled the big twin into a forty-five-degree bank that drove me into my seat.

I jabbed at my phone until Andy's name appeared. I hit the call button.
It rang in my headset.
And rang.
"This is Detective Stewart of the Essex—"
I killed the voicemail message.
"Dammit."
"Talk to us, Will. What are we doing here?"
"Stay low and gimme full power. Go! Go!" I pulled my face away from the window to focus on the iPad. "Stay with the highway!"

The acceleration pressed me back in the seat. I zoomed the iPad moving map until the small blue airplane icon raced across lines and markers.
Where was it?

I tried to remember. How far into the run were we when I saw it. Had we crossed the Highway 17 bridge over the Chowan River? Yes. That much I knew. We began our search where the highway cut a path inland through rural North Carolina. Away from the coast. Away from towns and roadside shops catering to tourists. How far in had we been when I saw the truck?

"What are we looking for, Will?" Earl asked.

"I saw it. I should have known, God damn it. I saw the truck." I bowed my head over the iPad and swiped the map to backtrack. It told me nothing. I checked my watch. We'd been on the hunt for less than twenty minutes, covering a distance of forty miles. We had been less than ten minutes away from the turnaround point when Pidge cranked us around to reverse course.

"What truck?"

"Andy sent me a text. She's been trying to call but we're moving too fast too low. There's a fire at the plantation."

"Son of a bitch." Earl got it.

"It was the goddamned firetruck. We passed right over it!"

74

"There! On the bridge!" Earl called out. I leaned forward between the front seats and peered over the instrument panel.

The truck ran in the left lane of the four-lane bridge. The way it surged past vehicles in the right lane, the way vehicles in the left lane moved aside as it approached, and the twinkle of flashing lights on the top of the cab told me they had assumed the role of an emergency vehicle.

"That's it," I said. "I can't get Andy on the phone."

"What do you want me to do?" Pidge asked. She heaved the controls to the left to set up a clockwise orbit around the moving vehicle.

Fire at the plantation. Not only would the truck have clear sailing, but any local police or marshals they encountered would wave it through whatever security perimeter they had set up.

"I need to get down there."

"And pigs will fly," Earl scoffed.

"Pidge, can you set me up with a stall?"

"Lemme get some altitude," she replied, pushing the throttle to full and heaving back on the controls. "Thousand feet okay?"

"What?" Earl spun in his seat.

Pidge pulled the nose of the Navajo up through the horizon, ten, then fifteen, then twenty-five degrees. She climbed like a demon.

"Go back there with him and get the door old man!" Pidge snapped at Earl.

"What the hell?"

"She'll explain after I'm gone. Get on the phone to Andy. If you can't reach her, call ATC. Somebody! Anybody!"

"Roger that. One forty. One thirty. One twenty..." Pidge counted down. "As soon as it buffets, I'm dumping the nose, so don't fucking linger!"

"What the hell are you doing?" Earl barked.

I slid down the steep angle of the center aisle and yelled back at him. "Earl, I'm going out. Get the door behind me!"

"Go! Go! Go!" Pidge let go of the throttles long enough to slap Earl on the arm.

I gave Earl credit for ceasing to question. He snapped open his belt and lunged out of his seat after me, although I wondered if he meant to stop me.

"Are you out of your goddamned mind?"

"One oh five! One hundred! Ninety! Get ready!"

The big airplane climbed steeply and lost speed rapidly. I snapped the latch on the door. It popped into the slipstream. I groped my thighs to confirm the presence of my power units and props.

"Here goes!" Pidge cried out. She jerked back the throttles to cut the prop wash. An instant before I dove for the door, I felt myself go weightless without *the other thing*. The cabin floor lost contact with my feet. Out of the corner of my eye, his face awash in shock, Earl gripped the arms of the two seats behind me.

The Navajo fell silent. The airframe shuddered as lift peeled away from the wings, inducing a stall. The nose dropped.

"Trust me!" I shouted at Earl.

I grabbed both sides of the door and heaved myself into the sky a thousand feet above the river and the ribbon of bridge that cut it. Behind me I heard Earl's gravel voice.

"HOLY SHIT!"

A BLAST of wind hit me, then died. Gravity dug in her claws and pulled me toward the river. I beat it to the punch.

Fwooomp!

"HOLY SH—!" Pidge cut Earl off by pushing the throttles forward. The Navajo engines thundered. The airplane fell away, gaining speed, spreading smooth air over her wings and finding fresh flight in Pidge's stall recovery. Pidge rolled into a steep right turn.

I tumbled through the air on a slight downward trajectory, my heart pounding, my arms tight, my hands on the edge of shaking, grateful that circumstances had given me only seconds to think about what I was doing.

I drew a long, slow breath, counted to four, then released it slowly. Feeling my arms and hands grow steadier, I carefully released the Velcro on my pants pocket and pulled out one of the three power units I carried.

The core muscle running down my center—companion to *the other thing*—flexed. I used it to right myself, feet down. There hadn't been time since Juárez to refine the concept of the safety loops I used to attach the power unit to my wrist. Holding it in my left hand, I pulled a prop from my pocket and snapped it in place with my right. I switched hands and thumbed the slide control. The unit responded instantly, pulling me forward.

A momentary search revealed that I was oriented in the wrong direction, facing north, away from the bridge. I twisted my wrist and accelerated in a tight turn, lining up on a track parallel to the four-lane bridge roughly five hundred feet below. High-pitched sound rose to my ears. I thought of birds, and worried about a collision, then realized that the truck used a siren to clear its path. It neared the end of the bridge.

I drew full power from the BLASTER in my hand. The prop's whine drowned the distant siren.

Like most things I've done without thinking, I collided with the realization that I had no idea what to do next. Calling Andy was out of the question. I had no way of dialing her, even if I took the time to dig my Bluetooth earpiece out of a pocket and push it in place. I prayed that Pidge and Earl would reach her.

Fire at the plantation meant two things. First, firetrucks would be given clear sailing to the front door. Second, it meant that someone at the plantation had set the fire to create an opening for the truck to slip through the marshal's security ring. The marshals would certainly be suspicious—but would they stop a firetruck with a burning building at their backs? Andy would warn them to be wary of a truck that had a tank on its back, but what if all they needed was to be within a few hundred yards? What if the tank carried explosives instead of men with guns?

I picked up speed. Wind tore past my ears. A new sound caught my attention. A familiar sound. I didn't understand how the BLASTER in my hand had suddenly developed a deeper tone.

Then it hit me. I twisted in time to see twin disks of propeller bearing down on me. Pidge had circled.

FWOOOMP!

I reappeared, curled into a ball and dropped. I cringed, expecting the props to shred my flesh and bones. Gravity jerked me downward. The Navajo flashed over close enough to see oil streaks where the engine breather tubes stained the flaps. I smelled exhaust as I fell from the sky.

Acceleration threw me at the river below.

Fwooomp!

Vanished, I continued a downward trajectory. Too fast to deploy the power unit—the relative wind would snap the prop off the shaft.

I uncurled my cannonball posture and spread my arms and legs like a skydiver. Wind pounded my body. The river rushed up at me. Against the roar of air passing my ears I heard the plane as it turned to orbit the truck. The siren sound below grew distant.

Three hundred feet.

Two hundred.

One hundred.

The wind diminished. My sprawling posture, designed to generate as much resistance as possible, took effect. I decelerated as the distance between me and the water shrank. The smell of the brown river rose to meet me.

I extended my arm and applied power. The dramatic result instantly changed my path. Slow, placid river water swept beneath me. My decent ceased. Skimming above the water, I aimed for the shore.

"You're off my Christmas list, Pidge," I muttered, climbing again.

Pidge and Earl circled to the east. Their orbit signaled that the truck had completed passage across the bridge. The small town of Edenton lay between the bridge and the plantation.

I had no idea what I intended to do if I caught up to the vehicle.

75

The truck exited Highway 17 and raced down an arterial street slicing through Edenton. Cross streets marked with stop signs posed no hazard to me, but major intersections hung stop lights high above the street on poles and wires. Telephone and power lines lined the road, crossing it at frequent intervals. Diving into one of those intervals would require precise timing.

Parked cars caused the street to narrow enough that drivers encountering the speeding firetruck were forced to swerve aside. More than once, accidents were avoided by inches.

I caught up and stayed high.

Hope rose sharply when the truck came to a stop near a multi-story square occupying one corner of an intersection. A sign on the corner said Edenton Police Department. I searched for an alert officer—one who might question a firetruck he'd never seen before on a thin city street with lights and sirens.

No one emerged from the building. No one jumped into a squad car to pursue.

I considered dropping to the sidewalk and rushing into the police station to report the situation.

Who are you again? And how did you come by this information? Take a seat while I get my desk sergeant...

The truck took a right at the Police Department intersection. Two blocks later, it turned left and roared forward.

I abandoned the notion of stopping and stayed with the big tanker. My vantage point revealed what a lash-up job had been done to create the fake firetruck. A pair of step ladders, probably bought from a big box store, hung on either side of the tank on crudely welded brackets. The light bar across the top of the cab appeared to be bolted in place, with wires dangling down the back corner of the cab. The flashing lights alternated blue and white—police lights, not fire department lights. The siren rose and fell like an old-school air raid siren, emanating from a box secured to the top hatch ladder with zip ties. Someone painted the vehicle bright red, but the job had been done with brushes. The brush strokes were blatantly evident, and the Paddington logotype and stolen bear image were faintly visible beneath the new coat of paint.

I saw all this from thirty feet high as the truck rushed down the small town street. The observations gave me a sense of superiority. Such a laughable effort would never pass close examination.

Oh, crap. They don't care.

They never meant for this vehicle to bluff past security. This was a battering ram. The likelihood that this was a rolling bomb, not a terrorist troop transport, loomed in my mind.

I became acutely aware of the houses lining the streets. Children on bicycles. Mothers pushing strollers. Here and now was not the time to try and stop the truck.

The lining of residential homes thinned. Open country spread on either side of the highway ahead.

A forty-plus mile per hour wind watered my eyes. I picked a spot half a mile past the last homes. I lined up an approach to the top of the tank where the small curved ladder arched up to the tank cover. From there I could pull myself hand over hand to the cab.

And then what?

I imagined jerking open the door and yanking the driver out, watching him tumble end over end while I jumped behind the wheel and took over.

Seat belt. Plus, he'll have a grip on the wheel. Plus the truck will immediately decelerate. Plus, the damned door will be locked! That crap only works when you have stunt men on the payroll.

Next, I mapped a route over the cab, down the front grille. There, I would release the hood locks and flip it up to blind the driver.

The hood release is on the inside, dumbass. This admonishment came into my head via Lillian's harsh voice. *You're getting nowhere faster than this truck.*

Which accelerated. The big diesel engine roared. Open road offered no resistance, not even sparse traffic. The driver stomped on it and what should have been a lumbering milk truck instead adopted the personality of a race car.

I pushed my slide control to the stops. At best, I estimate that I have clocked roughly sixty-five, maybe seventy miles per hour. Eventually wind resistance equals the thrust available. Limited battery power almost immediately causes my top speed to decay.

I needed to get down to the truck *now*.

I checked for wires. I saw none hanging across the highway, but the wire that kills you is the one you don't see. Nevertheless, I dove for the apex of the tank. The BLASTER prop screamed, vibrating the length of my arm. The siren on top of the truck howled.

My approach angle looked good. I closed on the ladder just as I felt my maximum speed waver. If the truck accelerated now, my chances of hooking it would evaporate. I flew with my right arm extended for the power unit, and my left arm tight against my body. Swinging my left arm to grab the ladder created instant wind resistance. My fingers brushed the ladder.

The truck abruptly swerved left, shooting to the other side of the highway. I saw why a moment later when a compact sedan flashed under me. Worse, the truck accelerated. By degrees, it pulled ahead.

By equal degrees, the strength of my power unit diminished. The tank inched forward.

My last chance lay in the ladder slung on the side of the tank. If I crashed into it, I might manage a grip.

I swerved. The move instantly cut my relative speed. The truck surged ahead. I threw out my left arm and groped for the last rung of the ladder. My fingers collided painfully, but I managed a second swing.

Just as my hand slapped the rung, the truck swerved wildly to the right, tires screaming. I looked up in time to see a flash of white wings and silver propeller discs cutting across the highway.

Pidge!

The Navajo sliced in from the side of the road, banked almost vertically. The left wing should have scraped the pavement. How it missed slamming into the truck cab baffled me.

The driver reacted as Pidge intended, jerking the truck to the right, cutting across the lane and leaving the pavement. The cab jolted. Steel over spinning rubber bounded and bounced into thick weeds and through scrub alongside the road. Clods of dirt flew skyward.

The ladder jerked me along with it. My hand had closed on the last rung. My extended body flew like a banner sailing in a storm.

Dust and dirt choked the air. I clamped my eyelids shut to shield them from debris. Hot slipstream from the airplane energized the tumultuous air. Vortexes swirled and slapped my body. I expected to hear truck brakes hiss, but instead the engine roared.

The ladder hanging on the side of the truck jolted up and down. The big tank heaved. The truck cut left again. The driver fought to regain pavement.

With a sharp lurch, the truck wheels bumped onto the road again. The driver nearly lost it, fishtailing wildly. An oncoming car swerved off the road, a fraction of an inch from collision.

Violence transmitted through the ladder lifted it free of the brackets and sent the entire length sailing with me attached.

I released.

The truck pulled away. The ladder clattered to the road and slid on the pavement.

"God dammit, Pidge!" I shouted. The Navajo was nowhere to be seen. "Next time warn me!"

My impulse to accelerate after the truck met with the realization that I'd lost my power unit in the melee. As the truck heaved up through its gears, regaining speed, I jabbed my hand in my pocket and pulled out a fresh unit.

Prop in place, I took off again.

This time I resolved to stay low, directly behind the tank. The time it took to deploy a fresh BLASTER gave the truck a quarter mile lead. Knowing it could eventually outpace me, I pushed to full power at once and raised my body to present the least wind resistance. The fresh power unit shot me forward a few feet above the pavement.

I caught up quickly. Drafting helped. The tank created a space of undisturbed air directly in its wake, sharply reducing wind resistance. So much so that in the last few feet I nearly collided with the rear of the big cylinder. A quick upward vector took me over the top where I met fresh, undisturbed wind and lost speed, but not before moving above the top center hatch and fixing a firm grip on the arched ladder.

Now what?

The driver accelerated until the diesel engine screamed at a pitch that matched the siren wailing just inches from my head. The noise pierced my skull. I spotted a wire wound up through the ladder. The wire split in two before entering the small gray siren box. I grabbed and yanked.

The effort paid off. One of the two wires broke loose. The screaming siren fell silent. Disabling it saved my hearing but did nothing to slow the truck.

We entered a wooded tract. Thick trees arched over the road. Branches swept by just feet from my head. The road curved to the right. In the distance ahead, I spotted shards of blue among the foliage. Albemarle Bay.

Something else appeared half a mile ahead. Slotted at an angle across both lanes of the highway, two black and white police SUVs blocked the road where the Siddley Plantation golf course bordered the thick woods. The vehicles looked small compared to the heavy cab of the truck. Judging by the acceleration the driver applied, he agreed.

Everyone involved knew what would come next. Behind the SUVs, figures bolted for the sides of the road, leaping across a small ditch and sprinting into tall grass. The truck driver built speed and aimed for the center point between the two vehicles.

I didn't think twice. I shoved hard against the ladder and sailed up and away from the tank. Branches slapped my face and arms, which caught and caused me to tumble. The truck lunged forward, leaving me behind.

The collision launched an explosion of plastic, metal and glass into the air. Chunks flew over the cab and banged across the top of the tank where I'd been. Both shattered SUVs spun in the road like tops as the truck plowed through. One of the two rolled into the ditch, chasing two of the officers who had abandoned their post, nearly catching them before the vehicle spun to a stop on its roof. The right front fender of the milk truck flipped into the air.

Pieces of metal, severed tires and SUV body parts clattered and danced on the pavement.

I fought off the trees. BLASTER in hand, I ducked below the overhanging branches and set off above the centerline of the road. I applied full power. I raced over the chaos and debris in the road.

The tree line ended. Clear sky opened above me. I desperately raised my arm to climb knowing what would come next.

Regaining their wits, the officers at the roadblock behind me opened fire. Handguns popped. I clawed for height to escape the line of fire. Bullets pinged off the stainless-steel tank. The truck roared on, undeterred.

Where are the marshals? Where are the men in black with automatic weapons that can shoot holes in an engine block?

The tree line bordered the Siddley Plantation golf course. Half a mile ahead, beyond fairways and water hazards, the plantation house appeared in its full glory. Although the front of the house faced the bay, the rear presented an elegant multi-balcony edifice overlooking terraced gardens that no doubt commanded six-figure fees for elite weddings. Or provided perfect solitude for Supreme Court Justices.

Please tell me you hear this train wreck coming! I begged of Andy in my head.

The truck followed a wide curve around the outer edge of the golf course. I aimed to cut it off.

I raced across a lawn, swerving between tall trees. I reached the antebellum façade just as the truck followed a circle drive around an expansive fountain and screeched to a halt on locked tires and hissing brakes. The building had a warm pink hue in the evening light. A smudge of dark air hung above one end. If the smudge represented the fire meant to open the door for this firetruck, it appeared to be out.

I looked for a squad of vested U.S. Marshals to emerge with rifles raised, making short work of the driver, possibly preventing the tank from opening to spill its cargo of suicidal gunmen.

Nothing happened. No one emerged from the building. No one occupied the porch or balcony. No one watched from the lobby windows as this fake first responder arrived.

Both truck cab doors popped open. The driver dropped to the pavement with an automatic rifle in hand. Two men jumped from the cab on the opposite side, weapons at their shoulders, hunting for targets.

I glided to a halt fifteen feet above the tank.

The driver hurried to the side of the truck, to the same control panel I'd seen used on the North Dakota highway. He produced the required key and worked the controls. An electric motor whined. A hiss and pop came from the rear of the truck. The driver watched the rear of the tank swung open.

I braced to see a squad of suicidal armed killers tumble from the tank.

Nothing happened.

The driver hurried to the rear of the truck. His two companions joined him. One of the two pointed his rifle at the building and maintained a watch. The other joined the driver in pointing weapons inward at what I assumed to be his own team.

Their aggressive stance made no sense.

The driver shouted in a language I did not recognize. He jerked the weapon back and forth, signaling for someone inside the tank to get down. From above the tank, I watched heads appear. I applied quiet thrust to the power unit and navigated a semicircular path to ground level. Skimming the pavement, I eased to the rear of the truck and took up a position behind the driver who continued shouting at the team disembarking from the tank.

They wore matching black military multi-pocket cargo pants and shirts under heavy vests. They carried the same deadly-looking automatic rifles as the driver. The similarity ended there.

Three men and a woman dropped to the ground, stiff and slow, shielding their eyes against the evening sunset. The woman held one of the men for support. He shifted his body and shielded her from the rifle aimed by the driver. The driver shouted at him. He shouted back.

If these people were here to conduct a suicide attack, their hearts weren't in it. The four from the tank cringed against the onslaught of what I took to be curses coming from the truck driver.

Prisoners. Each of the four carried a rifle. None displayed any expertise or familiarity with the weapons. None made a move to use their weapon against the men facing them. I made a quick guess that the weapons were either empty or disabled.

Odor wafted from the open tank. I recognized the scent from living in a farmhouse, surrounded by farm fields.

Ammonium nitrate fertilizer. With it, the scent of diesel fuel.

I eased to my right, past the driver, for a look inside.

Unlike the milk tank that carried Gloria Rilling and her son, this cylinder had a bulkhead just a few feet in. The four prisoners had been jammed together at the back behind a sealed steel plate that showed signs of recent welding. A tank within the tank.

The prisoners showed strain. One of the men dropped his rifle, which brought a new round of curses. The man facing the building façade swung around and hammered the rifle-dropper with the butt of his weapon, shouting words that convinced the man to pick up the rifle.

The tall glass-paned front door of Siddley Mansion opened.

A flash of hope disappeared the instant I recognized the tall man from Sergei Roane's bunker. His tan military shirt was gone, exchanged for kitchen whites. He stepped out of the building and walked toward the truck.

They put a man on the inside. And he's been busy.

Blood streaked his pants. He wielded a long knife in one hand, also stained. I looked past him. The interior, what I could see of it, appeared empty.

Where the hell is everyone?

The man in whites uttered new commands without shouting, leaving no doubt as to his authority. The two men from the passenger side of the truck hurried around to join the driver, forming a line. They jabbed their rifles into the backs of the three men and the woman. Still clutching one of the men, the woman pleaded in clear American English.

"Please! We've done nothing!"

The tall man in white calmly approached. He switched the bloody knife from one hand to the other. With his freed right hand, he drew a black handgun from behind his back. Without breaking stride, he raised it and fired.

Two shots.

Two shots.

The sharp reports hammered my ears and thumped my chest. As if turned to sacks of bones, the first two prisoners from the truck dropped to the ground. Blood glittered on the head of one. The other offered no indication of where he'd been hit, but the question of life and death had been answered.

"No!" the woman shrieked, clutching her companion.

Red rage blinded me.

Where the hell are the marshals?

The man in white strolled past the shocked surviving prisoners. He turned and joined the line at the back of the open cylinder, a line that now took on the ominous appearance of a firing squad.

"Go. Run. I give you a chance."

The remaining two prisoners recognized the lie yet took hesitant, helpless steps on the pristine brick inlaid sidewalk. They held each other tightly.

"Go!" the man in white shouted.

After half a dozen heartless steps, the man stopped and embraced the woman, turning her away from the rifles aimed at them. He drew himself erect, then lifted a hand to shield her eyes. The men at the back of the truck adjusted their aim.

I had only seconds and nothing in hand but the battery-powered BLASTER. I mapped out a move knowing it only worked in full gravity.

Fwooomp! I appeared and dropped to the pavement directly behind the man in white.

The two prisoners dropped their rifles and froze.

I pulled back my arm and swung for the fences. With the BLASTER wrapped into my fist, I landed a hammer blow on the vertebrae just above the white collar of the tall man's kitchen tunic. I felt a satisfying *crunch*. He sank to the ground the same way his two victims had. He dropped his handgun. I ducked and reached for it.

At the end of the firing line nearest the truck, the driver swung his head, saw me and with blazing eyes swept his rifle around. The handgun might as well have been on the moon. I pictured the levers in my head. Vanishing might cause a split second of confusion, but in the same instant I knew nothing would stop a burst from the rifle from finding me.

Before I could disappear, a huge fist flew past the back end of the tank and into the head of the driver, knocking it sideways. At the same time, another hand came up and closed on the man's outstretched rifle, jerking it skyward. The man went down.

Tom Ceeves, in a move displaying ballet precision, continued the upward motion of the rifle, flipping it and swinging it down like a club on the head of the second man in line. The gunman shrieked and dropped his weapon. He threw his hands to the crown of his head and howled. Blood seeped through his fingers. He doubled over. Tom ignored him and swung the rifle like a man burying an axe in firewood. The blow landed on the rifle of the third man and knocked it free. He staggered backward.

"Hey, Will," Tom said casually. He towered over the man he had dropped with his fist. He nudged him with one foot. "This one's dead."

I gawked, stunned as much by his sudden appearance as I was by the fact that Tom just delivered death with one fist.

"Wha—?" was all I could manage.

Tom conducted his kick test with the man in white who lay gasping. Tom flipped him onto his back. His eyes blazed, staring at nothing. "This one's dying. I think you snapped his neck."

"Where—what did you—?"

Tom ignored me.

"Leave it on the ground," he warned the third man who had recovered enough to consider retrieving his rifle. Tom kicked the second man. Still clutching his head, the man tumbled backward onto the pavement. The third man backed up beside him.

"Saw it coming. Donaldson and I just put out the kitchen fire. He saw this guy—" Tom tapped the man in white with his foot "—and went around back to cut him off. I came around the front. Ducked behind that hedge when they pulled up."

"Where's Andy?"

"Last I saw, collecting all the judges." He turned his attention to the man and woman locked in what they may have thought was their last embrace. "Who are these people?"

I stepped over the man in white. He quivered in the clutches of a seizure. His eyes rolled to slits of white.

"I'll make a guess." I examined the two prisoners who now looked at Tom with a new mix of fear and relief. The resemblance between the man and woman ran deep. "You're a preschool teacher from Chicago," I said to the woman. "And you just made a long trip from a prison in Ghana," I said to the man. "Brother and sister, yes?"

They blinked at me. Terror lingered in their wide eyes.

"Where are we?" the woman's brother asked through a thick accent.

"Long story," I said.

"*Who* are they?" Tom asked.

"Long story." I turned my attention to the last man standing. Up close, he sent a shiver down my spine. He aimed a hard-edged face my way. His eyes were cold. His entire body coiled at the ready, more than likely the product of harsh military training shared by his colleague in white. Entirely out of my league. Which is why I didn't see the flash of the knife in his hand until after I heard twin explosions behind me.

The knife dropped. The man dropped with it, missing part of the top of his head. I smelled cordite from the rifle Tom held to his shoulder. The barrel smoked beside my head. My right ear went dead.

"You alright?" Tom's voice was distant and muffled.

I think I said yes. He said something about the truck and keys. I watched him dismiss any concern for the man he just shot and drop to a knee to search the pockets of the dead driver.

"I need to find Andy," I told Tom. The shock and deafening rifle shots affected my balance. I felt unsteady starting up the sidewalk.

Just as I reached the two freed prisoners, the man closed a grip on my upper arm.

"Stop him!" he cried out. "Stop him!"

He pointed and pulled me around.

The man in white, wracked by tremors, held a cell phone in a clawed hand. He bared his teeth in grim determination. His hand shook. He stabbed his thumb at the screen.

I made one guess. Tom made the same guess and heaved himself to his feet. He took a single step and finished it with a sweeping kick that caught the man in white under the chin. The grinning head shot back and made a muffled snapping sound. He flopped to the pavement. The cell phone fell from his curled fingers.

Tom snatched it up.

"Son of a bitch." He jabbed at the screen. *"Son of a bitch!"*

He looked at the truck, then at me, ashen. He showed me the screen. His expression wrote the death warrant that the screen ticked off in seconds.

"Go! Will, go! You have a chance!"

Eighteen.

Seventeen.

Sixteen. A padlock icon suggested that nothing would stop the countdown.

Ammonium nitrate odor stung my senses.

Dammit! The truck!

"Andy!" I cried. I spun to face the building. The entrance, fifty feet away, might as well have been a mile away. I calculated that I would reach it just about the time the truck blew.

"She'll find shelter! GO!"

He was right. Even if I knew where to look, I would never find her. Even if Tom had the truck keys in hand, he would never get it in gear before it vaporized beneath him.

"Grab them! Bear hug! Do it!" I jerked my arm free from the man still holding it. I shoved him and his sister toward Tom. "Tight! Hold them tight!"

Tom didn't question. I stabbed my pocket for the last remaining BLASTER unit and prop. Tom dropped the phone. He lunged forward and threw his arms around the two people staggering toward him on the sidewalk.

On the run, I snapped the prop in place.

Tom folded the two adults into his arms like children. I hit them from behind—

FWOOOMP!

The sound thundered in my head as we collided. All three vanished. I closed both arms around the tight cluster and squeezed. The BLASTERs—one in each hand—answered my call for full power. The twin props screamed and pulled us past the tank truck in a dizzying acceleration.

The driver's second, still kneeling, still holding his hand to his head, shrieked. I didn't look back to see if his terror came from seeing us disappear or from finding the phone Tom had dropped.

Thirteen.

Twelve.

Eleven.

The numbers annunciated in my head courtesy of a time sense honed by instrument flying.

Acceleration under full power with a BLASTER can be astonishing. Except for my first, badly conceived attempt, I had never tried using two units. I never needed two. I feared that asymmetrical thrust would send me on a spiral. None of that entered my head now. Tom's bulk and the cargo of two grown people did nothing to slow us. We shot past the truck. I aimed for the broad strokes of blue-purple bay peeking between a regimented row of hardwood trees.

As if a giant hook had been driven into my spine, I felt a mental line play out behind me, attached to the truck bomb and the ornate mansion by the unanswered question of Andy.

She'll find shelter..."

How could she? How would she know what was coming? Would the walls of the mansion be enough? I wished I had looked to see if they were stone or wood. I wished I hadn't listened to Tom, even though I had no hope of making it past the lobby.

We tore through the air, through the stand of trees, across a manicured and regularly watered lawn.

Dozens of rooms in the house. She could be anywhere. She could be hiding. She could be in a safe room behind walls of steel.

She could be walking out the front door.

Don't think.

We accelerated at an astounding pace. Twin-unit power produced speed more rapidly than I've ever experienced. It would not be enough. A truck loaded with fuel-infused fertilizer—the very same bomb used to destroy the federal building in Oklahoma City—would produce a blast wave that would tear us apart.

Tear the building apart.

Tear my world apart.

The BLASTERS screamed. Wind whistled past my head. I felt my cargo tighten their grips on each other, turning muscle to stone. Someone may have screamed.

The dark blue horizon came into view. Just a few hundred feet from the front of the mansion the lawn ended in an abrupt drop, at least thirty feet, that fell to the water.

I saw a chance.

Eight.

Seven.

My head ticked off the seconds.

"Tom! Where was Andy?" I shouted.

The grass ended. A dirt and gravel slope met the water below. We soared over gentle evening waves lapping at the shore.

Four.

Three.

"I don't—!"

FWOOOMP!

I pulled the levers.

All four of us appeared and instantly dropped thirty feet. We hit the water hard. I slammed into Tom's back. I felt the impact from the others. We broke through the surface and sank.

First into darkness.

Then into an explosion of tan-green light. Blazing light. A shock wave distorted the surface above us and heaved the water around us. A hard metallic *crack*, louder than anything I ever heard, punched my ears.

We sank. Water, unable to compress and protected by the bank of shoreline above us, failed to translate the stunning blast into forces that would kill us. The line of sight blast wave raced over our heads into the bay.

Our water shelter didn't stop the debris.

Bombs dropped all around us. Large and small pieces dove through the surface, stabbing down through the water.

I sank until my feet made soft contact with mud and gravel. The water was cold at this depth. A depth that matched my despair. The light shifted back to darkness. A darkness that I would never emerge from. Not if Andy was gone.

76

I kicked and swam to the surface. What had been a placid evening bay now roiled, stormy and uneven. Small waves slapped my head. Saturated clothing and shoes pulled me down. Debris splashes broke the surface all around me. Shrapnel from the blast continued to fall. I paddled against sinking. My open hands told me that both BLASTERs were gone.

Two heads popped up nearby. The brother and sister. They gasped for air and grasped for each other. He spotted the shore and grabbed his sister by the collar, swimming and pulling her.

A search between frenzied waves showed me nothing of Tom. I cycled several lungs full of air, then swept my hands beneath the surface to plunge my body into the depths.

The bright tan-green color of the water had faded. Dark again, I could see little, but Tom's bulk formed a contrast just a few feet away. He flailed and clawed awkwardly. Panicked.

I aimed and kicked and pulled until I reached him. His arms worked furiously, thrashing and threatening anyone who came close. The man knew nothing about being in water. In a moment or two he would be finished. Drowned.

If he didn't punch me unconscious first.

I went low and worked into position to throw my arms around him. Without touching him—

Fwooomp! I vanished. The instant my body disappeared, the space it occupied in the water became a buoyant six-foot-one human balloon. I burst upward. Simultaneously, I closed my arms around Tom's torso. One of his arms came down. His elbow crashed into my shoulder. White pain seared up and down my shoulder, neck, and head. I held on. As a void without weight, my body formed a human life preserver. We broke the surface.

He gasped and spit and flailed.

"Freeze, dammit!" I shouted. "You'll drown us both!"

I had him from behind. My arms barely met around his chest. I wrapped my legs around his belly as best I could.

"Use your arms."

"I can't swim!" he cried.

"I don't give a damn. Fake it!" I shouted. "I got you. You can't sink."

He caught on. He lunged through the water, clawing for the shore.

It took a while. We rolled over several times. He caught fresh mouthfuls of water and coughed and spit. Our escape from the blast had carried us fifty or sixty feet out. By the time Tom's feet hit bottom close to the shore, he was spent. I felt him make contact and trudge forward. He stumbled and crawled the remaining few yards. I let him go.

I reappeared beside him and crawled out of the slapping surf. A few yards away, the preschool teacher from Chicago cried in her brother's arms. He looked at me, wide-eyed, but said nothing.

I had no breath to explain. Or time.

I staggered onto the narrow gravel beach and confronted the small cliff that had saved us from the blast.

Fwooomp! I vanished and tapped my toes. The launch took me up the face of the cliff. At the top, just as I cleared the edge, I reappeared and dropped onto mowed grass, landing on my hands and knees, still gasping.

When I looked up, I stood in Hell without the flames.

There was nothing left to burn.

A pall of rust-red smoke filled the sky, curling and roiling upward. The land in all directions was torn, streaked and sooty. The huge trees were gone. Not even the roots remained.

A crater smoldered where the Siddley Mansion had been.

No shelter. No safe room.

Nothing.

Gone.

77

I walked. I think.
    I wept. I think.

I don't remember Tom shouting at me, though he said so later. He cursed me for not answering, for leaving him on the beach. I don't remember Pidge slicing through the dirty, smoldering air, though she told me she and Earl flew the Navajo on a low pass over my head after nearly being torn out of the sky by a blast wave that broke windows two miles away. Pidge said she spotted me wandering away from the shore. By chance, she saw Tom with two more survivors below the cliff line.

I don't remember seeing the plane or the sky.

I don't remember feeling anything, though I would feel it later when an emergency room doctor shoved my left shoulder back in its socket.

I don't remember crossing the hellish landscape just beyond the perimeter of a forty-foot deep crater where the Paddington milk truck had been. Or wandering onto the undulating terrain that had been a golf course.

I remember a ball washer standing solitary, even though the trees surrounding it had been yanked from the earth by the supersonic blast wave.

I remembered Andy. Everything about her. Every word she ever spoke to me. Every moment she ever looked at me. Every casual touch. Every spontaneous laugh. A flood of Andy washed over my mind, teasing me with the knowledge that floods rise and overwhelm, but then recede and disappear.

I don't remember seeing the stupid little golf cart bouncing across the open fairway like a child's toy in the landscape of a carpet bombing.

I don't remember Chief Deputy Marshal Whitlock steering around the remnants of the truck bomb's engine block, seven hundred feet from where it had been when the tank blew.

I don't remember Andy leaping from the cart while it still rolled toward me. Her auburn hair flying. Racing over smoldering debris.

All I remember of that moment is that she materialized out of the flood of memories and words and kisses and scents that had overwhelmed my mind, and that she took me in her arms.

We fell to our knees on the scorched earth.

EPILOGUE I

"No. That's not him."

FBI Special Agent Leslie Carson-Pelham pointed at the high-resolution monitor providing the sole source of light in the stifling and seemingly airless van. I have been told that Washington, D.C., a former swamp, can be unpleasant in the summer. I should have figured the hot, heavy climate extended to the Potomac basin and the expensive gated suburbs of Virginia. Sunrise didn't help. Nothing resembling reasonable air managed to find us inside the surveillance van that Carson-Pelham drove when she picked us up at the hospital entrance. With the engine running, the van produced plentiful air conditioning, but apparently you are not supposed to run the engine on a stakeout.

Andy plucked at the buttons on her light summer blouse and fanned the fabric back and forth. I struggled not to enjoy the view.

"Isn't this a little obvious? Parked like this?" I had asked when the woman behind the wheel brought the van to a halt on the almost empty street.

"Heavens, every other panel truck and van on the streets of Washington has some sort of surveillance in it. Most people just assume it's for their nefarious neighbors, whoever or whatever they may be."

"Not comforting," I replied.

"You're sure he's coming here?" Andy asked.

Carson-Pelham nodded. "He'll be here."

. . .

SPECIAL AGENT CARSON-PELHAM found us at the hospital in Virginia Beach where Andy filled out forms for me to get my shoulder bone pushed back into its socket. We had settled in to wait our turn outside the ER when the woman appeared. I recognized her the moment Andy reminded me who she was. Mitchell Lindsay's gatekeeper. When she introduced herself, I learned that the late Deputy Director did not favor having a traditional executive assistant. He chose an experienced and fully trained special agent of the FBI. She immediately demonstrated just how much she already knew.

"Are you the disappearing guy?" she asked in a low voice after seating herself beside me on a plastic chair.

"No idea what you're—"

"Relax." Carson-Pelham studied me like a new toy. I returned the favor. She smiled. "Forty-seven. You're trying to guess. I'm forty-seven. I don't have the female hang-up about age that I'm supposed to have. In my twenties, I was young and stupid. In my thirties, I was ambitious and blind. I like my forties. They've been pure genius. God, if I only could have started out this way."

I wouldn't have been able to say whether she looked older, younger or precisely her age. She matched Andy's height, had closely cropped black hair that puffed up a little on top in a casual bed-head way, had a narrow but attractive face and wore a sleeveless black t-shirt over black jeans. She had a yoga fanatic's thin, fit physique and dark, highly alert eyes. When she spoke, her mouth favored left more than right, creating the impression of harboring an inside joke.

I'm lousy with faces, names and the memory of either. Aside from trying to block us from entering Director Lindsay's office, I remembered next to nothing about her.

"I know this isn't the time, but we have a lot to talk about," she said. "Are you okay?"

"They think my shoulder is dislocated."

"Ouch. That's going to hurt like the dickens. I did the same thing on a bobsled once."

"Bobsled?"

"Twenties. I told you. Stupid." She looked around the waiting room, then addressed Andy. "Karen Whitlock brought me up to speed. She said it was your idea to evacuate the Justices on golf carts, Detective. Well done."

Andy, seated beside me on her own uncomfortable plastic chair, squeezed my hand. The blast was more than four hours old. My clothes had dried, though my feet still squished in my shoes. From the moment Andy found me on the golf course turned no-man's land, I don't think we let go of each other. I didn't think I ever would again.

"We were about a mile from ground zero in the wooded part of the property," she said. "The explosion knocked us around. The chief justice caught a broken branch on his head. He'll need stiches, but otherwise he was okay. Chief Deputy Whitlock and I went back. We saw the helicopters come in. Where did they take the justices?"

"Harvey Point," she said. When Andy and I made blank faces at her, she added, "It's a defense testing facility up...well, nearby. The marshals got a call through to my office. Our team met them there. Last I heard, the Justices are all tucked away and being tended to on an undisclosed military base along with Kwame Mahame and his sister. Keep that information under your hat, by the way."

"That news feed is reporting little hope of finding survivors," Andy pointed at the muted screen mounted high in one corner of the waiting room. A graphic across the bottom shouted *Supreme Court Wiped Out.*

"Good." She seemed pleased with the misinformation.

The helicopter that picked me up along with Andy and Whitlock wore orange and white Coast Guard markings. The ride to Virginia Beach was a blur of noise, wind and revelation. Andy had to shout over the roar of chopper blades and turbines.

Andy, Tom and Donaldson had arrived at Siddley Plantation with Whitlock in the police SUV. Whitlock sent the police to set up the roadblock, then joined the on-site team. They collected the Justices and the Siddley staff in the dining room overlooking the golf course at the back of the building. When the fire alarms went off, the marshals decided the Siddley Mansion could not be defended. Andy put forth the idea to caravan everyone away in golf carts. They were well into the woods before the truck plowed through the roadblock. Tom and Donaldson volunteered to cover the evacuation. The kitchen fire had zero chance of being a coincidence, which meant at least one bad actor had the potential to either follow them or send the truck in pursuit. Andy last saw the two of them when she left with the golf cart caravan.

Gritting my teeth against shoulder pain that multiplied with each bounce in turbulence, I told Andy my half of the story. Around the time I finished, the helicopter made its approach to the helipad at Sentara Princess Anne Hospital.

We'd been waiting over an hour when Carson-Pelham found us.

"Where are Chief Ceeves and Special Agent Donaldson?" Andy asked.

"Your boss got picked up with the Mahames."

"Donaldson?" I asked.

"Chief Ceeves told our people that he and Special Agent Donaldson encountered someone in the kitchen. Chief Ceeves stayed to deal with the fire. Donaldson went after the man who started it."

"The man from the bunker," I told Andy. "Tall guy."

Andy pulled her phone and scrolled through the photo gallery.

"Him?"

"Yeah." I felt a cold grip on my spine, remembering the way the man walked out of the building holding the knife, the blood on his pants a stark sign of violence. "That guy is dead. But I never saw Lee…"

"May I see that?" Andy handed the phone to Carson-Pelham. "Ah. Colonel Juko."

"Colonel?"

"Intelligence officer for the Army of Ghana. Bag man for the 'Progressive Reformers'—or he was."

Carson-Pelham handed back the phone, then read my face. "They're still searching for Special Agent Donaldson."

I saw Andy steel herself against lost hope.

"Special Agent—"

"Please. Call me Leslie. My last name is a mouthful. Liberal parents."

Andy swallowed and began again. "Leslie, just what is it you think you know about us? About Will?"

"I know everything Director Lindsay knew. Including what you discussed at his cottage the afternoon before he was killed. I was his backup drive. His insurance. And now I'm yours."

"And just what does that mean?" I asked, feeling a sudden need to search the hospital waiting room for anyone in a suit and sunglasses.

"It means I rushed here to find you and assure you that who you are—what you are, Will—is protected. I came here to protect you."

"You came here to protect the story," I said.

"That, too."

"Protect Will in return for what, exactly?" Andy asked.

"Nothing, Detective." Carson-Pelham sat back. She bared her intentions with an open shrug. "We can certainly discuss your feelings on the matter, but as of this moment, you never walked into Director Lindsay's office. He never spoke to you. And nothing you did with the Director or at Siddley goes into a record of any kind—excluding, of course, Detective Stewart's valued assist with protecting the nine Justices of the United States Supreme Court."

"What about Mahame?"

"Mr. Mahame and his sister are safe. They've been placed in protective custody, pending the outcome of...let's just say, certain developments on both a domestic and international stage."

We must not have looked pleased.

"Oh, don't worry. There's no question that Mr. Mahame and his sister were innocents meant to take the fall. They're in no danger."

"That's not what that TV is saying," I pointed.

"Yes, well, we're letting a few parts of this little drama play out."

"We're supposed to trust you?" I asked. It might have been the searing pain radiating from my shoulder, but I was not in a trusting mood.

"Only if you choose to. Assuming, of course, I prove worthy of that trust."

The woman had a frank, open face. If she planned to double-cross us, she would do it with unquestionable finesse.

I glanced at Andy, whose teeth clenched, producing a prominence in her lower lip. Trust was not forthcoming.

"Also," Carson-Pelham added. "assuming you wish to finish this with me."

WE SWEATED in the parked van eight hours later, watching a monitor fed by a sophisticated camera mounted on the top of the windowless van. My shoulder ached, but not enough to make me tap the bottle of Vicodin nesting in Andy's shoulder bag. A pill would knock me on my ass.

I nursed another ache that no amount of Vicodin could dampen. A massive law enforcement and Homeland Security apparatus had descended on the blast site where Siddley Mansion once stood. Shortly before dawn, Carson-Pelham took a call from one of the investigators. She somberly reported that a search found human remains identified as Special Agent Lee Donaldson. She didn't elaborate and I didn't ask, but I could guess that when they said 'remains' there hadn't been much. Whoever designed the milk truck bomb had wildly underestimated its power. Nothing was found of the man in white, the driver, the two gunmen, or the two men killed by the man in white. They were vaporized.

Donaldson, we were told, had been far enough away to leave evidence.

It hurt more than I expected. The blast was less than a day old. Nothing about it felt real—certainly not the idea that Donaldson's buzz-cut demeanor was gone forever. Still, I might have felt numb to the news, if not for the pain brimming in Andy's eyes at that moment.

Carson-Pelham let silence speak for all of us, then she worked her phone screen.

"Fox News says Mexican police released the names of the terrorists who were smuggled across the border. The Mahames are being linked to a fundamentalist terror cell from Africa." Carson-Pelham scrolled. "They're having a cow about it. And the White House is all but declaring war on Mexico."

"Send General Pershing to get Pancho Villa," I muttered. "When do you plan to set the world straight?"

She didn't answer. "Your friends. Chief Ceeves. They all know about you, right?"

Andy explained the sequence of who knew and when. "And now you, of course," she added at the end of the list. "My turn for a question."

"I thought you'd never ask."

"Director Lindsay. Why did he go to McCauley's boat?"

"I had to postpone the director's meeting with you, if you recall."

"Because he had meetings in D.C."

"Yes. With them," she gestured at the sprawling house under surveillance.

"They approached the Director?"

She nodded. "Gently. Over a period of months. Then Roane invited him here, but even at that point Roane kept his cards hidden. When McCauley reached out for the meeting in Mackinac, we expected he had finally been given the green light to let the Director in."

"Why? That's a tremendous risk."

"They were looking for someone to have on the inside at the FBI, someone high up who would help them sell this whole terrorist theater production."

"But something went wrong," Andy said. "What?"

"I don't know," she replied. Genuine regret accented her voice. "Maybe the Director overestimated. Maybe something leaked, although the Director and I were the only ones who knew he was being courted. We may never know, but they backed out. And made sure not to leave any evidence."

"They burned his cottage on the island," I said.

"And with it the dossier I prepared. Or they took it, which is more dangerous. We don't know."

"Was Will in that dossier?"

She shook her head. "We did background on him. Right after you showed up. But no, there was nothing pointing to his involvement. I'm the only one who knew that the Director brought in the two of you—that he sent Will after Lonnie Penn's daughter. We knew she was Sergei Roane's wife."

"Why didn't you just pick her up from ICE custody?"

"She was never in ICE custody. Not officially. Those officers, once they saw a payday, made sure there was no record. When Lonnie Penn called out of the blue for help, we took a shot."

"They wanted someone high up to guide the investigation," Andy mused. "But someone else was already pulling the strings. They were hedging bets with Director Lindsay."

"Or hoping to use him to ensure that the real influencer remained deniable." Carson-Pelham abruptly focused on the monitor. "He's here."

She swiveled in her chair and checked the recording device tucked in my shirt pocket. She patted down my chest, following the twin wire leads to the microphones attached to my t-shirt collar. Out of one eye she caught Andy watching another woman's hands on her husband.

"Relax, Detective," she said smoothly. "If not for that ring on your finger, I'd be much more interested in you than your husband."

Andy blushed.

"Okay," she said. "You're on, Will."

I CUT the power and drifted. Their confidence made it easy. The location defeated surveillance and long-distance listening devices. They gathered around a marble fire pit beside a pool centered in the broad gardens of the estate. A trellis arched above the tiled patio, carefully covered in ivy to provide shade. Tall hedges formed a circle around the space, hiding it from outside eyes. The pool was the smaller of two on the estate, probably meant for more intimate recreation. Seated in comfortable patio furniture around the gas-powered fire, the men could feel well shielded from observation. The sky overhead added morning light to the fire pit flames.

A gentle glide took me to the trellis directly above their chairs. I closed a light grip on the wood framework.

Carson-Pelham had explained that Garcia Roane's estate in Virginia served his campaign to apply influence in Washington, D.C. She described the way he entertained officials at the highest levels of government, using expensive liquor and fine catering in the estate's backyard to spread his message of cartel reform and reconstruction. A recent interview for CBS News had been filmed in his manicured gardens. The estate's seclusion and electronic security eliminated the need to keep bodyguards close at hand. I saw no armed and muscled security lingering at a discrete distance.

Aaron McCauley sipped coffee and mimicked the country-club image I'd seen in the photo shown to us in Lindsay's cottage office. Garcia Roane, casually dressed yet formal and dignified, rose from his chair when the second guest arrived. Shorter and stockier than his son, he nevertheless shared his offspring's expressionless face. His hand went out and firmly clasped the fleshy paw offered him.

"Senator." He double gripped the man's hand.

"Garcia, my friend, I gotta tell you—you, too, Mac," he nodded at McCauley, "you have the touch. Lord a'mighty, you have the touch."

"Did we not provide everything we promised?" McCauley boasted. "Am I right?"

"Boys, they will burst at the seams at the White House. Nobody since the founding fathers has ever been in a position to nominate judges to all nine seats. A raging goddamned wet dream. That's what this is. A political wet dream that's going to lock my party in power for decades. Everyone on my side of the aisle is publicly calling for mourning and privately dancing a jig, itching to stamp those nominations asap."

The senator from Wisconsin sat down. His ruddy complexion suggested that hiking across the gardens to this secluded spot constituted significant effort.

"Icing on the cake, Senator Gianni," McCauley said. "Jay Manning phoned last night. He's ready to stroke you the biggest check your campaign has ever seen. He's on his way to Accra to finalize the mining contracts—post-dated, of course, for after the regime change. He already has initial logistics in place. I would imagine that means a nice order for some of those trucks built in your district, yes?"

"He's a fat slob, but his money's good and those fine trucks will let him cut the work force by twenty percent and pocket the profit." The Senator turned to Roane. "Garcia, my friend, I heard that your boy was injured. How is he?" The question oozed well-rehearsed concern.

"You are kind to ask, Reggie. His knee was badly damaged. He's flying to Boston tonight for the first of several surgeries to restore it. He will be cared for by the world's finest."

"Well, I wish him a speedy recovery. Is there any news of his wife and child?"

"My grandson? Not yet. There will be. We have excellent people working on it." Roane's responses were measured, as if counted by the word.

The Senator shook his head. From where I hovered, I could have spit on it. The thought was not fleeting.

"That is a shame, a crying shame, that a girl would run off like that. I wish you all the best."

More pleasantries followed. A young woman in a casual summer skirt and blouse arrived with a tray of finger food. The pleasantries continued until she disappeared from earshot.

"I'm going to jump right in, Garcia. Let's talk schedule. We got a lot of balls in the air. The White House is already talking funeral for those three fine justices—along with the rest of those liberal jackasses—from the Court. Of course, the President can't be seen to rush this, but I'm sure he'd like to include updates on the investigation with his public statement of condolences. When can we expect to get the evidence?"

"My people will see that it is leaked to your FBI team tomorrow. It will place Mahame and his co-conspirators at the border, at the safe house in Missouri, and on the way to North Carolina. By then, I anticipate that the investigation will produce their DNA at the scene."

"God willing," the Senator said. "Although from what I saw of that blast, DNA is about all they're gonna find. Your fellas might have overdone it."

"They had to be certain, Reggie. With so much at stake, certainty was crucial."

"My sources at State tell me that the order to close our embassy in Ghana will go out in the next twenty-four hours. That's the trigger that should put *el presidente* out of a job and open the palace door to the Progressive Reformers. I assume they're ready to move, Mac?"

"Have been for weeks," McCauley assured the Senator. "I personally helped them craft an urgent request to the United States for military assistance to help restore order."

"What about Nfuko?"

McCauley shrugged. "I impressed upon the new regime that they can't be seen as barbarians. They will express the right degree of reluctant willingness to extradite *ex-President* Nkufo to the U.S. to stand trial for the terrorism, but I've been assured that justice will be served before it comes to that."

"Good. Too much scrutiny might generate unintended consequences," the Senator said. "I gotta admit, I got a little nervous with that whole Lindsay business. I sure as hell thought we had him on board."

"It couldn't be helped," McCauley said. "But the Mahame Terrorist Cell—"

"Oh, I like that!" The Senator slapped his knee.

"I thought you would," McCauley laughed. "Right now, we're making them look very good for Lindsay as well as that business in Minnesota."

"Small change compared to the Supreme Court. Small change."

"The devil is in the details."

The Senator poured coffee from a carafe. "Then I would say we have this by the balls, gentlemen. By the balls. The President has been dying to move the military somewhere. They'll close up the border faster'n you can blink once that evidence is confirmed."

"Very well," Roane nodded.

"That should create demand that gives your profits a nice kick in the ass, Garcia," the Senator laughed.

Roane did not respond.

McCauley quickly filled the awkward silence. "Senator, did I see you playing golf with some of our friends from the hill last week? Tell me your score isn't improving or I'll never agree to another game with you."

The Senator took the bait.

I shoved off. A short glide took me past the circular hedge. I used a power unit to drop down to the lawn, where I grabbed the hedge and pulled myself into the prickly wall, out of sight.

Fwooomp!

I reappeared and settled on my feet. The recording device in my pocket had large, tactile buttons for Start, Stop and Play. I assumed it had been designed to be handled blindly. A small digital window showed me the progress of the recording. I touched Stop. It offered a prompt.

Replay?

I touched Yes and cued up the part I wanted. I touched Pause and dropped the unit back in my pocket.

Fwooomp!

A few minutes and some minor maneuvering put me back overhead while the Senator continued to boast about a shot on the sixteenth hole.

I reached in my pocket, rolled the volume all the way up, and touched Play. The speaker was small, but the voices were clear.

"Senator."

The three men below me froze.

"Garcia, my friend, I gotta tell you—you, too, Mac—you have the touch. Lord a'mighty, you have the touch."

"Did we not provide everything we promised? Am I right?"

"Boys, they will burst at the seams at the White House. Nobody since the founding fathers has ever been in a position to nominate judges to all nine seats. A raging goddamned wet dream. That's what this is. A political wet dream that's going to lock the party in power for decades. Everyone on my side of the aisle is publicly calling for mourning and privately dancing a jig, itching to stamp those nominations asap."

. . .

"What in God's name happened?" Carson-Pelham ushered me into the van and slid the door shut. "All hell is breaking loose. He's got his security people combing the place. What did you do?"

"Nothing much."

"Did you get it? Did they see you?"

She pawed at my shirt and pulled the device from my pocket. Not waiting, she pushed buttons until the voices played again. The excellent recording quality meant voice print analysis would put to rest any claim of fakery.

"What happened?" Andy asked.

Carson-Pelham stopped the recording.

"I got it. The whole thing."

"Why did the Senator blast out of here like that?"

"Well, the Senator is a little worried that the cat might be out of the bag."

"What did you do, Will?" Andy asked.

"I recorded it," I said. "Then I played it back for them."

Andy's eyes flared. She shot a glance at the FBI agent, who flopped back against the wall of the van.

"Oh...my...God," Carson-Pelham said. "You cagey bastard."

"Will, what were you thinking?"

"I was thinking the look on their faces paid part of the bill for Lee."

Andy slowly exchanged a veneer of stark concern for something softer, something warmer. Dimples appeared on her cheeks as she fought a smile.

Carson-Pelham stared at the floor. I braced for the speech, the one that declared what an idiot I was, the one that raged at me for blowing everything.

She chuckled.

"They're gonna kill McCauley. He's a dead man." She sat up abruptly and switched off the camera system and monitor. She carefully stowed the recording device in a hard-shell case. Casting a glance at me, she shook her head, grinning, and climbed between the front seats. She dropped in the driver seat and turned the ignition key. As soon as the engine started, blessed cool air gushed through the van's vents. "Guess I better go pick up the senator. I'll drop you off first."

"You're going to arrest a United States Senator? On the basis of this recording?" Andy asked.

Carson-Pelham laughed. "Arrest? Oh, no my dear. I'm going to invite him to bare his soul to the FBI before Garcia Roane dumps his severed limbs in the Atlantic." She turned in her seat and fixed a squinty gaze on me. "I'm going to like working with you, Will Stewart."

EPILOGUE II

I followed her from the hotel to the hospital. She used a lobby restroom to change into loose-fitting teal scrubs. She avoided the elevators, instead choosing the empty concrete stairwell. I gave her time to climb two flights before entering. I checked for cameras. None.

Fwooomp!

I vanished and gripped the steel railing to launch vertically. A perfect shot up the open center. I patted myself on the back for getting better and better at this.

I passed her on the third floor. She climbed the steps with her face upturned and steel in her posture. When the door marked 5 appeared, I grabbed the railing and pulled myself over. Her light approaching footsteps belied the weight she carried.

Fwooomp!

She made the turn on the landing below.

"Your mother is nervous."

She jumped and froze. A mix of emotions rushed her facial expression. Shock. Anger. Impatience. Resistance.

"Did you come to make small talk," Gloria said, finally settling on Dismissive. "Best we not talk at all."

She continued up the concrete stairs.

She met me on the fifth-floor landing. Her right hand pulled something from a shoulder bag not unlike the one Andy carried.

She pulled on a pair of latex gloves and squared herself to face me.

"What? No morality speech? No pleading with me about the stain this will leave on my soul?"

I thought about souls. Two in particular. "Milo's children…the little one had a thing for Disney fairies."

Gloria said nothing for a moment, then spoke softly, "Oscar and I watched Tinkerbell movies with him. She was his favorite. He wanted to fly like her."

I remembered the child's enchanted outcries above the rooftops of Juárez.

"Is that why you came? To help me? For Francisco and Daniel?"

"Who said I came to help you?"

She weaponized the teen *omigod* look and posture, flashing her true age if only for a split second.

"I don't like people who hurt children," I said.

"I could have done this without you."

"Really, Miss Obvious? *Mami? Can we stop in Boston on the way? I want to visit Fenway Park.*"

"Go Sox."

"Lame."

"I'm lame? *Lonnie, any chance I could ride along? I've never flown a Gulfstream jet.*"

"I haven't."

"I don't need you to watch over me," she said. "And I don't fear a stain on my soul."

"I don't fear a stain on your soul. But you clearly need me to watch over you. You mess this up and you'll wind up back in Juárez."

"You're a very strange man, Mr. Stewart."

"Did you just call me Mister?"

"You're older than my mother."

"*You're* older than your mother."

I leaned against the door and performed a quick reconnaissance through a small glass window. Better than I expected. She studied me, still assessing my intentions.

"Your mother is nervous because being honored at the Kennedy Center tomorrow night is a huge deal. Cut her some slack."

Gloria rolled her eyes.

"Third door on the right. He's got one guard outside. You were never going to get past the guard."

"And you are?"

"I don't have to." I took her by the arm.

"Are you seriously going to restrain me?"

"No. Get behind this door and face that way."

I expected her to jerk free, to fight me. She served up another rebellious teen face, a jarring contrast to the cold determination that drove her this far. Following her had been like following a tsunami.

"Just do it. And don't turn around until I say so."

She heaved a sigh and moved to the back of the door. She adjusted to face the wall.

"This is ridiculous."

"No peeking."

I waited a second to be sure. She stood obediently in place.

I pulled the door open and took one step in. The square-shouldered private guard outside Sergei Roane's hospital room door jerked his head to examine me, instantly alert. I recognized him. He led the cadre of men that raced to climb the water tower in pursuit of Milo and Maria. His had been the first face to rise over the edge of the roof. I calculated the mercy he would have shown Milo and his family and applied the null result to the moment.

I froze, stared straight at him, tried to look as guilty as possible, then quickly backed out the door and closed it.

I stepped aside. Gloria, her back to me, started to turn.

"No peeking."

She tensed. She drove her gloved hand into her bag.

A moment later the door burst open. The guard stepped through and faced me with deadly intent.

"Hi." I smiled.

I clamped a grip on his forearm.

FWOOOMP!

He winked out of sight. I lifted his weightless body up and over my head. Equal and opposite reaction pressed my feet to the floor. He let out a startled whoop. I heaved him toward the stairwell.

The door closed behind him.

Gloria turned. Just as her face came around—

Fwooomp!

I reappeared. The guard reappeared in flight above my head.

She caught me hurling two hundred pounds of bodyguard like a javelin. I let go and ducked to avoid his legs as gravity pulled his flailing body down. His face bounced off the handrail halfway down the half flight of stairs. He rolled onto the concrete steps, somersaulted, and folded into a heap on the next landing.

One leg pointed in the wrong direction. A gush of blood painted the side of his head. He moaned. Still alive.

"Go."

She gaped at me.

"How did you…?"

"*Listen to me. If you're going to do this, do it.*" My tone was not kind.

Her wonder vanished, replaced by one of Lonnie Penn's screen characters. The vengeful mother. The woman wronged. The victim no more.

She set her jaw and flared her nostrils.

She extracted a knife from the bag. It may not have been the same knife she had planned to use to take her son's life, but it came from the same murderous family. The deadly blade glinted shards of light. The curved tip and razor edge left no room for discussion.

She slipped through the door.

Stepped lightly down the hall.

And opened the door to Sergei Roane's hospital room.

DIVISIBLE MAN - THREE NINES FINE
January 17, 2020 to June 17, 2020
Break
July 19, 2020 to August 16, 2020

PREVIEW THE NEXT DIVISIBLE MAN ADVENTURE

DIVISIBLE MAN: EIGHT BALL

Will and Andy are drawn into pursuit of a serial sniper using high tech that never misses.

She walks in beauty, like the night
Of cloudless climes and starry skies;
And all that's best of dark and bright
Meet in her aspect and her eyes;
Thus mellowed to that tender light
Which heaven to gaudy day denies.

—

George Gordon
(Lord Byron)

DIVISIBLE MAN - EIGHT BALL
CHAPTER 1

Oh crap.

The hospital corridor lights burst from dim to blazing. People in scrubs materialized from all directions.

"That's my doctor," the girl hugging my neck whispered a little too loudly. "My nighttime doctor." I felt her move and point with an arm neither of us could see. We floated five feet above the carpet at the intersection of three wide hallways. The woman she pointed at hustled toward the room where I'd found this child.

Where did all these people come from?

I did not hear a PA announcement. No piercing digital alarm or squawking siren broke the semi-silence of the night shift. Yet a growing number of people in an assortment of medical attire converged on the recently empty hallway and this child's hospital room.

This is not good.

The child in my arms was number seven. Lucky seven. I started just after eleven p.m. and the first six went smoothly. Easy in and out. All of them asleep—all of them except this one. I've grown adept at simply closing a grip on an arm or ankle and pushing *the other thing* over their small bodies. A gentle touch, then—

Fwooomp!

The sound in my head jars me but the silence in the room remains unbroken. The child vanishes, creating an empty child-shaped cavern beneath fuzzy blankets. I give it a minute or two. I have no idea if duration matters.

Sometimes the sensation of going weightless seeps into the child's dreams and they stir or wiggle. None have ever fought it.

When it feels right, I release my grip.

Fwooomp! They settle back on the mattress, often stirring, perhaps reacting to the sensation of falling.

In. Out. Unseen. Easy.

Until number seven.

"Hey!" This girl spoke the moment she flashed out of sight. My gentle grip on her wrist shifted, telling me she sat up in bed. "Who's there?"

"It's okay."

The light blanket covering empty space squirmed and shifted.

"Are you invi—?"

"*Shhhhhh!*" I cut off her full-voiced question. "Yes," I whispered back. "And I'm not going to hurt you."

I expected her to pull her arm free. Instead, her free hand found mine. She probed up my arm.

"Are you a ghost?"

"No."

"Are you an angel?"

"Nope."

"Superhero?"

"You ask a lot of questions."

"Well, duh." She reached higher, found my neck, then touched my face. I felt her hand jerk away. "I can't see myself! I can't see my hand! How did you do that?"

A stream of answers, ranging from sweet to smartass, flashed through my mind.

"The truth? I have no idea."

There had been no time to gauge the child's age. Propelled by a blend of overconfidence and what had become a bit of an assembly line routine, I had moved into the room quickly, assessed that no adults slept on a spare bed or sofa, found her arm above the covers, and went to work without looking too closely. In the dark, she was just another sadly bald head indenting a pillow. In my haste, I failed to see that she was awake.

She occupied an adult-sized bed. From her voice I estimated her age between seven and twelve, although like many her age, her attitude suggested twenty-something.

She moved. The blanket wiggled on the bed. I guessed that she waved her other hand in front of her own face.

"Am I invisi—?"

"Yes."

"Cool! Is this a dream?"

I have used that gimmick, but only with groggy kids half in and out of sleep. This girl was fully awake.

"Nope. Keep your voice down, please."

She still had not pulled free of my light grip on her wrist. She moved on the mattress. From the way the sheets flipped off, I surmised that she swung her legs off the bed. An IV line followed her movement, then popped loose and dangled, dripping on the floor.

"It feels cool—I don't mean *cool* cool, but you know, like—"

"Water?"

"Yeah! Like going swimming!" She tried to stand. The act of pushing off the mattress sent us floating. "*What's happening?*"

I shushed her again and grabbed the bedrail with my free hand. She wiggled against the sensation of weightlessness.

"*I'm floating!*"

"That's part of the deal. We're weightless. Like astronauts. You. Me, too." I maintained a light grip. She seemed to be enjoying this, at least enough not to shriek.

"Why are you holding my wrist?"

"It only works if we stay in contact with each other. May I hold your hand?"

She thought it over.

"I guess."

I slid my grip away from her wrist and found her hand.

"Am I dead?"

I squeezed her hand. "Does that feel dead?"

She squeezed back. I lifted my arm and abetted her launch from the mattress. She giggled. To my surprise, she probed my arm again, found my neck and threw her free arm around it.

"This is the coolest thing ever!" she whispered loudly in my ear.

"It kinda is," I conceded. *In for a penny...* "You want to see something really cool?"

"Uh-huh!"

Off we went.

"What, exactly, do you do?"

Pidge asked the question less than twenty-four hours earlier. We flopped in a pair of ratty old lawn chairs and tipped end-of-the-duty-day beers at the Education Foundation hangar at Essex County Airport. A September sunset painted shades of orange in the western sky, hinting of fall. Warm light fell on us through the open hangar door. The Foundation's twin-engine Piper Navajo crouched at my shoulder. Pidge ranks among a handful of people who know about my ability to vanish.

"Sneak in. Zap sleeping children in their beds."

Pidge whistled over the lip of her beer. "Yeah...I wouldn't let that get around. This is that crazy Marshfield shit, right? I mean—you told me that you fixed that kid. What? Now you're taking that show on the road?"

"I didn't fix that kid. *The other thing* fixed the kid."

"Right. Any idea how?"

"No clue."

"FM."

"FM?"

"Fucking magic. Have you told Arun yet?"

Pidge, a little under five feet of coiled cobra with short blonde hair and a disarming pixie smile, is a hotshot pilot who can fly circles around every throttle jockey I ever met. I rank her as the best pilot on the roster at Essex County Air Service and it has nothing to do with the fact that I taught her to fly. She's also a dervish with a dockworker's foul mouth, but she transforms into the image of cotillion charm around Arun Dewar who is, nominally, my boss at the Foundation. Arun joined the Christine and Paulette Paulesky Education Foundation as a gofer and office organizer after Sandy Stone, Director of the Foundation, all but drowned in grant applications. When Sandy, a kindergarten teacher both by trade and in the depths of her soul, returned to her flock for the new school year, Arun took over the day-to-day Foundation work. Pidge, who I had always assumed would die alone in a bar fight at the age of ninety, fell hard for Arun. I credited the young man's English accent.

"No, I haven't, and don't you go spilling it during pillow talk either." Pidge might carry every pilot rating except seaplane in her wallet, but she will always be my former flight student. I shot her a warning glance. She shot back a sly grin. "I mean it."

"Relax. I pinky swore about your disappearing act and when I fucking pinky swear, Fort Knox takes notice."

We drank our beer and watched the Essex County Air Service hangar and office across the ramp turn to black silhouettes. Only Earl Jackson's office remained illuminated. I rarely see it extinguished before I leave.

"So, like what—you do this routine in hospitals when you're on Foundation trips?"

"Try to. On overnights. Plays havoc with my sleep time."

"Sleep is overrated. You ever think about going public? I mean—if it really works, there are a lot of sick kids out there…"

"Don't."

"Don't what?"

"Don't guilt me about this. Look," I said, "I have no idea how it works, but worse, I don't know why it works most of the time, but not all the time." The ache of a recent failure involving a young woman named Angeline Landry lingered, always within reach. "What happens when it works for nine kids and not for number ten? How do you think the parents will feel? How do you think the kid would feel? People expect perfection, or else you'll hear from their lawyer."

"Assholes. Lawyers, I mean. So, like tomorrow you guys have an overnight in St. Louis. You sneak out so Arun doesn't know?"

"Pretty much. I can hit ten, maybe fifteen rooms. Get in. Make the kid disappear for a minute or so. Then get out."

"Doesn't this scare the shit outta the kid?"

"They never know I'm there. Mostly. A few wake up, but these kids are accustomed to strangers coming and going at all hours, sticking them with needles, checking vitals, plugging in new medicine drips. Even the little ones are kinda worldly."

"How do you know when the kid is…cooked?"

"I don't. I don't know. I don't want to know."

Because that would mean knowing when it doesn't work.

"Not very scientific."

She said nothing for a long minute, prompting me to fill the silence.

"Sometimes…sometimes, I kinda feel it. Maybe it's just wishful thinking. But you're right. It's far from scientific."

"How do you know it works at all?"

"I have someone who loosely tracks the results."

Pidge lifted her eyebrows. "Someone else *knows*? Who?"

I held up a stop-sign hand. "Compartmental. He doesn't know about you. You don't know about him."

"It's that head doctor! The one in Madison."

"Jesus Christ, what does a guy have to do to keep a secret?"

"Yeah, you just keep tryin' there, partner. Your wife told me all about him. The one who got your ticket back. It's gotta be him. Steve-something."

"Dr. Stephenson."

"That's the one!"

"He's a neurologist."

"What does that have to do with kids who have cancer?"

"His reputation opens doors. I let him know where I've been. He looks into case results, don't ask me how. Remind me to tell you a story about him and Earl back in the day in Thailand."

"No shit?"

"Crazy story. Anyway, like I said, he's been quietly tracking the whole thing. Places I've been. Remission statistics. Doc says we're running about eighty percent."

She looked sideways at me.

"What?"

"Somebody's going to notice. You get that, right? Somebody's going to start asking how it is that kids are mysteriously getting cured at random hospitals. You watch."

"I think they know you're missing," I said to the girl in my arms. We hovered near the ceiling of the broad hallway.

"Really? What was your first clue?"

I liked this kid. A fellow smartass.

"How old are you?" She felt small, which was no reliable indicator. The disease killing her likes to shrink its victims first. I recalled that her scalp was hairless but could not picture her face.

"Eleven."

"Got a name?"

"Sure. Do you?"

"Divisible Man."

"That's stupid."

"I didn't come up with it. I know it's a little late for this, but would you promise not to tell anyone about…all this? If you promise, I'll tell you my name."

"I guess. Who would believe me anyway?"

"I know. It's crazy. I'm Will."

"I'm Amber."

"Cut it out. Really? You've got to be kidding me."

"What?"

"Amber?"

"What's wrong with Amber?"

"As in 'Amber Alert?'" As I said it, a deputy sheriff in full uniform hurried down the hall beneath us. His leather holster and belt creaked and squeaked. Keys on his belt jangled.

"Oh. I get it. Ha. Ha. Very funny."

Staff clustered around Amber's hospital room door now fanned out, checking adjoining rooms, opening closet doors, searching the unisex bathroom. Returning the girl to her own bed was not an option. A worried-looking woman in scrubs blocked the door. She held a phone to her ear and gestured at the empty room as she spoke. When she saw the deputy, she waved him to hurry to her. They traded words. The deputy lifted his radio mic to his lips.

"This is not good," I said, as much to myself as the girl.

Totally my fault.

The weightless aspect of *the other thing* had been problematic for me at first, and occasionally downright frightening. Drifting untethered, or worse, the risk of floating unabated to the airless edge of Earth's atmosphere, inspired me to engineer a means of propulsion. The solution came naturally to a pilot. I needed an engine and propeller. A few harrowing experiments with what looked like a small flashlight with an electric motor and a six-inch two-bladed hobby-shop propeller helped me hone the means to lift off and fly under control. Indoors or out. What had been frightening became exhilarating.

Along the way, I found what I can only describe as a core muscle that runs down my center when I vanish. It allows me to rotate and lever my body without the need for an anchor point. The discovery ended a disturbing tendency to knock over lamps and tumble out of control.

Between the power units, the ability to rotate in space, and a genetic love of flying, I had no one to blame except me for the fact that I invited Amber to go for a joy ride. We slipped out of her room and cruised down what had been the dim, nighttime hallway. We made a few turns, descended a staircase, and found the hospital's main entrance and lobby where I bumped the Handicap Entrance button and opened the front door.

We zoomed into the cool night, soared across the street fronting the hospital and explored a broad park at treetop level.

Amber's gasps and giggles paid her airfare. I flew her over forty-foot maple trees and initiated a series of dives and climbs over a placid pond. We skimmed the glass surface of the water. We followed the winding path of a running trail. We wove a low racecourse around empty picnic tables beneath a bloated moon. I made her shriek by colliding harmlessly with a row of tall arborvitae.

We had a blast.

We lost track of time.

Eventually I navigated back to the hospital, and back to her room.

Too late. All hell had slipped its leash.

The deputy taking up station at Amber's room door carried on an urgent radio conversation, no doubt calling in reinforcements or initiating a lockdown of the hospital.

"You ever wander off in the night before?" I asked.

"Me? No!" She sounded offended. "Am I going to be in trouble?"

Well, it sure as hell won't be me, I thought, instantly regretting that this child would take the heat for my impulsiveness.

"Just…give me a minute to think…"

I rotated and applied power to the hand-held propeller. Thrust pulled us away from the expanding search party. We cruised over a burnt-orange carpet embedded with a dizzying geometric pattern. Two more hospital staffers jogged toward us, bent on joining the search. Amber twisted against me as they passed. Her grip on my neck tightened, laden with tension and worry.

"What did you think of the flying?" I whispered, looking to lighten the moment.

"I love it!"

"You should become a pilot. When you grow up. You can take flying lessons and solo when you're sixteen. Get your private license when you're seventeen. Commercial license at eighteen."

She said nothing.

"Lots of women fly. The best pilot I know is a woman."

We retraced our path to the atrium where hospital signage sparked a plan.

"I'm not going to," she said faintly.

"What? Fly? Why not? You didn't like it?"

I felt her shake her head. "I'm not going to grow up."

Her matter-of-fact tone tied a knot in my throat.

"Don't be silly."

"This is my third time here. I had two remissions, but it keeps coming back. My mom and dad think I don't know what the doctors talk about, but I do. I know what's going to happen. I'm okay. But Mom cries a lot."

We soared over a staircase railing. This time there were no giggles and gasps. I aimed the power unit downward. We settled toward the first floor.

"Bullshit," I said.

"Daddy says that's a quarter for the swear jar."

"Bullshit, bullshit, bullshit. I owe you a buck. You ever been to Wisconsin?"

"My grandparents live in Wausau."

"Do you know where Essex is?"

"No."

"Well, your grandparents will know. Here's the deal. On the day of your sixteenth birthday, get your parents or your grandparents to drive you to the city of Essex. Get them to take you to the airport, east of town. You walk right in the office door and tell a lady named Rosemary II that Will said you get a free flying lesson. Got it?"

"Okay, but—"

"No buts. Promise me."

I halted our descent just above the lobby floor. I found the sign I was looking for.

"You mean flying like this?"

"No. Real flying. In an airplane."

"I like this better."

She had a point. "Okay. Well, then I'll give you both. Airplane, and this. Sweet sixteen. You'll be there. Trust me." I'd never made a promise like that before. It barely squeezed past my lips and left a sting in its wake.

"If you say so."

"I say so. Are you hungry?"

DIVISIBLE MAN - EIGHT BALL
CHAPTER 2

Except for a few operating coffee machines meant for third-shift workers, the stainless-steel shelves and tray slides of the slumbering cafeteria lay bare. The stoves were cold; the salad bars lay empty under sparkling glass.

Amber confessed that she wasn't hungry. She said it hurts to eat and makes her throw up.

I settled her in place on a plastic cafeteria chair and released her hand. She reappeared. Gravity embraced her. She gripped the seat of the chair as if it might launch her. Along with her naked scalp she wore the gaunt look and carried the thin appendages too often found in late-night TV ads meant to Save The Children. *Just a few pennies a day...*

All the pennies in the world weren't going to save Amber.

I maneuvered to the glass face of a snack vending machine, the kind that uses corkscrews to release treats. A small padlock secured the transparent front panel. I wrapped my hand around the padlock body and made it vanish. The border between the vanished body and visible shackle quivered. I tugged. The shackle snapped on the borderline. I dropped the pieces and heaved the door open.

"Here you go," I said. "My treat."

I feared she would reject the offer.

To my surprise, her eyes widened. She stood and took half a dozen steps to the unbound junk food riches. Her strides had a forced steadiness. Like a drunk trying hard to look sober. The idea of her wandering all the way from her room to the cafeteria in the middle of the night might test credibility. Her thin legs didn't look capable of the trip.

Something about the beckoning sugar and salty carbs awakened her. She held the open glass door and contemplated rows of gaudy choices.

"I have to go now," I said. She pulled her gaze free of the candy riches and searched for me in the empty air.

"Are you coming back?"

I pushed off and slowly floated toward the cafeteria exit.

"I might be back someday, but you won't be here."

A flash of resignation on her small face put a spotlight on my stupid choice of words.

"Hey! I don't mean it that way. You and I have a date for a flying lesson. Sweet sixteen. Promise?"

"Sure," she said. "Promise."

"Don't bullshit me."

"That's a buck and a quarter now. And I promise."

"For real?"

"For real."

She waved in the direction of my voice.

I didn't leave immediately. I watched her carefully pick out a Ritz cracker and cheese snack. Then a bag of Doritos. Then a Mars bar. By the time she retraced her steps to the chair and table, she clutched a load of goodies to her chest. She sat down and gingerly ate the Ritz crackers. She waited a moment, hesitant. Then she eagerly tore into the Doritos. I watched her munch and savor the chips, devouring the bag quickly and moving on to the next snack.

I never know for sure.

Except this time.

On the way out, feeling better about the night's work, I reappeared in a corridor long enough to flag down an orderly and report seeing a kid in the empty cafeteria who seemed to be eating the place clean.

DIVISIBLE MAN - EIGHT BALL
CHAPTER 2

I reached the TownePlace Suites hotel across from Spirit of St. Louis Airport just before four a.m. Zipping around behind a handheld power unit can be delightful, but it's dangerous at night when transmission and telephone lines become impossible to see and avoid. I traveled by Nissan rental car from the hotel to the hospital and back again. I parked in the hotel lot feeling tired but satisfied.

I feeped the car's door locks and hiked the full length of the silent parking lot, the penalty for being the last guest arriving at a hotel. The lobby was empty. The check-in desk stood deserted. I counted both as a blessing and hurried to the elevators happy to avoid a judgmental hello from a curious night clerk.

A few hours of sleep—that's all I wanted.

Arun's schedule lined up a full day of meetings and school tours. He had asked me to go along, or at the very least, meet him for breakfast to bolster his courage—being new to handling Education Foundation business trips on his own. I told him I wanted to sleep in. It felt selfish at the time, but it wasn't a lie. I told him I would check out at eleven and wait for him at the airport.

I planned to sleep up to the moment of checkout.

I slotted the plastic key card in my room door. The pessimist in me anticipated the card not working, necessitating a hike back down to the front desk for a new card.

The tiny green light flashed. The lock clicked.

I slipped into the room and had just long enough to wonder if I had left all the lights on before a woman's voice nearly stopped my heart.

"*Where the hell have you been?*"

Fwooomp! I threw forward the levers in my head and disappeared.

A tug on the core muscle jerked me off the carpet. An instant later I hung prone just below the ceiling, eyeballing a fire suppression sprinkler. The move startled me as much as the intruder's jarring inquiry.

She sat in the room's single occasional chair near the curtained window. Boyish dark hair, thin, dressed in a black blazer over a black t-shirt. Her dark eyes searched as the room door slammed shut behind me. Despite her angry tone and grim demeanor, her face gave the impression of suppressing a smile sprung from an inside joke. She carried a Glock semi-automatic handgun in a shoulder rig under her left arm.

"Christ," I said, "you scared the crap outta me."

Her eyes lifted toward the sound of my voice. FBI Special Agent Leslie Carson-Pelham rose from the chair.

"What are you doing here?" I asked.

"Do you always do that when you're startled?"

"Do you always break into people's hotel rooms?" I pushed off the ceiling and rotated to an upright position. The instant my feet touched the carpet—

Fwooomp!

—I reappeared. She blinked at me.

"Where the hell were you? I've been here for hours."

I glanced up at the ceiling. In an instant, I had not only vanished but, propelled by an instinct to move out of harm's way, had shot to the top of the room and swung to a prone position.

Without pushing off.

Without deploying the power unit in my pocket.

Without thinking.

Not for the first time, a strange emergency autopilot launched me at a moment of threat. Andy and I experienced a nearly identical move in a motel room in Montana seconds before gunfire tore apart the bed we occupied. The same thing happened over a frozen lake, where I hung helpless holding the drowned body of Andy's pregnant sister in my arms.

The first time it happened, it launched me and Lane Franklin out the window of a burning room. For months since, I've tried to replicate it, without success.

During the flashcard review of these events in my head, Leslie continued speaking to me.

"…to make this work." She fixed an angry expression on me. "Is your phone dead? I tried calling."

"I…uh…"

"Never mind. Let's go."

"Go where?"

She spotted my flight bag on the desktop. She hooked it and thrust it at me as she marched past me on her way to the door.

"I'll tell you on the way."

"On the way where?"

"A picnic."

ABOUT THE AUTHOR

HOWARD SEABORNE is the author of the DIVISIBLE MAN™ series as well as a collection of short stories featuring the same cast of characters. He began writing novels in spiral notebooks at age ten. He began flying airplanes at age sixteen. He is a former flight instructor and commercial charter pilot licensed in single- and multi-engine airplanes as well as helicopters. Today he flies a twin-engine Beechcraft Baron, a single-engine Beechcraft Bonanza, and a Rotorway A-600 Talon experimental helicopter he built from a kit in his garage. He lives with his wife and writes and flies during all four seasons in Wisconsin, never far from Essex County Airport.

Visit www.HowardSeaborne.com to join the Email List
and get a FREE DOWNLOAD.

DIVISIBLE MAN

The media calls it a "miracle" when air charter pilot Will Stewart survives an aircraft in-flight breakup, but Will's miracle pales beside the stunning aftereffect of the crash. Barely on his feet again, Will and his police sergeant wife Andy race to rescue an innocent child from a heinous abduction. *Will's new ability might make the difference between life and death...if it doesn't kill him first.*

Available in print, digital, and audio.
Search: "DIVISIBLE MAN Howard Seaborne"
Join our Reader Email list at **HowardSeaborne.com**

DIVISIBLE MAN - THE SIXTH PAWN

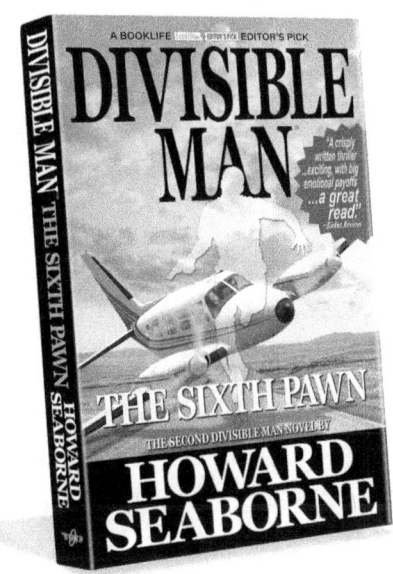

A *BookLife from Publishers Weekly* **Editor's Pick.**

"A book of outstanding quality."

When the Essex County "Wedding of the Century" erupts in gunfire, Will and Andy Stewart confront a criminal element no one could have foreseen. Will tests the extraordinary after-effect of surviving a devastating airplane crash while Andy works a case obstructed by powerful people wielding the sinister influence of unlimited money in politics.

Available in print, digital, and audio.

Search: "DIVISIBLE MAN Howard Seaborne"

Join our Reader Email list at **HowardSeaborne.com**

DIVISIBLE MAN - THE SECOND GHOST

Tormented by a cyber stalker, Lane Franklin's best friend turns to suicide. Lane's frantic call launches Will and Andy Stewart on a desperate rescue mission. When it all goes bad, Will must adapt his extraordinary ability to survive the dangerous high steel and glass of Chicago as Andy and Pidge confront the edge of disaster. **Includes the short story, "Angel Flight," a bridge to the fourth DIVISIBLE MAN novel that follows.**

Available in print, digital, and audio.

Search: "DIVISIBLE MAN Howard Seaborne"

Join our Reader Email list at HowardSeaborne.com

DIVISIBLE MAN - THE SEVENTH STAR

A horrifying message turns a holiday gathering tragic. An unsolved murder hangs a death threat over Detective Andy Stewart's head. And internet-fueled hatred targets Will and Andy's friend Lane. Will and Andy struggle to keep the ones they love safe, while hunting a murderer who is supposed to be dead. As the tension tightens, Will confronts a troubling revelation about the extraordinary after-effect of his midair collision.

Available in print, digital, and audio.

Search: "DIVISIBLE MAN Howard Seaborne"

Join our Reader Email list at HowardSeaborne.com

DIVISIBLE MAN - TEN MAN CREW

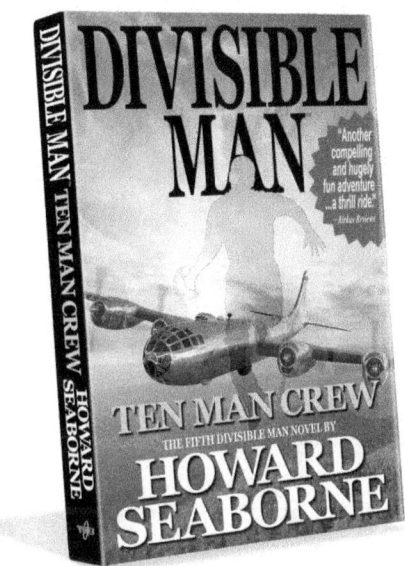

An unexpected visit from the FBI threatens Will Stewart's secret and sends Detective Andy Stewart on a collision course with her darkest impulses. A twisted road reveals how a long-buried Cold War secret has been weaponized. And Pidge shows a daring side of herself that could cost her dearly.

Available in print and digital.

Search: "DIVISIBLE MAN Howard Seaborne"

Join our Reader Email list at **HowardSeaborne.com**

DIVISIBLE MAN - THE THIRD LIE

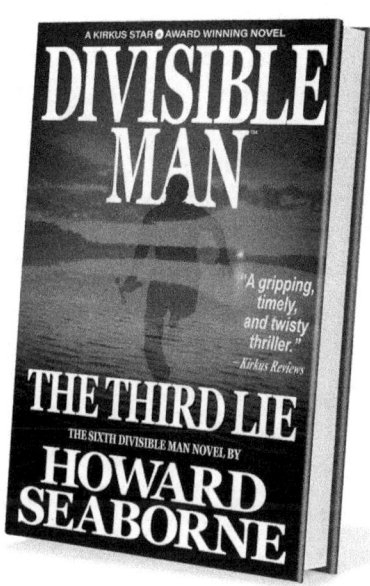

Caught up in a series of hideous crimes that generate national headlines, Will faces the critical question of whether to reveal himself or allow innocent lives to be lost.
The stakes go higher than ever when Andy uncovers the real reason behind a celebrity athlete's assault on an underaged girl. And Will discovers that the limits of his ability can lead to disaster.

A Kirkus Starred Review.

A Kirkus Star is awarded to "books of exceptional merit."

Available in print and digital.

Search: "DIVISIBLE MAN Howard Seaborne"

Join our Reader Email list at **HowardSeaborne.com**

DIVISIBLE MAN - THREE NINES FINE

A mysterious mission request from Earl Jackson sends Will into the sphere of a troubled celebrity. A meeting with the Deputy Director of the FBI that goes terribly wrong. Will and Andy find themselves on the run from Federal authorities, infiltrating a notorious cartel, and racing to prevent what might prove to be the crime of the century.

Available in print and digital.

Search: "DIVISIBLE MAN Howard Seaborne"

Join our Reader Email list at **HowardSeaborne.com**

DIVISIBLE MAN - EIGHT BALL

Will's encounter with a deadly sniper on a serial killing rampage sends him deeper into the FBI's hands with costly consequences for Andy. And when billionaire Spiro Lewko makes an appearance, Will and Andy's future takes a dark turn. The stakes could not be higher when the sniper's ultimate target is revealed.

Available in print and digital.
Search: "DIVISIBLE MAN Howard Seaborne"
Join our Reader Email list at **HowardSeaborne.com**

ENGINE OUT AND OTHER SHORT FLIGHTS

Things just have a way of happening around Will and Andy Stewart. In this collection of twelve tales from Essex County, boy meets girl, a mercy flight goes badly wrong, and Will crashes and burns when he tries dating again. Engines fail. Shots are fired. A rash of the unexpected breaks loose—from bank jobs to zombies.

Available in print and digital.

Search: "DIVISIBLE MAN Howard Seaborne"

Join our Reader Email list at **HowardSeaborne.com**

DIVISIBLE MAN - NINE LIVES LOST

A simple request from Earl Jackson sends Will on a cross-country chase. A threat to Andy's career takes a deadly turn. And a mystery literally lands at Will and Andy's mailbox. Before it all ends, Will confronts a deep, dark place he never imagined.

Available in print and digital.

Search: "DIVISIBLE MAN Howard Seaborne"

Join our Reader Email list at **HowardSeaborne.com**

DIVISIBLE MAN - TEN KEYS WEST

A terrifying incident lands Detective Andy Stewart in the grip of an indelible nightmare. A scheme to raise a fortune reveals that no life has value when billions are at stake. In this nail-biting adventure Will and Andy must enlist unlikely help to keep Will's secret from being exposed to the world.

Available in print and digital.
Search: "DIVISIBLE MAN Howard Seaborne"
Join our Reader Email list at HowardSeaborne.com

DIVISIBLE MAN - THE ELEVENTH HOURGLASS

A *BookLife from Publishers Weekly* Editor's Pick.

"A book of outstanding quality."

Will joins Pidge and Earl on a rescue mission that encounters a scene of unimaginable violence. The obvious explanation is impossible but grows equally impossible to ignore as the body count rises. Tensions spiral as billionaire Spiro Lewko, old secrets, and criminal lies push will to a breaking point.

Available in print and digital.

Search: "DIVISIBLE MAN Howard Seaborne"

Join our Reader Email list at **HowardSeaborne.com**

Printed in the USA
CPSIA information can be obtained
at www.ICGtesting.com
LVHW012340180824
788636LV00009B/514